By: B.L. Talley
Copyright © 2022, Brittnee Talley.
Second Printed Edition

All rights reserved. Printed in the United States of America. No part of this book may be used or reproduced in any manner whatsoever without written permission except in the case of brief quotations embodied in critical articles or reviews.
This book is a work of fiction. Names, characters, businesses, organizations, places, events, and incidents either are the product of the author's imagination or are used fictitiously. Any resemblance to actual persons, living or dead, events or locales is entirely coincidental.

REALM OF SHADOWS AND FLAME

Trigger Warning

While this book is a fictional work, it comes from deeply personal experiences and depicts heavy amounts of emotional abuse and self-loathing. The main character deals with a lot of grief and the loss of those close to her. There is also mention of attempted sexual assault. This book contains mature content and occasional swearing and is intended for more mature readers. Please note that if you are triggered by the above, or are not in a safe headspace to read content about the above triggers, please know that I value your mental health and do not recommend reading this book.

Book Playlist

For a curated playlist for the book, please scan the QR code below.

For those who continue to love not to spite the pain, but despite it. But mostly to my little sister, Bethany, who is the reason I continue to fight for love in this often cruel world.

I would do anything for you.

Prologue

My mother always put me to bed with stories of the sun and the moon. I was always told that the sun and the moon were destined for each other. That they were once lovers in another life, their timing forever at odds with fate. It was told as if it were some sort of romantic love story. One I should pine after or desire for myself. But, to me, it seemed cruel for fate to toy with those who dare to love.

An eternal game of cat and mouse.

The heart was such a fickle thing; love should not be given to those who dared not reciprocate. And so, I questioned her stories. Why did the moon have to disappear to let the sun shine? Why did the moon only glow in the aftermath of the sun's warmth? Why was it the moon was never respected in the ways the sun was?

It never made sense to me why the moon always came second.

Until today.

The day the boy fell from the sky, I finally understood the stories. I believed he was my sun, and I was destined to be his moon. But, unlike the stories my mother would tell, we were the exception to the ill-fated love fable. We would not end in tragedy, forever out of the other's reach. No, I would not let that happen. He would be mine, and I his for eternity. Equal in all things. Nothing would ever tear him from me. I would make sure of it.

Because I did not believe in fate.

REALM OF SHADOWS AND FLAME

CHAPTER 1

Panic seized my heart as the billowing smoke seared through my lungs, stinging my eyes. Fynn's body rose through the air as a menacing blaze of red and gold flashed through the sky.

Heat rolled through the forest in waves, the air rippling in the rising temperature.

My mouth was open, but no sound came out as I tried to scream. Seeing my partner violently transformed by an infernal heat, threatened to tear my heart from my body. I wanted to scream, to shout for help, to do anything but watch in horror…but I remained mute. Useless.

An agonizing scream ripped through his chest as he tore at his skin, still suspended high above the ground by nothing other than some godly magic I could not place. The clothing melted from his body as he writhed in the fire, burning, burning, burning.

A white light blossomed in the center of his chest as his body continued to rise high above the treetops. I could do nothing but watch as strange patterns branded themselves along his forearm, mimicking the movement of the flames.

A hiss of pain, not from him, but from me, broke me from my stupor. It was too hot and the smell of burning skin…it wasn't just Fynn, it was me.

I retreated to the edge of the glade, hiding in the shadow of a large pine, savoring the cool shade it provided. Panic clawed its way through my throat and a scream finally broke through my lungs when his back bowed backward, bending so unnaturally I knew it was broken.

I shielded my eyes when a flash of light exploded—spreading for what could have been miles—with golden fire. And then his body, bent and broken and altered beyond recognition, plummeted to the forest floor.

"Fynn," I screamed, but my voice was muffled in the suffocating smoke. I coughed violently, my breathing erratic as I squinted through the dark cloud of ash that now coated every surface

Terrified and frantic, I whipped my head around, searching for any proof that he was still alive, that whatever had happened might have been a dream. Some terrible, gods forsaken dream.

But it wasn't a dream. I could never be that lucky, because I knew what I would find. Fire had only one purpose—to destroy. It ruined everything it touched. Stole it from me. And when his body hit the forest floor, his charred corpse scattered into nothing but ash.

I broke into a run. For the first time in my life, I was running toward a fire. "Fynn," I screamed again, my mind racing. A cry of relief and shock escaped my lips as the ash began to shift, moving as if someone was digging through it. No, not through it…out of it.

A hand, perfect and unharmed, broke through the pile of ash.

Fynn Tirich was as glorious as the sun itself. The light in his golden amber eyes reflected the golden flame—the raw power inherited from the Sun God—that now danced beneath his tanned skin.

I was reminded at that moment, now more than ever, why I had pined after him for so many years. Even after my parent's death, even when I had retreated from all social interaction, I had always been drawn to him.

I couldn't quite describe it, but I knew from the moment I first laid eyes on him he was meant to be in my life…one way or another. Even my fearful heart could not shut him out. It was near impossible after he had saved my life all those months ago. That had been the start of a beautiful relationship between the two of us. One that I cherished.

"Gods, you're okay." My words were wet with tears as I fell to the ground next to him. I ran my hands over his body, reassuring myself more than him that he was unharmed.

"How?" I sputtered, still reeling from the myriad of emotions that swept through me. "Are you—you can't be, can you?" I didn't need him to confirm it to know it was true. Still, I held his face, staring into those golden eyes that now danced with flames.

A wide, boyish grin confirmed my suspicions. He only shrugged.

"I really am." His voice was pitched with excitement. He coughed, smoke still surrounding the both of us and brushed the remaining rubble and ash from his bare chest.

Fynn stood in one fluid motion, then stared down at his arms in awe. Swirling, golden tattoos now wound their way up his forearm to his chest. The fiery whorls met in the center, reaching for his heart in a clawing grasp. As if it were trying to claw it from him. Possess it.

I dug out a fresh pair of his pants from my pack, handing it to him to dress. We hadn't packed an additional shirt, but I was thankful we had planned for a few days of hunting—some spare clothing included—or the walk back into town might have been a little more than awkward.

When he was dressed and as perfect as ever, I sighed with relief. He was safe and alive. I had nothing more to fear. Yet I couldn't shake the nagging feeling that settled into my heart. Like an echoed warning from a voice I couldn't place. Familiar and yet completely foreign.

I took a steadying breath. "You always did like to make a statement." I carefully stamped out the remaining leaves that smoldered along the ground. Another fire in these woods would not bode well for me.

"It's a shame I didn't have an audience for such a spectacular moment." Fynn chuckled, sweeping blonde hair from his eyes. He surveyed the damage that had occurred in his fall, but he didn't seem to be bothered by it.

Only minutes before we had been walking through these woods, setting traps and checking the others laid throughout the worn path. We had established this routine together, hunting food and preparing it together. He didn't need the meat, but my sister and I did. We relied on it.

It would take years to repair this kind of damage, to let the great mother correct the course of nature and grow back the vegetation. Our hunting grounds would have to change. But I tried not to think of it, instead, I reminded myself of how grateful I was to have him still with me.

I had always been afraid of fire, and with my history, rightfully so. But I never feared Fynn. Never questioned him. I wouldn't start now. "What do you reckon Archer will think of all this?" I asked. I shook my head in mock disappointment. "Her favorite hunting post was just over there, and now it's only ash."

Even though I was mostly joking, trying to take the edge off, I recoiled at the thought of telling my younger sister that she'd have to find somewhere else to hunt. I had failed Archer enough in the last years and though it was only a tree…I hated to be the bearer of bad news.

Fynn reached out a hand for the pack, wanting to carry it. I let him take it, but in a graceful movement, he gripped my wrist and pulled me into him, his body flush with mine. I grunted at the impact, wincing at the way he held me. Gods he was stronger than I remembered. My hands rested against his chest and I wondered if he had become denser too, his muscles more compact than before.

His lips twisted into that wry smile I loved so much as he lifted my chin. "You know you could never be mad at me. You Orions adore me too much to ever seek retribution." His eyes sparkled with humor, and he winked.

I rolled my eyes, but I could swear at that moment, his face flashed with something darker, something that burned deep and ominous. I blinked and it faded just as quickly.

"Come on," I said, pulling away and walking back toward the trail. "Let's go home."

Despite hunting for most of the day, we had failed to catch anything. I would like to have blamed it on his godly claiming, but it would be a lie. Hunting had always been Archer's thing. Her skill with a bow was unmatched, yet she refused to kill deer.

But it didn't matter much anymore as most of the big game had disappeared from these parts of the woods after a forest fire nearly a year ago. Which left us resorting to trapping smaller game and pheasants until they returned.

Most of the time we only managed to capture one or two small animals. A couple of rabbits, or some small peahens that got loose from a neighbor years back and managed to survive this long. But we always made do. It wasn't as if I hadn't had my fair share of hunger these last few years. One more meatless night wouldn't kill us.

The part I loved most about it though, was the alone time with Fynn, to talk and get to know each other more and more. Most of our relationship had been physical up to this point and though I didn't mind it, I still craved something…more. Something fulfilling.

I never complained though, and Archer was content to let us wander the woods for days at a time. She took full advantage of it, using her afternoons to read book after book.

Fynn caught up with me, taking my hand in his and locking our fingers together. Warmth spread from his touch, hot and demanding.

"Something tells me you are going to be very popular when we get back to town," I said. "It's not every day the Sun God chooses a new host to be the Phoenix."

He jabbed his elbow into my side playfully, huffing in agreement. "It'll be exciting. I could do with a little change for once.

It had been over a hundred years since the last Phoenix died. Despite inheriting a significant influence of power from one of the original gods of this world, the Phoenix was not a true reincarnation.

True reincarnations had not existed within the Realm of Day since the Great War nearly a thousand years ago, fading into extinction. Even before then, few ever existed here and even fewer were written about, or permitted within our history books. Only stories passed down through the generations kept their legends alive.

Over the centuries, the kings of the Realm of Day ordered every last ancient text to be burned. Any worship or mention of the old gods, especially those pertaining to the Realm of Night, had been banned for centuries. Only the Sun God could be worshiped or spoken of. Though, even now, that was mainly for tradition rather than actual worship. There was no help to be found from the ancient being.

But those who were caught denying him, or sought another god for aid, were deemed traitors to the realm and quickly disposed of. Never to be heard from again.

Very little was known about the Realm of Night. Only a few stories told by my father were all I knew. But death wasn't a price worth paying for stories. Our life here in Firielle was predictable and peaceful. There was no need to disturb it.

I gasped softly as a light flickered in and out of view to my side. Fynn had already begun playing with his new magic. I closed my eyes tightly, willing away the fear that crept into me at the sight of red flames so close. One slip and even I might burn away forever. But I held my tongue, not wanting to ruin his fun. He looked like a child who had found a new favorite toy. One he would never let go of.

There were so many questions still running through my mind, but his rebirth as the Phoenix still rattled me despite him being unharmed. So I remained silent, letting him enjoy his new powers in peace as we hiked back.

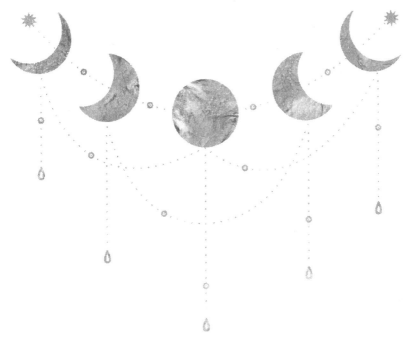

CHAPTER 2

My hometown of Firielle sat only a few hours north of the capital. It had its outlying farming villages and trading routes, but unlike most of the outer cities in Albionne, Firielle also had large schools and training facilities for the King's Legion. Many of King Tobias Sundan's warriors were from here. I hoped to one day be a part of it myself and was only less than a year away from completing my training.

After my family's death, Archer and I had taken a year off from school. During that time we became inseparable, both of us relying entirely on the other. I eventually finished my schooling and while Archer had finished hers, being two years younger, I spent that time hunting and saving money. We would need that savings as we now both attended training full-time.

Our friends had enlisted in the courses as soon as they were permitted to, but to my surprise, they all retook their first year of basics so I could join them. I never understood why they gave up precious time, but they had decided unanimously to do so and I was eternally grateful, though I suspected it had been Emryn who led the vote. Either way, I never would have survived this long without them.

I tried to wait another year for Archer so we could start together, but after some convincing from Fynn, I joined while she finished her last year of school. She promised she would catch up in no time and with her unmatched archery skills, I knew she would fulfill that promise.

Fynn and I exited the forest's edge, cutting through a worn path. My younger sister waited for us, her long, silvery-blonde hair tied back in its usual braid, tossed casually over her shoulder.

I watched with expected disappointment when her face fell, realizing we returned empty handed.

"I'm guessing it's broth and stale bread for dinner again?" Archer eyed us and closed the book in her hand with a snap. She placed it in her satchel, which certainly carried at least four other books she was rereading for the hundredth time.

I didn't have a chance to respond before her face contorted into a combination of amusement and confusion. Her jaw fell open as she glared at Fynn, realizing he was shirtless and covered with ash. Her jaw closed and then opened again as she tried to form a cohesive thought.

"I'm sorry...am I missing something?" Her gray eyes darted between us, searching for answers. "What exactly happened? You're both a complete mess."

"If you keep your mouth open maybe you'll catch enough bugs you won't need my broth and stale bread for dinner." I shook my head with mock annoyance.

"Very funny, Ren," Archer said, rolling her eyes. She stood, dusting off her legs from the grass and dirt that collected from hours of reading. She gestured to Fynn. "What in the world did you do?"

"Look for yourself." Fynn took a step back, letting his new markings glint in the sunlight. I could swear he was flexing his entire torso as Archer gawked at the new tattoos. "Pretty cool, huh?" His eyebrows wagged up and down.

He turned his arms inward, obviously flexing this time. He plastered on that dazzling smile of his, the one that could convince me to do just about anything, and confidence lined his chiseled features.

"Put them away before the arrogance blinds me." I dropped to the ground where Archer sat moments before, the soles of my feet still warm from stomping out the remaining embers in the forest. Despite not having a successful hunting day, I was exhausted.

He showed off his new powers, fire flitting between his fingers with ease as if he were born for this power. Archer didn't seem to be bothered, but my heart pounded in my chest, reminding me that I was still afraid. That fire was my enemy.

The haunted memories of my past flooded my mind, threatening to consume me, but I took a few calming breaths and repeated to myself that Fynn would never use those flames on me. He would always ensure I was safe.

I was safe. I was safe. I was safe.

When the memories abated, the terrified screams and crack of wood finally silencing, I folded my arms across my chest and rested my head against the tree trunk.

The shade it provided was cool and soothing, a welcomed relief from the heat of the afternoon sun. The Sun God provided our warmth and light, but often I silently wished for a touch less heat year round. It was always sweltering this far in the south. Even in the winter months.

Finally, calm, I opened my eyes and listened with amusement as Archer pestered Fynn with questions about being the Phoenix. She was always so curious. Sometimes, her incessant quandaries annoyed me, but I couldn't blame her in this instance. It had been nearly a hundred years since the last Phoenix died and no one I knew remembered what the world was like with a living one. With her thirst for knowledge, I doubt her questions would ever end.

I also had about a hundred questions to ask. Like, why had the Sun God waited so long to claim his next host? Why had the fifty-year rebirth cycle been broken now, of all times? What did it mean for our future together?

I held my tongue though, knowing I could ask him later when we were alone. First, I would let him be gawked at and praised by the townspeople first. They would never let it rest that Firielle had been the town to raise the Phoenix.

My mouth twitched to the side at the thought, my stomach filling with butterflies. I still wasn't used to being with Fynn, having him all to myself. It was a source of pride for me that I had been the one to entertain his attention this long. And now that he was the Phoenix too...

"Enjoying the sights, are we?" Fynn's voice broke through my thoughts. I must have been biting my lip absently while I stared at him.

I silently cursed myself for being so oblivious, but I couldn't help it. Any right-minded girl would stare the way I did if their partner was the Phoenix.

Even though the Phoenix was revered as the single most powerful being alive, it was the king who harnessed the power for himself. From the first Fae kings a thousand years ago until now, the Phoenix, and their Phoenix fire, belonged to them.

The alliance, if it could be called that, was originally established as a way to ensure peace among the land. It was only with the aid of the Phoenix that the kings of Albionne conquered the land in the name of the Sun God, effectively extinguishing the Realm of Night. Only one city remained in the realm to the north, tucked safely beyond the deadly pass of Mount Cresslier.

Fynn's hand rested reassuringly on my back, keeping me steady as we dropped off our gear and changed into fresh clothes. Cold water splashed across my skin as I washed away the remaining ash. "Do you think things will ever be the same again?" I asked, trying to fill the silence that seemed to eat away at me.

"Renata, this is something to celebrate, not worry about. This is good news." Fynn crossed the room, pulling me against his bare chest. I settled in, resting my head against him, my raven black hair a stark contrast between us.

"I know," I said. But the worry remained. Would likely never go away. "I just like the way things are now. I like this. Us." I gestured to my little house, the too-small bed we often slept in together.

"There is a life greater than this, and this is my chance. Our chance." He corrected himself.

For the last thousand years, each Phoenix served the king faithfully. Three had existed in the last millennia. Each one male, and each with a terrifying amount of power. And all had been Select Fae. Just like the both of us.

Select Fae lived on average around five hundred years, give or take, and each rebirth of the Phoenix lasted only as long as the host remained alive. While a Phoenix could 'die' and be reborn an undetermined amount of times, it would take more than a mortal weapon to permanently kill a Phoenix. An arrow to the heart or dagger to the throat was merely a hindrance to them.

But that was all I knew regarding them. Only the stories of those who had lived in the time of a Phoenix could attest to their lore. Other than that, only the king, the Phoenix, and the Keeper knew everything.

Fynn shook me gently, trying to sway my doubt. "It is an honor to have this gift from the Sun God. Think of the position I will have in the king's court. The gold and status I will be given. What else could we need? I could bring you and Archer to court, get a bigger house just for the two of us."

I smiled and nodded my head, letting his words take over. He was right. He was always right.

Unlike me, the idea of lifelong servitude to the kings never seemed to bother the Phoenixes, each one dutifully fulfilling their roles and keeping the peace. But even though this was what we had been taught, I wasn't entirely convinced it was peace that swept through the land but rather the fear of annihilation—and to prevent the Realm of Night from rising once more.

However, in the last century, when no Phoenix had been claimed according to tradition, rumors had started to stir once more. Doubt rising against the Sun God. Before now, no one had ever dared question him.

"I'd like that," I said, smiling for him. "I'd like that very much." He let me go, the feel of his arms around my waist still lingering as I finished getting ready.

From what I knew, the king was a good ruler. A just one. He maintained peace across Albionne, but occasionally, a whisper of speculation would reach our town, spreading rumors of his mercilessness and desire to end the Realm of Night entirely. With only the city of Asterion beyond the mountain lands, it made sense he would want to finish the work of his predecessors. But no king had dared try in some time for fear of the creatures that lurked beyond the shadow of the mountain.

I hoped the day would never come when the king would send his legion to the north. But if it were to happen, I did not doubt that it would be soon now that the Phoenix had returned.

I feared the threat of war, not for what it might bring down across the world, but that it might change the sweet and loyal male I loved. Fynn's confidence bordered on arrogance at times, but he always remained committed to whatever he put his mind to, sometimes even losing himself in the dedication. But this was a once-in-a-lifetime honor, and I loved him more than I ever thought possible.

As we left the house, finally ready to face what came next, I promised myself that no matter what came our way, I would do whatever I could to support him.

CHAPTER 3

It was naive to hope the event in the forest had gone unnoticed.

Trumpets rang out the announcement call and I flinched at the abrasiveness of it. There was only one reason they would sound when there wasn't a holiday or tax due.

The king was coming to Firielle.

Equal parts fear and excitement flickered through me. I'd never seen the king in person before, only the eldest of the princes once before, and that was a memory I liked to forget.

It was common gossip that the eldest prince was quite the charmer and had dark curls most girls would envy, even though he kept it short and tidy under his crown. But none of the gossip ever mattered much because I knew the truth. The prince was cruel. I often only held on to the town gossip to discuss it with Archer in the evenings. It was something our mother had done with me at a young age and I continued the tradition.

The thought of my mother made me pause. Even after all these years, the pain of her loss still stung. If she were here I imagined she'd gawk over the fact I somehow landed the eye of the most eligible male in town.

Fynn's hand laced through mine. He must have felt my surge of emotion because he said, "No need to panic." He leaned in and placed his lips to my forehead, reassuring me.

Together, his smile seemed to say. We'll do this together.

His comforting words left me feeling lighter and my breathing slowed as we approached the fountain in the center of town. Fynn rubbed my thumb with his, a reassuring gesture he had always done. The shuffling of feet caught my attention before I could pull him closer, and when we rounded the corner the town's whispers became louder, the crowd more dense. Hands lifted and pointed at his arms, the tattoos that swirled there.

"It's him," a man shouted. The crowd burst out into gasps.

"Praise the Sun God," shouted another, followed by, "Long may the Day last!"

A chorus of the phrase repeated. A smile tugged at Fynn's lips. He put one foot up on the tiled edge of the fountain and gave me a quick wink before boosting himself up.

I shook my head. Cocky bastard.

Fynn rotated on the fountain's edge, surveying the crowd who had gathered. All for him. He raised his arms in a triumphant gesture, gathering a loud response, and said, "People of Firielle, what you witnessed earlier was a gift from the Sun God himself." His voice was clear and confident as if he had been waiting for this moment for some time.

"I, Fynn Tirich, have been chosen." His fist pumped triumphantly. A ripple of fire glowed beneath those winding tattoos, shining brightly on the already captivating male.

The crowd erupted into a chorus of cheers, some even wiped away tears of joy. Everyone swarmed him at once, each one wanting their own precious moment with the Phoenix. The girls especially went feral, some even swooning as he held their eager hands.

I rolled my eyes, annoyed at the thought of others pining after him, but I stepped away from the crowd, content to let him have his moment of glory. As I backed toward the market stalls, I jumped in surprise as I bumped into a body behind me.

A small voice. "Watch it, klutz."

Relief washed over me as I turned to see Skye. Her brows were lifted and she folded her arms over black, fitted clothes. I blushed at the embarrassment of living up to the nickname she gave me years ago during an accident. One I made them promise to never bring up again.

"Sorry, I didn't see you there," I mumbled and looked down at the ground, kicking the dirt with my worn boots, still embarrassed.

"I'm not surprised." Her storm gray eyes crinkled at the corners.

I was glad the two of us remained on good terms ever since the incident with her brother. My relationship with Kaede on the other hand… had turned sour after I rejected his advances a couple of years previous.

"Kaede doesn't seem like he's going to be thrilled about golden boy over there becoming the Phoenix." She jerked her thumb over to a dark and brooding shape at the edge of the alley.

"I'm sure he isn't, but there's nothing I can do about it," I stated, shrugging my shoulders as I turned away from the tall figure disappearing into the shadows. "He can't mope around forever."

Fynn was still shaking hands and giving hugs, that bright smile still stuck to his perfectly symmetrical face. I leaned back on the stall post next to Skye and gave her a half smile.

"Yeah, he tends to do that. No matter the situation. Moody bastard." She straightened her back and pushed off the post. "But he's my brother, and I owe him my life, so I guess I'll suffer through it. Emryn seems to have turned him around though. But what's another few emotionally testy years when we have centuries?" She walked away in his direction, tossing her hand over her shoulder in an informal goodbye.

If I was being honest with myself…I missed Kaede. Well, the old Kaede, the one I knew and loved like a brother before he let my rejection turn to ire. Now it seemed like he couldn't stand to be within a few hundred yards without a permanent scowl on his face. It had been rough distancing from him. But he had confessed his love for me when he knew I had feelings for Fynn. I tried to let him down easy, but…it hadn't gone over well apparently.

I watched as Skye's split silver and black hair disappeared around the corner, contemplating whether I should follow her and talk with Kaede, but it was too late. Fynn was my focus now.

When I finally braved the crowds once again and made my way back towards him, the crowd began to split, parting in the middle. Trumpets sounded, notifying all of Firielle who was approaching. I glanced to Fynn, hoping to grab his attention and see his reassuring smile one last time before my world was turned upside down, but he was focused on the carriage rolling down the street.

When it finally came to a stop, the door clicked open immediately and my breath halted. It had been years since I saw him last, but I never forgot his face. Not once. Nor the things he had done.

Callax Sundan, Crown Prince of Albionne, and heir to the Realm of Day.

And behind him… My smile disappeared, my stomach churning. A strange rush of dread settled in my veins when I finally beheld the face of our king.

CHAPTER 4

The king of Albionne was shorter than I expected.

Somehow, I imagined the ruler of our kingdom would tower over his subjects. But he didn't. Though his piercing dark green eyes and spiked gold crown compensated for where his physical traits lacked.

Prince Callax, however, loomed over the crowd, lips curled in disgust. Annoyance plastered on his face, his nose upturned like the city carried a stench. He held himself with an air of arrogance, leaning against the carriage, hands tucked neatly into his pockets. Tanned skin from a lifetime in the sun, peeked through the rolled cuffs of his crimson top and his dark hair was swept to the side, perfectly manicured under his crown. Not only was he taller than when I'd last seen him, but new muscles coated his arms and torso. Thick brows lay atop his brooding, dark blue eyes, coated in shadows as he watched his father embrace Fynn.

Something like jealousy flashed through his eyes at the sight. But before I could second guess myself, he schooled it back to neutral, looking entirely unbothered.

Pretentious prick. If he couldn't at least hide the distaste in his face, then why was he even here? I hated the thought that one day, Callax would rule over us as king. If we were lucky, it would be centuries before it happened.

The prince's movements were calculated and precise, only shifting forward when his father did, a perfect mirror.

Many of our studies each year in school were focused on learning of the king and his doings. All of Firielle adored the Sundan family, though the queen was rarely seen or spoken of. We learned of his politics and the trade routes he opened, how he had established peace and provided new jobs for those farther north in the mines.

In comparison to the kings of the past, he seemed…mundane almost. Yet despite that, he had amassed the largest legion in history, preparing for a war that had yet to happen.

From what I could tell, there didn't seem to be any logical reason behind why he continued to gather such large amounts of trained warriors. But from what I could gather based on my instinct, and despite the good things he had done for the realm…I didn't trust him.

Perhaps it was bias brought on by my one interaction with the prince. The encounter had been short and brutal, but it was enough to know the kind of male he truly was. Glimmers of hatred and hollowness lay beneath those eyes. A male like that could not have been raised with love.

So perhaps it was only that, or perhaps it was because the smile on the king's face was a little too wide to be natural, but whatever it was, I didn't like him. And I liked even less that he couldn't tear his eyes from Fynn as if he were a prized stallion to be won and broken in.

A booming voice broke through my thoughts. "Citizens of Firielle, how blessed you are to have one of your own reborn as the Phoenix." The king's voice echoed through the square, inescapable and boisterous. They were eating it up. "It has been a long century as we have patiently awaited the return of the Phoenix. Today is a gift from the Sun God himself, one that should be celebrated. Long may the Day last!"

Echoes of the sentiment pierced the air around me. I grimaced, muttering the words in unison. Today wasn't a gift, it was a curse. I knew what was coming next and I could do nothing to stop it.

Like many other instances in my life, I was losing control over what was happening. Life had never been kind to me, so why would it start now? My heart raced, thundering louder and louder, and my legs swayed but I caught myself just before I fell.

I raised my eyes to see Fynn's reaction to the king's words. He looked like a lovesick puppy, eyes wide, soaking in everything the king said. Like he was the one who had given him this honor, this power. I was going to lose him and there was nothing I could do about it.

My chest constricted to the point of pain and breathing became difficult. I didn't have the time to go into a panic attack right now. I sucked in a deep breath and held it, counting to four each time, repeating the ritual. It was what my mother taught me to do when waves of emotion threatened to surface. She had always known how to calm me down in moments like this. I missed her dearly.

I shook my head, breaking through the haze of thoughts, and did my best to remain present.

The king continued his speech. "I am pleased to announce that because we have waited so long for his return, the Phoenix will begin his training at the palace immediately."

The crowd cheered at the announcement. They only increased in volume and ridiculousness when he gave Fynn a supportive pat on the back, beaming at the crowd. Fynn grinned back. They were a perfect pair.

I wanted to be sick. They were leaving now? He was already slipping through my fingers.

They stepped down, heading toward the carriage side by side, the prince trailing behind. The king hadn't even bothered to announce his presence.

Was Fynn going to leave without trying to say goodbye? He must have been too lost in the melee of events that he had forgotten. But I knew if I could catch his attention then everything would be fine. I yelled after him. "Fynn, wait!" Thankfully, his head turned in my direction before stepping into the carriage.

He waved once as I fought through the crowd. He cupped his hand to his mouth and shouted back, "I'll write, Renata. I'll write really soon." Behind him Callax rolled his eyes, disgusted, and shoved him forward.

With those final words, the door shut behind the three males. The sound of the whip cracked through the air and I flinched, watching him ride off without so much as a kiss goodbye.

Archer appeared from somewhere behind me and slipped her arm around mine. My shoulders slumped and I blinked back the tears stinging my eyes. I didn't have time to be sad, there were things to be taken care of back home so I shoved the feelings down into a box and closed the lid. But all I wanted to do was curl up in my bed and stay there for a long while.

"Come on," I said, tugging her closer to my side and draping my arm around her. Having her near always comforted me, made me feel safe. "Let's go home. We've got bread and broth waiting for us." She groaned and bumped my hip with hers.

Her voice dripped with sarcasm as she said, "How exciting."

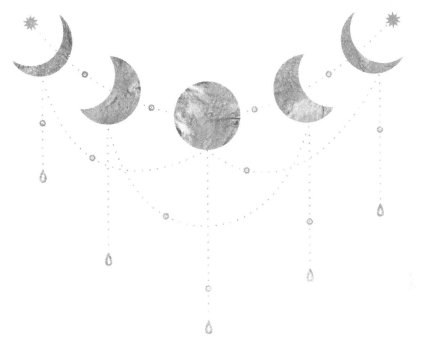

CHAPTER 5

The raging blaze pressed down, suffocating me as I choked on dark smoke. Flames roared up the walls and threatened me with imminent violence.

A banging on my door caught my attention and I turned my head, looking away from the mesmerizing trance of the flames.

"Ren! Ren! Wake up. We have to get out of here," Archer screamed on the other side of the door, rattling the doorknob. A short pained hiss carried through and I knew the iron handle must have heated beyond touch in the fire.

"I'm coming," I shouted, grabbing a spare shirt I had tossed on the floor the night before, and wrapped it over my nose. I dropped to the ground, avoiding the worst of the smoke, and crawled. I tried opening the door with the shirt, but it seared straight through. I scanned the room for something heavy enough to break the window, but I found nothing.

I cursed and said, "I need you to push as hard as you can, I'm going to grab underneath the door and pull." I had to get out. I couldn't die here. Not like this. Where were our parents? Were my younger siblings, Damian and Rellyn, safe too? Or had the fire already consumed them?

"I'm ready," Archer said. Together, we pushed and pulled on the door, but it refused to budge. I swallowed, fear gripping my heart and I coughed violently. Smoke sank toward the floor. The heat was unbearable as it continued to warp my walls, ruining everything it touched.

"Go get mom and dad. Make sure Damian and Rellyn are okay." They were only six and two years old, they were more helpless than either of us. "I'll keep working on the door. Just go." Panic crept into my heart, crushing whatever hope I had. I knew I didn't have time, but I would rather it be me than all of them.

I didn't hear a response, but the sound of her footsteps thudding against the floor reassured me some. A faint shout sounded and I could have cried from relief. The fire must not have spread that far, must have only been contained to my room.

Soon enough, three pairs of footsteps rushed toward me and my mother screamed my name. My father slammed his weight into the door, using all of his brute strength. He had always been strong and imposing. Tall, and handsome, and rugged, just like most other fae who made their living working on a farm and logging timber. In seconds, the door collapsed with a loud crack as he barreled inside. The flames roared higher in response, rising faster with the rush of air.

He covered his mouth, turning back and shouting at my mother to grab the youngest two. I sobbed in relief, releasing a pent-up breath. I hadn't realized until that moment just how terrified I had been. Just how afraid I was to be trapped in this room forever—fated to take my last breath while burning alive.

But as my father's shoulders sagged in relief to see me still unharmed, a loud crack sounded and the frame of my door snapped, caving in, burying my brother and sister's door behind a wave of flames.

I screamed for my mother, my father's face falling in devastation at the realization that saving his one daughter had likely sealed the fate of his mate and two children. Archer stood behind our father, her silver hair whipping behind her as she kept looking back and forth between the rooms, unsure of what to do.

"Girls, come with me," my father yelled over the flames. They filled my head with a dull roar, calling to me, begging me to become one, to join them as they tore everything apart. I only broke from the trance when my father lifted my nightstand with ease and threw it through the window. The rush of air fanned the flames and a blast of heat threw my hair back, singeing the ends as he swept me into his arms, protecting me.

I pounded against his chest. "We can't leave them, they'll die." My throat scratched with every word, the smoke coating it, sending me into coughing fits I couldn't shake. He didn't listen. Didn't seem to register my words as he lifted me with one arm, taking Archer in his other.

Despite my protest, he didn't respond. Pain flashed behind his starry eyes, his face hardening with his decision. Archer, on his other side, was frozen in terror as he lifted us over and through the window.

When we were far enough away from the fire, near the edge of our fence, he set us down. I looked up desperately into his gaze. I had never seen my father so scared in his life. Only once before had I seen him even slightly scared and that was when Archer had fallen from a tree and broken her ankle. But this was different. This wasn't a broken bone or a shallow cut from playing with knives. This was true fear.

Terror.

Tears welled in his eyes as he cupped Archer's and my face. Looking into both of our eyes he whispered, "My darling girls, I love you both so much. Your mother and I are so proud."

Archer, though a few years younger, silently sobbed next to me. She knew this was goodbye.

I refused to accept it. I had always been more impulsive, stubborn, quick to anger and slow to understand. I reached out and grabbed his hand as he pulled away. I whimpered, "Please come back. I need you."

His demeanor broke, tears falling freely down his ashen face. He knelt and held my face in his hands, wiping a tear from mine. "I love you so much, Ren. Trust that you will be okay." His bottom lip quivered. "If anything happens, you must promise me to watch over your sister. Stick together. 'Til the Night rises once more my darling girl. Always remember that." He kissed the *top of my head, then Archer's.*

I sniffed and nodded my head. "Remember to breathe. In, out, and count to four. If you can breathe, then you have control." His words were kind and soft, but his eyes were desperate, darting back and forth to the house that continued to be swallowed in the blaze. Every second that passed where he stayed to reassure me was a second I was stealing from the rest of my family. But he smiled lovingly. "I'll be back. I promise."

With those last words, he disappeared back into the burning house.

I hadn't accepted it yet, but I knew. As he ran into the flames, I knew this would be the last time I ever saw my father alive.

Archer clung to me and I held her in my arms. I took a deep breath, counting to four just like he instructed—as my mother taught me—and gripped Archer while we waited.

Archer and I called out for them, shouted and screamed until our voices were gone.

One minute passed.

Then two.

Three.

Still, no one emerged from the house. My panic rose and those steadying breaths disappeared. With each uncontrolled inhale, the flames rose and fell with it in time. A loud crack echoed throughout the world and the front of the house caved in, smoke billowing up toward the night sky.

I lost control then. Forgot to breathe entirely as I fell to my knees.

The fire roared higher as I continued to scream. he promised me he would be back, that he would not leave me. He promised, he promised, he promised.

Archer grabbed my shoulder and shook me. "Snap out of it. We have to go. Ren, wake up!"

I snapped awake, sweat drenching my clothes and bed sheets. Archer's hands grasped my shoulders, shaking me awake from my nightmare. No, not a nightmare…a memory. One which plagued me like a demon in the night.

I shivered, a cool breeze from the open window chilling my clammy skin. My nightmares were getting more intense because even the room now smelled like smoke. I sighed, wiping my hair from my damp forehead. Archer sat next to me, looking as exhausted as I felt.

"Sorry," I mumbled, embarrassed for waking her.

She looked at me with stormy gray eyes and sighed. "You don't have to apologize for having nightmares." She smiled softly and took my hand in hers. "I still have them too. It's okay to miss them. It's only been a few years."It had been five years. I was only fifteen when it happened and Archer only thirteen, so I knew she remembered the events just as well as I did.

I pulled her in for a hug and she crawled in bed next to me. After only a few moments, our breaths synchronized, the only sound filling the silence.

We were closer than most siblings I knew, save for Kaede and Skye.

After our family's death, we didn't leave each other's side for nearly a year. We even slept in the same bed for the next two years, both of us afraid that if we lost sight of the other we might lose them forever. But I promised her that no matter what happened, we'd always stick together. Nothing would come between us.

Nearly asleep, I felt Archer's arm lift from my side, pinky finger waiting mid-air. "Together?" she asked.

"'Til the Night rises," I answered, linking my finger with hers. Leaving them intertwined, we fell asleep. Mercifully, no more nightmares—or memories—plagued me for the rest of the night.

The early morning sun warmed my skin as I rubbed sleep from my eyes. When I moved to sit, I found my arm still pinned down, Archer asleep beside me. Her silver blonde hair splayed around her in a tangled mess.

She was usually so poised and perfect, but she was a laughable mess when she slept. Gently, I shook her shoulders, trying to rouse her. She groaned and swatted in my direction, obviously displeased. I chuckled and pushed her to the edge of the bed and off my arm.

"We're late," I said.

That woke her. Her eyes opened in a flash and she groaned, this time rolling off the bed and onto her feet.

We had accidentally slept well past the start of training for the day and didn't have time to drag our feet. We grabbed whatever bread was left from the night before and headed into town.

The new sessions of legion training had recently begun. I was entering my second and final year while Archer had just begun her first. If I could master the weapons courses and pass the final test, I would make it and be done. In second year, each training rotation lasted three months.

First, we mastered hand-to-hand combat, then the bow and arrow, followed by daggers and small blades—or a specialty weapon of choice—and we finished the year with swords. If you couldn't master the sword, there was no hope of achieving any rank in the legion.

Being born female had its disadvantages often enough, but it had been a blessing that my parents hadn't viewed it that way. We had been trained from a young age how to fight, but it was merely for survival and not for the thought of war. We had learned how to wield daggers and a bow and arrow. I could handle my own, and my aim was true enough, but my archery skills were lacking.

But Archer…she was the skilled one of the two of us. There was no target she couldn't hit. She took to archery as if she were born for it. Yet despite her perfect aim, she didn't like hunting. She understood its purpose and would do it if necessary, but never for sport.

She took after our mother in that way. Both in kindness and skill with the bow. And even though our mother never joined us for the hunt when we were younger, she could beat us all if she wished.

As the training fields came into view over the hill, two figures emerged from the edge of the woods. Skye waved, calling out for us to wait up so we could walk together.

Kaede and Skye were two of my closest friends—well, I guess Skye still was, Kaede on the other hand couldn't bear to look me in the eye.

After our parent's death, the two of them were one of the few constants in my life. So much changed following it, but their friendship stayed true. We had grown closer during that time, and looking back I wondered if that was when Kaede had fallen for me. I had never noticed it until it was too late. But even then life had been so chaotic that it wouldn't have changed my answer.

But even so, all my friends had remained loyal. Even if Kaede couldn't stand me. And I was eternally grateful for it.

Skye sauntered toward us, her black training gear matching half of her jet-black hair. The other half was an impossible shade of silver. She liked to joke she'd been struck by lightning as a baby, but there was no reason we knew of that half her hair actually lacked any color.

"Why are you two late? We know we are cause grumpy over here couldn't find his shoes." Skye winked, teasing Kaede.

He pushed her head away and rolled his eyes. When they landed near me, his playful annoyance faltered, turning into a scowl. Guilt pulled at my stomach, twisting. I shoved it down. Things had never been righted between us. But one day I might be able to talk about it, to fix whatever ill-will remained. I still had hope that day he would look at me and the hatred and pain would be gone.

"Late night," I replied, trying to avoid talking about the recurring nightmares. "And we all know Archer's no help with waking up on time."

Archer shoved me gently from behind, scoffing at the remark.

We all laughed together as we walked through the outer fence and onto the field where at least a hundred other young adults and trainers had already begun the day's drills.

CHAPTER 6

Kieran glared at the four of us as we walked onto the field. He pointed to the outer running ring and we knew what he meant without saying a word.

I hated running. Honestly, I didn't think there was much else I enjoyed less.

For every minute we were late we had to run a lap around the field and today's tardiness was a steep price to pay. Sometimes, as I ran, I daydreamed about sprouting wings and flying the laps instead. I wondered if flying would be a new part of Fynn's training, or if it would come naturally to him.

I had only managed a glimpse of his wings that day in the woods before they disappeared again, but I knew he had them. All Phoenixes did.

After we had completed our sixty laps, the four of us walked over to the center of the field where Kieran waited. Sweaty and winded, I downed a few glasses of water left in buckets for the trainees.

"Everyone to their respective stations. Let's make sure this doesn't happen again. Understood?" Kieran's dark brows furrowed, full of disapproval. We all nodded and Archer left for the first-year field, while Skye, Kaede, and

I headed for the weapons field where Senna and Emryn waited for us.

Apart from Senna—who had completed her training before all of us at an advanced rate no one could match—we had just finished our first course a few weeks prior. Hand-to-hand combat came easier to me than the rest. I spent the better part of the last few years of school in and out of fights. The boys in my class liked to tease me about my family's death, lighting little fires at my desk or making jokes about being an orphan.

I didn't appreciate their actions and I had no qualms with letting them know exactly how I felt. Except for Soren and Caldor. They were the only ones I dared not bother. Taking on boys twice my size wasn't always a wise choice, but it did give me an outlet for all my pent-up aggression. The bruises I got in the process only served as a physical reminder to the pain and I wore them proudly.

Skye bumped her shoulder playfully into Senna, accidentally knocking the quiver of arrows to the ground that she had pulled for us.

"Mind the arrows you two. We don't have replacements." Kieran's voice boomed a few yards away, his annoyance ringing clear.

"Sorry," Skye laughed, bending down to help pick up the fallen arrows.

Senna huffed, but not in true annoyance. "If you showed up on time, we wouldn't have this problem, you know?" She might seem upset, but Senna could never stay upset at her partner for long.

The two were paired at the hip and none of us were sure why a mating bond hadn't kicked in yet for them. Or why they weren't planning a bonding ceremony. They sure as hell acted like an unruly mated pair as it was. They were young, but it wasn't entirely uncommon for mates to be found this young. But once Fae found their mates, they were quick to celebrate and bind their love.

"You know you love me," Skye retorted, flicking her shoulder-length hair. She handed me a quiver of arrows and gestured for me to pass them to the others.

I gave a few to Kaede, but he took them from my hands without so much as a thank you and stalked over to the practice range where Emryn waited patiently.

Kaede didn't deserve Emryn. To be honest, none of us did. She was patient, loving, and loyal. It never bothered me that she was only a Quarter—or Lesser—Fae, fated to live the lifespan of a human. What bothered me was she only had a hundred years or less in this world. If she worried about it, she never let it show.

Maybe that was why she spent her time being so kind to us all. She always said there wasn't enough time in life to spend being cruel. She was the better of the six of us, or at least the most grounded.

The rest of us were all Select Fae. Most of the Fae in Firielle were, though a handful of Half and even fewer Lesser Fae lived among us. Humans were even less common, sticking more toward the smaller towns, or the cities to the north.

There was no technical class system in place, but with the way the king ruled and the mentality that passed down from it, there were still obvious differences. Many of us treated everyone the same, regardless of the percentage of their Fae blood, but there were those who held distaste for the lower blood status and their rounded ears.

Emryn was one of the rare ones who didn't quite look human. She was tall and lithe but still had that Fae-like quality to her face, her ears not blunt, but still lacked the same sharp point the rest of us had been born with.

But all of that didn't matter. Emryn could hold her own against any of us and we respected the hell out of her for it. Even Kieran had learned early on that she had every right to train alongside us.

Her strawberry blonde hair shone in the sun as she greeted Kaede with a glowing smile. Despite his poor attitude, he treated her well and she adored him.

I followed my group, making my way onto the field, slinging a large bow over my shoulder. The sight of them together made my heart ache, reminding me how much I missed Fynn.

Skye noted me staring and wrapped her arm in mine and began prattling on about what she and Senna had planned for the week. I was thankful for the distraction.

Senna led most of the training for and was exceedingly gifted in anything involving weapons or combat. She was usually reserved, but when it came to leading or strategies and skill, no one—not even Kieran—could beat her.

Everything about Senna, down to her appearance, commanded respect. From the way she held herself as straight as a sword, to how her braids wrapped around her head and the gold beads that shone in the sun, it all was so regal.

Senna bore the traditions of her people proudly, even though most of the people of Alira had dispersed throughout the continent. Very little was known about the Alirans. Over time, the traditions of her people faded. They became nomadic, their unique culture fading with time.

But despite it, gold adorned her ears, the cuffs on her wrists, the unique necklaces that lay across her throat, and the lines of tattoos across her arms and neck.

Along with her talent, Senna was a perfectionist. Even down to the angle of my knuckles as I notched an arrow.

"You'll never hit a moving target if you can't place the arrow correctly," Senna stated, raising her brows.

I lowered my wrist, correcting the placement. I sighed. "Thanks, Senna." I wasn't in the mood to bicker about technicalities today.

"I know you're hurting, and I'm sorry about that. But it doesn't excuse poor form." She moved to the next trainee in line, but I made a face of annoyance and without even turning around, Senna said, "For that, I want you to nock and un-nock your entire quiver ten times before you even begin trying to aim."

"Great, thanks," I muttered under my breath.

I spent the next few hours repeating her orders, then aiming down the range. I noted the angle of my wrist and knuckles as I released each one, not wanting to test Senna's patience. Sure enough, her advice helped, and my aim stayed true, only a handful of arrows straying from the inner circles. But mounted targets were never my problem.

After collecting my arrows for the hundredth time that day, Senna gathered us around. Behind us, a few others moved the bales of hay holding our targets and replaced them with wooden cages. My brows furrowed in curiosity.

"Those of you here have proven skillful enough in aiming at standard targets. But that won't help when your time comes on the battlefield." Senna spoke with authority as she paced back and forth.

There were roughly fifty trainees in our level; if I had to guess, more than forty were still here. The others rearranging the field behind us must be those who hadn't performed as well. I noticed Petyr was one of the few out in the field, a sweet kid I remembered from school. While he was kind, he never had much of a knack for anything athletic. He had made it this far in training, which was impressive, but seeing him fall behind wasn't a surprise.

Those who performed at lower levels weren't automatically kicked out; the cut only happened after completing each course section. So, Petyr, and the few others with him in the field, had just over two months to pick up the pace before their attempt to join the legion was over.

"Your task now is to kill five rabbits each by the end of the day. We have put up a small perimeter around the edges of the field, but the entire field will be open play."

Well…shit. I would not do well.

Senna continued the instruction, "Upon completing your task, you may take your kill and go home. If you don't wish to keep the kill, leave them at the edge of the fence, and we will donate them ." At least rabbits wouldn't be dying for no reason today, though I doubted any would die because of me. I usually relied on traps, or Archer, for catching smaller game.

Senna stopped her pacing and turned to the group. "You've all passed the first course, but this will show me how seriously you have taken your training and how much work you still have. We've given each of you a new quiver of specifically marked arrows; this way, you can't claim another's kill. Remember, aim carefully, and for the love of the gods, please avoid your fellow trainees." She gestured to the open field behind us, where the rabbits now ran in a frenzy. "Well... go."

I slung my quiver over my shoulder. This was going to be interesting.

It didn't take long for the better archers in the group to grab their kills and leave for the day. It had been only half an hour, and I had only successfully hit one. But even that one I only shot in the leg. When I retrieved it from the far corner of the field, I had to use another arrow to end its suffering—the poor thing.

A howl of pain from across the field drew my attention. Petyr lay on the ground on an adjacent range, clutching his thigh. A black-tipped arrow lay next to him. A few yards to my left, Soren, a pompous and cruel male, snickered. Next to him, his twin brother Caldor joined in on the mockery. I had no doubt it was Soren who shot his arrow at Petyr. His quiver was nearly empty, and there were flecks of blood staining his boots, showing he already picked up a handful of dead rabbits. The arrows in his quiver, sure enough, were tipped in black.

Out of the corner of my eye, Senna marched up the field, a fire in her eyes I had only ever seen once before when she had defended Skye from drunk, unruly males after a night at the pub.

Subconsciously, I took a step back despite being a healthy distance away already. I didn't want to be near her when she exploded on the two of them, but I would enjoy watching.

"What do you two think you're doing?" Senna's voice carried across the field, her careful control slipping ever so slightly. Senna liked Petyr, regardless of his skill. He was kind, and spirited, and eager to learn. It was hard not to like him. But I think that made him an easy target for the twins.

They had a long history of cruelty. They were the only two I never attempted to fight in our school days. I had taken their taunting silently, knowing if I reacted or tried to retaliate, they would have gladly beaten me to a pulp.

The arrow hadn't embedded itself in Petyr's thigh, so he would recover. But even if he could complete the archery course, there was a slim chance of his leg being in any shape to complete the last two. Like Emryn, Petyr was only Quarter Fae. And with a minimal amount of Fae blood, he would heal like a human. Slow and painful.

"It's not like he didn't have it coming. He's completely useless." Soren shrugged off his actions like they carried zero weight to his conscious.

Senna's jaw tensed, looking straight into Soren's eyes, the height difference not phasing her as she growled, "Do you know what else is completely useless?"

Soren lifted a brow but said nothing. If it were outside the training grounds, there would be a fight. But here, even Soren respected her authority.

She didn't wait for a response. "You two. Now go home. Don't bother coming back. Your training is over, along with any chance of making rank in the legion." Senna rocked back on her heels and folded her arms, waiting for them to move. She didn't flinch when they started to argue with her but arguing with Senna was useless. I had never known her to lose a fight, especially once her mind was made up.

Their arms tossed around in exasperation and anger, but she simply pointed her finger towards the fence. "Out."

A few curses and unnecessary gestures later, Soren and Caldor stormed away and out of view. The entire group had gone still during the interaction, observing how Senna would handle the scenario. Our eyes met, and I took a step forward, unsure of what I was going to say.

Before I could get any words out, she held up a hand, "You have an hour left, Renata. Finish your task." With that, she hurried to where Petyr was being carried away by Kaede and another trainee.

A soft hand landed on my shoulder, startling me. Emryn's kind smile greeted my surprise. "Sorry about Petyr, Ren, I know you were friends with him," she said.

"I knew him, but we weren't super close. It is a shame, though. Maybe it's easier this way rather than him failing out." I shrugged, trying to brush off my anger toward Soren and his idiot brother. The memories of their torment still played through my mind. Their cruel smiles and mocking laughter still sounded the same, even after all these years.

"Well, let me know if you want to talk about anything. I'm always around." Even sad and full of sympathy, her smile still reached her green eyes, lighting up her face. It was always lovely to have Emryn around; she always knew exactly what to say. She had a gift for it. Emryn tucked a stray strand of her perfect strawberry blonde hair behind her ear and patted my shoulder in farewell. "Good luck with the rabbit hunting. You're doing great."

"Thanks, Em."

I spent the next hour chasing around whatever rabbits were left on the field. A few had attempted to dig burrows into the ground, but the heat of the day had hardened the ground, and I was able to grab two in quick succession. Perhaps it was cheating since they weren't running around much, too distracted with hiding to notice their imminent doom. I managed to kill one more before the afternoon was over, still falling short. But I held my head high as I brought four of my needed five over to the edge.

Senna and Skye stood together, leaning against the fence. Skye finished a while ago but had stayed around to spend time with Senna. I missed that with Fynn. It had only been a short while, but I missed his laugh and how his thumb rubbed over mine, calming me. I hoped he would write soon… I didn't like the empty ache that filled my chest in his absence. Like part of myself was missing.

"I guess four is better than zero," Senna said, taking my bow and quiver from me, and placing it in the rack with the others. "Better than expected, but you'll have to practice more, Renata. I don't want you to fall behind. It would be a shame." She was so blunt that sometimes it was hard to tell if she was being kind or sarcastic.

"I know. I promise I'm trying. I'll have Archer work with me more." I dropped two rabbits into the pile, removing their arrows and keeping the other two. It would be good for an easy dinner, and the other I could preserve with some salt.

She nodded. "Rest up, and I'll see you tomorrow. On time."

I rolled my eyes and mumbled I would try my best.

Archer waited for me at the gates, having ended just a few moments before I did. The sun was beginning to set, and she looked just like she had this morning, barely a hair out of place and no sweat from the day's work. I don't know how she managed it, but that was Archer, always so effortless.

"How'd it go?" she asked.

I grunted in response, shrugging my shoulders. "Could have been better, could have been much worse."

"I guess I'll have to whip you into shape." Her smile was infectious as she teased me.

"Yeah, whatever. Come on, let's go home." I dangled the rabbits in front of her. "Dinner is on me."

CHAPTER 7

Another restless night of memories and nightmares plagued me.

Fire and ash surrounded me in the woods, the roar of a fire flaring behind as I ran. The smoke of the burning trees seared my lungs. I was nearing the forest's edge, the afternoon sun beginning to peek through the thinning trees when I stumbled.

My foot caught and twisted, a loud snapping sound rang in my ears. The fire neared with every ragged breath, racing in time to my heartbeat.

I winced and braced for more pain as I attempted to pull my foot free, but it was stuck. I needed to get out. Even though I was to blame for this fire somehow, I didn't want to die for my mistakes.

I attempted to snap off the branches holding my foot hostage, but the angle it had twisted at left me unable to apply the proper pressure to free myself. Behind me, a large tree cracked and buckled from the heat, toppling to the ground. The sound was too similar to that of beams in my home breaking, trapping my mother.

Fear and anger raced through my mind and a wave of heat swelled, reminding me I had only a few moments left before the destructive flames consumed me.

Twigs cracked, and footsteps sounded. I perked up, listening. I was sure no one had come into the woods that morning. Few people ever did, only the tradesmen who traveled north or a farmer on occasion.

A shadow grew and Fynn stood over me, hands on his hips, not seemingly worried about the fire at all. He cocked his head to the side, a look of bewilderment crossing his sharp features. "You sure know how to get into quite the predicament, don't you?"

I was at a loss for words. His bright golden-amber eyes pulled me in, swallowing me whole, and I couldn't manage to get any words out. I gestured awkwardly to my foot, as if that was answer enough.

Stupid. Stupid. Stupid.

He looked at the flames with concern now, and said, "Let's get you out of here. And quickly." I swallowed and nodded in agreement, words still failing me.

Strands of his golden, shoulder-length hair fell from his half-up knot and down in front of his eyes. He worked his knife back and forth across the thick branch. "Fynn," I urged, worry creeping into my voice. His pace quickened in response.

But it wasn't working fast enough. In a last ditch effort to free me, he placed the knife between his teeth, wrapped both hands around the branch, and pulled.

With a deep grunt of effort, the branch finally snapped, and my broken foot slid from its grasp. A sigh of relief escaped my lips but it was soon replaced by a pained gasp.

"Come on," he shouted, a sense of panic resonating deep in his voice, the flames now only a few paces away. He secured his hands under my arms and hoisted me to my feet. He ducked his head underneath my left side and helped steady me as we ran.

Heat burned the back of my neck, singeing my hair. The smell of burning flesh flooded my memories. I couldn't let it end like this. We were so close. Almost free.

The pain was excruciating as I tried to balance my weight on it, but I had to keep going, even if it hurt. I spared one last glance and realized too soon that it was a mistake. Terror flowed through me, gripping my heart in its claws. The only thing keeping me from an irretrievable panic was knowing that Archer was waiting for me back home.

No. I would not let myself die here. I would not leave her alone.

The thought screamed in my mind, spurring me forward. For a moment, the heat seemed to dim, the flames pausing as if they had heard my silent plea. Fynn readjusted his grip and I bit down on my tongue to keep from screaming as we escaped into the clearing.

I woke with a start. Instinctively, I reached for my foot, phantom pains whispering through the bones.

Sighing with relief, I let the blanket fall back into place. I took a deep breath, counting to four each time, waiting as my heart returned to normal. I lifted my arms and stretched. I wanted to lie back down, but after a nightmare like that I knew I wouldn't get much sleep, even if there were only a few more hours before sunrise.

I swung my legs over the edge of my small bed. Most often, I enjoyed the company of my sister as I slept. The warmth and comfort she provided kept me calm and steady. But on nights like this when I was restless and couldn't settle my mind, I appreciated the solitude.

Though we were young when the fire that took our family occurred, I knew she remembered the haunting moment as well as I. I let the guilt of it settle in my mind, curling up next to the other pain and memories I kept there, waiting to rise up.

I shook my head absently as if the motion alone could remove some of the guilt. But guilt was not so easily shaken.

The chilly night air invigorated my senses. Cool grass met my bare feet as I walked over to an old oak tree in front of our yard, and I took a moment to appreciate the feeling. The night was always a welcomed relief. I leaned my head back against the rough bark and looked up to the heavens. I stared at the stars, the constellations, the light of the moon.

I loved everything the night offered. It beckoned to me, welcoming me in its dark embrace. On days when the heat of the sun blazed on, the night was my solace. My salvation.

I loved the light, but you could never stare at the sun the way you could the moon. The sun was a constant, always there, always the same, forever the same path from start to finish—never wavering. But the moon was endless in its change.

It waxed and waned with the days, growing and fading through time. Some nights were brighter and other nights it disappeared altogether. It served as a reminder that though it brought light to the darkest of nights, the moon—even in its eternal glory—needed to rest.

I spent the next hour in the company of the moon, counting stars and finding familiar constellations. One in particular always stood out, the easiest to spot on a clear night like tonight. Orion.

A warm smile spread over my lips at the thought. The night sky always felt like home. Familiar. Like we were a part of each other despite their mystery and endlessness.

Our father told us stories of the gods and stars as children. He loved acting out Orion's myth for my sisters and me. Most of the origins were lost over the last thousand years, but enough had passed down through generations to remember that Orion was a valiant warrior. One who was loyal to, and fought only for, the Realm of Night. His loyalty, honor, and sacrifice allowed for his story to be forever written in the stars. An honor never bestowed on any Fae ever again. It was told that he was sent to be with his mate, but her name, too, had been lost to time.

My mother, however, preferred to tell us of the sun and the moon. And though I never had the heart to tell her, I always favored my father's stories of love, courage, and the night stars. Somehow, the stars seemed to hold the truth of the universe. I only wished I could read them.

So, I found myself doing what I did most nights when my mind was plagued with nightmares of the past, and my heart ached for those I had lost… I looked to the stars and wished.

My lack of sleep caught up to me over the next week. My nightmares doubled and the emptiness I felt without Fynn began to show. My temper was shorter, my smile smaller, and my will to do menial tasks waned. The only thing that kept me together and pushing through the week's training, was our one night off.

For the last two years, the six of us, and occasionally even Fynn, went to a local tavern to drink and play darts. I opted out of some of the outings more than I'd like to admit in recent months.

Fynn kept me occupied and I stole every moment alone with him I could take. Often, we spent them at his home talking or taking part in other…extracurricular activities. My heart skipped a beat at the reminder and ached with loneliness. His physical presence wasn't the only thing I missed. A week was the longest we had been separated and in that time I had yet to receive any type of correspondence.

The six of us, still sweaty and worn out from the day's training, made our way into town, ready to release some pent-up energy and likely annoy the tavern in the process.

"I can't believe Em bested Senna," Kaede said, laughing as he draped his arm around Emryn and spun her around. She giggled and kissed his cheek, the two of them never afraid to show how much they were in love.

"I can't believe we get free drinks out of it." Skye winked at Senna who only rolled her eyes but pulled her closer.

Earlier that day Senna had kept us all behind an extra hour, wanting a little friendly archery competition. She bet that if any of us could beat her, she'd pay for drinks. Emryn had split her arrow in two.

"I can't believe I missed it," muttered Archer. She threw her hands up in mock annoyance. That was the one thing that occasionally bothered her. Because she was younger than the rest of us, even if only by two years, she often missed out on inside jokes and small events like today.

It was a significant downside that I hated, especially since she was as integral to the group as any of us. But regardless of what happened or what separated us at times, they never let anyone feel excluded. Even when tensions rose between Kaede and me, they would allow for breathing room, but ensured we never missed any outings. Well, until Fynn came around and I opted to be with him. But the invitation always remained.

The tavern was crowded when we arrived, typical for the week's end. Thankfully, we had an in with the barkeep, mainly due to the absurd amount of money we spent each week and always had our table in the corner reserved.

I was only three drinks in when the dizziness set in. I usually wouldn't drink to wash away worry or anxiety, but this week had been a lot to handle—both physically and emotionally—so I made an exception for myself this one time. The world dulled with each sip and I finally relaxed some.

"I still can't believe what happened to Petyr," Skye said, grumbling. "Soren deserved to be given lashings for that." She slammed her drink down against the table, emphasizing her words. "Yes, but I had to think long-term. Giving only lashings to someone who enjoys pain would have done nothing, let alone check their egos. But banishing them from the legion permanently will leave a stain on their family legacy. That is a pain you cannot outrun." Senna's lip curled almost imperceptibly as she spoke. She placed her hand on Skye's arm, calming her. For most couples, it was a small show of affection, but for Senna, public romance was a rarity.

"Well, I would have done both if it were up to me. Seems like the fitting consequence," Kaede mumbled, downing the rest of his drink.

"Let's be thankful you weren't," Emryn joked, and a surprised look crossed everyone's faces, shocked she would aim a joke at Kaede.

I tried to hold back a laugh, but my common sense had drowned in my liquor and I threw my head back, roaring with laughter. The others joined in, the sound contagious. Even Emryn giggled, looking to her partner with soft eyes as she covered her mouth.

"It wasn't that funny," grumbled Kaede. "At least your precious Fynn wasn't here to see you come in last against all your friends."

I tried not to care, I really did. I told myself to keep my mouth shut, to not bring up the one thing he was still sensitive about, but the anger rose. Not all at him, just…in general. And I couldn't keep it in.

"You don't always have to be such an asshole." I downed the last of my drink, slamming it a little too hard on the table. I shouldn't be going after him like this, shouldn't try and coax out a fight. I knew that we both had tried getting over this, moving past it. I thought I had, but… "Just because I dared to tell you 'no' once, doesn't give you a right to—"

"Watch it," Kaede growled and rose from the table with a start, knocking his chair back. Emryn put a hand on his arm, attempting to calm and coax him back down. He growled, his eyes still anywhere but mine, focused instead on the space above them. "Do not speak to me of rejection. Not when you're the one who pines like a lovesick puppy after a boy who's given you no attention until recently. We all know he doesn't deserve you."

"Don't you dare speak about Fynn like that." My shout rang through the tavern, drawing unwanted attention. Archer grabbed my arm, attempting to pull me back down, but I shook her off. I started to say something else, but a male appeared at our table, his posture making it clear he was unsure whether he should interrupt our spat.

"Petyr, I'm so glad to see you're okay." Emryn stood and embraced the male as if he were an old friend. But friend or not, Em's kindness knew no bounds.

Petyr blushed, his cheeks flushing from her sudden embrace and the public reminder of his injury. His leg was bandaged, but besides a slight limp, he seemed okay. "Yeah," he said sheepishly, "I'm okay. A little sore and upset, but I should count myself lucky."

"Soren should be lucky we didn't sic Kaede on him," Skye muttered, raising her glass to Petyr. "Why don't you sit? Join us."

"I'd love to, but I'm here on official business from the palace. I took a job as a messenger after the incident, but I may be able to work my way up to a guard eventually if I heal well enough." He pulled out a folded piece of paper. It was small, but I could see a large red seal even from across the table. The royal seal.

My heart skipped a beat. "Is it from Fynn?" I asked. My voice cracked.

"Sorry, Ren, but no." He smiled in sympathy. "Actually, it's from the king. It's addressed to all of you. Well…everyone except Emryn, I'm afraid." He winced.

Emryn only smiled as if it didn't bother her. It sure as hell bothered me.

What could the king possibly want with all of us that excluded Emryn? She was as much a part of the group as any of us. But if it was from the king, then I had no clue what his intentions could be. The only plausible reasoning I could find was that he didn't see her as an equal due to being Quarter Fae.

As it had been for centuries, the Select Fae viewed themselves in higher regard than any other 'lowers'. But my parents had raised us with the notion that life was precious. Whether it was five hundred years as a Select, or a mere hundred as a Quarter. My mother always said life was meant to be lived and not wasted, so why did it matter the expectancy fated to us at birth? I never questioned her teachings, but it wasn't a common belief in Albionne. Especially in Sunsbridge.

Senna held her hand out expectantly and Petyr offered her the letter. Emryn dug through her pouch and handed Petyr a gold coin. "Thank you."

He accepted the coin and left without another word. I wondered if we'd ever run into him again, or if life would carry us in separate ways.

I focused back on Senna, eager to hear if there was any mention of Fynn in the king's letter. We waited as she read it silently.

"Well?" prompted Archer, sounding as anxious as I felt.

Senna set the parchment down on the table and looked me in the eye as she said, "We have been summoned to Sunsbridge. We are to report immediately."

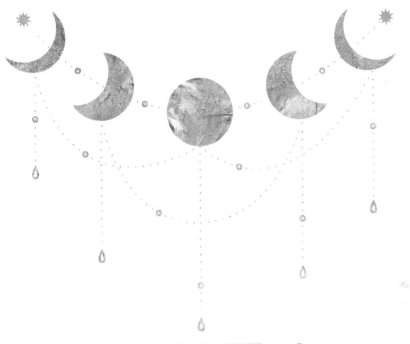

CHAPTER 8

Outside the tavern, the late hour of the night did little to hide who waited for us. If anything, it seemed to bend around him, the stars I loved so much betraying me as they illuminated the light in his eyes.

Sitting atop a tall golden horse, wearing a deep red cloak and a gold crown atop his midnight curls…was Prince Callax. Next to him were five saddled and ready horses, along with riding cloaks for each of us. All except Emryn, of course.

Kaede stepped forward, facing Callax. Both males sneered at the other with blatant distaste. If I wasn't so concerned about what this summons meant and why the king sent his son to fetch us, I would have found the encounter…oddly attractive. Despite my ongoing issues with Kaede and my justified hate for Callax, both men were incredibly handsome.

Where Callax was tall and imposing, Kaede was his opposite. Kaede carried himself without that air of silent authority, his size enough to command respect. His dark hair brushed the nape of his neck, framing his angled eyes and sharp lines of his clean-shaven face.

Callax glared over the bridge of his nose, not a hair out of place. "All of you are required at the palace. Immediately." His voice was clear and demanding. It wasn't a request. "Choose a horse and let us be on our way."

Still inebriated, none of us were in a fit state to ride, but when the king called, there was no choice. My hope of seeing Fynn propelled me onto a horse, my legs shaky.

The prince eyed me as I settled into the saddle, but I ignored him, and a strange sort of electricity charged the air between us, waiting to snap. I fastened the provided cloak over my shoulders and kept my eyes forward, but still, the weight of his gaze persisted. I darted my eyes toward him, letting my distaste remain evident, and a flash of shock and what looked to be fear swept across his face. Before I could react, he settled back into his usual scowl.

Kaede stood his ground, arms folded. Callax, clearly not impressed by the show of disobedience, turned his horse to better look down on him. Leaning forward, he said, "Are you deaf as well as dumb, bastard?"

Kaede's eyes flared with rage. He didn't take lightly to the term. He never talked about his home life before his parents abandoned them, but we all knew it was a subject best left alone. "I will not come unless Emryn is permitted to as well." His arms folded across his chest in defiance.

Emryn placed her hand on his arm and shook her head. Softly, she said, "Go. I'll be fine here." Her smile didn't reach her eyes. Emryn never let on whether or not her status as Quarter Fae bothered her, but it was in moments like this when the inequality seemed to get the better of her constant optimism.

"No," Kaede grumbled. Again, he faced the prince who grew more impatient by the second.

"Why is it the Lesser Fae girl is imperative to your obedience to your king?" His voice remained calm.

"If she goes, then so does Emryn." Male protectiveness flared across his features and I could swear Callax's eyes softened for a heartbeat, as if he understood.

The prince's brows rose and his gaze settled on me, assessing me as if he were trying to figure out if I was worth the hassle. "And what is it about this one that makes inviting along an almost human justified? You do realize she will stand before the king, and the king…well, we all know his prejudices."

"I can hold my own," Emryn snapped.

Pinching the bridge of his nose in annoyance, Prince Callax said, "Fine. Find your own horse and meet us there. The king specifically requested the lot of you and I fear there would be more consequences if there were one less than one more. So be quick, or don't bother coming at all."

Kaede gave a curt nod at the approval and put a hand on Emryn's back, leading her down the street to the stables.

"The rest of you…" The prince glanced at my sister, Skye, and Senna who had all taken their place beside me. "We haven't got all night, the king awaits."

With that, the four of us followed the prince back to the palace where only the gods knew what fate awaited us.

"Are you truly as awful as your friend seems to make you out to be?"

We had ridden in blissful silence through the night, no one daring to speak or ask questions until now. I kept my mind focused on Fynn, on not letting Callax get under my skin.

"Depends on who you ask."

"I'm asking you."

"I'm an absolute delight," I said, keeping my eyes forward, my voice bored.

He huffed a laugh. "Seems like it. Do you know why the king summoned you? I've been trying to wrap my head around it all night. I've seen your training scores, talked with Kieran myself and I can't seem to understand why in the world my father…who expects nothing less than perfection, would add your name to the list?"

My jaw clenched. I truly had no answer, no guess that could be better than his other than the fact that perhaps Fynn had something to do with it.

"Does it matter?"

"I suppose not. But I'll find out sooner or later, Miss Orion. I always get my way."

"Not if Fynn has anything to do with it," I said, regretting the tone of my voice. I should not be speaking to the prince this way, but there was something about him that grated on my nerves.

Callax only tipped his head back and laughed. I took the opportunity to spur my horse forward, placing myself next to my sister instead of him.

The sun was cresting over the eastern hills as we rode into Sunsbridge. It was quite the feat that none of us had fallen asleep during the journey. For me, it was likely the amount of focus I required not to spill the contents of my stomach, but we made it without incident. Kaede and Emryn caught up to us about an hour after we left and kept pace with ease.

I stared in awe as we rode through the lower city, the cobblestones damp from the early morning mist. Large storefronts displayed a myriad of wares and gadgets I'd never seen and shops full of beautiful gowns and formal attire lay around every corner. I smiled at the unfamiliar sights. Everything was new and exciting here.

It was still early, but the streets teemed with life. Shopkeepers dusted off their windows and opened their doors, preparing for the day's work ahead. The smell of freshly baked bread wafted through the streets and my stomach grumbled. I'd eaten nothing in nearly a day now, having only filled myself with drinks at the tavern. I hoped they would offer us breakfast and fresh clothes before our audience with the king. And before I saw Fynn.

The gates lowered behind us as we crossed a long white bridge leading to the upper city. Streams of water gently flowed beneath, leading to the ocean, its salty breeze gently blowing through my hair. Once through the large golden gates, we were met with an imposing wall of granite, gleaming in the morning sun. Black borders lined the hundreds of windows and flecks of gold scattered through the stone. Ornate sconces held torches at each doorway, their shadows dimming as servants and workers rushed back and forth across the manicured lawns and gardens which teemed with blood-red flowers. I had never seen blooms like these. They were dark and lovely and covered in thorns.

Despite the beauty of the castle, the architecture and spiked archways loomed above with severity. The white was inviting, but the structure was entrapping. As if once you stepped into the alluring complexity and walked beneath the vaulted ceilings, you'd be caged forever. It was dizzying to think about.

Callax stopped at the stables and dismounted, handing his reins to a young stable hand. The rest of us followed suit and dismounted with varying levels of success. Poor Archer had only ever ridden a handful of times in her life and despite her never-ending grace, she nearly tumbled off. I would have laughed had I not been utterly exhausted.

Callax instructed us to follow him and proceeded toward a side entrance tucked between two rows of deep green trees. The yellow blossoms attached to each branch gave off a sickly sweet odor and I held my breath until we passed through the door.

The palace was equally striking on the inside as the outside and somehow managed to be even more intimidating. Callax's deep red cloak brushed the floor as he swept through the halls. The color matched the same as the banners lining the corridors, bearing the golden crest of the realm—two twining snakes around a spiked sun.

My thighs ached in protest as we wound our way up the flights of stairs. Finally, we stopped halfway up the tower where six large doors lined the alcove at the end of a long corridor.

Callax placed his hands behind his back, standing tall, and said, "Two of you will need to share a room as there is one more than expected." He glanced at Emryn who stood silently next to Kaede, their hands intertwined. "I don't care who, figure it out among yourselves. Your belongings, along with a fresh bath and breakfast are in each of your rooms."

I sighed in relief, my stomach rumbling in answer to his words. Food and a bath. Both of which I desperately needed.

"You have two hours before the king expects you in the throne room. New training gear has also been provided. Wear them." He turned on his polished heel and proceeded down the stairs, calling out one last remark before disappearing down the spiral staircase. "And for the love of the gods...please bathe. You lot reek like a lower city sewer rat."

An hour later, clean and polished and tucked into a plush robe, I wanted nothing more than to fall into the large four-poster bed in the middle of my new room. I had never had more than one pillow, but with how many lay across the bed, it looked like a cloud. It was almost enough to convince me to ignore the king and take a long nap instead.

"Want to just skip the whole thing and take a nap?"

I jumped, not expecting to hear another voice in my room. I must have left the door open.

Archer leaned against he door frame, her arms folded, hair still damp and tucked into a long braid. She was dressed head to toe in black training gear that was far nicer than anything we could ever afford. Not a scratch or scuff to be seen.

"You read my mind." I let myself smile as she walked into the room, hopping onto the bed.

"You'd better get ready." She tucked one hand behind her head and gestured to the clothes at the edge of the bed. "We only have a half hour and none of us even know where the throne room is or how to get there."

"She's right you know." An all too familiar voice reached my ears and my heart fluttered at the sound.

"Fynn," I gasped, emotion cracking my voice. I bounded the few paces still separating us and leaped into his arms. He held me tight, squeezing me as he chuckled.

"I missed you too, Renata." I nestled my head into the crook of his neck, sinking into his arms, and breathing a long sigh of relief. The familiar scent of cedar and ash filled my nose. I lingered there, breathing him in.

In just those few moments, I could feel the pang of loneliness in my heart subside. He was all I needed and everything was right in the world once more. After a few more seconds, he pulled away and ran his hands down my arms. "Come on," he said, "get dressed and I'll take you all to speak with the king."

His crooked smile reassured me and I knew he'd answer all the questions lingering between the two of us. I trusted his judgment and left his embrace.

Archer slipped off the bed and exited the room with him, leaving me to change.

CHAPTER 9

With my hand firmly placed in his, Fynn guided us through the maze of corridors and stairwells leading to the king, pointing out things we ought to know along the way. The way he spoke made it seem as if we would be here for a while. I had no idea what the king could need from us, but there was no scenario in my mind where we would be required to stay long-term.

According to Fynn, just down the hall were the healer's quarters and infirmary, and at the other end was another alcove of rooms identical to ours where he was staying.

As we neared the throne room, we walked under the massive portraits of the royal family. The Sundan line went back for the last thousand years. Each portrait lined up in historical succession grew more severe in the angles of their face and the harshness of their eyes. It made sense why I had felt an innate distrust toward the king, even only having seen him once.

Two guards were stationed outside the gilded doors. Fynn motioned towards them and they heaved them outward, obeying his command. We stood as a group, Fynn and I at the center. My nerves were on edge, the anticipation and exhaustion blending into a slurry of chaos. But after a deep breath and count of four, I nodded that I was ready and Fynn led us inside.

Towering columns of white stone rose to the ceiling, ornate carvings decorating the tops of each. Snakes, carved in striking, realistic detail wound around the base, framed by lush green plants. Though plenty of light streamed in through the floor-to-ceiling windows behind the throne, a myriad of gold sconces held flaming torches.

The regality of the spacious room was almost painful to look at. I had spent my entire life living at the edge of Firielle, where my only change of scenery was when I went into town or the woods. The soft rolling hills and bright green trees of my hometown were the only places I worshiped any kind of deity. I'd been happy with my world before today, but seeing this city, this palace—and this room alone—showed me there were beauties to find in this world I hadn't known possible.

I gasped a little as I took it all in. Fynn squeezed my hand as if to say, I know, I felt the same way.

Sitting on his throne atop the small dais, raised above the rest of the room, was King Tobias. Next to his throne, stood five Fae all clad in black, Callax being one of them. But it was the two faces beside him, the ones I detested that made my lip curl.

Soren and Caldor.

Next to Senna, Kaede hissed in disapproval. I turned to Fynn, whispering as softly as possible. "What in the hell are those two doing here?"

He whispered, "They're with us. The king will explain."

Maybe he didn't share our distaste for the males because he wasn't there the day Soren shot Petyr, or perhaps the king had his reasons for having them here, but either way...I didn't like it.

I quieted as the king eyed me warily. A too-wide smile grew across his face as his arms outstretched in a welcoming gesture. "Welcome to Sunsbridge," he said. His voice was inviting, but his eyes were cold. "I apologize for the rush in your arrival, but I promise it was for good reason. The five..."his voice faltered, eyes darting between Emryn and his son, trying to piece together why there was one more female here than expected. He cleared his throat. "The six of you have been summoned here to the palace at my behest."

"As you know, your friend is now the Phoenix. This is a tremendous honor and one you should count yourselves lucky for. Not only that this blessed event occurred in your lifetime, but that is one you call friend."

I smiled a little at his words, my heart bursting with pride. I did count myself lucky.

The king continued. "Now, it is your great privilege that I extend an offer. As you know, one can achieve many ranks within my great legion, but there is one that has not been established for some time. One offered only to a select few and led by the Phoenix himself. They are known as the Ira Deorum."

Ira Deorum. The name felt ancient and powerful.

"The eleven…twelve of you, will be advisors to and aide the Phoenix. I have chosen six of my own, as has the Phoenix. You are here at his behest." He nodded at Fynn, a smirk of some hidden knowledge flashing through his eyes. "He will lead you all in assignments and tasks for the crown. I will send you where I see fit, and you will do as you are commanded, either through my own or the Phoenix's delegation.

"You will begin your training today. You will continue with the regular courses set for the legion, but you will be required to outperform in every category. Merely passing the courses will no longer be acceptable. There will be no weakness. No mercy. And no exceptions."

I swallowed hard. While single combat was something I did well in, I wouldn't deem myself exceptional. And I wouldn't categorize myself as above average in anything, let alone archery.

"Just because you have been brought here for this honor, does not mean you will make it to the initiation ceremony." He eyed the six of us. "Upon completion of your training, we will host a ball in honor of the return of the Ira Deorum. If you have not been cut by then, you will face your final trial set by me." A cruel smile spread over his face. His wide mouth only added to the sense of foreboding. "Pass the trial and you are in. Fail…well, the shame will be more than enough, but let's hope it doesn't come to that."

A shiver ran up my spine. I didn't want to know what would happen if one of us were to fail, but I couldn't imagine a scenario that ended well if we were to embarrass the king in any way.

"Prince Callax will lead you into your training." With a dismissive wave, Callax as rigid as a board, walked off the dais, the king's chosen following him out. But as we left the room, he uttered one more phrase, no warmth remaining in his commanding voice. The words would haunt me for months to come.

"Do not disappoint me."

The training room expanded so far back I couldn't tell all that lay inside. Equipment lined the walls along the entrance with every weapon imaginable. Adjacent to the endless supply was a wall of jagged and uneven stone, made to look as if it were hewn directly from a mountain itself. Ropes, ladders, poles, hand wraps, and a table full of vials and bowls I could only assume were for poisons, lined the opposite wall.

The further we walked through, the more that revealed itself. Towards the back was a maze, pits of mud, water, and sand that took up a sizable chunk of space. And in the center of it all sat a platform raised off the ground—a sparring ring.

Fynn squeezed my hand and said, "I'm training separately with the Keeper, Ilvar, to focus on my new abilities so I won't be here most of the time. But I'll see you for dinner." He kissed the side of my cheek and whispered good luck as he walked away.

After the twelve of us took an inventory of where we would be training, a deep, booming voice echoed. "Two rows, single file. Line up in the center. Now." I whipped my head up, locating the speaker. Standing above us in a viewing box was an average-sized male. He had a salt and pepper beard, long wiry hair swept into a low knot, and a scar running the length of his jaw. Intense was the only word I could think of.

We did as we were told. I stood across from the prince and stared him down, not bothering to hide my distaste. In the training room—as was standard tradition—everyone was an equal and therefore, fair game.

Kaede stood across from Soren, Emryn was opposite Caldor, and the other three paired up against Skye, Senna, and Archer but I didn't know their names.

"Senna. Mavenna. You two are up first. Please step up to the platform." The male above us commanded, and the two did as they were told. Senna tied back her long braids with a leather cord she kept around her wrist. The other Fae female, Mavenna, followed suit. She was nearly as tall and wide as most of the males, her legs and arms proving her physical capability. But the sheer size of her made me nervous. Even though Senna could hold her own against anyone, the last thing I wanted was to see my friends get hurt.

"You will fight until one of you is unconscious or thrown out of the ring. Whichever comes first." The unknown male stepped to the side as another joined him. The king. He must be here to monitor us. No pressure.

Senna was born for battle and it showed. She dodged every punch Mavenna threw her way. She had yet to throw one of her own, but it was a typical strategy for her to assess the opponent and calculate their moves before determining her own. I watched as she eyed her opponent's legs, then hands, then face. Looking for tells and signs that would give away her next moves.

After only a few moments, Senna raised her arms, ready to fight back.

It was quick. Mavenna landed a blow or two to Senna's shoulder, but she moved with wide steps and took up too much room. Senna noticed the same thing because she let Mavenna back her into a corner.

I watched as a grin grew on Mavenna's face, thinking she had her trapped. But when she moved to throw the final blow, Senna ducked and rolled to the side where she only crouched and watched as Mavenna's swing propelled her forward into thin air.

Her balance buckled as she attempted to correct the step, but with no more platform available, her foot met open air and she fell to the ground in a tangle of limbs.

Senna stood, straightening her back, and acknowledged the males above. They did not provide any applause or approval. They simply said, "Emryn. Caldor. You're up next."

Even though Emryn was as good, if not better than the rest of us, she was still less Fae than anyone else here. I didn't doubt she was the only one who wasn't even Select. Emryn was tall, but not nearly as tall as Caldor, and easily half his size. My heart beat faster, and I reached for Archer's hand. She must have been worried too since she squeezed back, both of our hands clammy from nerves. I took a glance up at the king, and a small smirk crossed his lips as if he was hoping to enjoy seeing a Lesser Fae beaten down by one of his chosen.

Before they could say 'begin,' Caldor was swinging, aiming directly for Emryn's face. She dodged the first few punches, but the third and fourth landed squarely on her jaw and then her gut. Her breath caught in unison with ours, all of us concerned.

Kaede's fists clenched, but we all knew there was nothing we could do. Caldor wouldn't seriously injure Emryn, or at least I hoped so. Surely, they would stop the fight before it got too serious. But Emryn kept taking the blows. One to her stomach, the next to her hip, then her chest.

She sat on the ground, blood trickling from the edge of her mouth. Despite the blows, she continued to fight back. Caldor had the larger half of the ring occupied by his pacing, waiting for her next move.

"Oh, come on, Emryn," he teased, his voice lilting, trying to goad her. "Show me how hard a Lesser can really hit." He put his hand out and motioned for her to come at him.

Her eyes flared with confidence and something else I couldn't quite place, but it seemed like…excitement. As if she were enjoying this game. As if she didn't mind getting pushed around while she waited to make her move.

"Well, since you asked…" Emryn swung her long leg out and swept it beneath him. His ankle buckled, but he didn't fall. Instead, he stumbled back, tripping over his leg. In an instant, Emryn was on her feet and placed three blows back-to-back. A punch to his gut made him catch his breath, a direct blow to his center had his hand protecting his chest, but it left his head wide open. Something Emryn predicted.

She didn't hesitate a beat as she placed one final uppercut directly under his large, square jaw. His head snapped back, and he stumbled over the edge, landing flat on his back. The sound of the mat and his body echoed through the room. He was out cold.

Emryn wiped the blood dripping from her split lip. She turned to the king and gave the tiniest bow, but I suspected it was more in mockery than respect. It seemed there was more to her than just the kind friend we all loved.

Archer, Skye, and Kaede went one after the other. Archer lost her match, but it was expected as she had not had training with hand-to-hand combat yet. I worried about what that would mean for her in the coming months, but the worry faded to the back of my mind as I was more concerned about my duel with Callax.

Pyne, the female who sparred with Archer, was the same age as my sister and had yet to start section training like the rest of us. She must have excelled at something, otherwise the king would have had no reason to select her. She was tiny but quick, and even though Archer was fast, she had no practice in physical fighting.

The two of them lasted longer in the ring, a little more evenly matched, but by the end, they tired each other out. In a misstep, Archer stumbled off the platform.

Skye, like Pyne, was tiny and quick. Her match with Kell didn't take long. I knew Skye and Kaede had put in time with each other after hours to practice their weapons and skills. But Kell was strong and won at the last second.

Kaede and Soren were second to last, leaving Callax and me to end the session. My nerves danced on edge, my hands shook, and my stomach turned. One more, only one more to go.

The two males were evenly matched when it came to size and height. Both launched immediately into action, attempting to tear the other apart. I had seen many fights throughout the years and participated in many too. But the sight of the two of them was something else entirely. The sheer amount of anger that emanated from them could be felt throughout the room. Punches continued to land in a frenzy, neither getting the upper hand until Kaede landed a rough blow to Soren's chest, winding him. Before Kaede could rush to the other side of the platform, Soren took two bounding leaps and crossed with incredible speed.

I didn't have time to close my eyes before Soren, his face plastered with rage, hit Kaede square in the nose. A crack sounded, and I didn't need to see the spurt of blood to know it was broken.

Stunned by the pain, Kaede paused long enough for Soren to sweep his leg underneath Kaede, sending him toppling over the edge.

A satisfied smirk passed over the king's face when I looked up. The other male stood; stone-faced with his arms crossed over his chest. I couldn't tell what he had been thinking, but there was at least no shadow of pleasure over the brawl.

My heart pounded faster, my hands sweating, and it felt like all the eyes in the room were on me.

"Callax. Renata. Please step forward," the male called out.

I took a shaky breath. I tried to use my breathing technique to calm myself, but it did nothing. I had fought before, many times, but I'd never fought Callax. And I had never fought in front of the king.

We were all equal in the training ring, and I knew they expected me to give my all regardless of my partner or their status, but this was the prince. Would they punish me for ruining his pretty face or spilling his blood on the floor? Assuming I could beat him. I had never seen Callax fight, had never seen him train. I had no clue what was waiting for me.

"Begin."

My heart jumped in anticipation, and I immediately put my hands up, knowing I needed to protect my face and head before anything else. Callax didn't move, he just... winked.

"Poor Orion...you know, I think I finally have the answer to my question. You're only here cause of Fynn." He circled me, forcing me to move in tandem with him. He was trying to get under my skin, trying to get me to react and slip up in anger.

"Watch your mouth, prince." I knew these games. I had been an unwilling player my whole life. I had listened to Soren and Caldor tease me for my losses for years now. They still riled me up, but I learned to breathe through the worst of it, channeling the anger into my training.

"Feisty. I like it. I can see why the Phoenix likes to keep you around. I should thank him for bringing you here." His words agitated me, grating in my mind. I tested his boundary and took a step forward, closing the gap between us, forcing him to make a move or bring him close enough to attack. "Though, I can't imagine he'll stay entertained by you for long if you can't keep up." His eyes grazed my body from head to toe, looking at me with cold eyes.

I gritted my teeth. I, of course, already had the same thoughts. I should be flattered—honored, even—that he chose me as his partner and now to be part of his guard. I knew Fynn must have been the one to request my presence, but Callax made it seem like a pity choice and not because he wanted—or needed—me here. Now, I only questioned how I could ever be enough for someone as perfect as he.

My lip quivered, and he smiled coldly. He hit the nerve he wanted, and it pleased him. Bitter anger coursed through my veins. I needed to hit something. Hard.

I launched myself at Callax, and the thought of being the one to break the pretty prince's face fueled my actions.

Only a few inches from my target, Callax stepped to the side, spurring my forward momentum with a shove. My head snapped against the floor with a loud crack.

Callax's smug face was the last thing I saw before the room faded to black.

CHAPTER 10

Something wet and cold pressed against my forehead. I tried to open my eyes, but the intense pounding in my skull was enough to make my vision blurry. I pressed my palms to them, trying to rub away the pain, wincing at the pressure.

"Welcome back." I recognized Fynn's voice immediately and tried to sit up, but his strong hands held me down, forcing me to stay put. "Heard you took quite the fall today."

"I'm just glad you weren't there to see it," I chuckled, but it turned into a pained groan once it escaped my lips. Gods, my head was killing me.

"Don't worry, Camilla will be right back with a tonic to ease the pain as you heal." Fynn wrapped his fingers through my hand, rubbing his thumb over the back of mine. I loved the little things like that. The reassurance of his touch always comforted me. It made me feel a little more secure. But at this moment, it only reminded me of Callax's words before I fell.

I can't imagine he'll stay entertained for long…

The words replayed in my head, taunting me. I pushed them down, ignoring the bile rising in my throat, and focused instead on Fynn's touch.

"Who's Camilla?" I asked. Still unsure where I was. I had yet to open my eyes through the pain.

"A human healer. She's one of the few here that attend directly to the thirteen of us if need be."

"Well, I'd say it is 'need be' today."

An unfamiliar voice approached from the side. "Quite the bump there, miss. This should take the pain away in a few minutes." The lilt in her voice was soft and comforting. "Just make sure to put a cold compress on it tonight for an hour or two, and you'll be right as rain."

"Thank you, Camilla. I can give it to her if you don't mind." Fynn let go of my hand, and I felt him lean over my body to grab the vial. The clink of glass sounded against his rings, and then a tiny noise escaped Camilla's lips. A whimper almost. I could tell from her tone alone she found herself entranced with Fynn's presence. I knew because I had been the same way once. I rolled my eyes behind my eyelids and pushed down the pang of jealousy that flared.

Calm down, I told myself. I knew I was being irrational, but Callax's antagonizing words still hung fresh in my mind.

"Here, drink this." He placed the cool glass against my lips. The bitter liquid ran down my throat, and I hoped it would take effect quickly. A drop of the tonic escaped my lips and dripped down my chin. Fynn's hand wiped it away, and he cradled my face until the pain subsided.

She was right. It only took a handful of minutes until the throbbing eased. Only a dull ache remained.

"Hey," I groaned and tightened my lips in embarrassment.

"You have to make sure you stay in one piece. You have a bad habit of winding up in painful situations." He cocked his head and raised an eyebrow.

"Yeah, I know." It was so nice to see his face without anyone else around. I had missed him—more than I wanted to admit. But seeing him now, smiling at me with love and affection, made up for it.

"I'm going to grab us some dinner since you missed it. I'll meet you back in your room shortly. Love you." He kissed my cheek, and the words warmed my skin.

"I love you too," I whispered. My heart steadied at his words, and the warmth spread through my body.

I swung my legs off the bed and tested my stability. I swayed a bit, the blood rushing from my head, but I stayed upright. Luckily, Fynn pointed out where the infirmary was earlier, so I knew my room wasn't far away.

"Let me know if you need anything else, miss," Camilla shouted from across the room, the volume making me wince. I waved my hand over my shoulder and muttered my thanks.

The corridor, unfortunately, looked the same leading in either direction. I had a fifty/fifty chance of getting it right, so I went to the right, hoping my prediction would be correct. As I turned, I bumped into a tall, rigid body. "Oh, I'm so—" I stopped.

It was Callax.

"The hell are you doing here?" I hissed. I wasn't in the mood to see him. My head ached in response as if it knew he was the reason it hurt.

"That's not any way to talk to your prince." He crossed his arms, leaning against the stone wall. Pure male arrogance seemed to radiate from him.

I scowled. "If you weren't in my way, then I would have no problem ignoring you completely." That wasn't true. But, then again, I hadn't had the opportunity to test the validity of my statement, so it wasn't a complete lie.

"Oh, I doubt that very much, Miss Orion." He stared at his fingers, assessing each nail as if they were somehow more interesting than I was. "Besides, I've come to give you some advice."

I shook my head in disbelief. "Do you really think I want to hear what you have to say?"

"You'd better keep up. You missed the last half of the day, and even your little sister managed to catch my father's eye with her archery skills." That didn't surprise me. There had yet to be anyone who wasn't impressed with her accurate aim. "And the others all have qualities that prove useful. You, however..." He looked me up and down again. I pulled my arms in tighter, trying to hide from his roaming gaze. "Have yet to prove your value. Take my advice, and practice more. Train harder. Learn something useful, or leave. Otherwise, my father will lose interest. Even if the Phoenix specifically requested you, you will become nothing more than an afterthought. Easily discarded and easily forgotten."

The last line hit me harder than I had expected. A flash of pain tinged my face, and Callax softened a little as if he realized he had gone too far. He brushed his hands through his perfectly set hair.

He turned away, walking past me, when I blurted out, "Why are we forming this group when there are no wars to fight? What could the king possibly need from us that a Phoenix can't do on his own?"

He paused, back still facing me. "As I said, learn something useful. You'll find my father does not take kindly to those who question him." I threw my hands in exasperation at his non-answer.

"Oh, and Miss Orion…" he called over his shoulder as he strolled down the hall, hands in his pockets. "Your room is in the other direction."

The smell of food hit me before he entered my room. A roast, fresh bread, potatoes, and brightly colored fruit filled the plates Fynn carried. I sat up immediately, ready to devour everything. I hoped he had already eaten because I could easily consume both plates.

"Oh yes, please," I said, extending my hands out impatiently. He handed me the plates and sat down, stealing some of the fruit, popping it into his mouth before leaning back on the pillows, one hand under his head.

"Thank you," I mumbled between mouthfuls of bread and meat. Gods, this was good. I had always enjoyed food, but since my parent's death, I didn't have the luxury of sweet fruits and spices. So this meal was a small piece of paradise.

I didn't say anything else while I inhaled both plates, Fynn's hand tracing the edge of my thigh. I felt like I could burst at the seams, but I was happy and full.

Fynn extended an arm, inviting me to lie down next to him. I leaned back and curled up into his side, resting my head on his chest. For a moment or two, I listened to his steady heartbeat and savored his earthy scent, content to just exist with him.

It had been some time since we did this last. Or had a moment to just enjoy the other's company without interruptions. I had missed it dearly.

"Yes?" he asked.

"What?" I looked up, confused.

"You only breathe like that when you have something on your mind."

I held back a smile. "No…" I loved that he knew that about me. That he knew my tells and body language. It made me feel seen. Loved.

"I'm sure you have lots of questions, I did too. Ask away." He combed through my raven waves with his fingers. I was tempted to brush it off and just soak in these few precious moments. But I had been waiting for over a week, and the questions pressed to the front of my mind.

"What was it like?" I whispered, thinking back to the moment I had seen him scream as white-hot light seared into his chest and down his arms. Exploding like a newly made sun.

For me, the moment was only anxiety and nerves. Fire had claimed my family, and I was forced to watch as it nearly claimed him too. But his was a gift from the gods, not a curse of damnation.

He looked to the ceiling, recalling the memory. "It was sudden and painful, but it was over quickly. There was this intense heat that formed in a tight ball in my chest. I honestly thought my heart would burst, or maybe something similar to your panic attacks, but it wasn't." I was familiar with that painful sensation. They happened semi-regularly and had been common for as long as I could remember. But I could see how a sudden onset of one might worry someone. Especially if they had never experienced it before.

"As the pressure built, I heard a voice in my head. This deep, thunderous voice. I thought I was going crazy, but it said, 'Fynn Tirich, I claim you as my host. You are claimed as a loyal servant to your realm's one and only god. You are bound by this power. You will live by my will. You are the chosen, the Phoenix.'"

I stared up at him, his eyes glazed. He took a deep breath, coming out of the memory. "And then…it all exploded." His hand stopped moving through my hair and he clutched at his chest absently as if he still felt the pain. "As I was lifted in the air, I felt the fire, the blinding heat rush through my veins and sear down my arms, branding me with these marks." He lifted his other arm to show the tattoos I absently traced. "The next thing I knew, I was on the ground and the world faded away. I—I died." He swallowed hard. "But then I felt the world again. The light beckoned me back and I heard your voice. I sifted through the ash, and I was alive again." He looked down and smiled, his thumb tracing my cheek. "I'm glad you were there, Renata. I'm glad it was just you when it happened."

The words made my heart melt. "I'm glad I was, too."

He kissed my forehead and asked, "Okay, next question?"

I contemplated the multitude of them but finally decided. "Where are your wings?" I realized I had not seen them since the explosion. "Aren't Phoenixes known for their legendary wings?" I sat up and searched his face, eager for the answer. I hadn't asked, hoping he would offer, but I desperately wanted to see them.

He chuckled as his mood shifted, his smile growing. "Oh, I have wings." He said it with such pride I knew they must be spectacular. Just like everything else about him. "Would you like to see?"

"Let's see what kind of wingspan the hose of the Sun God has been blessed with." I winked, smiling coyly.

He took my arm and pulled me off the bed with him, empty dishes clattering behind us. We were out the door and running down the hall, still barefoot. I laughed at the spontaneity of it all. "Where are we going?"

"Do you trust me?" The playfulness had my heart as light as a feather. Moments like this were the memories I knew I'd keep forever, tucked away in my heart for the days when life was hard.

"Of course," I said breathlessly. We reached the bottom and Fynn threw the door open as we walked onto the perfectly manicured lawn. My bare feet in the cool grass had me pausing to appreciate the feeling.

He dropped my hand and paced a few steps away, making sure there was plenty of room. "Ready?"

"Yes, please," I grinned.

I watched him peel off his shirt, which I wasn't sure was necessary but appreciated it all the same. He planted his feet wide, straightening his back as he rolled his shoulders. There was a shimmer of light and the grin on his face grew into glee as two massive wings appeared from behind him.

I marveled as they unfurled. Beautiful, enormous, feathered wings spread out wide behind him. They were as wide as he was tall if not more so, tapering to a delicate point. A deep crimson red coated most of the feathers, but as they trailed off, they faded to a deep burnt orange bordered with gold. Flecks of gold speckled throughout, decorating the edges of each delicate feather.

Each one was long and immaculate, the smallest still nearly the size of my forearm. He shook them out, the soft whisper of them a song on the wind. Beautiful was not the right word for how he looked. He looked…god-like. He was god-like, because the host for the Sun God stood before me, in all his glory. And he was mine, all mine.

In the setting sun, his golden tattoos flickered in the light. I could see why he hadn't wanted to keep them there at all times, the rooms were not built for him, nor the beds.

I stared for a moment more, mouth still open wide, afraid to breathe in his presence.

"Pretty cool, huh?"

"I have no words. They…they look like flames." The thought of fire triggered that innate response, causing the briefest moment of panic. But Fynn wasn't a threat. I loved and trusted him. I repeated the last phrase in my mind, forcing myself to ignore my own mind and trust him.

I had yet to ask about the rest of his abilities, afraid to see the flames brought to life before me. It was better to wait, to adjust to this, and then I could determine how I felt going forward.

I took a step forward, lifting a hand reflexively, wanting to touch the feathers. "Can I?" I asked, wanting permission first. There was a moment of hesitation, but he nodded and folded one in, bringing it close so I could admire them.

Ever so softly, reverently, I ran my fingertips along each row of feathers. He breathed sharply. He answered before I could ask. "They're sensitive.

I've caught on quickly though, learning how to summon them and fly. Flying is..." He shook his head, trying to find the right words. "Flying is something else entirely. I can't explain it. But I can show you." His face was wicked with mischief.

Before I could say anything, Fynn stepped forward and locked his arms under mine. In a flash, his wings unfurled and lifted high. In a powerful downdraft, we shot into the sky.

CHAPTER 11

I used to dream of the night sky. Long before I was plagued with nightmares of death and flames, the darkness opened its arms to me, welcoming and unending. I dreamed of soaring over the world, crossing oceans, harnessing the wind. Power and freedom at my beck and call.

But I had not dreamed of such things in a long while. No, those dreams had died along with my hope. With my family. It had been some time since there was happiness. Joy.

The sudden leap upward jolted me, sending me into a panic, my stomach leaping straight into my throat. I scrambled, my arms and legs flailing as the earth rapidly disappeared. I shut my eyes tight and held onto Fynn for dear life. Clinging to the only safety I could find.

"I've got you. You said you trusted me," Fynn shouted over the wind, his laugh infectious. I couldn't form words. "Open your eyes." His voice softened when he noticed I had tucked my head into his shoulders.

Our ascent slowed to a stop, the wind now only a gentle breeze. I took a deep breath and counted to four, slowly prying one eye open, placing my trust in him. What lay before me was nothing but a sky of deep blue and gold, the sun slowly disappearing behind the mountains beyond the city. I gasped, drinking in the sight before me, my worry washing away.

I had never seen anything quite so breathtaking. From this high, the world stretched on for miles in every direction. Below me lay the palace and Sunsbridge. The people seemed like tiny ants. Little fires flickered in houses and windows, reminding me of stars. Beyond the city were rolling green hills and a deep forest of thick trees to the right. The palace lay behind it, and below the cliffs lay the ocean. I could the roads extending far into the country. I had never been beyond Firielle's walls before and in just one moment, Fynn had shown me…everything.

Those dreams of flying, of freedom, and excitement, and adventure all came rushing back. Like I could keep them within my grasp and conquer anything or escape anywhere in just a few strokes of his wings.

"Show me everything," I whispered breathlessly. "I want to see everything."

Fynn nuzzled his face against my cheek, kissing me softly, grinning against my lips. "For you, I'll give you the world."

I shrieked as he tossed me in the air. The brief free fall both exhilarated and terrified me before he caught me in his arms once more.

I wrapped my arms tightly around his neck, never wanting to let go. He beat his glorious wings once, and we were soaring.

I couldn't wipe the smile from my face and my cheeks ached, but I didn't care. I wasn't typically a jealous person, but this gift he had, it was something I would envy every day for the rest of my life.

He set me down gently and I took a moment to reorient myself with stable ground. He tucked his wings in tight and watched as they glimmered out of existence.

"Where do they go?" I asked, curious how his magic worked.

Magic didn't used to be entirely uncommon. Small magics had been used for centuries, mainly in healing and small matters such as plant growth, but that kind of magic was so small it was trivial. Only the gods and their direct lines often carried any kind of useful magic in their veins, but it had been a thousand years since the old gods were around, so the magic died out with them.

"They're not gone, exactly, more like… in between." I gave him a puzzled look and he continued, "I don't know how to explain it, or if I should, but it's like a little pocket of space I can store them in. Ilvar calls it aether." He rolled his shoulders, adjusting. "They're still there, I can feel their weight, but they cannot be felt or seen by anyone else. It allows me to move in and out of doors easier, that's for sure." He breathed a short laugh and reached for my hand. I wrapped my fingers around his and we walked back inside, the cool stone reminding me I had forgotten my shoes. I shivered.

Fynn recounted the last few days of his training, telling me of his Keeper and all that he had begun to teach him, how Ilvar was one of the few Fae that had any direct contact with the last Phoenix. And how most of the Phoenixes in the past were withdrawn and secretive, keeping their knowledge only to themselves, a privilege in its own right. He told me how Therion, the Fae male who had overseen our first day of training, was teaching him to use a sword before the rest of us would.

There were no written recordings about the workings of a Phoenix's power, only the words passed down from Keeper to the Phoenix himself. If books had ever been written or were found, it was considered treason of the highest degree and punishable by death. The Phoenix was the advantage of the king, and keeping that information, and the Phoenix himself a secret, was the way to ensure that.

As he continued, a worrying thought passed my mind. "Fynn…if Ilvar won't even write these things down, should you be telling me? It'll be months before any of us are technically a part of the Ira Deorum, and I know I'm your partner but won't he be mad? Would the king be mad?" Worry crept into my voice. I remembered the king's parting words and I felt like having this knowledge only put me in danger.

He pulled me in close and wrapped his arm around my shoulder. "I'm not worried. I'm the Phoenix, remember? The information should be mine to do with as I please. Besides, I love you, how could I be a good partner if you didn't know these things about me?"

"Yeah," I said, letting his logic wash away my worries. We reached my room and I stopped in the doorway. "Will you stay with me tonight?"

"Always." His eyes warmed. He liked being needed. Liked me needing him.

We curled up in my giant bed and he held me tight, rubbing my hair with his hand until I drifted off to sleep.

I dreamed of flying that night.

When I woke, I stretched and felt for Fynn next to me, but he was gone. His half of the bed was already made, and I imagined he must have left for his training.

Not wanting to miss breakfast, I dressed quickly. I knocked once on Archer's door and didn't bother to wait for a response, barging in. I was shocked to see Kaede and Archer exchanging an object and having what seemed to be a pleasant conversation.

"What's going on?" I asked, genuinely curious.

"Let me know what you think." He dipped his head in goodbye to my sister and breezed past without acknowledging my presence.

"Wow, so nice to see you, Ren. I hope you have a lovely day." I muttered as he passed by, mocking his voice, letting him know he could have at least acknowledged me. "You too, Kaede...how kind and thoughtful."

Archer chuckled. She moved to put away whatever he had given her, but I grabbed her arm and pulled the book from her hand. "Since when did Kaede learn to read?" I joked. "And when did you two become book best friends?" I flipped through the book, trying to glean its contents.

She snatched it back and looked at it like it was a delicate, precious thing, "This isn't the first time he's done this. It's been going on for a few years now. Whenever he finds an interesting title or reads something he thinks I don't know, he brings it to me." I must have been making a sour face because Archer gently hit my arm with the book.

"Ow, what was that for?"

"You know, Kaede's a sweet guy once you break down his tough exterior."

I knew. I'd known that for years before this new version of him. But that wasn't the Kaede I knew now. The version of Kaede with us here couldn't bother to think twice about me. He was still bitter. Part of me wanted to understand, but the other part wanted to tell him to deal with it.

"I'm glad he's nice to you," I said in defeat. I wasn't going to bother arguing so early in the morning, not after I had had such a lovely night. "He can be really nice if he likes you."

I sat on the edge of her bed and flopped backward, sighing both in exasperation at Kaede and the contentment of the previous night.

Archer sat next to me, "Is there something you're not telling me?" she asked. She knew there was, but she was being polite. We always knew when something was bothering the other. We were too alike. Even though there were only two years between us, I was convinced Archer and I were twin souls, one-half mine and the other hers. Too often, we would find ourselves saying the same thing simultaneously, having the same thought, or thinking the same way. Sometimes it spooked me, but for the most part, it was amazing to have someone in my life who could know what I was feeling without asking. To know I was seen and understood completely.

I rolled to my side, facing her, and squealed with excitement. I spent the next fifteen minutes explaining in detail the experience of flying and Fynn, the Phoenix powers, and everything else I could think of.

When I finished, she said, "So unfair...when do I get an all-powerful partner?" We laughed, curling up next to each other.

"Patience, my child." We giggled, and I pulled her up off the bed. "Come on," I beckoned her to follow me out the door. "I don't want to miss breakfast."

CHAPTER 12

Therion wouldn't listen to my arguments about why it was a bad idea to pair the two of us up, he only said that the decision had been made and to learn to get along. Some weird peace and harmony garbage I didn't care to listen to. So from here until the end of our training, I was stuck with the self-righteous prick of a prince.

"If you lowered your elbow, your aim would improve." Callax didn't even bother to look over at me as we shot arrows at targets impossibly far away.

"If you stopped telling me what to do, maybe I could concentrate long enough to hit something." I scowled but kept my eye on the tarted. I missed the center to no surprise, but it was close. I lowered my elbow and let it fly. I watched as it landed dead center. I cursed softly, he had been right.

I slowly looked to my right, hoping to find him occupied, but there he stood. Smirking.

"Are you always this stubborn?"

I ignored him and continued to swap out the style of bow I was using, learning to string new ones and get used to the feel of them all. It was tedious, but useful, and found that the long bow gave me the most control.

Therion rotated us in our pairs, in and out of his direct training. I loathed working with him more than the archery practice…which was saying something.

"Lower." Therion's stick whacked against my thighs and they screamed in defiance. I was not built for this kind of movement.

I sat deep in the squat, my hips lower than my knees, trying to work on my range of motion, but my body kept refusing. Therion demanded I should be able to stretch and bend my body into submission, but my hips merely just…stopped after a certain point. I didn't understand the importance of all this groundwork. Stretching and balance seemed so…mundane. All this time he had us working on movement I should have been spending on honing my weapons skills. Those were the true tests of whether I would make it or not.

Despite my level of athleticism, having spent most of my younger life wandering trails and hunting, it didn't seem to aid me here. After our parent's death, Archer and I had to learn to rebuild our home with the help of some locals. I was capable—more than capable—but for whatever reason, I could not bend over backward. Literally. Which was precisely what Therion was trying to get me to do now.

I fell over sideways, landing on my head. I would have a headache from this later. I glanced to my left and to my surprise, found that Callax was upside down, folded in half. It was almost comical, his back arched in a near perfect semi-circle. He took it a step further, kicked one leg up over his head, somehow defying gravity and landed on his feet.

I must have been staring in bewilderment because Callax raised his brows. "You need to work on your flexibility."

"What do you think I'm doing?"

"Do you want some help? I know a few other things we could do that could get you to bend like that."

I scowled and turned away, refusing to let him see the color rushing to my face. I had never met someone so…forward.

"As I said, Miss Orion, learn something useful or leave."

Prick. If he could bend his back like that, then I was determined to do so as well.

I attempted the move a handful more times, but each time I fell on my side or head. Mercifully, Therion called the morning session quits and released us for lunch.

The days passed quickly, blurring together. Our archery course was nearing its end, and thanks to Archer and the lessons she spent time giving me, I improved to just shy of acceptable.

Therion still publicly shamed me whenever my form was off, but it wasn't nearly as bad as when we had started. Every night before crawling into bed with Fynn, I spent a handful of minutes stretching. I wanted to ensure I wouldn't have to face Callax's mocking and smug attitude when the next day rolled around.

Everything he did tested my patience and every day I restrained myself from spewing profanities at the prince. Fynn brushed off my opinions of Callax, not wanting to hear about my time with him or how he made me feel.

Fynn now had a close bond with the other six in our group and spent much of his spare time with them, calling them his friends. It bothered me some, knowing that Soren and Caldor were a part of that group. The rumors of the twin's activities with the women of the court had circulated, and it was apparent their behavior remained the same. But Fynn was allowed to choose his friends, even if I didn't like them, so I kept my opinions to myself.

Even though I would never admit it out loud, or ever confess it to Fynn, having Callax as my partner rather than one of my friends, had done me some good. He pushed me to try harder, if only out of spite. I refused to let him be better than me, so I dedicated my time to ensuring there was nothing to criticize. It still pained my ego when he gave me tips that panned out to my benefit, but I never acknowledged it either way.

As for my friends, we hadn't had much time to converse in the last weeks, so it was often left up to Archer to inform me of how their training was going.

Her little book swaps with Kaede gave her moments to talk with him, and I knew she was close to Emryn too. They had always been friends, but since coming here, Emryn and Archer would spend hours a day talking and trading tips.

Emryn had shown her new ways to style her hair and she eagerly absorbed every bit of information. She tried to pass along the tips to me as well, but I couldn't figure it out. I was content to sit and let her try to teach me, soaking in the moments together.

I hadn't admitted it to anyone, but being here offered some strange relief. I didn't have to worry about money or meals or any regular tasks that typically landed on me to fulfill. The training was hard, but it was a different kind of hard. One that didn't challenge me emotionally.

I loved Archer, but I felt responsible for everything in our lives and it was like I could breathe for the first time in years. I felt guilty about these thoughts, and I still loved being her sister, but it was hard. Harder than I liked to admit.

"I see your skills are improving." Senna sat down next to me, Skye beside her. This was high praise coming from Senna. She rarely gave an outright compliment, especially regarding skills or training.

"Thanks," I said, between mouthfuls of chicken.

Our group had gathered in one of the many courtyards around the palace, deciding to enjoy the sun's warmth instead of eating inside. We sat in a lazy circle, sprawled out over the grass. Emryn draped her legs over Kaede, and he traced circles on her legs with one hand, eating an apple with the other.

It was nice to see our group like this. To have us all together for a brief moment. We spent the last few weeks occupied with training from dawn to dusk, so by the time the day was over, we were ready to crash as soon as we returned to our rooms.

"Did we all forget what day it is?" Emryn sat up from her slumped position, her face beaming with excitement. The rest of us tossed questioning glances, hoping someone else would speak up.

Senna, thankfully, saved us from continued embarrassment and asked, "No, what is it?"

"I can't believe we've forgotten for this long. It's the week's end…" she trailed off, expecting us to finish her thought, but we stayed silent. "What do we do before our day off?" She probed the group once more, waving her hand as if her gestures would pull the answers out of us.

Finally, it dawned on me, but Archer spoke before I could say what we all were thinking. "Drinks."

The group gave a collective ah in realization and cheered in excitement.

Emryn squeaked in delight. It made me smile to see a slight sense of normalcy back in the group, even if for only a moment. Emryn held the lot of us together. She was a light for most of us, and I don't think we had ever truly been mad with her. The rest of us had spats and disagreements throughout the years, though it was mainly Kaede and me.

Kaede and Skye had their usual sibling rivalry, Archer and I would occasionally go a day without talking if one of us hadn't gotten enough sleep, and Senna, Kaede, and I all had disagreements. Usually about training or about the fact that Kaede couldn't stand me.

Senna and Kaede had the biggest egos, so they butted heads the most, but it was nothing a good group outing, and a few drinks, couldn't resolve. Thankfully, since being here in the palace, there hadn't been time for any old spats to resurface. Seeing the six of us have genuine fun together would be a welcome relief.

"It's settled then." Emryn's grin lit up her eyes, and she clapped her hands. "We'll meet tonight, an hour after training, and find a good tavern!"

I saw Fynn walking through the corridors, Therion and Ilvar at his side. I stood quickly and bid the group a quick goodbye, promising I would see them later for drinks.

I caught up and grabbed his arm from behind, getting his attention. "Hey," I breathed, winded from the sprint across the courtyard. Therion and Ilvar nodded at me, though not entirely pleasant, and told Fynn they'd catch up with him the following day. His training never seemed to end.

Tomorrow was supposed to be a day off for the both of us, and I had hoped to spend it with him. I loved his dedication and the hard work he put into his role, I admired that about him. But sometimes, I wished we could have a few uninterrupted hours other than just before bed. I missed him.

"Do they not give you time off to rest?" I asked, only half joking.

"No. But I don't mind. It keeps me busy and gives me a purpose." He shrugged his shoulders as if that was all he needed to say.

I nodded my head, not necessarily understanding what all his duties were as the Phoenix, and I left the subject alone. There were a few debates the last few nights over what exactly it was he did and why. He always liked to share his day with me, and I loved to listen to his voice. But when it came to specifics lately, he shut down the conversations, not wanting to share, suddenly becoming too tired to continue.

He spent more time than the rest of us training, so I understood he needed more rest. But I had become anxious over this space that was beginning to form between us. It wasn't like him to be so distant or not to seek me out every spare moment he had. It was confusing, but I gave him the benefit of the doubt and gave him space for the changes in our lives.

At the end of the day, we loved each other, which was what mattered most.

"What is it, Renata?" He asked. His thumb rubbed absently over mine.

"Oh, um, the group and I are going to go for a night out in town and grab some drinks like we used to. We've been so busy and haven't had a chance lately." His hand dropped from mine, and a strange emotion passed through his face I hadn't seen before. "I figured you could use a night out, too, and come join us." I hoped the promise of a good time would entice him to agree.

He glanced from me to the corner that Therion and Ilvar had disappeared behind. He seemed distracted. Preoccupied. "I can't." He pinched the bridge of his nose. Something he did when he was frustrated. "I've got duties I have to fulfill. You wouldn't understand. But you should still go, of course." His tone was soft and gentle, but something else was behind those words.

Had I done something to upset him? Was it the group? I pushed the thoughts down, trying to ease my accelerating heart.

I had half-expected the answer, but it was still surprising.

"I understand. Don't have too much fun without us." I tried to smile like normal for him, but it was strained.

We said our goodbyes, and he gave me a parting kiss.

He's just busy, I told myself. Being a Phoenix can't be easy. I tried to rationalize the thoughts in my mind, and even though I justified his absence, a strange, new feeling nagged at my heart.

CHAPTER 13

"Don't you dare bring that up," I laughed.

Archer grinned as she teased me, the mood light and carefree after four rounds of drinks. But Archer continued with the recounting, a story in which I embarrassed myself beyond reason and the main reason Skye called me a 'klutz' from time to time.

After a vaguely threatening gesture, and an attempt to cover her mouth to stop the story, she held her hands in surrender, giving up. If I hadn't been so inebriated, I could have sworn that even Kaede looked down at his drink and smiled at the encounter.

The tavern we had all chosen to go to was one of the few places near the palace. It was the largest in the upper city and patrons bustled in and out. The smell of fresh food and boisterous clientele had drawn us in, reminding us of home. It wasn't the same as it used to be and we didn't have a reserved table, but it did the job. What mattered was that we were all together, even if Fynn had opted out.

The thought of him missing brought my mood down a peg. His rejection of joining us wasn't what stung the most, but rather that he had dismissed me as if I were an inconvenience. Being the Phoenix came with a lot of responsibility, but it was more than either of us realized. But perhaps the way to bridge that gap was to be more present for him and to understand what he was going through.

Reading wasn't my favorite thing, that was more of Archer's lane, but if anyone knew where to ask or how to research, it was her. I knew the books containing information about it were banned or burned, but maybe there was something—or someone—who could help. No matter how convoluted or far-fetched the idea might be.

Someone snapped near my ear, breaking me from my thoughts.

"Sorry, yes?" I looked up to see Skye, her face full of impatience. She was small and determined and her slicked back hair was coming loose from its low knot.

"Senna's idea…you in?"

The group was all looking at me, having already agreed to something while I was lost in thought.

"Always." I nodded a little too enthusiastically.

Senna broke her stiff silence. "You didn't hear anything I said, did you?"

"No," I muttered into my drink, distracting myself from her gaze.

She only rolled her eyes. "While we're all getting better, Therion will introduce group training soon, and we need to make sure we stand out from the other six." She eyed all of us individually, making sure she had our attention this time. "They're decently cohesive and I would hate to see us fall behind and not have anyone pass the trials."

I nodded in agreement. She was right. I hadn't thought much of the trials since the king had mentioned them. I was too concerned with getting through the archery course to really dwell on much else.

"What the hell are the trials, anyway?" I asked. I could gather from the name alone that it would be some grand test of our skills, but the legion training had never included such a thing.

Senna's eyes darkened, but Kaede spoke. "The trials are meant to push us to our limits." I was surprised he bothered to answer my question. "From what I've gathered, none of us will know what we will be tested on, but only that we must be ready to excel and prove our skill from any of our areas of training. What area that is, will be chosen by the king. But that is all anyone knows. Which is why we must make sure we're all excelling in each of our areas. If one of us fails, it puts the entire Ira Deorum at risk."

I tried not to take that too personally, but I had a feeling it was aimed at me. But if what he was saying was true, then it made more sense why Therion was so focused on even the small things. We truly had to be elite, not just a brute force like the legion. Those who made it to the legion were well-trained, but agility and stealth were not their specific focuses. Fire, aim, kill. That was the goal for them. Where they were a hammer, we were to be a blade, finely honed and lethal. Ready at all times to protect and serve.

Kaede twirled the bottle in his hands, focusing on the swirling liquid inside. "Therion wouldn't give me specific details more than that, but if we fail the trials at any point, whether we have one task or many…it's not good. He was vague, but the king isn't going to let us leave with our new skills and knowledge if we fail." His voice trailed off. I had never heard Kaede be anything but confident and sure of himself, but the way he talked tonight, he sounded…afraid.

Silence fell over the group as he finished. The gravity of our situation squashed the jovial mood. Only five months remained before the trials—five months to become as skilled as possible. And out of all of us, I was the one who put us at the most risk.

My stomach sank thinking about it. I knew I needed to be better if there was any hope of surviving the rest of this year. I needed to offer something more to our unit. Skills, yes, but also knowledge.

"Okay, enough with the doom and gloom," Skye said, interrupting my train of thought. "We're here for fun." She jumped up, her seat scraping against the floor with a loud groan. She whipped around and pulled something from the wall nearest us, a wicked grin on her face as she held out a handful of darts.

"Gather round, my friends." She waved the darts in the air for us to see. "The rules are simple, all three in or you're out. Last one standing buys the table another round." She looked like a fox, ready to play.

Senna rolled her eyes but held a hand out to Skye. She handed them over without question.

Skye raised a brow to Kaede. "Brother?" she asked. He groaned, but rose from his chair, holding his hand out too.

I only shook my head, leaning against the wall as I waited for my turn. An elbow jabbed into my side and I turned. "Reckon you'll even place this time around?" Archer laughed at her question, and I shoved her shoulder.

"This will be easy," Senna said, cracking her knuckles.

Senna landed three with ease, all within the inner circle of the board. Emryn laughed and the musician played a lively fiddle piece, picking up the mood. My foot tapped slowly in my shoe, growing faster with the tempo. I couldn't help but smile at the tune. It made me want to laugh and dance.

"Oh, you're so on." Emryn snatched the darts from the board and took her place behind Kaede. It would take us many rounds for the first of us to miss, and we would keep drinking until one or all of us became too inebriated to see straight. As was tradition.

Skye was usually the first, her small frame only allowing her half the tolerance of the rest of us. She was already slurring her words, another drink in hand. "This is so much fun. I've missed this."

"How many have you had?" I laughed as she stumbled back to the table.

"Not enough, my lady," she mocked a bow and spun back around to Senna.

Senna only raised a brow but watched over her with loving intent. Senna may not say much, but the look in her eyes always gave away how she felt. Even if she refused to join in while Skye danced around her in circles, drink sloshing.

We all laughed at the sight, even Kaede. His arms wrapped around Emryn's waist, his head resting on her shoulder. He looked content. Happy. My heart warmed a little at the sight. No matter how we might fight, he was still my friend and I wanted them all to be happy.

I took the darts from Emryn and handed them over to my sister. "Think you can win this?" I asked.

"I'm offended you'd even ask." She grinned and landed all three with practiced ease as if she hadn't had anything to drink at all. I shook my head in amazement. She never failed.

"You…" Senna pointed to Archer. "You need another drink." We all laughed and gods did it feel good. For the first time in weeks, my worry melted away and it felt like old times again.

We all cheered, letting our drinks spill as we inhaled more and more. Eventually, we all grew too drunk to continue the game without risk of injury so we joined in on the dancing and general celebration in the tavern. As the night began to wind down, a strange surge of emotion washed over me and I looked at all my friends, only feeling love for them all.

I held my arms out wide, drink spilling. "You guys are the best, you know? Come here." I pulled Archer and Skye in under each arm. Emryn wrapped herself under Skye's arm, Kaede under hers. The five of us looked to Senna, waiting for her to complete our little circle.

"My love…" Skye crooned, her voice dripping with sweetness. "Be a dear and join us."

Senna crossed her arms and leaned against the wall. "Not a chance." She tried to feign seriousness, but couldn't help the smile that pulled at the edge of her lips.

Skye shuffled the group over to the wall, entrapping Senna. Begrudgingly, she let us envelop her, pulling her away from the wall pocked with holes from misplaced darts. Together, we spun, moving in time to the music.

We spent the rest of the evening drinking, and dancing, and laughing. We walked back to the castle together, speaking too loudly to be discreet, but none of us cared. We had each other, and everything was going to be okay.

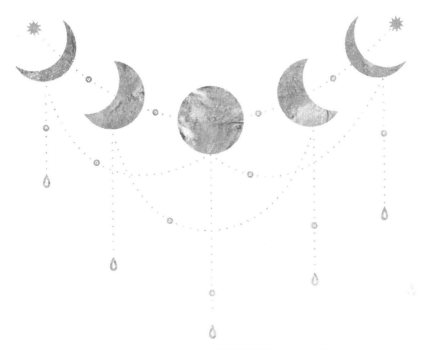

CHAPTER 14

Callax was mildly annoyed at my adeptness with the knives, and I took it as an ego boost. Seeing his smugness falter when my blades hit the target dead on made the day's soreness worth it.

"Don't let it go to your head, Miss Orion," Callax grumbled, displeasure clear in his voice.

I looked at him blankly, trying to appear bored and indifferent. Gods, I hated him. He was insufferable.

"If you spent half as much time thinking of insults to throw at me as you did throwing a dagger, then maybe I wouldn't have to waste my day listening to you prattle on." Without so much as a glance toward him, I tossed two thin knives, hitting the target directly next to each other.

From his private session with Emryn and Caldor, Therion watched and gave a silent nod. His small acknowledgment of approval filled me with pride. For a split second, I felt I might have a chance of surviving this. That maybe there was hope for me. But Callax ruined the fleeting moment.

He leaned close to my ear, his hot breath tickling my skin, "Miss Orion, you think too highly of yourself and your friends. I'd be careful if I were you." A chill ran down my spine, the sensation of his voice in my ear too intimate for my liking.

"Oh, and do be a dear and give our precious Phoenix my love. Although, maybe I should pass the sentiment along myself, as it seems you two don't spend much time together anymore."

"He's busy," I snapped, obviously flustered.

I wasn't sure if I was trying to convince him or myself.

My aim was off for the rest of the day.

Group training finally began and we spent hours running basic drills. Therion had us start with the smallest of things, a simple movement flow that ran us through squats, lunges, and rotations. As we worked on synchronizing our movements, he spouted information about the Ira Deorum.

"The Ira Deorum has existed for as long as we have had a Phoenix. Simply put, Ira Deorum means 'Wrath of the Gods.'" He continued to pace before us, his hands folded behind his back, watching intently and using his long stick to slap anyone who fell out of pace or moved too quickly. I knew I would leave the room with a few welts on my arms and thighs. "A thousand years ago, when the Realm of Day began conquering the continent, their original purpose was to serve and protect the king. But as the legion grew over the years, the kings took a step back from fighting on the front lines, and the roles shifted. The main priority is to serve and protect your Phoenix and king."

My heart swelled with pride at the thought. Fynn. We would swear to protect Fynn. I knew he was capable on his own, even though we had yet to see a display of his power. I couldn't think of a scenario during this time of peace where we, or even the Phoenix, would be necessary.

"You are to serve as the extension of the Sun God. The only god we acknowledge. And the only god who grants us the power of the Phoenix. Anything the king demands, you will do. Without question and without mercy." He met each of our eyes directly as he stated those last words.

I wondered if the day would ever come when we would have to enact punishment without mercy. I was no stranger to death, and no stranger to pain. But no mercy? Surely there would be some leeway regarding what justice the king needed us to enact. I prayed the peace that already prospered would keep and our skills would not be required.

By the end of the day, my lower body was on fire. Callax and Soren both pushed their way to the front of the twelve as we continued our drills without Therion. Both were trying to assert their dominance.

Mavenna and Pyne were smarter, like the rest of us females, and let the males deal with the physical fight for leadership. It was obvious that the two were trained in weaponry before their legion training, putting them ahead. But even though they were aggressive, ever since that first day, none dared to question Senna or her qualifications. Even Therion respected her opinions and rarely needed to advise her. His sessions with her and Mavenna were merely a formality.

Thankfully, the day drew to a close, and we were ready for a hot meal and an ice-cold bath. Before we left for the dining hall, I stopped Archer. "Can I ask you something?"

"Sure, what do you need?"

"I need some help locating information for a few things. Can you take me to the library?"

"Um, of course!" Her face lit up at the idea. I don't think there was much more in life Archer enjoyed besides her books. She could get lost for days. I had assumed she spent most of her free time in the library as I wasn't with her most nights.

"Could we go now?" I asked, wanting to avoid the attention of the others. I didn't need them knowing I was searching for knowledge of any kind.

"Follow me."

White columns rose to the ceiling, each one topped with intricate gold ornamentation that glistened in the light. Beautiful and extravagant chandeliers hung along the main walkway, lit with hundreds of candles each. A balcony ran along the edge of the second floor, fencing in additional materials while each alcove held cushioned seats and vases of red poppies. Magic echoed throughout the room, so full of knowledge and wonder. I could see why Archer loved this place.

I breathed a low whistle of appreciation. "Cool, huh?" Archer said, admiring the books as we passed. "Do you know what you're looking for exactly?"

"I think I need to look for history books. Specifically about the Realm of Day or maybe if some of the archives might have old texts."

Her nose scrunched as she thought about it. "I don't know…most books here don't have any documented history past the last thousand years, so you won't find much on the origins. But even recent history is sparsely documented. Especially anything regarding the Phoenix. There might be one section where there are archived dates and lists of battles that the kings led. But none of them really mention much besides the dates of the previous Phoenixes. When they burned all the old texts, they were pretty thorough."

I worried this would all lead nowhere, but I said, "I'll take whatever we can find."

"What is this for exactly? You know this is dangerous, right?"

I avoided her critical gaze, pretending to be enthralled by the books we passed. "Just some research."

We entered a new section toward the back of the library, one cornered off by open silver gates. "This is the history section and archives of the realm." She gestured to the meager four shelves, only one of which contained a full stack of books. A large table lay in the center, an assortment of books, quills, and ink lay across it. There were more shelves toward the back, but those were empty too, with dust collecting in the corners.

"What happened to all the books?"

A shuffle of feet made me turn. I saw no one else here, but the light was dim enough that the tall shelves could have hidden whoever was there. "They were burned, as you well know." A gravelly, old voice grumbled as a scholar appeared from behind the furthest shelf. He wore the same brown robes as the other scholars in the library, but his beard was longer than most. It was wiry and reached his mid-chest, more white than black speckled throughout.

"Hi, Cyrus." Archer's voice rang through the quiet library, but she didn't seem to care.

"Hello, little moon." The grumpy male sounded pleased to see her.

She gestured to me. "Ren, this is Cyrus Godrell, one of the best scholars here in the library. Cyrus, this is Ren, my sister."

A myriad of questions filled my mind, but I only asked, "Little moon?"

She shrugged. "He's just called me that after the first time we met. He can help you find almost anything, he's truly a godsend." He smiled at her and she waved goodbye as she disappeared back into the main library.

His eyes seemed to peer into my soul, searching for something. I felt bare. It made me slightly uncomfortable, and I shifted on my feet, waiting for him to break the silence.

"What is it you seek, Lady Orion?"

I opened my mouth to ask why he referred to me as 'lady', when I was anything but. Our family was anything but noble, only simple farmers and healers. I wondered if Archer had told him of our past, of how we lost our family, and how if we were to ever marry and have children, the Orion name would die with us. Instead, I said, "I need whatever information you can find for me about the Phoenix."

"Ah, you wish to know more about Mr. Tirich, our newest Light Phoenix." His joints creaked as he shuffled behind a shelf, beckoning for me to follow him. I rounded the corner and found he already had a book in hand. "I'm afraid this won't answer any of your questions, but it is all we have."

I knew it was naive to hope that the castle would contain answers not readily found outside its walls. There was a long history of Phoenixes in the realm stretching as far back as the realm's existence. As far as I'd been taught, anyway. "Is it truly all there is?"

He huffed a short laugh at my impertinence. "This is all. Only the Keeper and the king know anything else and you'd be a fool to approach them about it. The king burned all but one book, and that includes most dates and basic information." He handed me the too-thin book and moved back to the table. "I think you'll find that the king does not like to share what he deems to be his. And this includes knowledge."

I nodded with defeat and thanked him for the book and his time. Before I left, a phrase he used snagged in my mind. "Cyrus, you said the 'Light Phoenix.' What did you mean by that?"

"Do not ask questions you are not ready to hear answers to, Lady Orion. Make sure to keep your findings to yourself, no matter how small." His words were a dismissal.

In silence, I packed the book into my satchel and headed to my room, unsure what to make of the conversation.

CHAPTER 15

I flipped through the old pages as I walked, trying to make sense of its contents. There was a short page of names, listing families and dates of the past Phoenixes. Below the dates were the causes of death. The only ones legible were the two listed as 'natural causes.' From what I could gather, they served the king and lived out their natural life span ranging a couple of centuries each, only one meeting the full five hundred years of the Select Fae. Which seemed odd seeing as it was rare for Fae to die of any serious illness or injury. Let alone Select Fae, which all of them had been. No Half or Lesser had been chosen, though I doubted the Sun God would choose a host that wasn't to their full potential.

Even though Fae no longer had true individual powers, only the small residual magic, my mother claimed to be from a long line of Fae descended from the Moon Goddess herself. But that had been a taboo subject and had only ever been brought up once in passing. A slip of the tongue, but I had always remembered that.

My father never offered up his heritage, but the name Orion was a give-away as to where his line had come from, but we were not permitted to ask. I figured he'd always tell me one day how the Orions came to live in the Realm of Day, but that time never came. Stolen by the fire.

By the time I reached my room, I had quickly scanned through most of the pages. An occasional name or time frame stood out, but nothing was helpful. I closed the book and stashed it away once more.

Fynn lay shirtless on my bed, his deep golden tattoos glinting in the candlelight. He was reading a scroll of some sort, but he put it away hurriedly when he heard me come in.

"What are you reading?" I asked, setting down my bag, not wanting to bring the book out while he was here. I wanted it to be a surprise, to prove that I was invested in his life.

I quickly changed, pulling on a loose sweater he loved and light linen pants. I crawled onto the bed next to him. "Nothing you need to concern yourself with." He tapped my nose with his index finger, smiling, and leaned in for a kiss. I met his warm lips, wanting nothing more than to melt into his embrace. I missed him. My body missed him.

My brain began to shut down, letting my body relax and meld into his, his arms wrapping around my back in answer. But his comment lingered, and a foul taste filled my mouth. I put my hand on his chest and pulled back, resisting the urge to run my hand over him.

"Why not?" I asked, trying not to sound hurt. "I think it would be good for me to learn, don't you? After all, you said whatever you learned about being a Phoenix was yours to share. I'd love to learn about it all." And I did want to learn. I wanted to find a way to connect with him. I knew he loved our time together, but he prided himself in his job.

His warm smile faded ever so slightly, his eyes losing that lustful glint I had been desperate to see.

"Renata, I appreciate that you want to help, but let me take care of it, okay? You focus on finishing your training, then we'll have more time together." He rubbed his hand over mine, attempting to reassure me. But I didn't want to let him handle this alone. I'd seen how my mother and father had shared their lives, how they supported the other unconditionally. I wanted that too.

"Don't you think it would be easier to let me in?" My eyes searched his, looking for a way in. "When you took me flying, it was the most exhilarating moment of my life and you enjoyed it too. We could be a team if you'd like."

He pulled back at my words, my heart beating faster. This wasn't the reaction I had expected. He was usually gentle and kind, but his eyes had changed. A subtle darkness deepening that gold. Their warm fire now cold.

"That was a mistake. One that won't happen again." My stomach dropped. My stupid heart raced, beating at a dangerous pace as the room began to spin. The one sure thing in my life slipping out from under me.

He said it with such finality, such severity. Tears brimmed my eyes. I hadn't prepared for this, for him to turn so…cold. If he didn't notice my panic before, he did now.

In a flash, his demeanor changed, the iciness melting away into realization. "Renata, I'm so sorry. That came out worse than I intended, but you have to understand."

"But I don't, Fynn. What did I do wrong?"

"Nothing, just…just let it go."

"Let it go? We haven't even picked it up because you keep shutting me down."

He pinched the bridge of his nose. "You don't…you wouldn't understand."

I fought the urge to shout, to scream that this was exactly the point. "Give me a reason and I will let this all go. But don't shut me out and not expect me to wonder why. I want more than this, more than just passing moments and short conversations only when you feel up to it. I want a relationship. A partnership. This…" I gestured between us, my words thick with tears. "This isn't that."

He sat up, tossing his hands in exasperation. "What do you want me to say? That you don't understand, that you never can or will because you'll never have power like this? That you couldn't possibly grasp the weight of being responsible for a whole realm?"

"I don't have to live your experience to empathize and support you."

"I don't need your support, I need you to be safe. So I don't have to constantly worry about you. I want you to do your job and be there for me at the end of the day, just like you always have been."

Did he truly think so little of me? That a warm, safe body to crawl into bed with at night was all I was good for? This wasn't him. This wasn't the Fynn I loved. An unfamiliar ache built in my chest, threatening to tear me apart. Like the walls of a house ready to crumble.

I put my hand on his chest, searching for the familiar warmth I once clung to. "I want to be there for you, but I don't know how to do that if you won't let me." I felt like I was doing something wrong, punished for trying to do what I knew best, and I didn't know why.

He gripped my wrists, wrenching my hand away. "I said no." His eyes darkened at my protest. I had never seen him this angry—or angry at all—now that I thought of it.

I recoiled, but he held on tightly, staring me down with what I could only describe as rage. Fear blossomed in my chest.

The smell of smoke filled the room, his golden eyes flashing dark red, flames igniting within them. Something was very wrong.

"Fynn," I said, my voice thick with surprise.

I smelled burning flesh before I felt the pain. His tattoos glowed lightly in the dim room. But I couldn't pull away, couldn't stop it as a red-hot pain seared into me, flowing from his hands and to my wrist. I tugged back, trying to wrench free, but he held on tight, that look in his eyes piercing me to my core. It wasn't Fynn staring back.

I cried out, but kept my voice low, not wanting to alarm anyone next door. "Fynn, let go." My breath was ragged, broken into small gasps. "You—you're hurting me."

The heat only intensified and for a moment, and I wasn't sure he would ever let go.

My mind raced back to the night my family died. To the roar of the flames and the screams of agony. Even then I hadn't been burned, only felt the heat. But now…his hand—this pain—only made me realize that they had not died peacefully.

I wanted to erase the memory of it all. To take back this moment and my stupid words.

I said again, "Fynn, please." But all I could hear was the echo of my family, trapped, burning to death in the walls of their own home.

My last cry shook him, and he finally released me. His eyes returned to their normal amber, his tattoos dimming. Shocked, he looked at his hands, to the smoke trailing between us, my skin burning bright red.

He burned me.

He reached out and I scrambled back as quickly as possible. I cradled my wrists against my chest, searching for a bucket of water or anything to cool the burning flesh. But there was nothing.

I backed away, but he was too fast, his hands on my shoulders, shaking me. "Oh gods, I'm so sorry, I…I just got so frustrated, I don't—I don't know what happened."

"Let go of me." I didn't recognize my voice, those words. I shouldn't be afraid of him. He was my safe space. My home.

But I was terrified.

He sank back onto the bed, my words like a physical blow. He placed his head in his hands, hunching over as he repeated the words 'I'm so sorry,' over and over.

It felt like more of an attempt to placate himself than an actual apology.

A sick part of me wanted to forget my pain, to ignore it and comfort him instead. He was hurting too and his power was still so new. Maybe he didn't mean to. He was right, I had pushed to far, I should have stopped the first time he said no.

The rambling thoughts halted when I moved, the pain in my wrist flaring, reminding me I needed to tend to it before justifying his actions.

I closed the door behind me, not wanting anyone to walk by and see him like this. He didn't need that. When I rounded the corner, heading toward the healer's quarters, I slammed into a large, dark body.

Kaede.

"Watch where you—" His low growl stopped mid-sentence, noticing me cradling my burnt wrist, clothes disheveled, my face red with tears. He took a step back, taking in the full view of the mess I was.

I kept my head down, not wanting to meet his judgmental gaze.

His hands hovered over my burnt flesh, not touching it but wanting to. His voice was deep as he said, "Who did this?"

I turned to the side, trying my best to avoid the shame that filled my words. "No one, Kaede…please, just let me be." It was better when he ignored me.

"I won't ask again, or I'll get Emryn and Archer. Who did this to you?" I felt the deep timbre of his voice roll through me and I knew he meant it. I hadn't heard that kind of sincerity in his voice in years. Seeing this side of Kaede, the side that cared, the friend I missed…I couldn't stand it.

"Please, just drop it. *Please*." I couldn't say the words. No, because saying them made it real.

The shaking in my voice must have been convincing enough because he backed up a step, running a hand through his hair. "There's only one person who could—"

"Kaede, stop," I demanded, but my voice cracked. "I just want to go to the healers."

With a sigh, he stopped his questions and agreed to let me go, but walked with me, one step behind the entire way. It was comforting to know he still cared, that there might be hope to fixing this thing between us. To being friends again.

It was almost enough to distract me from the pain.

Almost.

CHAPTER 16

Camilla bandaged me up, gently rubbing in a salve to pull the heat from the wound. She had never treated an injury caused by Phoenix fire before and said the healing process was bound to be slower. If the marks healed entirely at all.

I received a few glares from the human healer as she pulled pieces of burnt cloth from my skin. I knew she knew who burnt me, it wasn't exactly like many people could do such a thing, let alone leave a burn mark in the shape of a handprint. But when I told her it was an accident from trying to start a fire in the hearth of my room, I knew she didn't believe me. Thankfully, she let the matter be.

I arrived at training the following morning with bandages still wrapped around my arm. Even though I tried pulling my training gear down over it, the sleeves were just shy of long enough.

To my dismay, it caught Callax's eye. "Trying to get my sympathy by feigning an injury? That's a new low, even for you." He didn't look at me as he continued to fling the knives.

We had accelerated to moving targets earlier than some of the other pairs and practiced outside in a grove of enclosed trees. The poor rabbits were yet again our targets. His knife flew through the air and pinned one against a tree mid-jump, red staining its white fur. At least he always made quick, efficient kills and was never needlessly cruel to the animals.

"It was an accident, and I require none of your attention. It would actually be nice if you left me alone for once."

"Not a chance. You wouldn't survive here without me. Besides, you like the attention. Especially since it's evident you're not getting any…attention at night, given your poor attitude." He winked, and something snapped within me.

I whirled, my knife still in my hand. I had no intention of letting it kill him, but maybe I'd make him bleed, see just how pretty his insides were.

He didn't even flinch.

"I don't need you," I gritted out, the words acid on my tongue.

Callax smirked. "What? Are you going to tell me that you can win this thing on your own?" He broke from my grip with ease, disarming me in seconds, the knife now at my throat. He pressed it in, biting against my skin. "Clearly."

I held my breath as he took a step back, flipping the dagger in his hand and handing it back to me. "If you're going to threaten me, Miss Orion, I suggest you follow through. Otherwise, you'll find that I won't be as predictable."

I reached for the blade, my fingers grazing his. My breath quickened, my lips parting as his deep blue eyes locked on mine. They glinted with madness, something dark and dangerous swirling beneath. I almost lost myself in their depths.

He leaned in, our hands still touching, a current running between us. But I snapped out of it, ripping my hand free, along with the dagger.

His eyes cleared and he took a step back, then disappeared back into the castle without another word, leaving me alone for the rest of the day.

I wasn't sure what had just happened, but while I had a strong distaste for the male, I wasn't sure I was ready to push his limits to see just how far he was willing to go.

I spent nearly every night with Cyrus down in the dark recess of the library. I grew to enjoy the old scholar's company. He was wise, and kind, and enjoyed spouting random facts. I found myself listening to every story he told and liked to imagine that if I had a grandfather, I would want him to be like Cyrus.

I groaned as I leaned back into my chair, stretching. My knees popped with the motion, and Cyrus lifted his head. "Aren't you a little young for your joints to sound like that?"

I laughed. "Yes. But I think that's what happens when you spend hours training with someone who refuses to take it easy. Today, I was thrown to the ground more times than I'd like to admit." I rubbed my knee absently. It wasn't injured exactly, but it wasn't in peak condition. We had run drills on how to disarm someone, and today was my turn to be the armed opponent. Callax had taken every opportunity to throw me to the ground, and my body ached in protest.

Cyrus held up a wrinkled finger and stood. "I'll be back shortly, Lady Orion." He patted my shoulder as he passed. "I have something back in my chambers for your knee that will do the trick."

"I can visit Camilla later, no need to worry about me." I tried to protest, wanting him not to bother with something as simple as an aching knee, but he kept moving.

"I'll be right back. Keep up your research."

I poured over another useless book filled with only census information, dates, and occasional locations that weren't blacked out. I was nearly ready to pass out from boredom when Archer walked in. She carried a stack of books under one arm and read one in her other hand. I huffed a small laugh as she sat next to me and didn't pause her reading. I mumbled a hello and returned to my book.

Moments later, Cyrus returned carrying a small vial of light blue liquid, "This should do the trick."

I took the vial from his hands and sniffed it; it smelled floral and sweet.

"What is it?" I asked.

"It's an old recipe I learned from my father, who learned it from his father. Even the healers here would not have this, as it is brewed from a flower that doesn't grow in the south anymore. I've had this for as long as I can remember. One vial will last for years, and you only need a drop."

"Won't you need it?" I tried to offer the vial back to him, but he shook his head.

"I feel you will get more use from it than I."

I pulled the dropper from the top and placed a single drop on my tongue. I was surprised by the flavor. It tasted of lavender and honey. Almost instantly, the ache in my knee disappeared, and I flexed my leg back and forth. The usual click that accompanied my movements ceased.

"Wow, that's incredible."

He smiled, and I thanked him, pocketing the vial. We resumed our research in companionable silence. When I was ready to call it a night, a string of information caught my attention. I straightened and brought one candle closer, trying to ensure I wasn't just seeing things.

Cyrus noticed my change in demeanor and motioned for Archer's attention, tapping her arm. "Little moon." She perked up at the nickname. "Go fetch me a book on the history of weapons from the Scholar Myrna, would you? He knows the one I'm talking about."

She smiled at him and placed her book upside down on the table. "Sure, I'll be right back." He muttered his thanks, and she walked away.

As soon as she was out of earshot, he leaned in. "What is it you found, Lady Orion?"

"I'm not sure, Cyrus, but...I'm confused."

His face tightened, the wrinkles around his eyes deepening. "Let me see." He pulled the book from me before I could hand it over. I watched as his eyes poured over the information. He looked at me, perplexed. "What did you find? I see nothing here but family names and dates." He motioned to the book, waiting for me to point it out to him.

"That's exactly it." I rotated the book and pointed to a name halfway down the list. "See here, it says Cassius and Claudia Orion. Those are my parents' names. The only other time I have heard the name Orion was when our father would tell us stories of the legendary warrior who fought for the Realm of Night."

He took a sharp breath at the mention of the Realm of Night. It wasn't talked of often—or ever. It was the reason the wars had started so long ago.

I continued, "Cyrus, they never lived in Solterra. They were born and raised in Firielle, just like my siblings and me. My father always said that his father was a farmer and tradesman just like he and that he had grown up in Firielle and never stepped foot outside. My mother claimed nearly the same story, but her parents had died as a young girl, and she spent her life working as a nursemaid in town until they were bonded and had me." Cyrus was still, but I could see his eyes searching mine, looking for an answer to the question I had yet to ask. I knew he wouldn't have an answer for me, he hadn't known my parents, but the information didn't add up. "How could these records show them being in Solterra when I would have been two? They always told me they were from Firielle. My father was an only child and, therefore, the last of his line. Archer and I are the only Orions left. So, if these names listed are my parents, then why did they lie?"

My hand was still pointing at the familiar names on the page when he pulled back and snapped it shut. His face was stern and serious when he spoke, "Lady Orion, you will not speak a word of this to your sister, do you understand? Some questions should not be asked in such public places." I looked around, we were as far into the library as one could get, and none of the other scholars ever came near here.

Archer's footsteps sounded against the stone, indicating her return. I realized he had sent her in search of a book he did not need. He leaned in and, in a hushed whisper, said, "We will speak of this later. There is much you do not and cannot know right now. But for now, you will forget you ever saw this. Understood?"

I nodded in agreement.

"Here you go! Sorry it took so long to find the book. Scholar Myrna is quite old and slow." Archer gave a short laugh and handed Cyrus the book.

"Thank you, little moon. Now, if you two don't mind, I think I will call it a night and close up. I will see you two later."

We picked up our books and walked out of the library. The silenced questions still rang through my mind. Why had my parents lied to me?

The days sped by quicker than I would have liked. I wasn't ready to face Fynn, but we still needed to talk.

I had agreed to meet him for dinner after training, but I still felt uneasy, even when I knew we could only move forward if we were able to talk. My wrists had healed in the days since the incident, but a faint red ring was still evident on my skin, serving as a reminder of what he was capable of.

Thankfully, he kept his distance and stayed out of my room during those days, giving me space. He had written an apology note and sent flowers. Twice. But I placed them in the corner and tried not to think about it.

I felt so conflicted over it all. I knew deep down his behavior was unacceptable and if this had happened to Archer or anyone else, I would tell them to leave. But no one knew about it, and it was an accident. I knew he truly hadn't meant to hurt me, but the nightmares that had been at bay for the last few months resurfaced. I often awoke to the lingering smell of smoke and my skin hot to the touch.

On top of it all, we had less than two weeks left of the training course before moving on. While I excelled at daggers, sword mastery was up next, and I had no experience. I had a nagging feeling it would be more complicated than I would like.

"Are you ready?" Skye snapped her fingers by my face, trying to gather my attention, my head still in the clouds as we packed our gear.

"Right. Yes, let's go."

I was distracted and shook my head, trying to clear out all thoughts of Fynn. I could think of something else for the next hour.

Hopefully.

The six of us walked out to a courtyard tucked behind the stables. We had been training together for the last few weeks outside our normal practice with the twelve. Senna drilled us until we couldn't move, but we had improved our team skills.

"Think you can handle this? Without, you know, maiming somebody?" Skye winked as she passed a handful of weapons my way. I rolled my eyes. I knew exactly what she was referring to, and I tried to push the less-than-ideal memory away, but it did bring a smile to my face.

"Yes," I said, grabbing the daggers and sheath of arrows. "I doubt he even remembers. Besides, it was four years ago, and it was raining. We all know it was an accident."

"Reckon the baker feels the same way?" Kaede's deep voice was full of sarcasm, trying to rile me up. There was something different about him after the night he found me in the hallway. Softer, almost.

The five started laughing while I holstered the weapons in their place. One dagger on each thigh, two at my waist, and one around my ankle. The events that caused Skye to nickname me 'klutz' also involved the lot of us having a foot race and some poor aim.

"I apologized, okay? And besides, he banned me for life, so I think we were even."

"Gods, I miss his bread." Emryn brought her hands to her chest and feigned tears of sorrow. Her sarcasm made the group laugh even harder.

"He is the best baker I've ever known. Even better than the cooks here," Archer chimed in. "It's too bad I was banned even though I wasn't the one who maimed him." She glared at me, but it was all in jest.

Kaede shrugged his shoulders. "Guilty by association."

Once we were all strapped up, Senna positioned us across the field, staggering our locations. "Is there a reason we're using actual weapons?" I shouted from across the courtyard.

"If you want to learn, you'll learn. So don't make mistakes," she shouted back.

I sighed. This was going to hurt.

Archer took off first from the back, running towards Emryn. When she got close, Emryn matched her speed, and Archer tossed a dagger her way. Emryn caught it without pause and threw it at a nearby tree, severing some rope and releasing three buckets positioned on a low branch, each filled with apples and water. Directly above me.

I ran to avoid the spill and pulled out an arrow, turning around to shoot two of the falling apples into the tree's trunk. I silently patted myself on the back, congratulating myself on the shot.

Simultaneously, Kaede jumped and grabbed another apple mid-air. He rolled into his fall and tossed it to Skye, who threw her daggers, aiming at the apple. They were supposed to hit the tree closest to Archer, but it missed, instead nicking Emryn in the arm.

"Close, but not quite," Emryn yelled, grabbing her arm. Luckily it was only a scratch, her leather gear taking the brunt. We didn't stop. Senna ran directly toward us, and we gathered to form a step. She jumped and was boosted into the air, first by Kaede and me, then Emryn and Skye. Together, we propelled her up and towards the wall. She soared high and caught the lip of the nearest window at least twelve feet off the ground. Catching a foothold in the stone, she hoisted herself up into the window, grabbing a small red cloth tied there.

It wasn't perfect, but we did it. While the exercise itself would never fold out exactly like this on a battlefield, it tested our coordination as a group, how we could pass weapons to those in need on the field, or how we could communicate even with multiple things going on at the same time.

Senna had us run the drill five more times before the hour was up. Skye managed to miss Emryn the rest of the time but I got hit by the falling apples at least twice, and Archer dropped a dagger handoff. By the end, however, Senna gave us her approval.

CHAPTER 17

A warm hand slipped into mine. My heart froze for a beat too long. "Fynn, you scared me," I squeaked, holding back a whimper. The act of being touched sent a jolt through my chest. I didn't think I was afraid, just…wary.

"I was hoping to surprise you, I should have made a noise or something, sorry." His face fell and a surge of guilt rose in my chest.

"No, I'm sorry. You didn't do anything wrong." I smiled reassuringly at him, and it seemed to do the trick for both of us.

"Ready?" he asked.

"Yes, I'm starving."

Hand in hand, we walked through the palace gates and down the streets of Sunsbridge to a local dining establishment. They welcomed us without hesitation and sat us at the best seat available. I supposed being the Phoenix had its advantages.

Over dinner, I listened to him tell me stories of cities far away and how he stayed with the nobles there, learning all he could about the realm as a whole. How it worked, how the people were, whose loyalties could be trusted. I made a mental note to commit the information to memory since I would serve at his side soon enough.

But my favorite was listening to him go on about how beautiful the countryside was. How if I thought Firielle was beautiful, that I needed to visit the cities to the east. There, they were surrounded by endless grasslands that ran right up to the sea. The soft rolling hills a seamless extension of the water. And to the west, the Sunstone Steppes stood tall and desolate, a strange type of beauty that bordered the opposite sea. The Steppes were home to ancient stone mines that shone like gold when the sun hit just right.

I envied him, but it helped some knowing that a life with him might grant me the same opportunities.

Until I had come to Sunsbridge, Firielle was all I knew. I was content with my life there. And even though Sunsbridge wasn't that far away, everything felt different and new. The music was unique, the food, and sights, and smells so vastly different to back home. But the one thing that spurred my desire to see more of this world, was when he had taken me flying.

It had only been the once, but for that brief moment, it felt like I could breathe again. The freedom and exhilaration was unlike anything else. Almost like hope—a promise of a brighter future. I wanted to feel that again.

Reality pulled me back down when Fynn took my hand in his, reaching across the table. I had forgotten all about the other night for a moment, lost to the memory of flying.

I downed another glass of wine, the sudden touch sending me back to the night, his hand around my wrist. But I pushed the memory away, storing it in a little box far away, wanting to enjoy this moment with him when things almost felt normal again. He had apologized, why not move forward and let things be?

"Renata, I want you to know how sorry I am for that night," he said. Sadness passed through his eyes and this time, I let myself believe him. Seeing the love on his face, the desperation to have me back, softened my heart. He was a good partner, thoughtful and kind. Everyone always told me how lucky I was to have him.

"I know," I said, barely more than a whisper.

He smiled softly. "I need you. I want you to know how important you are." He focused on our hands, trailing his thumb along mine. "I only acted that way because I've seen things, know things, that I never want you to endure. I only want to protect you."

I straightened at that. I had taken care of myself and Archer for years now, if there was anything I could handle, it was this. But despite that, some small part of me wondered what it would be like to give up that control I desperately clung to. To not have to fight anymore. "I'm capable of taking care of myself," I said.

"I can't help but think of the night I first fell for you. You were so scared and hurt. I wanted nothing more than to help you. To make sure you were cared for. I know you can take care of yourself, you always have, but I want you to let me do it now. And if you keep trying to take on my burdens as yours…" He trailed off, shaking his head. "I couldn't forgive myself if you got hurt."

"I'll do my best going forward," I promised.

He smiled and it warmed my heart. For him, I would try. And if I couldn't, I wouldn't let it show around him. "Thank you," he said, lifting my hands to his lips and kissing it.

I only nodded, pulling my hand back and resting it on my lap, trying to ignore the scar. If nothing else, I was glad to put the matter to rest.

An hour, and a delicious round of dessert later, we paid our tab, giving our compliments to the chef. He tried to let us go without paying, but Fynn insisted. He was always good that way, ensuring everyone was treated fairly and compensated. It was something I noticed about him before he ever noticed me.

We walked lazily up the hill back to the castle grounds. Eating that much was a mistake because my sides ached in protest from the climb.

"Maybe you should just fly us up," I joked, laughing as I struggled to breathe, the food pushing my stomach against the confines of my pants.

Fynn's good mood shifted, his muscles tightening. He released my hand, the warmth disappearing with it. I hadn't meant to push his boundaries. I forgot that one of the reasons I had gotten myself burned was because I mentioned flying together. Fuck.

"I'm sorry, I forgot," I pleaded, trying to get him to look at me, but he kept his gaze focused on the gates ahead.

"I told you to leave the subject alone." His voice was dark, the softness in his eyes gone.

"I'm sorry, Fynn. It was just a poorly timed joke."

"I'm going to go to bed. I'll see you later."

I opened my mouth to protest but only sagged at the thought of continuing in this cycle. We walked through the gates, and instead of following me down the same path, he stalked off in a different direction.

I called after him, thanking him for dinner, hoping to soften the goodbye. He tossed his hand over his shoulder in acknowledgment and didn't look back.

My heart sped up. I had just fixed things, and now we were back to square one. I struggled to keep the tears at bay, forcing them to remain where they were as I refused to acknowledge the sharp ache in my chest that felt like my heart was tearing itself apart. Silently, the tears fell.

I wiped them away one by one, but they didn't stop. I passed each floor at a slower pace than usual. My mind felt far off, like it was trying to leave my body. My feet shuffled mindlessly beneath me, following some unknown force as I replayed the conversations over and over in my head until they faded into the background.

It was only when the tip of my boot caught the edge of a loose stone I snapped out of the haze. I didn't recognize this part of the castle. The stone was darker, older, and less light found its way through the deep, red-stained windows. But when I turned, hoping to retrace my steps, I was met by a tall figure leaning against the wall.

Callax.

Quickly, I wiped the last of my tears from my eyes, hoping he would think I was rubbing them from exhaustion.

"What are you doing here?" I demanded, my tone harsher than I had expected.

I had no desire to banter with the prince at this hour. The torchlight of the dimly lit hall glinted off of his small crown. I hadn't thought of Callax as a royal in a while. He had become a regular part of my routine, and this part of his life slipped my mind. But here in the hall, Callax looked regal. His crown fit perfectly, like it was molded to his skull. It sat atop his black curls, complementing the gold buttons of his dark crimson attire. He must have come from a royal dinner or political event.

"Me?" he gasped, feigning shock. He clutched his hand to his chest. "I should be asking you the same thing, Miss Orion, seeing as you are intruding in the royal wing."

Shit. I didn't realize I wandered this far. I was on the complete opposite side of the castle.

"I'll be on my way then." I moved, but Callax stepped in between me and the doorway. Annoyance crossed my face. I was in no mood to play games.

"Leaving so soon?"

"You're the one who told me to leave," I said.

"I said no such thing. I was simply stating where you were."

"I'm sorry." I mocked a bow. "May I please go now?"

He tilted his head back and forth as if contemplating my request. "You know, I am a little bored. The meeting I just went through nearly made me want to jump out a window, and I find myself in need of entertainment." He took a step forward. I retreated, backing slowly toward the wall behind me.

"Care to...entertain me tonight?" His eyes roamed slowly over my body, taking in my evening attire and landing on my red, puffy eyes. His demeanor changed ever so slightly when he realized I had been crying. But when he spoke, that sly mockery and lilt returned.

"Is something wrong between you and your dear little Light Phoenix?"

There it was, that word. Light. Cyrus used that same phrasing the night Fynn burned me. Light Phoenix.

"Mind your business, prince." I spat the last word. I wanted to be anywhere but here.

He took another step forward. This time I was nearly against the wall. I changed the subject. "What did you mean by Light Phoenix?" I searched for a response in his eyes, but he took the final step forward and pinned me against the wall with his proximity.

His hand landed above my head and leaned in, towering over me. "Miss Orion, I suggest you watch your tongue." He looked over me again, but this time it was different. Panicked, almost. "Wouldn't want to see that pretty little head of yours...misplaced." The way he said the last word had me swallowing hard. At that moment, I realized just how close we were. How close Callax's mouth was to mine. "It would be a shame if it came to that. I can think of a few better places for it to be." He winked.

Using his free hand, he lifted a finger to my chin, pausing before his skin grazed mine. His hand shifted, and like a puppet, I echoed his movement, my head following his hand.

The lack of touch was electric. The static between us was the only thing connecting us, pulling me in—an invisible string tightening its hold.

The thread went taut inside my chest as his hand hovered around my wrist, directly above the fading scar.

I hadn't told him how I got the burns. I hadn't told anyone. But the way he looked at me...he knew.

His teeth grazed his bottom lip. My heart raced.

I wasn't entirely convinced it was out of panic.

My eyes met his, and I had never realized the blend of colors that lay beneath those long, dark lashes. Colors that illuminated in the torchlight. Black, deep blue, and flecks of silver, all swirling in one beautiful dance. They reminded me of the night sky. I was mesmerized.

Despite his proximity, he never touched me. He always kept some sort of space between us, save for when we were training.

"See something you like?" His words flowed from his lips like honey, and he curled them into a wicked grin. "I'd be more than happy to show you more," his whisper tickled my ear, and I felt a sudden rush through my body, raising the hair on my arms, sending an electric bolt through my chest and down...I jerked free from his grasp.

"Keep your hand and filthy intentions to yourself," I snapped, wanting to be anywhere but here. I made my way to the stairs and ran as fast as I could manage, my heart still racing.

"See you in the morning." His voice echoed through the stone halls.

I didn't look back.

CHAPTER 18

I wasn't sure where I was going after the encounter with Callax, I only knew I needed to get away. It was late, but the library was still open and I found myself making my way to the back where Cyrus was packing away his quills and ink.

"Cyrus," I breathed out, still winded from my race down here.

"Lady Orion, it is late. What are you doing here?" His brows raised in surprise, and his voice was hushed.

"Light. You said Light Phoenix the other day. And tonight, I ran into the prince, and he—" Cyrus cut me off.

"The prince?" he said, closing the book with a loud snap. "Lady Orion, I told you not to speak of such things aloud for fear of the consequences that may befall us both."

"It's only a word, Cyrus, and no one is telling me anything." I felt childish, but I was frustrated. Everyone knew more than I did, and I hated not knowing. I hated feeling incapable and inferior, and I was at a loss. What else was I supposed to do? "The books you gave me led nowhere except to questions about my parent's integrity, and I can't keep going on like this with

Fynn if I know nothing about anything." The words fell from my mouth in a breathless string. Familiar, burning anger ran through me, my temper always giving way to the same sensation.

Cyrus gathered his belongings. "I suggest you watch your tone and volume." He walked past me and waited for me to follow at the gates, but I stood firm. I wasn't leaving until I got an answer. I had been taken from my home against my will, forced to train for an elite group I didn't ask to be a part of, my partner selected for an honor no one would tell me anything about, and I was just supposed to go along without any protest? No. I needed something—*anything*—to keep me sane.

"I can't do this," my voice threatened to break, and I swallowed the tears, "I need answers." I crossed my arms over my chest and leaned back against the table. I felt guilty for demanding something like this from him, but I had always felt safe around him and didn't know what else to do. I was helpless.

He debated internally before heaving a long sigh. He turned and motioned for me to follow him. "Follow me. And try not to make so much noise."

I obeyed.

Cyrus led me through corridor after corridor as we wound our way down through the castle. The normal white stone giving way to dark, dingy gray, overrun with water damage.

"Where are we going?" I asked, but he waved his hand in dismissal. I followed him for minutes before we finally stopped at a large door with heavy iron locks on the outside.

"Where are we?" I prodded again.

He ignored me and pulled out a set of keys.

When I walked in, I realized we were in his private chambers. It was smaller than I expected from the size of the door, much smaller than the rooms given to us upstairs. I looked around. Medicinal posters lined the wall and small vials of strange-smelling liquids lay strewn about with scrolls and quills. It was messy, but it looked lived-in and well-used.

Cyrus shut the door and locked it from the inside. He sighed heavily and paused a moment before turning around to face me. "Lady Orion, I apologize for my bluntness earlier, but you must understand that the subjects of which you ask me are strictly forbidden to discuss. Even the scholars know little to nothing about it." He strode over to the bed and sat. "I hoped to have more time to figure out for sure and to find the best way to tell you, but if the prince is using the term 'Light Phoenix,' then I fear we may have less time than I thought." He grabbed the lone chair at his desk and pulled it out, gesturing for me to take a seat.

"What are you talking about?"

"A thousand years ago, my great-grandfather was one of the first scholars to serve the Fae Kings. He was charged with knowing everything there was about the Old Gods and the Phoenixes. He was the original Keeper." I pulled back at his choice of words. Did he say Phoenixes? As in more than one?

"The Fae King at the time valued knowledge and desired to know all he could. My great-grandfather was the king's personal scholar, dedicating his life to gathering all the information. The king was loved, but the more he learned, the more power he craved. He recruited the Light Phoenix and began to claim more land in honor of the Sun God, no longer content with half of the continent which had been granted to the realm after the Great War."

I had learned of the Great War in school years before. It was all we were allowed to know of the old gods. We were told the Gods of the Moon and Night conspired against the Sun God and his throne. Jealous of his power and the beauty of Day and demanded they share the power between them. It was a long battle that divided the gods, and the realms. But eventually, the realms compromised, the north went to the Realm of Night, and the south went to the Realm of Day. A clean divide. But now, Asterion was the only remaining city in the Realm of Night. It lay just beyond Cresslier Pass, a mountain range no one dared cross in centuries.

A thought passed quickly through my mind. If King Tobias was so set on keeping the truth hidden, was this why he was amassing a legion? Would he dare attempt to take the last city?

"And so, the old king utilized his Light Phoenix and the Ira Deorum.

One by one, he dispatched them to every city, collecting all the knowledge surrounding the Old Gods. Once he collected every book, scroll, and tablet regarding this, he had the Light Phoenix burn them all to ash." The thought of flames and millennia of knowledge being taken away in a matter of minutes made me sick. "The king had grown selfish and angry in his search for more. He decided that if he wanted to rule it all, he needed absolute control. He began to burn those who continued to teach of the Old Gods. He burned every temple, every school, every man, woman, and child, who dared to continue to pray to them. He deemed them traitors to the crown and rid the world of those who opposed him."

"And the Phoenix just went along with it?" I couldn't imagine Fynn going along with a plan as heinous as that. Maybe he would go along with burning books, that seemed like the easiest part of the plan to swallow, but…murder? No mercy? It had always been taught that the Sun God was the one true god. That he alone provided the lands with fertility and prosperity through the kings and Phoenixes together. But the Phoenix was the host for the Sun God's spirit. That was why he was imbued with so much power.

"Yes. Some Light Phoenixes have been just as cruel as the kings. But…" his voice trailed off just then, looking around the room and hesitating as if he wasn't sure if he should continue. He took a deep breath but eventually said, "There is so much more to our history and your family than you know. The king has a weapon. A god-made blade of death. Forged from sunstone and welded in Phoenix fire. It's sole purpose was to kill even a Phoenix if used correctly. It was a weapon forged in the time of the Great War."

Just then, Cyrus stopped speaking and walked to the door, leaning against it as if to hear something outside. I heard it too. The shuffle and clank of metal in the distance. It was probably guards on their nightly rotation.

"You must go. Now." His voice was hushed, but I could see the urgency in his face and the panic in his eyes.

"Cyrus, what's going on?"

He didn't respond. He only proceeded to push his bed to the side of the room, revealing a trap door under the edge. I looked at him, concern seeping into my features, my eyes widening. He beckoned for me to get in.

I shook my head. I didn't like small spaces and the thought of going underground without a light of any kind—without knowing where I was—terrified me.

"If you value your life, you will do as I ask. Please, get in." The command and desperation in his voice pulled me toward the hole, I knew he was being serious, but I couldn't imagine what threat was so imminent I needed to leave this way. I sat on the edge, feet dangling inside.

"Let me help," I pleaded.

"No. I must deal with this on my own, my lady." He reached under the edge of his bed and began fumbling around with something I couldn't see. A soft thump sounded, and he grabbed whatever he had been reaching for, handing them over.

Books. Ancient, very worn books.

"What is this?" I asked, looking from him to the books and back again.

"Everything my great grandfather could save was passed down to his son, and his son, and then to me. This is everything I can give you." His eyes brimmed with tears as he spoke urgently, "I'm sorry we didn't have more time, but please read these. And do not, no matter any circumstance, share them with anyone if you value their lives. Hide them at all costs do you understand?" All the kindness in his voice was gone. Cyrus stared through me with an intensity I didn't want to question.

"O-okay," I stuttered, still in shock. The steps grew closer, and three loud bangs on the door shook me.

"Promise me, my lady. Promise me you will guard these with your life."

"I promise."

He nodded sharply and grabbed the trap door, "Follow the tunnel until you see the light. The grate will open from the inside. Hide the books." He pressed his hand to my back, urging me into the darkness. "One more thing. I know it is hard, but you must decide what is more important. Your love for Mr. Tirich—and loyalty he does not return—or the truth?"

I paused at the thought, but he continued, his voice hushed and full of emotion. "If we are not to see each other again…goodbye, Lady Orion. 'Til the Night rises once more. My only regret is that I couldn't tell you sooner."

He put his hand to his heart, and his long brown robes fell, a small tattoo I had never seen revealed from underneath. "Please give my love to my little moon." With that, he pushed me over the edge, down into the space below, plunging me into the darkness.

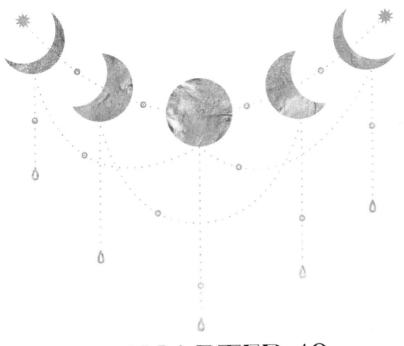

CHAPTER 19

The acrid smell of filth and rot assaulted my senses as I ran. I trudged through the shallow water, mud and filth kicking up around me. I hugged the ancient texts, protecting them from the spray.

Eventually, a sliver of light peeked around the corner. I tried opening the grate with one hand, but it was too heavy. I didn't want to set the books down, but I didn't have a choice. I found a rock a few steps back that seemed a little higher than most and balanced the four books on top, hoping they wouldn't fall over and into the murky water beneath.

With both hands, I pried open the grate. It was rusted and creaked loudly. I prayed to whatever gods were out there that no one would hear. If someone found me like this, I doubted I'd be able to talk my way out of it.

Setting the grate aside, I paused, listening to hear if any guards were nearby. When there was no sound, I clutched the books tighter and ran back as quickly as possible.

The flicker of candlelight and shadows danced beneath when I got to my door. Fynn must be waiting for me as I was sure I hadn't left a candle burning earlier. He had been so angry earlier that I didn't expect he would want to see me again tonight. Cyrus had made me promise that under no circumstances was anyone to know of the books. I knew Fynn didn't like me searching behind his back, and seeing more books would only lead to questions. But where could I hide them? I hadn't brought my satchel with me, and I needed someone I could trust not to pry or ask questions.

My first thought was Archer, but she was too curious. She would know how to push me into telling her everything, and I wanted to keep her safe and keep my promise to Cyrus. The one part of his promise I knew I couldn't keep, at least not yet, was telling her goodbye for him. I couldn't bear the thought tonight.

I didn't know what would come of Cyrus, and guilt washed over me. I was going to be sick. Whatever happened, those guards didn't sound like they were stopping by for a late-night visit. I would check on him tomorrow.

I hoped he would still be there, back in the library, like nothing had happened. A voice deep down told me he wouldn't be there, but I pushed it back down, not wanting to confront the reality of the situation. It was easier not to think of it.

I found myself quietly knocking on a door. A moment later, the soft shuffle of feet and the faint click of her lock. Emryn's strawberry blonde hair was plaited in two, green eyes full of sleep. "Ren? What is it?" She leaned against the half-open door, squinting in the dimly lit hall.

"I have a favor I need to ask. Can you keep a secret?"

She looked me over, curiosity and concern forming on her tired face, but she just nodded. "Of course. Anything for a friend."

I sighed in relief. I knew she would, but I was still tense. I pushed the stack of books forward. "I need you to store these for me. Keep them hidden. No one can know you or I have these."

Confusion flickered over her face. "Is everything alright?" Concern filled those luminous green eyes, and it took everything in me not to break right then. She was so genuinely concerned, and the weight of the entire night seemed to knock into me at once. Fynn. Callax. Cyrus. All of it. I was tired, and the emotional wave I had been riding was catching up.

I shook my head, blinking back the tears. "It's better if you don't ask, and please don't read them. It's important these stay hidden and unread, Em. Please."

She took the books, tucking them under one arm, and wrapped the other around me, pulling me close. "Whatever is going on, you can trust me. I'll keep your secret. I just hope you're taking care of yourself." She smiled and held a hand to my cheek for a moment before disappearing behind her door, closing it softly.

A single tear fell down my cheek as my heart warmed from her kindness.

None of us deserved her, she was too pure. Too good. I didn't know what I would do without her.

I thanked her and bid her goodnight before walking across the alcove to my room. I took a deep breath and paused outside my door, steadying myself.

Fynn was asleep, thank the gods. He must have been waiting for me, hoping to reconcile. He looked so peaceful and worry-free when he slept.

I undressed quietly and curled up in bed next to him, careful not to wake him. I fell asleep to the soft sounds of his breathing and tried to dream of simpler times.

I woke well rested for the first time in what felt like forever. I stretched and rolled over, placing my hand over Fynn's chest, ready to cuddle up next to his warmth. We had our issues, but I craved the comfort of his touch.

But he wasn't there.

I opened my eyes to see where he might have gone and saw him standing at the end of the bed, reading an archive book from my satchel I'd forgotten to return to Cyrus. My heart dropped.

I did my best to keep my voice from shaking. "What are you doing?" I tried to play it off, as if pretending everything was okay would somehow let him glaze over the fact I'd gone against his request and continued my research. "Why don't you come back to bed?" I patted the empty spot next to me, trying to seem as inviting as possible.

He ignored me, eyes scanning the book.

"Fynn?"

He slowly and quietly closed the book, raising his eyes to me. They were cold and dark–empty. It was something I had never seen before. I swallowed hard.

"You promised," his voice was soft but unmistakably angry.

"I promise this one was left over from before." It wasn't a lie. But I wasn't about to tell him about the new ones I acquired. Some part of me deep down knew this wasn't right. That he shouldn't be hiding all of this from me, but seeing him now—this angry and hurt—I wanted to ignore it all and comfort him. I could deal with my emotions later. What mattered right now was fixing us. He had come back last night for that very reason.

He took a quick step forward, and I pulled my hands back without thinking. I hadn't meant to make it so obvious, but some part of me remembered the last time he'd gotten like this and instinctively moved my hands.

The fire beneath his eyes stopped swirling, and he blinked back into the room. "I'm so sorry. I didn't mean to scare you."

"I know," I whispered, "I'm sorry too." I looked down at the pillow and hung my head. I was so tired of this. Loving him was supposed to be easy. So why was it so complicated?

He sat on the bed gingerly, trying not to startle me again.

"Can I hold your hand?" He reached out, waiting for my permission this time. His eyes had returned to normal, and I appreciated the gesture. It comforted me to know he was trying, but every apology felt....desperate. Like he was clinging to me as much as I was to him.

He held mine with both of his, absently stroking my hand with his thumb like he always did. He turned his head towards the floor, letting it hang between his shoulders. "Renata, I can't have you seeking all this information about Phoenixes, old gods, history, or anything like that. The king is...he's very intent on what he wants." He hesitated on those words, looking as if he had said too much already. "I've told you what I can, and I just—I need to know you're going to listen to me." His head still hung low, reflecting over his words, and seemed full of sorrow. "I need you to promise me. For real, this time. Please. Please don't go seeking more information. You don't know what it can cost. You don't know how it hurts me to see this." He lifted his head. "I'm trying. But please don't make this harder."

Pain and sadness welled in his eyes. My heart sank at the sight. I didn't want to hurt him. Maybe I owed it to him to try.

I held my hand to his face as he leaned into my palm. "I promise. I won't go back anymore. For you, Fynn, I promise." I meant it. I was still terrified of what had come of Cyrus, but surely he was okay, right? I couldn't sacrifice what I had with Fynn for a couple of questions. I trusted him when he said he would tell me all I needed to know.

I needed him.

We spent the next hour holding the other, content in companionable silence.

Two weeks passed, and I had forgotten about Cyrus. Part of me wanted to satiate the curiosity of his fate, but I knew Archer had been to the library in the days since, and she made no mention of his absence. That thought made it easier for me to reconcile the fact I had yet to tell Archer he said goodbye.

Fynn and I had mended things over that night, and he still spent most of his spare time training with Ilvar, occasionally joining the twelve of us during our group sessions. He even asked me to stay behind from our group outings going forward to have private dinners with him instead. I was sad to miss out on precious time with my friends, but he was trying–giving me more of his time when he could—so I took what was offered.

Emryn kept me up on the group gossip whenever I missed an outing, so it worked out. Kaede was perpetually grumpy, Archer gossiped about a handful of cute guards she had seen, and Skye and Senna left early for private walks each night.

We were progressing well as a team too. Unresolved tension between the two sides was still present, but for the time being, the angst had dissipated.

Except for Callax.

He increased his torment and snide comments during training, which left our sessions annoying at best.

Though I hated Callax, he had become a suitable partner over the last five and half months, pushing each other in our own strange way. The lingering distaste between us fueled my desire to improve. It was the one thing he was useful for.

The repeated motions of my daggers as I knelt, swiped, stood, rotated, and swiped again all kept my heartbeat steady. But my stomach still roiled like something was wrong. I couldn't place it, but there was something off about today.

Callax and I worked in unison for the next hour, tossing daggers between us and repeating the same flow of motions on the torn bag until it was committed to muscle memory. The loud thud of a body thrown on top of a mat sounded from behind me. It wasn't uncommon, but the severity of it drew my attention. I turned in time to see Archer tossing her hands up, trying to protect her head as Soren brought his fist down onto her jaw and then to her temple. She tried not to make a noise, but a whimper escaped her lips and blood trickled down her brow as he continued to land blow after blow without stopping.

I had never seen a group of people move so fast. Kaede tackled Soren off my sister and onto the ground in an instant. Caldor jumped to his defense, but Senna had the hilt of her ax around his throat, pinning his back to her front before he could do any damage.

Pyne moved to free Caldor and, knowing Senna would not go down easily, grabbed a pair of brass knuckles from the table.

Emryn and Skye were across the room from each other, and both ran to stop Mavenna and Kell before they could attack Senna from behind.

Archer lay on the ground, clutching her jaw, dizzy from the attack. Red coated my vision, and my mind blanked as I launched myself forward. I was going to kill him. I was going to break his fingers, one by one and watch as he screamed.

Time slowed in my rage. Fire roiled in my veins. Whatever strange strength lay beneath was beginning to surge, and I was tempted to let it continue to build, but I pushed it back down. If I was going to end Soren, it would be with my own bare hands. However, Kaede seemed to be doing an excellent job of it so far without me.

As I was nearing Soren—Kaede still on top, fighting to keep him down—two hands grabbed my arms, and I came to a halt. I struggled and screamed against my attacker, but loose black curls swayed into vision, and Callax's sneer greeted me. He hooked one leg between mine and yanked back, bringing my backside flush against his front.

I snarled, putting all the hate I could muster into my voice. "Let me go, you pompous prick, or I will sever your hands and make you wear them like a necklace." He had both of my wrists in one massive hand. With the other, he quickly removed the two daggers from my belt, disarming me. He must have assumed I would use the daggers to pin Soren's hands to the floor so Kaede could beat down on him.

He would have assumed right.

Before I could maneuver away, he whispered in my ear, distracting me. "I could get used to you like this. Hands tied, writhing, speaking those foul things as you're pressed against me."

I tossed my head back, a loud crack and a painful stabbing ran through my scalp where his teeth had sunk into my skin. I hit my mark. "You fu–"

His words stopped as I threw my weight forward, and he stumbled to the side, releasing my hands. I broke free and scrambled to my feet, ready to throw myself on top of Soren.

"Enough." Therion's voice boomed as the training room door burst open. He strode in, angry, Fynn and Ilvar at his side.

Oddly enough, Fynn looked at me, his gaze almost… approving of my actions. Like he was proud of the violence.

Archer managed to sit up, and the rest of us stood at attention, waiting for our inevitable scolding. Ilvar stared Soren and Caldor down, disappointment evident in his gaze.

"Even though this has been thoroughly entertaining, and I hate to cut the bloodlust short…the king requires your presence." He paused, looking at all of us. "Clean yourselves up. All of you are to report to the king. Immediately."

I expected him to break up the fight, shame us for our childish behavior, or tell us how we were supposed to be a cohesive unit—the legendary Ira Deorum. We were a far cry from that, and the title alone should shame us. But instead, he praised our violence.

We were not ready, and with only three months left before the trial and Initiation Ball, I feared we never would be. As individual groups of six, maybe. But together as the twelve. No. There were too many unresolved differences between us, and I had a feeling it wouldn't be fixed before our time was up. And Therion had now given his approval over our discordance.

I broke the silence, moving to help Archer stand. I rubbed the blood from her eye and wrapped my arms around her as we walked out, making sure to give Soren a promise of future retribution.

I wasn't sure what the king wanted from us, but I didn't have a good feeling.

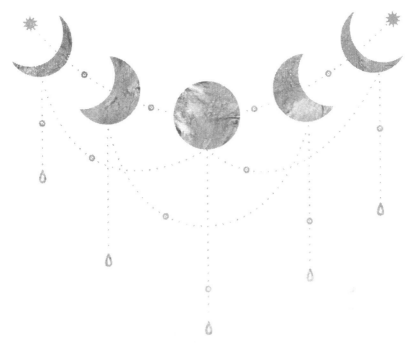

CHAPTER 20

We stood in a line as we faced the king, the twelve of us disheveled and bruised. We all bore small spattering of cuts and bruises, but the only thing that hurt was my ego.

I wanted to keep my eyes down, avoiding the disdain on the king's face, but it was rude to ignore him. His silence seemed to stretch on forever, the wind blowing through the large open windows, making the banners with the royal sigil flap in the breeze. The two snakes and sun emblazoned in the center seemed to come alive with the movement, pulling me in, mesmerizing me.

"You are the twelve. The elite. The Ira Deorum." I could hear the anger rising in his voice. "And yet here you stand, bloodied, and bruised, because of what? Because none of you can get past your schoolyard squabbles?"

Soren lifted his head and, quieter than usual, said, "Therion instructed 'no mercy' your highness. I was only doing as I was told."

King Tobias rose to his feet, "This is your unit. You do not turn on those who would have your back in battle. If they can't trust you, then how are you to trust them when they could hold the key to saving your life? No mercy, yes, but there must be respect."

Soren bowed his head and looked at the floor. My lips tugged up in a smirk, basking in the glory of his being chided by the king. The feeling was short-lived. "Miss Orion, I suggest you wipe that smile from your face. You are the weakest of the lot, and you'd better consider your position very carefully." My smile faded, and I fought the embarrassment, biting the inside of my lip.

"Things have begun to change in the realm. We are no longer at peace. Rumors of plots and uprisings have spread, and I will not tolerate it. I will not tolerate my elite guard fighting like children. Do you understand?" We all nodded. "If you are so keen on disobeying basic rules, then you will suffer the consequences." I swear he looked directly at me, making sure the words sunk in.

My mind went to Cyrus, had he told him? It wasn't likely. If Cyrus was as serious as he had claimed to be about hiding that information, then the King would likely have had him killed or me. Executions were usually public, so I would have known if Cyrus was dead. His next words stopped my rambling thoughts.

"You are to finish your training in forty-five days. Keep up or get out." His eyes bore into me.

My heart dropped. Archer turned her head to look at me, panic in her eyes. Neither of us had picked up a sword. We needed all three months to dedicate our time to master it for the trials. We still didn't even know what would occur in the trial.

I tried to reassure her, but it was hard when even I wasn't full of confidence.

"However, your time will start when you return." Confusion spread through the group, but Fynn, Therion, and Ilvar's faces remained unchanged from where they stood. They looked ready as if they had been waiting for this.

"You are to leave in two days for Alynta. There have been rumors of Fae of all classes, and even humans, who have been talking of the old gods. Wind of a newfound rebellion has risen, and there are speculations of those who wish to leave the Realm of Day. This cannot be allowed. Poison like this will spread, and it needs to end. Now."

The words, 'no mercy,' rang in my head. I swallowed hard. I was afraid of what that might entail.

"Your Phoenix will guide you in this first mission. He is your leader, and you are to follow his every command. This will test your cooperation and prove you are more than mere trainees. You are my champions. Albionne's great warriors. The Ira Deorum. Go, and end this corruption before it infects my lands." He dismissed us with a wave of his hand.

We bowed and turned to leave one by one. As we walked out of the throne room and back to our chambers, I heard his voice, just as he had said the first night we had arrived.

"Do not disappoint me."

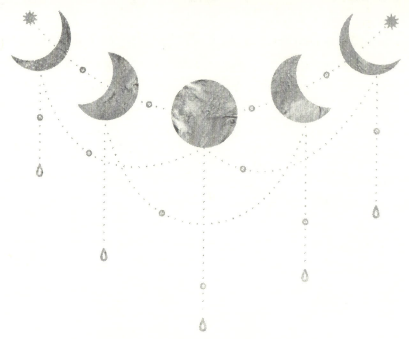

CHAPTER 21

Cyrus's last words echoed in my mind. Was my loyalty and devotion to Fynn more important than the truth? The fact my parents might have lied to me about my past still bothered me. I rationalized it in my mind over and over again. Was it really that big of a deal? It was only a location, but I didn't know if there was more to it or if this was all. Maybe they were ashamed of their past? Maybe their families weren't good people. Perhaps they had a complicated history and were trying to escape and build a better life for us. The possibilities ran through my head but knowing they lied about where I was from didn't sit right with me.

There was also the matter of gathering knowledge regarding Fynn and his mysterious Phoenix past and present. Emryn still had the books, and no one had come in the middle of the night as they did for Cyrus. Surely, he was okay. If the king knew what he gave me, his execution would have been both immediate and public, along with his pursuit of whomever he had given the books to. I told Emryn to keep a hold of them until I was ready.

I came to the conclusion to Cyrus's question, that yes, right now, my loyalty and trust in Fynn came first. He was my partner. We belonged together like the sun and the moon. He was my gravity—my center. I shined because of him. I would gladly come second to his glory if it meant I was destined to be by his side.

I would respect his wishes even if I didn't fully understand his reasons.

The rest of the evening passed by slowly. My friends all went out that night, wanting to drink away the scolding from the king. Fynn requested I stay in with him while he did some extra training but told me he would refrain from using his fire around me.

I sat in the cool grass beneath a tree and watched his muscular body flow smoothly through his motions. The sun slowly set over the stone wall bordering the cliff, and the golden sky glistened off his skin. Light danced around his flame-like tattoos, curling up his arms and chest. The center point where they almost touched glowed a faint red like his heart was the source of power.

It was mesmerizing. I wanted to know what it felt like. To have power like that.

He caught me staring, a wry smile crossing his lips. "Like what you see?"

I did. I really did.

I didn't know what came over me, but I blurted, "Can you teach me?"

He paused but eventually said, "Okay."

I sucked in a breath of excitement, surprised he had agreed.

"I know you've been trying lately and haven't pushed me. I appreciate it. This is simple enough. I don't see any harm to it." He offered his hand and waited for me to take it.

He positioned me in front of him and extended my arms while I matched my stance to his. He held my wrists gently, careful not to squeeze too hard and frighten me. It was so fluid and smooth but made me feel strong. As I moved through the motions, I realized it was almost a dance. Reflecting the way a fire would move and extend itself through the air.

It was almost sensual. As we continued, heat rose in his hands. It was soft and warm, not aggressive and scorching. The warmth grew and somehow, I felt myself cooling down. My normally overactive heart paced itself, slow and steady—beating in time to the rhythm of the dance. It wasn't angry and bitter, but calming.

Fynn broke my train of thought and released my wrists, spinning me to face him. We were both covered in sweat, glistening in the sun's fading light. He stole my breath with how beautiful he was. His hand brushed against my cheek, and I leaned into it. We stayed like that for a moment, and I stared, feeling my body relax in contentment. His touch always grounded me.

His thumb glided over my smooth cheek, and I smiled. "I love you," I whispered. I could feel it in my chest, spreading throughout my body. Like a burning ember taking root.

He pulled me in close, wrapping me in a tight embrace. "I love you too. So much."

The sun shone through his fair hair, his golden tattoos softly glowing with power. He truly embodied the Sun God's spirit. He was to be honored and respected. At that moment, I committed never to pry again. The Sun God provided these lands for us, had made our lives possible, and had never led us astray. He blessed Fynn, and through that, he blessed me. I should be grateful.

Who was I to challenge a god?

I strapped myself with weapons. A dagger on each thigh, two at my waist, and a belt across my chest carrying a hunting blade. We strapped bows to each horse, but Archer and Kell were the only two to keep them on their person. The rest of us carried various knives and specialty weapons. Fynn and Callax carried the largest swords, and Senna had a pair of axes strapped to her back.

If we rode fast, it would take us a few days to get to Alynta. It was a small town, more of a space for transient use than anything else. But a decent population had grown there from those who did not want to travel between cities for supplies and market days.

It had been centuries, if not the entire millennia, since there had been temples and sacred buildings dedicated to worshipping the old gods, so who and how these rumors spread was unknown to me. The towns were small enough, everyone knew everyone, and the whole town usually shared the same mindset concerning the beliefs and opinions of the king. Had there been an outsider who spread their ideas? What could have incited a change? I wanted to discuss it with Fynn, Archer, or Emryn, but I knew better.

The less we knew, the less we asked, the better. I committed not to push things with Fynn, and I would hold to that promise.

The first few hours passed by with no issues. We were still half asleep, trying not to sway out of the saddles. By noon, most of us were irritable at best. Pyne and Kell were bickering over who could take Mavenna in a fight, and Skye teased Kaede about his grumpiness as of late.

Kaede was usually a male of few words, but even fewer had been spoken in recent weeks. I chalked it down to his need for dominance as he and Soren were constantly at odds, trying to best the other each day. In actuality, it was probably Senna who could best us all, but she never goaded her strength, opting for stealth and strategy rather than brute force. She'd make a fine general one day.

"You don't have to be so grumpy all the time. It's good for you to smile now and then," Skye said.

Kaede rolled his eyes, "I do smile. You wouldn't know because you've never given me a reason to."

That was a lie, but they both knew it. Skye and Kaede had a great relationship, but Kaede was more reserved than Skye. It was usually in private or close moments where the two shared inside jokes or laughed. It was sweet if you had the opportunity to witness it. His smile was slightly crooked, but his teeth were a brilliant white against his olive skin, his canines slightly longer than the rest of his teeth. Skye shared that feature with him. His upturned, blue-green eyes was a fitting look for him. They were a chaotic blend, rimmed with a deep blue that was almost black.

The sudden stop of our troop pulled me from my thoughts.

Fynn dismounted his beautiful white stallion and led us to a stream we had been following. I groaned and leaned over, releasing the tension that had been building in my lower back. I wasn't sure why Fynn hadn't opted to fly to Alynta ahead of us, he could have been there in half the time.

Once we all gathered near, he said, "We'll take a short break here, water the horses, and then continue. Stretch your legs and eat something. We still have a long way to go before camp tonight."

Senna grabbed our wrapped lunches from her sack and handed me one.

"Thanks," I said, lifting and stretching my legs. I was not made for riding long distances.

"Are you ready?" she asked.

I furrowed my brow. "For sword mastery?" I inquired.

She nodded.

I breathed in deep and sighed. "Honestly...no." It was the truth. I wasn't ready. I didn't think I ever would be. "I have a good grasp of using knives, but I've never used a sword before." All the time spent with my father and sisters in the woods had barely gotten me through the archery course. Swords weren't of much use when hunting.

"To be honest, Senna, I'm worried. About me. About Archer. I just...I don't know what I'm supposed to do." I looked at the bread and meat in my hands, and suddenly I wasn't hungry anymore. I pulled off pieces of the small loaf and fed them to my tall, golden horse.

"You'll master it. I have faith in you. We all do." She was serious, and there was a look of belief in those stern, golden eyes. Those words meant a lot to me. If Senna Ayre, the fiercest warrior I had ever known, believed in my success, then I did too.

I smiled my thanks. We continued to eat in silence, and Archer sat next to us, the same bread and meat in her hands.

Archer caught Senna's attention between mouthfuls and asked, "I don't think you've ever told us about your tattoos."

"I haven't." She didn't look up from her food.

I think we had all been a little intimidated when we first met Senna, and now that I thought of it, she hadn't ever really explained anything to us. I knew she descended from the islands of Alira on the east side of the continent. It was an old civilization full of culture, light, and music, which had dispersed over the centuries, spreading out between wherever the people landed. I didn't know much, but everyone knew they were a beautiful and ancient people who decorated their bodies in golden tattoos and gold adornments wherever they could.

"Sorry, let me rephrase that," Archer chuckled, clearing her throat. "Will you tell us about your tattoos?"

"Good luck," Skye laughed and plopped down next to Senna, followed by Kaede and Emryn, forming a circle.

Senna shot Skye a look I didn't quite understand, but Skye's eyes widened in surprise as Senna told us the story of her people.

Long ago, Alira was full and thriving with the people of the sun. They worshipped and danced and spun sunlight into their very lives. It was a beautiful way of life, one that praised the Sun God for giving them everything they had. It was a bountiful and prosperous island full of life-giving fruit and grains. The tattoos, she explained, represented the old ways when the Alirans would spin pure sunlight into their skin using special tools lost in the great fire.

Her tattoos ran down her body in perfectly straight lines to represent the flow of the sun's energy through her body. She turned her head and pulled up her sleeves to show the one long line of gold running from behind her ear, down her neck and shoulder, all the way to her hand, where five rays flowed from the line onto the back of her hand and ended at the knuckles. She traced her tattoos with reverence and respect.

Her face became more serious as she continued the tale of her people.

It was the most we heard her speak in one go and were all entranced.

She told us of a male who deemed himself worthy of being the Phoenix. He had run a sun temple for nearly a century, and when the Phoenix of that time died, he built a sacrificial pyre in the middle of the town. While preposterous, many Alirans followed the idea, believing the city was worthy of the honor.

He built a large glass structure that would reflect the sun's power and direct it to himself. He intended to absorb the directed light and, therefore, its powers. He knew he would light on fire, but he believed that even when he did, the flames from the sun would honor him and his offering—selecting him as the Phoenix.

The Sun God did not find the man worthy. When the flames lit the pyre, he burned, along with the entire town. It drove the people out and into the countryside, but the fire continued to rage on, decimating the lands and forcing the people of Alira off their island and to the mainland.

Over the years, there have been those who have tried to return to rebuild their towns, but the fire obliterated the lands, rendering them infertile and incapable of sustaining life.

And so, the people of Alira became nomads, wandering until they found a resting place. Over time, the culture and practices dissipated, and wearing gold adornments was her family's way of honoring their heritage.

We all stared at Senna in awe. We all respected her before, but there was a newfound sense of reverence. The culture and history of her people were fading, and she was continually doing her best to honor and preserve it in her own way. Conformity was easy, but what she was doing was admirable.

We finished our lunch in silence as she continued with more stories of her lost people.

The rest of the journey to Alynta was hard and fast. Only in the moments during meals were we able to rest and stretch. My back and thighs ached.

Just beyond the hill in front of us, Fynn came to a halt, trails of smoke winding their way into the sky. It was nearing dusk, but we had finally made it.

He circled his horse around and said, "Before we head into town, there are a few things you must know. First, this is where your cooperation and communication skills will be tested. We will spend as much time here as we need until we root them out at the base and extinguish this rebellion before it can spread." This was a different version of him. The Fynn I knew and loved may have made mistakes, but he was not cruel. "Second, there will be no prisoners, no questioning, and no mercy. Whomever we find in opposition to our king, to our god, will be terminated." An uneasy look passed between the six of us. The other six, his 'friends,' all nodded as if this weren't an issue.

He moved his horse up a few more feet and faced us one last time, fierce determination written over his handsome face. It was not Fynn who faced us but the Phoenix.

"We are the Ira Deorum. We will not fail our king."

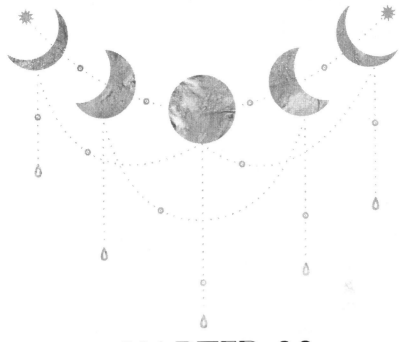

CHAPTER 22

Our blood-red capes rippled in the wind behind us as we rode into town. Leading us all was the golden-haired Phoenix on a massive white stallion. Golden crests of the realm pinned our capes closed abreast our left shoulders–the snakes and sun–glinted in the dying light of the day.

I pitied whoever looked up at us as we rode through town. Invading their home, intent to up-root the lives of fathers or mothers, or whoever dared to defy the king's wishes.

We stopped at a small inn and purchased seven rooms. The innkeeper looked scared out of his mind as he handed us the keys and instructed us where the stables were for our horses. We ate a quick meal and went straight to bed, exhausted from the day's journey.

I was restless, pacing back and forth, chewing my nails. All the worries about Cyrus, the new deadline, and everything else settled into a pit in my stomach. Fynn took notice.

"What's wrong?" he asked, motioning for me to lie next to him so he could hold me. He wrapped his arms around my waist, spreading his warmth as I rested my head on his bare chest.

"Everything and nothing at the same time. I trust you, and I trust you to lead this team, but I don't think I trust myself." I distracted myself from his stare and focused on my fingers at his chest.

"What do you mean?"

"I don't feel ready for all of this. I know you chose me, but I can't help but feel it was only because you love me and would feel guilty for not picking me." I could feel his head tilt and look down at me, but I ignored him. "We all know that Kaede, Senna, and Emryn are better than me. Skye is getting better every day, and even Archer has her insane skills with the bow."

"Have you not noticed your skills with the daggers? Renata, you're doing great."

"I've never picked up a sword before, and now King Tobias wants us to cut the training time in half?" I held back the tears that stung my eyes out of frustration. I hated to cry in front of him, but I felt so lost. "I don't think I'll make it, Fynn. The sword is going to be the reason I fail. And if I don't pass the trials and make it to initiation…" I trailed off, not wanting to finish the thought. But there was no need. We both knew what would happen if I didn't.

He rubbed my shoulders in silence while he thought.

I took a breath and focused on the feeling of his fingers on my skin, how the physical contact connected us, grounding me. I could feel the tension bundle in my muscles as he pushed against them. It was painful, but the good kind. I leaned into it.

"You're going to be fine. I promise."

"You don't know that," I said.

"I do. Because I…" he paused for a fraction of a second, but I still heard it. "I trust you. Just like you trust me. Okay?" He shook my shoulder, trying to get me to laugh or smile.

"Okay," I agreed, but my smile was forced. I didn't believe it, but I wanted to. I wanted to because he said he was doing the same for me.

"Get some rest. We have a big day tomorrow." He kissed me quickly on the forehead and rolled over, tucking his leg around mine. It didn't take long for him to drift off to sleep.

We split into groups of four. Fynn took Soren, Caldor, Callax, and Kaede. Senna was to lead Mavenna, Kell, and Emryn, and I was left to take Skye, Archer, and Pyne.

I had never led a group before, but I would try. Fynn gave me a small smile of reassurance when he announced the teams, letting me know he purposely took the troublesome males and gave me Archer. It felt slightly divided to know all but one of the males were going with him, but I pushed the worry away. He wouldn't give these groups without reason.

"My group will take the center of town. Senna, take your group north and circle to the east. Renata, you take the south side and circle up west. Take your time. This doesn't have to be done in one day. We need to speak to as many people as we can. Get them to trust you, and if necessary, apply force. If they don't respect us outright, we will make them fear us. Understood?" I hesitated but agreed.

We were up early, but the town's shopkeepers were dusting off their windows, baking their bread for the day, and readying their wares. "Skye and Pyne, you two go off and search that side of the street. Archer and I will take this side and work our way to the end. When we've talked to everyone, report back, and we'll compare notes and move on." They nodded and walked off towards an elderly male sweeping his shop porch.

Archer and I headed to the bakery, and I grinned a little. It may have been out of selfishness that I chose this side, but I craved fresh bread. There wasn't much I loved more than freshly baked bread.

"Good morning," a portly Fae with fading brown hair greeted us. He didn't look up from his kneading as we walked in.

"Good morning," Archer and I chimed in together. At the sound of the two strangers, he lifted his head. I smiled in response, and his eyes widened. He quickly wiped the sweat from his brow and dusted his sticky hands on his apron.

A breath of surprise left his lips before he said, "How can I help you this morning?" His eyes flicked back and forth between the two of us. I couldn't tell what his expression was trying to convey.

I smiled, trying to ease the tension, and pulled out a couple of silver coins placing them on the counter. "We'd like some bread and maybe some sweets if you have them too, please? Whatever this will get us." I nodded to the coins on the counter, but he didn't move. He had noticed the golden snakes and sun across our chests. I looked down and back to him. "Oh, we're only here on some business, please don't mind us." That didn't seem to clear the confusion or surprise, but he nodded and busied himself with grabbing a few small rolls and three pastries each. They smelled so good I swear I floated on the scent alone.

As I took them from him, our hands touched briefly, and he pulled back. "I'm so sorry, my lady. Please forgive me."

"Is everything okay?" I handed the bread over to Archer, exchanging a confused glance. She didn't understand his behavior either.

"I—yes, of course, my lady." He bowed his head and looked sheepish. "Everything is going to be just fine. Thank you." His surprise morphed into something else.

"Do you mind if we ask you some questions?" Archer took a step forward. He nodded timidly but agreed to listen. "Do you know of any strange meetings going on lately? Or maybe whispers of those who wish to live… differently? Or perhaps elsewhere?" Her voice was gentle, guiding the question without force. She worded it better than I would have, encouraging him to talk rather than confront or accuse him.

He took a sharp breath and whispered, "No, there is no secret group here." He seemed genuine, but the tone led me to believe otherwise. He must be used to denying this, and I suspected most of the town would as well. I didn't blame them. Admitting to such things meant certain death.

"It's essential that you tell us the truth," I urged him softly, "It would be much appreciated if you could help us. I promise we'll keep you safe."

His hands shook, and I could hear his heart beating faster from behind the counter. He knew something. But I didn't want him to face any unwarranted consequences. He had been so kind and was only trying to make an honest living here. Regardless of if he took part, he didn't deserve it.

"I take no part in such things," he confessed, using his hands to emphasize his words. "But if there were to be anything of such nature, it would take place in the town library. I can't say for certain, and you didn't hear it from me. Do you understand?"

Archer and I smiled reassuringly, "We understand. Thank you." A petite young male stepped out from a door leading to the kitchen. As we waved goodbye, his mouth fell open.

We closed the door, and swore I heard him say, "Is that her?"

Archer and I continued down the street, forgetting all about the boy as we devoured the delicious bread. I would be sure to go back for more if we stayed a while.

"I have a feeling most of these people are in on something," Pyne said, frustrated they hadn't gleaned any helpful information.

"It's only day one," Skye said, looking rather annoyed, "Besides, it doesn't help that you're scaring everybody."

"Well, if they don't know that defying us means death, then how will they ever talk?" She threw up her arms, frustrated.

"Did you try being nice?" Archer asked, giving her a skeptical look.

"Nice gets us nowhere."

"It got us an answer."

Pyne rolled her eyes, but Skye asked, "What did you find?"

"A baker gave us the mention of a meeting potentially taking place in the library, but he was adamant he didn't know for certain."

Pyne mulled over the information. "I guess it would make sense. It's a public place and lots of areas in the back to hide and whisper."

I said, "Other than some strange looks throughout the day, we didn't get much else. I think most people either don't know or are too scared to tell us. I say we go without our cloaks and sigils tomorrow, see if we can't appear less... intimidating. Maybe they'll trust us and open up some more." Skye nodded. Pyne didn't like the idea but kept quiet. "We'll run it by Fynn tonight and pull together the information. We can make a final decision in the morning. For now, let's eat and get some rest."

As we walked back towards the center of town, we heard a commotion and the sound of glass breaking. We ran through a back alleyway that smelled horrendous and had animal entrails falling out of an overflowing bin. The smell alone nearly knocked me back. We were behind a butcher shop.

The back door swung open, and an elderly man wearing an apron covered in blood flew out. His head hit the bricks of the alley wall, and he slumped to the ground in a heap. Still alive, but dizzy and disoriented. He wasn't Fae, his rounded ears confirmed as much, and blood streamed down his neck. By the stench, I could tell he was the butcher.

I turned quickly to tend to the man when out of the door stormed Soren and Caldor. Fynn leaned against the doorway, satisfaction written on his tan face. Behind him, Kaede and Callax remained in the shadows, their black hair and leathers blending into the darkness.

Soren grabbed the man by his apron and pulled his body a few feet off the ground, bringing his face close. Hovering next to him, Caldor glowered.

"You will tell us what we want to know, or defying us will be the last thing you do," Soren growled, sick enjoyment twisting his face as he shook him violently.

I watched in shock and horror. I glanced towards Fynn, curious if he would let this behavior play out. Surely, he would stop him, right? I knew he said no mercy, but this man was human, Quarter at most, but he had no way of defending himself. No mercy would only apply to those who openly defied us and fought back. It shouldn't apply to those weaker and less capable than us.

Caldor kicked the man in the ribs. He groaned in pain, clutching his side as blood spilled from his lips. But still, he said nothing. Soren dropped the butcher to the ground and pulled out his sword. Archer and I gasped audibly.

Fynn only seemed to notice us then. His facial expression did not change, but a tiny sliver of surprise lit his eyes.

"What in the gods' damned realm do you think you're doing?" I yelled, furious. I stormed towards Soren, Archer right behind me, one hand on her bow. I had my daggers out before I realized and stood, ready to fight him, not caring that Caldor would back him up or that Archer and I were in no position to take the twins in a fight.

"Stand down, Renata." An air of authority and power I had never heard him use filled his voice. It reverberated through me and I paused, my hands loosening on the daggers. I moved back involuntarily.

"What?" I whispered. "Why?"

"We are the Ira Deorum and will show no mercy against those who stand against the king or me."

I said nothing, staring in disbelief as he continued, "This man has openly defied us and has refused to speak. He has information that he is withholding and will be punished for his crimes against the crown. If he wishes to stay silent, then he shall. Forever." The golden amber of his eyes had turned dark, and the swirls of power roiled behind them, threatening.

I didn't have time to scream before Soren drove his sword down into the man's chest. He didn't fight it and went limp, his hand falling from his head. Lifeless.

This wasn't happening. It couldn't be. I wanted to turn and run, but Fynn's stare held me in place as he stated, "We will meet you back at the Inn."

They left, and I stood stunned in the reeking alleyway, the butcher's blood pooling at my feet.

CHAPTER 23

I opted for a hot bath instead of dinner.

I had no desire to be near Fynn, but it was hard when we shared a room and bed. Thankfully, he was going over the debrief, so I had a few moments to myself. He would just have to hear the day's report from Archer for all I cared. If he wanted to speak, he could wait.

The warm bath cooled my temper and relaxed my sore muscles. I still ached in places I didn't know were possible from the long ride. Secretly, I hoped this mission would take us a few days longer so I could recover fully before getting back on my horse. I wouldn't mind staying with the people here either. Despite some of their frenzied or awed looks when we approached, they were kind and generous. I had yet to get a solid answer from anyone during the day's inquiries, but part of me didn't want to.

I soaked in the tub until the water grew cold, and even then, I didn't want to move. Bathing gave me time to think and calm my mind. It had become my safe space.

The only thing that could have made it better would be sweet-smelling salts. They were typically an item I splurged on before being called to the castle. But there, it was readily available. I took full advantage of it. Especially when training made me smell less than desirable by the end of the day.

There was a soft knock on the door, and Fynn entered without waiting for a response. I sat up and leaned forward, bringing my chest to my knees. I wasn't afraid to be on display for him, but it felt like he had become someone else after today—someone I didn't trust.

The kindness in his eyes was gone. I didn't want to bare my naked body to this new version—a stranger.

"Hey," he whispered.

I averted my gaze, unsure of how to respond. He knelt by the side of the tub and reached for my hand. He held it there, waiting for me to take it, but I didn't move. I wasn't ready to let him touch me yet. I wanted to trust him, to open up to him, but I couldn't. Not yet. Not until he explained his actions.

His hand fell to his side, a soft sigh escaping his lips. "I'm sorry about earlier. I want you to know I never meant to talk to you that way."

I bit my lip, not trusting my words. Normally I would fight back, argue, or try to convince him, but my heart fell.

"I have to be strong for the others, to lead, and show them how we must act."

Tears stung my eyes. I blinked, trying to hold them back. I did know, and yet despite that, it still troubled me. Why did it have to be this way?

"You know what the king expects of me. I have to make sure I meet that demand. It's a lot of pressure, and I don't think you quite understand it. I'm glad you don't understand it. I wouldn't wish this burden on anyone else, but I have to ensure I am the best I can be."

I lifted my eyes from my knees, "I know." The words were hushed. Defeated. I resigned myself to him at that moment. It was easier than fighting, and I couldn't muster the energy for it. I couldn't plead my case to him yet again. I felt like I was stuck on a wheel, spinning out of control as we repeated this painful cycle.

He stood and extended his hand, beckoning me to leave the cold water. I accepted and let him wrap a dry towel around me. I still felt numb, distant from it all, but his warm touch centered me and brought me back to the room. He could always bring me back because I revolved around him. He was my sun…and I wasn't sure what I was without him. If I was anything at all.

I let him tell me about his day. It was strange to be comforted by the same voice that cut so deep.

The following day continued with much of the same: strange looks, hushed whispers, and dead ends. Fynn hadn't liked the idea of leaving our cloaks at the Inn, so we had decided it was best to keep them on.

The face of the lifeless butcher kept appearing in my head every time a human or Fae showed any fear at our questions. Guilt twisted my stomach when I replayed his death, the pool of blood, his lifeless body. I wanted to understand Fynn, but it was hard to comprehend the extent of what was happening. I didn't want to be complacent, but what was I to do if I had no solid information? I hated the idea of blind obedience, but it was the path of least resistance.

"Do you think any of them will tell us anything?" Archer sighed, tossing her arms in resignation.

"Not dressed like this, no." I fiddled with the pin that held my cloak closed on my left shoulder. My fingers ran over the twisting forms of the intertwined snakes. My finger pricked the edge of the sun, and I flinched. I brought it to my mouth and tasted the metallic tang of blood. I unpinned my cloak, hiding the sigil from view.

"What are you doing?" Archer lifted a brow in curiosity.

"We don't have the luxury of waiting until we find someone willing to trust us." If they didn't trust the king, they wouldn't trust us either. Fynn could argue all he wanted, but I felt the people would open up more if we weren't wearing the crest so brazenly. "The others are out there doing gods knows what to those who won't talk. Isn't it better to just see what an hour or two like this can do?"

Archer looked uneasy, but she nodded hesitantly and draped her cloak over her arm. Without the king's sigil displayed on our chest, we looked like regular Fae folk. High-end Fae, but a step in the right direction.

It didn't take long for my plan to work. I had suspected it would, but a small rush of pride filled my chest when I recognized that I had been right all along. I should have trusted my instinct from the beginning.

"Hi there, how can I help?" The shop lady was short and petite, only coming up to Archer's shoulders, her hand full of sewing pins as she worked on a dress. Her beautiful silver hair and worn face indicated she was Quarter Fae, maybe Half if she was a couple of centuries old. She had aged beautifully and looked friendly. It was a nice change of pace.

"We had a couple of questions for you, if you don't mind?" Archer smiled warmly at her, and she looked up from her work. Her smile wavered slightly, and she dropped her pins on the floor, scattering every which way. Her eyes widened like many others we had come across in this town. We quickly leaned down and helped pick them up for her.

"Oh, please, please, my ladies, do not bother yourselves with this. I'm so clumsy. Let me clean." She tried to shoo us away, but we didn't move.

"It's truly no bother at all. What is your name?" I asked, and we handed her the pins we had collected. She kept her eyes lowered, and her head bowed as she took them from us.

"Anya. I suppose I can try and answer what I know. Whatever the two of you may need, I will try." I knew removing our capes had helped, but this seemed too easy.

I focused back on her and continued my questions, "We've heard of some rumors that there is a group here that meets in secret. Maybe at the library, or somewhere near the town square? Is this true? If so, can you give us any more information?"

The shop attendant chewed her lip and wrung her hands, debating internally. I could tell she knew something. I smiled reassuringly, praying it would ease some of her worries.

She took a breath. "There is a group, rather large, which meets twice a week either in or near the library. Now, I've never been, mind you." Her eyes darted between the two of us as if trying to gauge how much of that lie we believed. If she knew this, the odds were she had intimate knowledge of it, but I didn't press, letting her continue. "But there have been whispers around the town of those seeking a new home. A long-forgotten city that would solve our problems."

"What problems?"

"You've seen the town, my lady; surely, it's obvious to know we are not well-off people. Life is hard here. Ever since the king cut off the trade routes, we have struggled to make ends meet. Humans and Fae of all kinds are trying to find a way just to make it by,"

I interrupted, holding out a hand, "Wait, what do you mean ever since the king cut off the trade routes? I thought this was a major waypoint between cities."

Her eyes brimmed with tears, "It was, for a short time, decades ago. But about twenty-five years ago, King Tobias discovered our mountains in the west were filled with a rare stone thought to be depleted thousands of years ago. Ever since that day, he's cut off our town and pulled all males of age to go mine. He steals them away." The hatred and loss were clear in her worn face. The creases around her mouth deepened, and her lips tightened as she spoke. "Most never return. And if they do, they are gone for ten years."

Her revelation shocked me. I hadn't heard of this. What stone was worth the sacrifice of trades and jobs, and livelihoods? "What stone could be that important?" I asked.

"I'm not sure, but from what I know, it's an ancient one, brought to this realm by the Sun God himself. One used to forge a weapon in the Great War." Her voice was hushed; she knew this was not information to be shared aloud, even though no one else was in the store with us.

When neither of us responded, still stunned in silence, she continued, "Most don't return, and those that do, their bodies are so worn from the constant mining that they can hardly work for years after. He took my husband from me. He died in the mines, slaving away. He never came home." Her tears began to fall, and she choked back a sob, "Eight years ago, they took my son, my sweet Talon. I haven't heard from him since." Her voice dropped off, and she buried her head in her hands, succumbing to her grief.

Archer took her hand and guided her to a nearby bench, letting her rest.

"This city you mentioned," I gently pressed, "how is it you came to know of this? And why do those who seek it feel it will be their answer?" I had a feeling I knew which city she was referring to, but I didn't want to be the one to speak the words aloud.

She looked at me then with wariness as if I should have already known the answer. "Soon after King Tobias cut things off, a young Fae couple passed through town on their way south." She smiled fondly at the memory, "I only remember this because we used to own an Inn next door. I knew everyone who passed through. We took the couple in for a few nights. The female carried a young Fae child in her arms, only a year or two by the looks of it. A wee little thing with raven hair and cobalt eyes. Both were beautiful creatures, the kind of beauty I hadn't seen before. They were Fae, like most of us, but this family was different. Something that felt ancient—sacred, almost."

Archer looked at me from the corner of her eyes.

"They were only here a few nights, but the stories they told were of love and acceptance and a city that filled the night sky and reflected moonlight. It was an old city, just beyond Cresslier Pass."

I took a sharp breath. I had been right; she was talking of the capital in the north. But to get here, one would have to travel through Cresslier Pass. There were no stories of those who went through and returned to tell the tale. The mere mention that three Fae could come through the pass was quite the story. Near impossible. But something about this story made me want to believe.

"She told us if we could let go of our prejudice and trust in the Night, we could find our way. I thought it was all myths and legends, stories designed to entertain, until eight years ago." She looked at us again, and her eyes bore into us, searching, "There was a shift. Something changed. A Fae male wearing a cloak and sigil I'd never seen before came through town, looking for something or someone and asking for a girl with raven hair and cobalt eyes. But when he came to me, I had just lost my husband. I was inconsolable and remembered nothing." Anya sighed, shoulders slumping, "So, finding nothing, he left. Months later, I recalled seeing that sigil once before when a Fae couple with their infant passed through. An infant with raven hair and cobalt eyes." She stared past my eyes, straight into my soul. I averted my gaze. "I told a few people of this, and it sparked something. Something I wanted no part of, so I stayed out of it. Soon after, humans and Fae alike left, never returning. My best guess is they all either died or made it through somehow." Her voice shook, and Archer interrupted.

"Through to where Anya?" she asked.

"Cresslier Pass. To the hidden city of Asterion."

"Is this why there have been secret meetings? To organize escape groups?" Archer pressed.

She nodded, "Yes, my lady. The king has been sending a rotation of guards to find out who, but so far, he has only succeeded in rooting out those who have already left on their journey and killing them. He's only managed to find a handful over the years, but those who were caught were slaughtered. Their bodies left on the road, only to be found months later during trade season."

They were escaping. The king was upset because he was losing subjects, faithful men who were stolen to serve in captivity for a decade. I never trusted King Tobias, but I never had a solid, factual reason other than my gut instinct. This…was despicable. Evil. To steal away husbands and fathers from families, to kill those who only wished for a better life—it made me sick. And now Fynn had killed an innocent man who was only trying to protect his friends. A man that had likely served his time in those mines, too, only to receive a cruel fate for wanting to decide his fate. My stomach churned, and I pushed down the bile.

"Before we go, this sigil you mentioned…could you describe it to us?" She nodded and disappeared behind her counter, returning a moment later with a scrap of paper. She sat for a minute, her hand hovering above the page, but then she began to draw. It was a rough sketch of lines and a few curves, and when she handed the paper over to me, I studied it for a minute. One line ran down the middle. At the top, centered in the line, was a crescent moon and five lines below. Two on either side of the center, angled in the shape of wings. It looked familiar, almost like a bird. I pocketed the paper.

"Thank you, Anya. You have been a great help." I handed her a few gold coins for her cooperation. She waved her worn hands in refusal, but I insisted,

"Please, it's the least we can do." She thanked us and took the coins.

As we walked away, a chill ran through the town, and I swung my cloak back over my shoulders, not thinking about the shop window still in view. I turned to wave once more, and the gold sigil of the king flashed in the sunlight. I would never forget the look of horror that washed over her face.

CHAPTER 24

I debated for hours whether I should tell Fynn. I wanted to be loyal like I promised but interacting with the people of Alynta and hearing their desire for freedom made me question where I should place my faith. It reminded me of Cyrus's lingering question. What was more important—the truth or Fynn?

I thought it was Fynn. I wanted it to be. But the more I learned, the more I had this nagging sense of doubt. Were all the legends of the Realm of Night true? Anya had mentioned Asterion, and more and more references that had all been banned continued to show up. It made me wonder how deep King Tobias's hatred and ambition ran and what lengths he would go to accomplish his goals.

"Are you going to tell Fynn?" Archer asked. She played with the clasp of her cloak.

I didn't have an answer. I didn't know. The thought of the butcher still played in my mind, and the idea of Fynn or Soren or any of us harming sweet Anya gave me a pit in my stomach. I don't think my loyalty extended to the torture of innocents. But if I had no choice, would I blindly follow the king's bidding?

"I don't know," I muttered. "I don't think so, but I can't imagine it would end well if he found out we were lying."

She nodded in agreement. "Let's figure out what everyone learned and go from there."

She was wiser than her years.

We met with Skye and Pyne, and followed the streets to the town square. It felt half abandoned, and the sense of dread was thick in the evening air.

"Where's Fynn?" I asked Skye.

She shrugged.

Out of the library in front of us strode Fynn, walking towards us with confidence. A look of triumph was arrogantly written on his face as he said, "Everyone, gather your things. Meet me at the top of the hill outside of town in an hour. Soren, Caldor, Callax, Kaede, you four stay with me. Ren, Emryn, and Mavenna pack the rest of our stuff. We won't be long." His grin didn't reach his hollow and empty eyes.

We returned to the inn and put away the few belongings we each brought. I didn't know what Fynn had planned, but we were leaving, and that was what mattered. It meant Anya, the baker and his son, and anyone else we had spoken with who were too scared to talk, would be safe. It meant they would live to fight another day, to find a way to escape.

Archer and I had yet to discuss our conversation with Anya, but I knew we would need to as soon as we had the privacy to do so.

I secured the horses' saddlebags, double-checked the straps, and refreshed our water skins. We rode in silence to the top of the hill, where we waited. As we sat there, I admired the town once more. Hoping it would be some time before we were sent out again. They deserved peace.

The pinkish hues of the sunset fell over the town, wrapping it in a warm blanket. I would have admired it if it weren't for the suffering I knew lay beneath.

I closed my eyes and listened for the soothing sounds of the town's routine. But my breath caught in my throat.

Silence.

It wasn't natural for a town to be this silent—without noise or chatter.

Then, a scream echoed, filled with terror. A deafening explosion followed.

It took me a moment too long to register what was happening before a ball of fire exploded from the bell tower directly above the library. The shock wave reached us, forcing me to dig my heels into my horse to keep steady as they all reared in the air, terrified. The wave of heat scorched us, eliminating the chill from the air.

Flames spread in a cloud of destruction, the heat warping my vision. From the center of it all, triumphant and god-like, rose Fynn.

His mighty Phoenix wings, red and gold and coated in flames, propelled him upward into the sky. He hovered, watching the destruction unfold beneath him. The screams of terror filled the air. Horrific, pained screams echoed as flesh burned, searching for their lost loved ones in the wreckage.

The powerful downbeats of his fiery wings only fanned the flames. They encompassed him, his red wings blending seamlessly with the fire, their burning tendrils wrapping around his arms and licking at his feet. He alone could survive them.

Looking at him now, I recognized him for what he was. He might have been the host of the Sun God, but at this moment, he was no better than death himself.

Stunned, I stared in shock, my body unmoving in the horror of it all. There was nothing I could do. Half the town had been destroyed in the blast, and the rest would soon catch on. Their homes. Their shops. Their livelihoods. All destroyed because of the beliefs of a few.

I could feel the perfect version of him, the one I had held on to so tightly, beginning to slip away like ash in the wind. I was losing him.

There was no mercy. This was not an act that could be justified…this was cruelty. And he reveled in it.

I leaned over and emptied my stomach's contents.

To my left, Kell, Mavenna, and Pyne grinned. The flames flickered dark shadows across their faces. To my right, my friends all watched in silent horror. There was a clear divide.

There were those who were loyal to the king—cruel—and without mercy. And then there were the six of us, who sided not with the king, but with the plight of the people.

We would never be united, no matter our duty and service to the crown.

But the time for questioning was over. There was no going back.

As we rode back, one question kept nagging at me, carving into my mind with its incessant need. What was more important, the truth or my loyalty to Fynn?

For the first time, my answer changed.

I needed to find Cyrus.

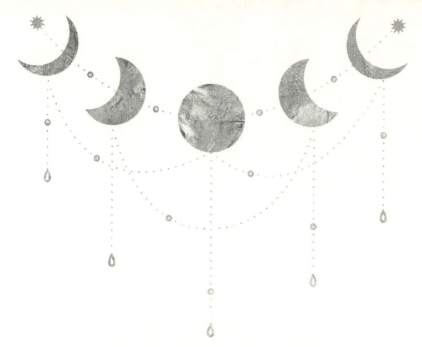

CHAPTER 25

We returned to the castle, left with less than half a day to rest and recover before heading back to training first thing in the morning. Tomorrow we would start our last and shortest course—sword mastery. I sighed, tired from the day and anxious for the next. I wanted to crawl into my warm bed and melt into the blankets.

I didn't give Fynn a chance to talk to me as we stabled our horses. Instead, I grabbed my gear and headed straight inside. I'd put off seeing Cyrus for far too long.

It had been weeks since I last saw him, and I'd yet to go back and find out what exactly happened. I figured if it were important enough, he would have sent a messenger, but the nagging guilt of the consequences of my choices ate at me.

After quickly changing, I wound down the stairs to the library. I strode straight for the back, my soft-soled slippers nearly throwing my balance. I knew that this was where he would be if he were here. Where he always was. I missed his worn face and fun facts. I had let my poor judgment get in the way of keeping his company. I wouldn't let that happen again.

The other scholars gave me strange glances, shock written all over their faces at my sudden barging in. I reached the golden gate, sectioning off the small archive, and pushed it open. The hinges squeaked in protest as I walked inside. But the figure inside was neither Cyrus nor anyone I had expected to see here.

Callax.

"What in the hell are you doing here?" I growled, trying to hide my frantic search for Cyrus. Unless he was lying on the ground behind a shelf, there was no chance of him being here. My heart fell. Everything usually here… was gone. The only things remaining were the chairs and table at which Callax sat, haunting the space where Cyrus should be.

No.

No, no, no, no. I tried to push the worst of the thoughts from my head in the last weeks without visiting him. I had refused to think the king was capable of such a cruel act, but I had known. I had known and refused to acknowledge it. The painful and bitter memory of loss swelled in my chest, growing frantic.

"You know…" he said, not even glancing my way, keeping his interest focused on his nails. "You have a bad habit of maintaining poor etiquette. I am your prince. You will acknowledge my presence with 'your highness' or 'my prince.'"

I snarled. "You have a bad habit of being an asshole. I couldn't give two shits about the way I treat you. Besides, it's not as if you don't deserve it." He shrugged, not denying my claims. "Now, where is Cyrus."

Callax looked up from his nails. I hadn't noticed his appearance until then, his face hidden under tangled curls. He looked haggard. Worn. His beautiful black curls lacked any shine and hung limply around the nape of his neck. Dark circles rimmed the bottoms of his eyes, making them look hollow. The sallow color of his skin exaggerating his sharp features. There was a new darkness to him, one that wasn't there before. It leeched all the vibrance from his eyes. I might have been concerned for his well-being if I didn't hate him.

"Didn't you know?" he asked. My heart leap to my throat. "The night you were with him, my father sent guards to detain him." I shook my head. Cyrus had been right all along. I naively assumed he was all right, maybe just sulking a bit from my poor choices.

"No," I whispered, afraid to hear what came next.

"Yes." His sunken eyes met mine, and there was no gleam in them as he said, "He is to be executed at dawn. And you are to blame."

I stumbled back, hitting a chair behind me. I sank into it before I fell. My heart raced in my chest, a dull roar in my ears building.

"How did you do it?" Callax leaned across the table and searched my face for an answer. "How did you manage to escape his room without the guards finding you?" He looked distraught as if Cyrus's fate affected him as much as it did me. But Callax was cold and incapable of feeling that way towards anyone.

I took a moment to catch my breath and placed a hand on my chest. Trying to steady myself. "I don't know what you're talking about," I lied again.

"Don't be daft. We know it was you. You were with him earlier that night; the scholars told us as much. But what my father can't figure out is how you managed to evade him." He looked genuinely curious.

"I don't know what you're talking about."

"Why he didn't give you up is a mystery, but he's willing to die for your secrets. You seem to earn the loyalty of those around you and I can't determine why."

A dull roar built in my head, drowning it all out. I felt myself slipping out of my body. Though I could still hear Callax, I was numb, like my body wasn't my own.

"It's only a matter of time before my father proves that you're taking things a step too far." He spat the words and pushed the chair back with a loud groan. "It would be in your best interest if you stayed far away from the execution. It would only serve my father's theories of your involvement. If you're going to continue to lie to me, then fine. Just…watch your back." A moment of near concern slipped in his voice, but the hardness of his face did not change. "Your usefulness is waning." He lowered his head and turned to leave.

"Why warn me?" I hissed, my voice barely audible. Why was Callax acting as if my fate mattered to him? He didn't like me, and I loathed him. We were not friends, had never been so. "What does it matter to you?"

"Because for some reason, you matter." He paused at the old golden gates. "And because there is something else at play here. Something they have kept me in the dark about. And despite your recklessness or opinion of me, there are people I care about, and lines even I won't cross." He didn't give me a chance to respond before he walked out, hands running through his hair.

I stayed in the chair a while longer, unable to move. The weight of my actions slammed into my chest, pinning me in place. It was my fault. Cyrus was going to die because of my reckless curiosity. Why couldn't I have just listened to Fynn the first time?

He was right. Gods damn it, Fynn was right. I shouldn't be looking where I didn't belong. The king suspected my search, and if he was willing to torture Cyrus for weeks without answers and order the destruction of an entire town and its people... I didn't want to imagine what he would do to me. I was supposed to be fighting for him as part of the elite, and if he confirmed his suspicions I would be as good as dead. It wouldn't matter if I was the Phoenix's partner. He would kill me without a second thought.

Fynn might even encourage it.

I shuddered at the thought.

The worst part was that Cyrus would die, and I hadn't even read the books he sacrificed himself for. I had gone right back to Fynn and forgotten all about him. Gods, what would Archer think? My stomach turned at the thought. I swallowed the rising bile.

Another person in her life. Dead. Because of me.

All I wanted was to be happy. Instead, it only led to more grief.

Cyrus's execution would be a public affair used as a message to the people that defying your king would end brutally. Coupled with the fate of Alynta, this would solidify the king's power. It would shake the country awake. The peace would be broken, and I wondered how many more cities out there knew about the ill intentions of the king or if they were as ignorant as I had been.

I needed to get the books back. I needed to read them. I needed to figure out why the information in them was worth dying for, even if it meant going behind Fynn's back.

He had broken my trust. I owed him no loyalty.

CHAPTER 26

I knocked softly on Emryn's door. It was late, and the last thing I wanted to do was walk in on her and Kaede amidst certain…activities.

She opened her door, wearing a silk nightgown, her strawberry blonde hair flowing in waves over her shoulders. She was stunning, even after having ridden for nearly two days straight like the rest of us.

Emryn beamed, pulling me in for a hug. I wrapped my arms back around her, giving her a quick pat, letting her know there was no need to extend the hug longer than necessary. I loved physical touch, but I was not much of a hugger outside of Archer or Fynn.

Still breathless from her embrace, I said, "Do you remember those books I gave you a few weeks back?"

"Of course, come in." She moved aside, letting me into her room. It was clean and organized, just like her appearance. She had a few books on her nightstand and her leathers for tomorrow already laid out. She was much more prepared and organized than I was. I was more of a 'toss on whatever is clean from the floor' kind of girl.

"Please, sit." She sat on the edge of her bed and motioned for me to do the same.

"Oh, I just need the books, and I can get out of your hair." I tried to protest.

"Absolutely not." She folded her arms and looked up through her brows, daring me to defy her. I conceded.

"Are you going to explain?" Emryn folded her legs beneath her and waited for me to talk. Emryn and I had talked plenty before, especially when I was in the giddy phases of being romanced by Fynn.

"About?"

"Seriously, Ren?"

"What?" I shrugged, trying to play it cool.

"Don't. I can see right through you. You might fool everyone else, but I can tell when your moods shift and how you act when you're frustrated or upset. And don't act like we all didn't witness what happened in Alynta." Her knowing eyes looked right past mine and into my soul. I sighed, knowing there was no point in trying to hide from her.

"I don't know, Emryn." Tears welled in my eyes before I said anything at all. She reached her hand out and rubbed mine while I told her the last few months' events. The ups and downs and how I felt like I was being tossed around emotionally. I don't know how much time had passed, but I unloaded nearly everything, unable to stop.

I was careful to tiptoe around Cyrus and the events leading to his death, not wanting to involve her more than she bargained for. I also conveniently left out the parts with Callax pinning me to the wall or his alluding comments during training—or how I felt guilty for not telling Fynn about it even when nothing happened—but I laid it bare.

Her arms extended, and I leaned forward, sobbing into the safe embrace. She ran her hands up and down my back, letting me cry. She didn't try to tell me it was going to be okay, or that I was crazy, she just let me cry it out. She was the older sister I never had but needed. Being the eldest daughter came with so much weight and expectation. Losing my parents threw me into a role I never asked for but fulfilled regardless. It was heavy, and Emryn was here to take it for me. Even if only for a moment. The relief she provided, the space she held, saved me more times than I could count.

That was what often made Emryn so special to us. She made space for us, not letting our actions or words impede ourselves. She held room in her life for all of us individually, and we felt safe with her. Free to love, and feel, and express ourselves. I don't think we ever did the same for her, too caught up in our own lives to make sure the one who cared most was also cared for.

I sniffled. "I don't know what I'd do without you."

She smiled warmly and said, "Ren, you don't have to carry this by yourself. You aren't meant to go through life alone. We're your family, not just your friends. Let us in. Let us help you." I took a shaky breath. I wanted nothing more than to tell her about Cyrus and the information that might be in the books I endangered her with. But I didn't. That was one burden I would carry alone.

"I know. Thank you."

"I will say this, and then I'll keep my mouth shut…I think it'd be wise if you got some space from Fynn. We all do, but we've been too afraid to say anything. Something is going on with you two. I don't know what it is and it's not my place, but I feel uneasy about it. I'm not saying you need to leave him, but I want you to know that there are others in this world who want to love you. You just have to let them." She squeezed my arm gently. "Just be cautious, okay?"

"Emryn, I…I want to apologize for how things have been for too long now. Between Kaede and I. I know it throws us all off when we bicker. I thought we had moved past it all ever since…"

"Since he told you he loved you?" She finished my thought, speaking aloud what none of us had really talked about.

I looked down at the floor. "Yeah, since then. I just want you to know how sorry I am for letting it go on this long."

"You don't need to be sorry. Kaede loves you, we all do, he just has a funny way of showing it sometimes. He's a male, they're egos are fragile. But the way he acts, avoiding you…it was more than you just denying him that day. He's made peace with that for a long while now, but I think you should talk to him. Mend this all before it turns into something bigger. Something you can't fix."

I chewed on my lip, thinking about it. She was right. She always was. With the way things were going right now, I needed my friends more than ever.

Emryn leaned back and reached between the space of her bed and the wall. A soft rustling sounded, and she pulled out the four books hidden in the frame. "Here." She extended them towards me, and I pulled them close to my chest.

These were the cost of Cyrus's life. Part of me wanted to throw them across the room, and the other wanted to protect them.

"Thank you, Em, for everything."

"I love you, Ren. We all do." She patted my shoulder, and we stood up from the bed. I turned to say goodnight, and her green eyes shone in the light of the torches lining the hall. They were the eyes of someone so full of kindness and love that anyone who crossed her path should consider themselves lucky.

She moved to close the door, bidding me goodnight, but I stopped and looked her in the eyes one last time. "Out of all of us, you deserve the same love you give. I hope you know that."

Her eyes brimmed with tears, but she blinked them back and thanked me. And with that, she closed the door, and I couldn't help but feel like my heart was a little lighter.

Back in my room, I stoked the slow-burning fire, beginning to heat some water for a bath. I wanted to relax as much as possible before being forced to show my weakness with the sword in the morning. Once it was ready, I slipped out of my clothes and dipped a toe, testing the temperature. The water scalded my foot, turning it red, but hot baths were one of the few times I preferred the heat. I scooped a handful of lavender salts from the bowl next to the tub, letting it fill the room with its refreshing scent.

When I was clean and my skin sufficiently wrinkled, I slipped on my plain nightgown and settled into the warm covers of my bed, a handful of pillows surrounding me. Knowing his last few hours were at hand, I tried not to think of Cyrus as I read.

I opened the book, the old spine cracking at the movement. The title read, 'Sun, Moon, and Night. A History of Albionne's Original Three.' It seemed like a good place as any to start.

'Before the realms or gods, there was only Chaos. The Infernal Chaos was born of the Cosmos—creating, destroying, and playing as he wished. There was no ruler, no balance, no order. Over the eons, he grew bored. From this, he created a new world. A new order, where he could come and go as he pleased. And so, Chaos plucked a star from the sky and created the Sun God.

But it wasn't enough to have only light in this new system. Chaos stole shadows from between stars and mixed them with his own to create the God of Night. The two gods were equal but opposite in their glory. But in their opposition, each resented the other. So, Chaos created a third who could bridge the gap between Day and Night. She would not be as powerful as either, so as not to upset the balance, but rather an equal harmony of the two—a bridge. She would have the power to harness both light and dark and exist in both day and night. And so, the Moon Goddess was created.

Chaos was pleased with his new system and retreated below the mountain to rest. With Chaos gone, the three gods began their new order and named it Albionne.

For centuries there was peace and harmony, but the Sun was a jealous god. Over time, he grew resentful of Night's affinity with the Moon and courted the goddess. The two became inseparable, ruling together over Albionne with their light. In his grief, Night hid away in the northern mountains, keeping to his shadows. But together, the Sun and the Moon molded new creations, bringing them to life with their magic. They called them Fae.

The Fae were strong, long-lasting creatures who would live in the lands and cultivate life there. Seeing the Fae grow and prosper brought pride to the Moon. But the Sun was a jealous god. He felt it unfair that he had to share his power with the Fae.

While powerful, they were flawed creations, and he craved perfection. The Sun God retreated to the skies, no longer desiring to be around his shameful creations. However, the Moon loved the Fae. She did not understand why the

Sun God would leave his creations unattended and unappreciated. She tried to convince the Sun God to return and keep her company, but he refused.

In an attempt to please the Sun God, the Moon Goddess molded a new creation—one without magic. Humans. They were simple creatures with short lifespans, but she loved them dearly. The humans contained no magic, but they were kind and loyal, and she hoped they would appease the Sun.

They did not.

Waning in strength, the Moon realized she could not rule alone. The original three had been created to keep the balance, and in his infinite recklessness, Chaos made the Moon flawed. She did not compare in strength to the Sun or the Night, that much she knew, but in her loneliness the Moon Goddess had grown weak. She could no longer shine on her own.

The Moon believed the Sun to be her only option for strength and decided it was better to be with him than to be lonely and weak. And so, she retreated to the skies to be with her lover.

In her absence, the Sun became eternally bitter. He gave her attention and took it away as he saw fit, over and over, until it had become a pattern.

First, he gave only a little, keeping the Moon in the dark, providing only a sliver of power. Then seeing her devotion, he would give a little more. Days would pass, and he would grow appreciative of her needs and attention, slowly allotting more power each day. When she had finally rejuvenated, the Sun would grow jealous again, fearful that she would become too strong at her full force—the full Moon—and so he would retreat. Each time she recharged, she tried to return, but it never lasted long before his withdrawal weakened her.

At first, only a sliver disappeared from her strength, but over the following days, she depleted to half. And then, within two weeks, she was completely drained—the New Moon. Void of all light and power.

Over and over, this pattern repeated. The Sun gave and took as he wished. While the Moon suffered, the Sun enjoyed this rush of power. He reveled in the control.

The Moon Goddess tried many times to leave the skies and return to the lands she missed, content to lose her powers if it meant she could live in *peace. But the Sun refused to let her go.*

Back in Albionne, the Night missed his companions. He was content to roam the land on his own, but centuries had passed, and the Fae needed another ruler. But the Sun and Moon had not returned from the skies. Alone in his world, the Night sought Chaos, hoping to plead with him for their return.

Chaos did not desire to deal in the affairs of the gods, but he was upset to learn the Sun and Moon had left his land. He desired control above all and they had defied him. He had created them for this purpose, and they abandoned their responsibilities. Yet, they were out of his reach. So, in return, Chaos created many lesser gods and goddesses to rule the lands and keep Night company. They were not as powerful as the original three, but they were gods in their own right.

The Sun grew angry upon learning this. He took the Moon Goddess, and together, they returned to Albionne. It didn't take long for the Sun to exert his dominance over the lesser gods. He split the lands and created a realm of his own to rule over with the gods, Fae, and humans alike to serve him.

With their return, Chaos was pleased, and retreated to the heavens where gods could return to rest.

But no longer in the skies or under the Sun's control, the Moon escaped, desperate to reconcile with Night and regain her power once more.'

I closed the book and placed a hand on my chest, feeling my speeding heart beneath. Why was I reacting this way? It was just a story of the gods. Gods I had never known the origins of or had been allowed to learn. It felt strange that this information had been forbidden.

Questions swirled through my mind, but my eyelids had grown heavy, and I knew if I stayed awake much longer, my performance would be less than desirable in the morning.

I curled into the pillows and drifted off to sleep. I tried not to dream knowing they would only plague me with memories of Cyrus…reminding me that he was going to die because of me.

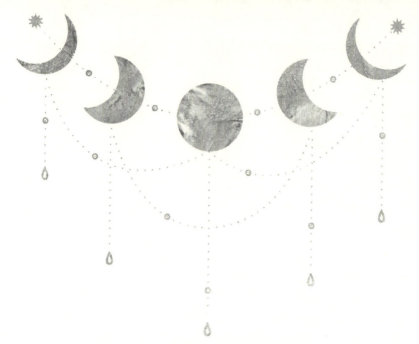

CHAPTER 27

I was terrible at using a sword. It had been nearly a week since we returned from Alynta and a week where I had been too exhausted to read anymore. The training was also a welcomed distraction. I was too tired to make time to see Fynn, but every night he seemed to be caught up in political meetings or extra training with the Keeper, so my absence didn't phase him.

We had only just picked up the actual sparring weapons today. The rest of the week had been countless hours of tedious footwork drills. I was unprepared for how intense learning to use a sword would be.

The weight of the wooden practice sword felt off-balanced in my hand, like something was missing, while my other wasn't sure where to go. With my daggers, I knew to use both arms, both had a place to be, and both hands had practical uses. But with a sword, I felt off.

Pain radiated across my lower back as Therion's cane snapped across my skin.

"You are going to break your wrist if you can't manage to hold it upright, Miss Orion," Therion said, whacking my forearm next. I flinched but adjusted my arm, leveling it. I would never survive in an actual battle if I couldn't hold it with one hand.

"Again," he said. I positioned my legs and held the sword out. I followed through with the flow he taught us that morning. The weight of the blade made my shoulders and back ache. Developing a new skill always meant developing new muscles along with it.

I brought it to my face and did as he asked: lunge, block, retreat, forward again, overhead, side, parry, retreat. I repeated the drill, and every time Therion slapped my arm, correcting my poor form until I made it through without correction.

"Good. Now do it ten more times."

I held back a sigh of frustration and continued. My muscles screamed, but the alternative of failure wasn't an option.

Even after completing the ten additional rounds, I repeated the drill. I needed to get better—I needed to succeed. Time was no longer an option and I had twice the catching up to do. If my muscles hated me and I had to take ice baths instead of hot ones for the next six weeks, that would be the price I paid.

I watched the others and their techniques in between sets, committing their movements to memory. I listened to the advice and implemented it with as little complaint as possible. I would do whatever it took to succeed. I would survive this.

I took my time leaving the training room at the end of the day. I was exhausted and worried, and I could feel it draining me. I leaned my forehead against the doorway and sighed.

"Tired already?" Callax's voice grated in my ears. Apparently, I wasn't the last to leave. I sighed and hit my forehead twice on the frame. Sweat dripping from my slick hair at the impact, and I wondered if I hit my head hard enough he'd think I had gone mad and leave me alone.

"What do you want, Callax?" I asked, irritation seeping into my voice. If he could tell I wasn't happy to be talking to him, he didn't let it show.

He sucked his teeth, tsk-ing with disappointment. "Now, now, Miss Orion...that isn't any way to speak to your prince. This seems like quite the habit you're beginning to take on. I don't know that I like it." His brow raised, disappearing behind a lock of stray hair. He cocked his head and leaned back on one leg, surveying me.

"The way I speak to you isn't my top priority at the moment." I gestured vaguely to the training room, knowing he knew exactly what I meant. "Go complain to your father if you really care. Now let me pass, I'd like to leave and you're getting on my nerves."

"Nerves, is it?" He winked an annoyingly beautiful eye at me. The hollows of his cheek were sunken and dark circles still haunted his eyes, but a little life had returned to them as if sparring with me all day had given him something to look forward to. "That isn't how I'd describe your body's reaction when I had you pressed against the wall."

I stiffened, remembering when he had cornered me in the hall.

"That is none of your damn business," I snapped.

"When a lady as stunning as yourself responds that way to my presence, I'd say it is."

"Leave me alone." I readjusted my bag, trying to signal I was finished with the conversation.

"You were wise to stay away." His voice was softer, less grating. I swallowed and stopped, remembering Cyrus had been executed early this morning and that I hadn't been there to bid him goodbye.

The weight on my chest doubled, settling on my heart. I knew it was what he would have wanted, and I knew that it would have been detrimental had I shown up. Though I disliked Callax with every fiber of my being, he was right. Maybe that was why I pushed myself so hard today. It was my punishment for causing Cyrus's horrible fate.

"Do you feel guilty? Knowing it was all your fault?" he drawled.

Anger flashed before my eyes, and I whirled. "What the hell do you know about whose fault it was? You can't prove I was there, so do me a favor and back off."

I shoved my finger into his chest, emphasizing my words with a sharp jab. My bag dropped to the ground, and my chest heaved with anger, my breath catching in my throat. I hadn't expected to be so angry, but I was. I was furious. At Callax, at Cyrus, at myself. I was mad at the king, at Fynn, at the world for putting me in a situation I wished I could excuse myself from. I seemed to have lost all control. Everything decided for me by fate, or gods, or men in power.

And I was sick of it.

Hurt passed over his face along with what seemed to be sadness. But he only looked down, using his height to intimidate me, to make me feel small and weak. And that was hard to do as I was not small or delicate.

"Tell me, Callax, what do you know about whose fault it was, you sniveling, pretentious, stuck-up, good-for-nothing excuse of a prince." I pushed closer, wanting him to see my bared teeth and rage-fueled expression, wanting to assert some form of dominance over him. To make him see me for who I truly was.

He bared his teeth. "Be that as it may, Miss Orion, I know a thing or two more than you. One of those is how to handle a sword properly." He glanced down his nose at my hand lingering on his chest.

"I am handling it perfectly fine." I removed my finger.

"You are falling behind. I could help you, you know. You need only ask." His voice lowered, eyes darkening.

"The last thing I need is your help." I spun on my heel and moved to storm away, but he grabbed my wrist, pinning my arm to my back as he shoved me towards the wall.

I stomped my foot on his heel.

He sucked in a sharp breath but kept his grip tight. This was not a position I wanted to be in. There wasn't much I could do with my hand behind my back, but I was sure as hell going to try.

I bent my knees and threw all my weight forward, trying to get him off balance. He stumbled a foot or two, taking me with him, but I had miscalculated his strength. His movement only pulled my arm higher, my muscles threatening to rip under strain.

I held back a cry of pain and swept my foot behind me, aiming for his knee. It was nearly impossible to tell what I was doing when pain blinded me. My foot grazed the side of his knee, accomplishing nothing. He corrected his footing and hoisted me from my crouch, throwing me face-first against the wall.

This time, he grabbed both my hands and twisted my wrists inward. I tried to yank free, but each movement brought more pain. His body pressed against mine and his curls brushed my temple—the rough edges of stone biting into my skin. I could feel his breath dance along the edge of my ear, and a trickle of something wet and warm slid down my cheek.

I grunted with the effort and turned my face in the opposite direction. His chuckle was dark and low. I felt it vibrate in my back, rolling down to the base of my spine.

He placed his mouth close to my ear. "Miss Orion," he purred. His voice was like silk, sliding over my skin, teasing me like a predator with its prey.

I sucked in a breath and held it, refusing to breathe in anymore of his scent. I tried my best to look disinterested, but my heartbeat betrayed me. It pounded louder, harder, against the wall.

His voice tickled against the edge of my pointed ear. "That's not any way to behave, now, is it?" I struggled against him, but it only made our bodies rub together in ways I wasn't sure I...didn't like. I was flustered, and he knew it. He knew the effect he had on my body, but not necessarily my mind.

"You are the most infuriatingly stubborn and insane person I have ever known. You both irritate and intrigue me. But your behavior is horrendous." I thrashed against him once more, but he held firm. "A good lady should respect her prince. Worship him." He moved a strand of hair from my face and swept it behind my ear. "On her knees, preferably."

"You sick bastard," I spat.

"Maybe so, but even then…" He freed one of his hands, grasping my wrists with only one, and pressed his hips against my backside, pinning me down. I could feel every inch of him.

I didn't think it was his intention. He wasn't dishonorable. Flashy and forward, yes, but not dishonorable. A tiny gasp escaped my lips.

"You seem to be responsive to a firm hand." I could hear the sick satisfaction in his voice.

I wanted to say something, but my body betrayed me. I couldn't describe why, but I was glued in place, held tight to him as if by some invisible string.

Heat pooled in my center, and I was afraid that if I were to speak, it wouldn't be the insults I intended.

If my body was rebelling, who knew what my tongue would do. What it wanted to do.

"I'm going to let go now, so be a good girl and behave for your prince while I finish speaking." He growled, "Do I make myself clear?"

I grunted and nodded, but I wasn't going to listen.

The pressure lifted, and I whirled around. I slammed my hands to his chest and shoved. He had braced himself, expecting my rebellion. Still, my strength knocked him back one step, letting me move away from the wall. I pulled my hand back, curling my fingers into a fist, ready to ruin his perfect nose.

I wanted to see him bleed. To see him fall to his knees before me, submitting to my strength.

But he caught my fist and twisted. I had no choice but to buckle under the pressure, falling to my knees at the foot of the prince.

His eyes darkened. His smile wicked. "That's a good girl. Now beg."

I bared my teeth. "In your dreams."

"Don't worry, love, you already do." His eyes glazed over with a dark lust, piercing me with such intensity I couldn't look away. He was enjoying this, and a sick, twisted part of me was too. My heart continued to race, the growing heat spreading from my stomach, moving down between my legs, pooling with desire.

He twisted my arm, and a tear slipped from my eye, mixing with the blood.

"I said let me go," my voice was softer but still defiant.

He released my hand and squatted down, his eyes now level with mine.

He lifted my chin, his thumb wiping away the blood before resting on my lips. He pushed into my mouth, parting my lips, sliding it against the tip of my tongue.

"And I. Said. Beg."

The authority in his voice shook me to my core. His voice darkened, and I was overcome by a roaring desire for the male I despised. I wanted to be disgusted, but I wasn't…

Instead, I was on fire.

The rage that usually ran like fire in my veins thrummed with a new kind of power. It was slower, lazier, and pooled in places I didn't expect. We stared at each other a moment longer, neither of us saying anything.

He leaned in, bringing his mouth closer to mine.

I mirrored his movement. The anticipation heavy on my breath.

Before our lips could touch, he stopped and whispered, "You look your best on your knees, Miss Orion." He let go of my chin and stood, leaving me panting beneath him, the sudden absence of his touch a slap to the face.

"If you want to learn how to use a weapon properly before your time runs out…you know where to find me."

And with that, he casually walked out of the room. Hands in his pockets—an annoying swagger in his step—he disappeared into the dark hall beyond, leaving me brimming with hate and desire on the floor behind him.

CHAPTER 28

What the fuck was wrong with me?

My legs shook as I climbed the last flight of stairs to my room. I had never been more grateful for Fynn to not be waiting. The cold wood of my door pressed against my shoulders as I slid to the floor.

What the hell just happened? I looked at my hands and pinched my arm, trying to ensure I was still in my body. Callax had a way of getting on my last nerve and under my skin simultaneously. I wanted to punish my body for betraying me. The feeling of his thumb on my mouth lingered, the metallic taste echoed against my senses. I scrambled for the tub, needing to scrub his touch from my system.

I grabbed a bucket and filled it with cold water. The heat still pooled low in my abdomen, and I wanted to remove it, to claw it out of me. Even though nothing had actually happened, I hated that I liked it. Hated I responded the way I did instead of fighting harder. But mostly, I hated that in that moment, I had forgotten entirely about Fynn.

I dipped a toe into the frigid water and shivered. Perfect.

Before I could second guess my choice, I put both legs in and sank beneath the water, freezing the desire out of my body.

It was miserable but effective.

I quickly washed off the day's grime and rinsed my dark hair. I wrapped my soft robe around myself and crawled into bed, grabbing my book. I was tired and desperately needed to sleep, but I needed a distraction. Hopefully, it would hold the key to ensuring I didn't dream of Callax that night.

The Moon Goddess escaped to the north, knowing the Sun would never venture that far. There, the Fae basked in the warmth he provided and worshiped him with gifts and sacrifices.

The Moon Goddess hid in caves for months, trying to break the pattern she had grown accustomed to. She wanted nothing more than to shine on her own, but she could not break the pattern she had been molded to fit. Her power would wax and wane for eternity.

Overcome with grief, the Moon Goddess wandered, searching for a new home, hoping to find the God of Night and reconcile with him when she was ready. Unknowingly, she wandered near the city of Nox Arctus, the capital of the north, home to the God of Night.

She stumbled upon Night one evening, painting the dark sky. He carefully placed the stars, creating endless patterns and stories, all for the enjoyment of the Fae in his land.

This intrigued the Moon Goddess. Never before had she seen such a powerful god carefully craft art and love into his domain.

The Moon had once known the Night well, but in her search for the Sun's love, he had become a stranger once again. Fearing his anger and judgment, she watched in silence for weeks from the shadows, noticing the detail he put into painting the sky with his love. Each night a new story—new stars and new life—was placed into the heavens. He was careful, considerate, and contemplative. Everything the Sun was not.

With time, the Moon remembered that she had been created for both gods. He was much a part of her as she was him, and she need not be afraid.

One night, the Moon noticed a discrepancy in the star's usual patterns from her watch in the shadows. A path of light was missing, carved out from the sky. Blank. Empty. She wondered if the Night had grown lazy or if he had done this on purpose.

Eventually, she left the shadows and confronted him as he painted the skies. He did not flinch nor back away at the sight of her waning glory as she had expected. Instead, he took her hand and pointed to the night sky. He told her to look and carefully guided her hand across the blank space on the canvas.

Confused, the Moon told the Night that he had made a mistake. She prompted him to fill the space, wanting nothing left blank so she might marvel at it once more.

But the Night only explained that he had carved this space for her. When the Moon did not understand, he told her how he had watched for centuries as she shied away from her power and beauty. How she had sat in the shadow of the Sun for too long. He told her how, every night, he watched in agony as the most beautiful creature he knew had fallen destitute in search of love and companionship. He pointed to the skies and explained, 'This, my love, is for you. Whether you choose him or me, this path is yours alone to take. The Sun God cannot take it from you, for this is the Realm of Night. I have blessed these sacred mountains, and he cannot intervene here. Here, you are safe, welcomed, and loved as you are... phases and all. My moon, you are my love, my light, my glory—I worship at your feet."

I paused, needing to breathe to fully understand what I had just read. So little was known about the Realm of Night, let alone the Night and Moon. The sparse information we were taught in school only informed us how they were evil, sadistic gods. And how they had tried to condemn the world into an eternal night, forcing the sun to fight valiantly on our behalf.

This was why we worshiped only the sun. This was why worshiping the old gods was banned. Or so we had been told.

Everything seemed so backward. From the few chapters I read, the Sun God was the one who was sick and twisted.

I kept reading.

'It was only a matter of years before the two gods became a bonded and mated pair. The Night honored his mate and crowned her as the queen of his realm, ruling by his side over their people.

The Moon abandoned the Sun God entirely, reveling in her new path in the night sky. Peace prospered in their realm; every human, Fae, and god were treated fairly and equally.

In this new era, gods and Fae bonded and bore children together. The product of these bonding's produced different classes of Fae. Their lifespan longer than a human's, but not as long as the gods themselves. Over the next thousand years, the bloodline would be diluted, creating the different classes of Fae.

The Realm of Night flourished under their reign, and after a time, the love between the Night and Moon made way for a new magic, one that never before existed. One that defied the laws of the universe.

The Moon had become pregnant with a child.

This was unheard of. Only Chaos had the power to create godly life, but the bond between the two gods surpassed the threads of Creation and paved a new way.

No gods since have ever produced a god-child.'

The words stopped there. I flipped through the next couple of pages, hoping it was a trick of the dimming light. But as I scanned the book, multiple pages were missing or torn out. Some of it was because of the sheer age of the book itself, but others looked fresh. As if it had been removed on purpose. For the rest of the book, I could only learn that the Moon gave birth to a female child named Astera R— something. The words Phoenix and dark and night were often paired together, but like the name, most of the text was blacked out.

I sighed and closed the book. I only managed to learn a few things, but none of this seemed like it was worthy of being forbidden by the king. Why would the king want to make sure no one knew about the gods of old? There had been a war, but what possible ideology or teachings were there that was so heinous?

My lids beginning to droop, sleep weighing heavy on them. I placed the book back behind the headboard and curled up on my side, pulling as many pillows and blankets around me until I was as comfortable as possible.

Thankfully, I did not dream of Callax.

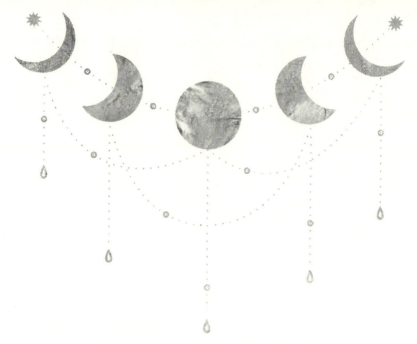

CHAPTER 29

"You can't keep coming to me like this." The sweet lilting voice brought me out of my daze.

I groaned as I came to, remembering why I was here. Therion switched up the pairs earlier that day, forcing us to learn how to fight other opponents and once again, I had lost. Only this time, Soren had taken every second to make sure I knew how much he detested me, beating me over the head with the pommel of his sword before knocking me unconscious.

"Hey, Camilla." I grabbed the cold rag she placed on my head and moved to sit up. I winced at the sharp pain in my side, and her tiny, human hands pressed my shoulders back into the bed. Humans were so fragile. The late afternoon light leaked through the open windows into the healing room, and I could see through her skin. The red and blue veins peeking through thin hands.

But it wasn't her skin that had caught my eye. A silver ring, wrapped around a chain, dangled from under her smock as she leaned over me. It bore the same symbol that Anya had drawn for me. She noticed my lingering gaze and quickly tucked it back, hiding it from view.

"Your ribs are still mending. I need you to lie down for at least another hour, so they heal properly. Otherwise, you'll be stuck with sharp pains in your side until it's re-broken and reset."

I sighed. She was right; it was better to wait it out. I closed my eyes, trying to ease the pain in my head, but it was no use. I'd have to wait for that one out too. "Any chance you have more of that tonic from last time?" I asked.

"I gave you some when you were brought in and unfortunately used the last of the batch for the day. You lot have a tendency to need it frequently."

"I understand. Thanks anyway."

I heard her shuffle off to a table nearby, and I tried to sleep, but the memories of the fight kept resurfacing. It was beyond embarrassing. I knew I was terrible at wielding a sword, but it felt so much worse knowing I hadn't been able to hold my ground against Soren. He was bigger, yes, and had years of experience on me, but I felt like I should be able to fight him. I knew it was unreasonable to expect that of myself, but I did.

As I lay there, not sleeping, the image of her ring appeared again, and I knew I had to ask. "Camilla?"

"Hmm?" She was preoccupied and didn't look up from her desk where she was mixing some new tonic.

"Your ring, I've seen that symbol before…it's for the Realm of Night, is it not?"

She sucked in a sharp breath, her eyes darting around the room in a panic. But there was no one here besides us. I would have heard breathing or a heartbeat, so I knew we were safe.

She stood from her desk and came over to my side, "Miss, do not speak so loudly of such things." Her eyes were wide and pleading.

"I'm sorry, Camilla, I didn't mean to frighten you, I just—I feel like that symbol is following me, and I've never noticed it on you before."

"I usually keep it tucked into my top or leave it in my room." She slipped it off and placed it in her apron pocket, patting it for good measure. "What do you know of the symbol?" She pulled her stool up close to the table.

"Not much," I admitted. "I only heard of it from a shop owner in Alynta. That and one of the scholars." I hid my wince remembering the same symbol tattooed on Cyrus's wrist.

She flinched. Anger and sadness filling her eyes.

"It was a shame what happened there, I—I wish I could have stopped it." I looked away, not wanting her to see the shame and guilt I still held, knowing I had not been able to stop the destruction. Destruction caused by my partner. If I had just talked to him, convinced him a little more... maybe he would have stopped. I knew I hadn't known the outcome beforehand, but still... the guilt was tearing me apart.

"I was from Alynta." Her voice was barely above a whisper. "When I was a girl, my father and brother were taken to serve their time in the king's mines. My mother was older when she had me and developed a weak heart. After they left, she lasted little more than a few months before her heart gave out. I found her dead one morning, just lying in her bed. It looked as if she had cried herself to sleep and wore her poor heart out." A single tear fell from her eye. She quickly wiped it away. This pattern of heartache and tragedy seemed to be repeating itself.

This wasn't the story of one person, one family; it was everyone outside of Sunsbridge. How many others in the castle came from there or surrounding cities? What else had the other cities endured at the hand of King Tobias?

"When she passed, I waited for as long as I could, but we were poor, and my mother did not have any savings. So, I came with a caravan of other women and children who had suffered similar fates. We left together—most of us walking the whole way—and made our way south to Sunsbridge, looking for work wherever we could find it. The separation between Fae and humans is obvious wherever you go, but it worsened the further south we traveled. No one wants to hire strange humans or Lessers, which most of us were. I lucked out, and my mother had taught me how to make tonics and salves from nature, and I began selling what I could. Eventually, someone from the palace found me and took me in. I was one of the lucky ones. Many others died of hunger or left for another city, hoping to find a way to live."

I was speechless. "I had no clue, Camilla. I'm so sorry." I reached out a hand to comfort her, but she didn't accept my gesture. She stood up and dusted off her apron, "I'm all that's left, and I've made a name for myself here. My mother gave me her ring, hoping I would someday find my way out of this cruel realm. She had talked of one day escaping to Asterion, but she refused to go without my father and brother. And when she died, I vowed the same."

"What happened to them? Did they ever come home?"

She shook her head, "No. They didn't." With that, she walked away, back to her table, ending the conversation.

I closed my eyes again and waited in silence until the hour was up.

Sweat coated my palm and my hand slipped on the pommel, my fingers clenching. His sword clashed with mine over and over, each swing harder than the last. I gritted my teeth, concentrating on the balance of the heavy weapon. I would not lose. Not again.

The weapon fell from my hands as my arm twisted under the pressure. I lunged to pick up my fallen sword, desperate to finish this to the end, to wipe that smirk off his rugged face. He merely stepped in between me and the blade as I fell to the ground, a look of smug satisfaction plastered to his face.

I had known there would be consequences to my loss yesterday with Soren, but I hadn't imagined that Therion would make me publicly fight Callax. After I went down, Callax had won in a spectacular feat against Kaede, impressing even Therion.

Though Callax spent most of his life training, he continuously, and annoyingly, kept improving.

As I predicted, I was an embarrassment to the group. Even Archer and Skye, who had just as much experience wielding a sword as I did, held their own against Kell and Mavenna.

Callax and I were barely on speaking terms. We'd grown accustomed to each other's company, and I trusted him only enough to have my back in a fight, but it didn't make us friends. His continued unannounced offerings and unwelcome advances only made me more irate with him. Yes, he was the prince, but he was not someone I would ever consider a friend. He pushed me to my limit one too many times.

From the corner of my eye, I could see Soren and Caldor leaning casually against the wall, laughing, and pointing towards the ring. I knew they were laughing at me, talking about how Soren had enjoyed beating me senseless.

I had been dealing with childish males for too long and was sick of their insolent behavior. To beat me at a skill was something I expected, but to be cruel without reason...I was sick of it.

My mind went blank, and all I knew was that I wanted more. I deserved more than this. I deserved to win for once. I was ready to prove my capability here and now. I could feel the thrum of power flicker beneath my skin, and it propelled me forward, urging me to use all of my strength and win.

I twisted, placing my legs firmly underneath, and using whatever strength was left in my thighs, I launched myself at him.

My sudden move took him by surprise, I had abandoned my sword, despite this being a sparring match, but I didn't care if I broke the rules. I knew Therion wouldn't stop me.

My arms wrapped around his thick, muscled torso, and the blow knocked him off balance, sending him stumbling backward. He kept his footing, but I wanted him on the ground. I wanted him to know what it was like to be beneath me, to be forced to look me in the eye as I took my victory.

The memory of him leaning over me while I sat on my knees made my body flush with heat. I knew he wouldn't let me live it down if he managed a victory.

Part of me, deep down, wanted to hesitate. Would it be so bad to have Callax on top of me?

Gods, what was wrong with me?

I shoved the thought deep down and crouched, sweeping my leg under his. I grinned as he fell to the ground, knees buckling underneath him. He reached for his sword, which had fallen from his grasp. I moved my feet.

But as I readied to drive my knee into his chest, a firm hand gripped my braid and yanked. My head snapped back, throwing off my momentum. His legs twisted between mine, flipping me over.

I was on the ground in an instant, but I never made impact. His hand cradled the base of my skull, preventing it from slamming into the hard mat.

I screamed in frustration.

But I was still underneath him. He was stronger, and there was little hope of getting out. I flailed my legs, but he only sat his weight back onto my hips, pinning me down. I tried to punch, scratch, or claw at any surface I could find, not caring about technique, only blinded by anger.

My nails found his face, and they tore through his rough cheek. Three uneven lines of red followed the scrape of my fingers. Good, let him be reminded of me every time he looked at his face. Let him remember I hated him, that the sight of him filled me with anger.

His hand left my hair and wrapped around my flailing wrists. Calloused hands held me down, pinning them above my head.

He was so close. I could feel the heat of his breath caress my skin. A drop of blood from his cheek dripped down through his dark stubble and strong jawline. I didn't flinch as it fell onto my cheek.

A small smile twitched on his lips as his attention darted from my eyes to my lips and back. He was enjoying this.

"Get off of me." My scream echoed, bouncing off every surface. A hush fell over the room, and I could feel their eyes focus in on the two of us. On me. Usually, I would hate the attention, the judgmental gazes, but I was too distracted by Callax to care.

My outburst shook his demeanor, and those deep black and blue eyes swam with more emotion than I could discern. Fear, loss, longing, confusion, and hatred all combined into the endless flecked expanse of midnight.

Tears stung my eyes. Why was I crying?

"Why can't you just leave me alone?" I knew my outburst was somehow directed less at this moment and more towards his behavior in general.

"Why?" The boredom in his tone dissipated the frustration and my anger returned, sparking through my veins. If I weren't so distracted by his weight on top of me, I would have sworn I smelled a hint of smoke. "Does my attention irk you so, Miss Orion?" My name rolled off his tongue like smoke—husky and breathless. I could feel every part of his body that met mine, his legs, his hands...his hips.

Every place our bodies connected warmed with frustration.

He leaned in closer, closing the gap between us. "Is my body on yours not enough? Too much? Do you need more?" His voice rippled through me. A shiver raced down my spine, every nerve standing on edge.

"I don't need anything from you," I lied through my gritted teeth, turning my head to avoid smelling him. Sweat and blood mixed with his tobacco and vanilla scent. It was intoxicating. I had never reacted to Fynn like this before. Why Callax of all people?

He shifted his hips ever so slightly, and I couldn't swallow the involuntary moan that escaped my lips.

Every sense was heightened. Every nerve burned with desire.

One hand released my wrists and dug into my cheek as he pinched hard, jerking me back to face him.

He leaned down to my ear, his warm breath tickling against my ear. "What I need, Miss Orion is to hear you make that sound for me over and over again."

I shivered. His teeth grazed at my ear, and I sucked in a sharp breath, biting my tongue to stop the sound building in my throat.

Shit.

My face flushed, and I wrenched my hands, prying them from his clutch. I shoved him off, and he moved with little hesitation this time. I grabbed my sword and stormed off in a huff. I needed to get out, to be anywhere but that training room.

As far away from Callax as I could manage.

I found the nearest balcony and threw open the doors. Stalking to the edge, I leaned onto the railing and lifted my head to the sky, breathing in the night air, free from his scent.

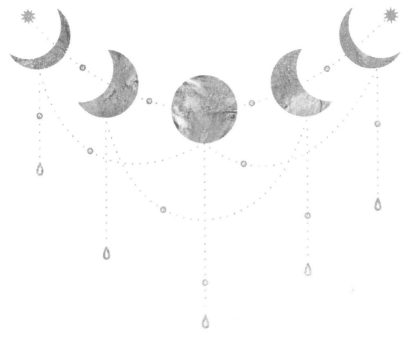

CHAPTER 30

Losing was becoming a habit. I didn't want to slip into this pattern.

I had survived without my parents for years, raising Archer and ensuring she was always fed and cared for. I knew I was capable in that way, but I needed to be better everywhere else. I had to be. I owed it to her to prove it was possible, that she shouldn't be worried.

We both had taken on enough hardships as such a young age, and though I had to deal with the brunt of it all, I wanted her to live as carefree of a life as possible. It was my one wish for her as her big sister.

Archer must have heard my loud thinking because a small knock sounded on my door. Her silvery blue eyes peered around the corner, and I beckoned her in, scooting over on the bed to make room.

She curled up next to me and handed me a lemon scone.

"What's this for?" I asked.

She crinkled her brow like I should already know why she had offered it. "It's bread. It's not going to heal a bruised ego, but it'll do the trick for now."

I chuckled. She was right. There wasn't much more in this world I loved more than bread. I think sweets were a close second, though.

Our mother had often baked us bread whenever we were sick or needed comfort. The smell always brought me back home, and we both kept up the habit of eating a lot of it when we were sad or upset.

I chewed on the sweet scone as she told me about her past few weeks. So much had been going on that we hadn't had a moment to sit together as just sisters, not trainees, and talk about our lives. "Pyne is okay, kind of annoying, but pretty decent as a partner overall." She reached over and stole a small corner of my scone, "She's good with a bow too, so it's been nice to have someone push me to be better."

"You already know you're the best. Has she ever beaten you?"

"No," she laughed and stole another piece of my scone. "So, what's going on with you and Callax lately?" She elbowed me in my side, and her brows rose.

"Absolutely nothing," I said.

"We both know that's a lie." She tilted her head and gave me a look that pushed me to spill the truth.

"The truth," I sighed. "Gods, I can't stand him. He's arrogant, bossy, pushy, and gets on my last nerve every day."

"So, you like him?"

I nearly spat out my scone. "I'm with Fynn."

"I know, but it doesn't mean you don't like Callax, too."

"Callax is an asshole, and besides, I love Fynn. There's nothing else to say." I nibbled on the scone, trying to distract myself from her line of questioning.

"Is love enough?" She turned to me and waited until I looked at her before saying, "Loving someone doesn't mean you're obligated to stay with them. Sometimes loving someone means letting go."

I turned and stared at the ceiling, fighting back the tears beginning to form in my eyes. She was wise beyond her years, and those words opened a well of emotion I wasn't expecting.

I hadn't ever considered leaving Fynn. This was just our life. If we made it through these next few weeks, we would be fine. I knew we would. We had to be.

I took a deep breath, counted to four, and steadied myself before saying, "It's…complicated. I have to hope things will be okay. I don't think I could handle it if they weren't." I stared at my hands as I spoke, picking absently at my fingers. "He's done some shitty things, but I haven't been my best either. I could always do more or be better for him, so I can't blame him. I should try harder to be what he needs." I felt my shoulders slump forward. "I shouldn't be adding to his burdens."

Archer interrupted my rant, her voice soft and kind. "If he can't see how amazing you are now, as you are, then he doesn't deserve you." A tear escaped my eye and fell down my cheek. Her words meant more to me than she would ever know. But it didn't change anything.

"How did you get so wise?" I asked, trying to change the subject.

"I've had to deal with your emotional ass every day."

I choked on the last of my scone, breaking the tension. We both started laughing. The kind that relieved tension and filled the soul. The sound made my heart swell. I hadn't felt this way in some time—years, perhaps.

She was all I had left of my family. We were it—the last of the Orions. I wished nothing more in the world than to have our family back, but having Archer here with me made me feel like things were going to be okay.

My happiness was interrupted at a sudden reminder that I hadn't told her about Cyrus… guilt turned my stomach, and I turned to her. "Archer, there's something I need to tell you. It's about—"

Another knock on the door made me pause mid-sentence.

She sat up, wiping tears from her eyes from the laughter. She moved to get the door, but a second later, Emryn strode in. Her satin nightgown matched the color of her strawberry hair. Her green eyes shone excitedly, "I heard laughter, and I can't believe you two didn't invite me."

"Well, come on then." Archer pushed me to the side, making room for Emryn. She giggled and hopped over the edge into the middle of the bed.

"So, what are we gossiping about?" Emryn wagged her eyebrows at Archer. "Is it boys?"

I looked back and forth between them. "Wait, Archer, is there something you're not telling me?" I couldn't believe she had kept something so important to herself. Her cheeks flushed, and she gave Emryn a look that screamed, I told you to keep your mouth shut. Emryn only grinned and gave a big wink, knowing fully what she had done.

"Are we talking about Archer's crush on the scholar boy?" Skye and Senna burst into the room, carrying wine and cheese.

"Wait a damn minute," I held up a hand and looked around at the girls surrounding me. "You're telling me you all knew about—wait, what's his name…"

Emryn leaned in. "Laken," she whispered, grinning in Archer's direction where she sat unamused.

Exasperated, I exclaimed, "You all knew about this 'Laken' boy, and no one bothered to tell me?"

"You've been busy," Senna stated and placed a cheese board in the middle. Skye passed around the bottle of wine, not bothering with any glasses.

It was my turn to blush. I had been preoccupied as of late. I felt terrible that I'd neglected my friends and sister, but I felt like I was constantly being pulled in every direction. I could only handle so many things at once. I popped a few cubes of cheese in my mouth and looked away, "I know. I'm sorry, you guys, everything's just–"

Skye leaned over and placed her hand on my leg, and a shiny gold ring sat on her hand. Her ring finger, to be precise. "We know Ren. We don't blame you. There's been a lot going on." She glanced at Senna, and a wide grin spread across her face. "For all of us."

I grabbed at her hand, realizing what she was hinting at. "Holy gods, are you guys actually a bonded pair for real now?"

Even Senna, stoic and regal as ever, burst into a grin. "Yes, we are."

We all squealed, a loud symphony of glee, and ignoring the cheese lying on the bed, we all leaned over and wrapped our arms around the two. Senna held the wine above her head. "You're going to spill the wine." But we knew she didn't care, it was just Senna being her usual self.

"Oh my gods," Emryn looked like she was about to cry and beamed, "I'm so happy for you guys. When? How? Where? Tell us everything."

Senna nodded at Skye and began to speak, but Emryn held up a hand to pause her before running out of the room. We all looked around, confused, but a moment later, she returned, Kaede in tow. He seemed a bit miffed that she woke him from sleep for a girls-only moment. His hair ruffled, and he was shirtless. But he let Emryn drag him in, and she sat him down next to us.

"What's going on?" he asked, rubbing sleep from his eyes.

Skye dismissed him with a hand. "He knows already."

"What? Why him?" Archer asked, baffled.

"He's my brother," Skye stated as if that was reason enough. It was, but at the moment, she must not have put together that Skye would share it with Kaede and trust him not to tell Emryn.

"It was small, and only us two," Senna explained, "We wanted it to be intimate. For it to be just us for a while." She squeezed Skye's hand, and her face softened, the love for her partner evident in her eyes. "It's been just less a month now. We did it right before our mission to Alynta. We only started wearing our rings this week when we were certain." She lifted their hands and kissed Skye's finger where the ring sat.

"Certain about what?" I asked.

Senna grinned from ear to ear. I had never seen her smile spread so wide. She squeezed Skye's hands and then looked at us, that goofy grin still on her face. "The mating bond…it finally kicked in."

My eyes bugged out of my head. I put my hand to my chest, overwhelmed by the declaration. Mates were not entirely uncommon, most Fae had a mate out there somewhere, but the odds of finding them in your lifetime were rare. My parents had been mates, and I knew a handful of others who had been so lucky. Mating bonds were a serious and highly respected union. Most Fae only became bonded pairs—similar to marriage for humans—and honored the bonding as if they were a mate, but it wasn't the same. The bond didn't run as deep.

Each Fae experienced acknowledging their mate differently. For some, it was immediate, but for others, it could take years. It all depended on the situation and how open the Fae was to the other. "When I finally agreed to go forward with the bonding, it clicked. I knew I wanted to be with her for as long as I lived, but I had been hesitant about the whole ceremony aspect of it all. But, when she suggested we could do it privately, I agreed, and… it just snapped into place." Her grin turned into a soft smile of adoration towards her mate, her eyes never leaving Skye's.

Seeing Senna so outwardly happy and expressive, even if only in the confines of this room, made my heart swell.

"We're so happy for you two." Emryn leaned over and gave them another hug, then leaned back against Kaede, letting him play with her hair.

I was surprised he came into my room, but I was glad he was there. This was a moment that we would all remember, and though the tension between the two of us had never really been fully resolved, it made me hopeful that in the future, we could reconcile our differences. I offered him a small smile from across the bed, and though he didn't meet my gaze, he came close.

He didn't smile in return but gave me a slight nod as if to say, I'm glad I'm here, and maybe things will be okay one day.

I would take it.

We sat like that for hours, laughing, talking, and sharing wine and cheese, celebrating our friend's love for each other. This was a moment I knew I would remember for a lifetime. Moments like this made the bad days worth it.

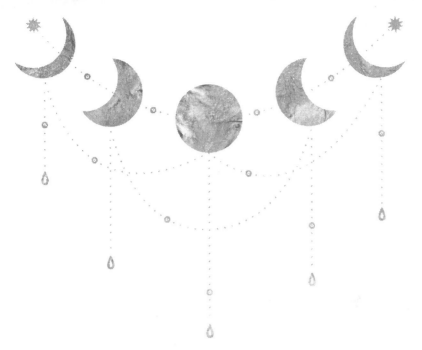

CHAPTER 31

There was something about the night before that made me feel like I could accomplish anything. Perhaps that was why I thought asking Callax if he would teach me to wield a sword was a good idea. He had nearly dropped his sword mid-swing in surprise.

I contemplated asking Kaede, seeing as he was my friend, but we had just started to stand each other, and I didn't want to push it. I knew it would not end well if we were locked in a room together with swords. Although, maybe taking our frustration out on each other could be beneficial to both of us.

I didn't particularly imagine Callax and I alone with sharp weapons would end well either, but I had to ask someone.

To be honest, Callax wasn't my second choice. He had been my third.

My first was Senna. She was the logical and best choice, but when I approached her she told me she had been called to assist the legion's training and to start sitting in with the Generals. Before this new promotion of sorts, we all knew it was obvious that Senna would lead the King's Legion in one way or another, it was only a matter of time.

So I decided to ask Callax.

He laughed in my face, but had agreed upon me accepting three conditions.

First, I was to maintain my health at all times. I was to go to bed early, to eat regular meals and snacks in-between and to avoid any unnecessary drama. The last bit made little sense, but he said I needed to keep my mind focused and clear.

Second, I was to do things his way or not at all. I swallowed my pride, but I begrudgingly accepted.

Third, I wasn't allowed to complain. I laughed in his face at that one. I told him I would agree to the first two, but never to the last. Complaining would be the only way I could survive this. He tried to hold his ground, but after a few minutes of staring him down in silence, he let the condition slide.

So, this was how I found myself here—two hours after training had ended—sweaty and lying on the ground.

"You could have given me a warning," I groaned, rolling to my side. I pushed myself up, trying to stand.

"Actually, stay down." His heavy boot connected with my back, shoving me back to the ground.

My face landed in a pool of my perspiration, and I grimaced. "What the hell was that for?" I asked, face smashed against the floor.

"You're weak." There was no teasing or arrogance behind his words. He said it flatly—matter of fact.

"That's why I'm here," I grumbled. "Against my better judgment."

"Your body is strong, but the specific muscles you need to focus your strength are weak. During the day, we train skills, specific movements, motions, weapons, but what you need is a broader scope."

"We do warm ups and stretches in the mornings. Is that not enough?" I asked.

He scoffed, foot still on my back. I was getting annoyed.

"Don't laugh at me," I snapped through gritted teeth. "Remove your foot before you lose it."

He didn't. Instead, he relieved only enough pressure for me to push up to my forearms. His weight returned, and I braced myself against it.

He leaned down and adjusted my leg. "Stay there, and hold it." My abdomen ached and my arms shook. "Your core holds your power. Every movement you do stems from your core. If it's weak, then you're weak." He removed his foot, trusting I'd stay in the position, and squatted down. He was still above me, but his voice lowered when he said, "You are pathetic and weak. Only the strong survive."

My arms were shaking, and I knew my body would give at any moment, but I gritted my teeth, determined. "No."

"Then prove it."

I stayed there, straight as a board, for as long as I could. When I finally caved and fell to the floor, it felt like I'd been holding it for hours.

It wasn't even a full minute.

"Like I said," he said. "Pathetic."

His jab struck a chord, and I shook. I pushed to my feet, tilting my head to meet his gaze. "Don't speak to me that way." Heat traveled to every part of my body. There was something about his eyes that dug into my soul.

It felt like he hooked invisible talons into my mind and latched on. There was no denying that I was drawn to him. But I fought it, pushing the heat down, and dared him to fight me back. I wasn't going to let him talk to me this way. "I may be weak, Callax, but I will not stand here and let you talk to me that way. I have dealt with enough shit from everyone else, and I am done taking it from you." I pointed a finger at him, demanding his attention. "I deserve respect, regardless of how strong or weak I am." I was shaking.

He stared, silent, those swirling eyes looking more black than blue today. The corner of his mouth twitched with pure male satisfaction. "There she is," he purred.

I took a step back, confused. I had expected a biting quip or for him to impose his height over me. To exert his dominance. Instead, he stood still, staring at me with a proud look on his ordinarily arrogant face.

"Fight back, Miss Orion. Do not let others stand in the way of your success. Just because they are bigger, or taller, or have more brute strength, does not mean you are less than." He took a step forward, closing the gap between us. "Train. Fight. Win. No matter the cost. Mercy is not weakness, but the strong do not falter." I could feel the heat of his breath on my face. "Do not make yourself smaller. Yield your power to no man." His smile was gone, and his face was stern.

Something like desperation or panic, lay hidden beneath his cold, steely gaze.

Where was this coming from? Callax had always been cocky and arrogant, always teasing me and pushing my limits, so I hadn't expected words like this to come out of him. But he was dead serious, like he had thought of this on more than one occasion.

"Why does it matter to you?" I whispered, my voice shaking under his gaze.

"That's none of your concern."

"It involves me. It is my concern."

"Because we are the same," he shouted. "Because the same desires drive you. Because I see the way he treats you and I want to kill him for it."

My chest rose and fell quicker—erratic. Speaking like this, about the Phoenix…it was treason. I shook my head, trying to fight this. Him. "And what exactly does that change between us?" The words escaped my lips before I could stop them. I wasn't sure what answer I was searching for in the question, but he took a step back.

"It changes nothing." He looked to the side, avoiding my stare. "Not while your heart still belongs to him." He picked up his gear and quickly walked out of the room, leaving me to wonder why I suddenly felt empty and alone.

His words rang through my mind, forcing me to face the lingering question Cyrus had posed before he died.

Was I willing to give up myself, my knowledge, for my blind loyalty to Fynn? How deep did his hold on me really go?

I needed another cold bath.

I relaxed into the warmth of my bed, my muscles screaming at the movement, and picked up the last book in the small pile Cyrus had given me. In the back of my mind, a nagging reminder that the trials were only days remained. I had done my best not to think of it and to focus instead on my training, but it was drawing near. I wouldn't be able to ignore it for much longer.

I flipped through the pages, seeing how much of it was blacked out or torn like the previous ones, but this one only had one page of missing information. I sat up a little straighter, realizing this one might hold more detailed information. I was eager to devour it.

I flipped through a hundred pages of history and background on the legendary Arderan Orion, the Fae warrior who led the Realm of Night's army. Near halfway through the book, I stumbled upon something new that piqued my interest.

'Astera Renata, daughter of the Moon and Night, perished in battle at the hand of the Light Phoenix, Razael. She led the Legion of Night, side by side with her mate and General, Arderan Orion.

Astera and Razael fought atop Mount Cresslier, surrounded by shadows and flame, in a fight heard across the lands. Astera gravely wounded Razael by severing one of his wings with her twin nightshade blades. Mined from the base of Mount Cresslier and sealed in moonlight in the temple of the gods, Astera's nightshade blades were weapons of death. They were the one thing that could kill the Light Phoenix. Both blades—deadly to even the gods—were forged from extremely rare material. Only the Realm of Night's inner circle, The Court of Infinites—made of six powerful gods—bore weapons of nightshade.

However, after this battle and the untimely death of Astera, her weapons were the only remains of their great struggle. The field was empty when they searched for her. Her soul had ascended to the heavens—where gods could find peace in the eternities.

Arderan Orion collected his mate's blades and returned with his legion back to Nox Arctura.

The Realm of Night mourned the loss of their princess. In her grief, the

Moon Goddess retreated into shadows behind the world, and the night fell void of stars.

During their time back in the Night Realm, the Court of Infinites came to the understanding that both blades must be used simultaneously to end the Light Phoenix permanently. Orion abandoned his weapons, choosing instead to use his mate's blades to honor her and end the Light Phoenix.

With his renewed motivation, Orion consulted with his God and Goddess, and they agreed for him and the remaining court to end things once and for all.

So, the six gods followed Orion in search of Razael. After weeks of searching, they found the Light Phoenix in the south of the land, near the sea. There, the Sun God's followers had built a castle of white and gold. Wasting no time, Orion and the Inner Circle launched an attack on the castle. The Sun God proved to be a coward and stayed in the skies, leaving the protection of his realm to the wounded Light Phoenix and his dwindling Inner Circle.

Over the next few days, battles between the gods and the Light Phoenix commenced. On the last day, Orion and Razael fought atop a nearby hill, and the battle was nearly as loud as the one between Phoenixes.

I paused and closed the book. The information swirled in my mind. There was a lot to process, but one word stuck out, one that made little sense. One that whoever was censoring these books must have forgotten. 'Phoenixes.' As in more than one.

There had never been more than one Phoenix at a time. After the death of the original Phoenix, each one that came after had been the host for the Sun God. The Phoenix himself had never been a true Reincarnation, but even then, only one existed at any given time.

The words Light Phoenix swirled in my mind. It never made sense why Callax and Cyrus had always referred to the Phoenix that way. Outside of the two of them and these texts, I had never heard this unique phrasing before. But the existence of light meant there was dark. If the Light Phoenix came from the Realm of Day, did that mean–no, it couldn't. Surely, I would have been taught about it before. I knew the king had censored the worship of the old gods, and if there was another Phoenix, would it also be the host for a god? But the reference had been to the battle between Astera and Razael... and Astera was a god, not a host.

My mind swirled with too many theories and questions to be left unanswered, so I opened the book and finished the last few paragraphs.

'But Orion was not Astera. He did not have the strength of the gods or a Phoenix. Even though Razael had been stripped of his ability to fly, his strength and flames overpowered Orion. Ever the loyal soldier, Orion continued to fight, despite the fatal injuries. In one last surge of energy in his mate's name, Orion used Astera's twin nightshade blades and severed Razael's head.

The world shook with anger as the Sun God rained fire from the skies at the loss of the Great War. But the gods of the Realm of Night did not desire to rule over the entirety of Albionne. Balance was required, and neither the Night nor Day could rule in entirety. They only desired peace for their people, a safe haven for Fae, humans, and gods to exist together in harmony. Following the loss, many gods of the Realm of Day ascended into the heavens or fled to the north, seeking refuge.

The Court of Infinites returned to Nox Arctura and brought Orion's body back before their king and queen. Still grieving their daughter's loss and now Orion's, the God of Night bestowed an honor on Orion. One which had never been given to any Fae before, or since. The God of Night ascended Arderan Orion to the heavens to be with his mate, his love and devotion forever written in the stars.

In their grief, the Night God and Moon Goddess left their realm and returned to the heavens, leaving their granddaughter, Cassia Orion, to rule over Nox Arctura. To honor the love and life of her parents, their daughter renamed the city of Nox Arctura. It was now to be called Asterion—a combination of her parents' names.

Over time, the gods each faded—or were killed by the wicked Fae kings of Day—and returned to the heavens. On occasion, the gods would reincarnate, keeping their bloodline magic alive, but this too faded, becoming rarer. For reasons unknown, Astera remains as the only known god to deny reincarnation.

The wicked kings of Day, still under the influence of the Sun God, began to push the borders of their realm, pressing into the territory of Night. For a time, the Night fought back, but without a Phoenix to lead them, they were no match. And, in an attempt to keep Asterion safe, the last of the Court of Infinites set about protecting their capital.

Unable to find their way through or to break the wards set by the old gods, Asterion remains untouched.'

I went to turn the page, but it was the last. The rest ripped from its binding. I sat in my bed, reeling over what I read.

There hadn't been a known existence of a true Reincarnation in hundreds, if not a thousand years. It would make sense that if the Sun God never fully reincarnated, he might have never allowed the other gods in his realm to do so. And if there were gods that reincarnated, staying in Asterion where they were safe, would make the most sense.

Knowing any of this for certain was impossible. It was possible that Cyrus had known more, but it was no longer an option to ask.

Before I could close the book, a sketch and some scribbled handwriting on the back page caught my eye. I recognized the handwriting as Cyrus's immediately. I had become acquainted with the scholar well enough to recognize his lazily scrawled marks with ease. Some of it had smudged, but the drawing was clear. Two blades, side by side, each with a beautifully detailed pommel, one wing protruding from each, winding its way up the base of the blades. And when placed side by side, they formed one pair of beautiful wings. Wings that looked exactly like Fynn's.

In the corner of the page were four words. My heart stopped.

Dark Phoenix—Orion Family?

At the sight of the swords and my family name, I was transported back in time.

Suddenly, I was back home. My father opening an old chest made of metal so blue it shone black, flecks of gold inlaid in the clasps that locked it. Beautiful black and cobalt blue wings were carved into the top, and behind it were a handful of silver stars—the constellation of Orion.

In the memory, my father beckoned me forward, showing me how to adjust the wings. A lock clicked, and the chest opened. Inside were two twin blades wrapped in cloth as black as night. He carefully lifted one out and placed it in my young hands. It was heavy. Solid, but beautiful. In my hands was a blade made of nightshade.

The edges glinted in the moonlight, the lines mimicking that of flames. On the handle, winding its way up the base, was half of a beautiful wing—one matching the pair atop the lid.

I stared in wonder and felt a familiar echo in my mind calling out, singing to me. As if it wanted me to bring the other one out–to wield them together. Before I could reach for it, my father folded the blade back in its cloth and placed it with its twin.

He held my hands and, reverently said, "These blades are sacred, Renata. They have been passed down in our family for as long as the gods have existed. They were mine long ago, and one day they will be yours. As the eldest daughter of the Orion family, they are yours by birthright. When you are ready, I will teach you to use them. Until then, you will hold no other sword. They were made for you. Only those with the blood of an Orion have the power to wield both simultaneously. One day, you will be stronger than any other Fae."

I grinned at my father. "I'll be strong like you, dad?"

"No, my darling girl," he whispered tenderly, "you will be even stronger than I."

I laughed, the innocence of my childhood resounding through the memory.

He closed the lid, and I saw a flash of silver, bright and beautiful as moonlight, but I didn't have the time to follow the memory before I was back in my body.

I instinctively reached out my hand to the empty air around me. "Dad," I cried, the memory so vivid and real. I wished more than anything I had hugged him at that moment. But I was only eight. I had not known he would die before he could ever teach me to wield the blades.

Tears fell from my eyes, and I curled onto my side, blindsided by the memory. One I had forgotten about. One I would hold on to dearly for as long as I could.

It wasn't until I was on the verge of sleep, slipping in and out of dreams and memories, that I sat straight up—the realization dawning on me. I quickly got dressed and ran to get Archer.

"Where are we going?" Archer asked, her voice nearly drowned out by the thundering of hooves.

"Just trust me," I shouted.

"Trust you? You dragged me out of bed to go on a ride. The trials are tomorrow, for gods' sake."

I grinned and spurred my horse faster, giving Archer no choice but to keep up.

"Home," I yelled over the wind.

We were going home.

CHAPTER 32

It was two hours past midnight by the time we arrived back in the familiar streets of Firielle. The town had long since gone to bed, only one or two stragglers wandering from the taverns and into the streets. It was strange being back.

It had been almost eight months since we were summoned away in the middle of the night. We passed the bar where we had been drinking that night, and memories flooded back. I missed the banter, the spats between Kaede and me, the normalcy of it all. I missed the usual routine we established for ourselves. But there was no going back. Even if we were somehow all allowed to come home at the end of this, our lives would never be the same.

As we rode up the hill to our house, flashes of memories flickered in and out of my mind. Walking to training with Kaede and Skye, late-night girl talk, staring at the stars on nights when the terrors prevented me from sleeping. The good, the bad, and all the in-between that happened here at our tiny house atop the hill.

The town all volunteered to help when our house had been rebuilt. Two young girls stricken with grief would never have been able to complete the task on their own. Our father had been a woodsman, cutting and distributing lumber from the forest to the town. He was kind, and caring, and generous with his time. He often gave out firewood for cheaper than necessary, or even free to those struggling. Everyone adored him, and the town took care of us for a time after they passed. After a few months, the food stopped flowing, and the house was rebuilt. They returned to their everyday lives, and Archer and I were left to rebuild ours on our own.

Few things had survived the fire that night. Whatever was left, I had moved to the attic after the house was rebuilt. I had to care for Archer, and the constant reminder of our pain hindered my stability. Parts of me regretted hiding away the few items left, but it was the only way I could cope.

I had forgotten about the chest. It had been the largest thing to survive the fire, the black metal covered in ash and soot when we sorted through the rubble, but it was there—not having even a scorch mark from the flames.

"What are we doing here? We have to go back." Archer dismounted with me as I walked towards the house.

"I promise we'll be back in time. There's something you need to see, and I needed a place to talk to you where no one could hear." I pushed open the door, and the familiar scent of pine and oak filled my nose. I took a deep breath and reveled in it. Home had been a foreign concept for a long time. The heady scent was more comforting than the stone walls of the castle.

I looked at Archer and could tell she felt the same way, a small smile curling the edges of her lips. I grabbed her hand, "Come on," I said, dragging her to the back of the house.

I pulled down the hidden hatch and dropped the ladder.

She looked confused. "You pulled me from my bed in the middle of the night to ride for hours, only to show me…our attic?"

I rolled my eyes and started climbing, "Just trust me, okay?"

The dust floated through the air, reflecting in the moonlight. I grabbed a candle and matches from the windowsill and lit it, illuminating the attic. It was stacked with various crates where we had stored linens, winter clothes, and miscellaneous items over the years. An old armoire and a stack of blankets sat in the corner, hidden in the shadows. I made my way over to them.

"I'm pretty sure the castle has extra blankets. You just had to ask," she drawled, sarcasm dripping from her voice.

"Shut up and help me move this," I said and kicked the blankets to the side, grabbing one edge of the armoire, Archer the other. Together, we slowly moved it a few feet to the side, scratching the floor. And there, in the dark, back corner, lay the metal chest from my memory.

"Whoa," Archer breathed, "where did that come from?"

"I don't know." I shook my head. "I had a memory of it earlier, and I think there's something in there for me. I just—I needed to see."

"What is it?" she asked.

"I'm not entirely certain. Here, come help me." I walked back to it, ducking under the sloping roof, and grabbed one side. Archer held the other, and we dragged the heavy box out from deep in the shadows.

Using our hands, we wiped away the thick layer of dust that had accumulated on top of it. A thrum of energy ran through my hand, and a sharp gasp from Archer made me turn. Our eyes met, and I knew she had felt it too.

I looked to the wings emblazoned on the top and smiled. "Watch this," I said. I ran my hands along the ridges of the wings, admiring the detail and beauty. It was cool to the touch, but the sight of it warmed my heart. Something about this discovery made me feel connected to my parents, to my past and lineage. It felt ancient. Powerful.

I grabbed the edge of one wing and moved it upward, then ran my hand along it to the other and repeated the motion. A small click sounded, and the locks opened, echoing loudly in the silence.

Archer's eyes were wide with anticipation. I flicked the clasps on the edge open and lifted the lid.

I expected dust to flow out from the interior, but there was none. Instead, there was a rush of air. It smelt of night air and fresh pine. A wave of memories flooded through me. My father holding me high above him, pretending to let me fly. My mother, sitting in the grass with us girls, pregnant with little Damian, telling us stories. Archer and I using our first bows in the forest with dad.

Tears brimmed in my eyes, and I let the feelings rush through me. The ache in my chest intensified and I couldn't stop them from falling.

I knelt in front of the open chest, one hand still on the half-open lid. I had lost so much and only wished I could have it back. Even if only for a day. The grief consumed me, and I succumbed to it. I wanted to wail, scream, and yell, but I only hung my head and sobbed.

Archer knelt, embracing me. A small trickle of her tears hit my neck, and I knew she felt it too. She had felt the rush of air and the sudden flood of memories. She was young when they died but old enough to remember it all clearly. I sometimes forgot that I wasn't the only one carrying the weight of their loss.

We spent a minute or two holding each other, not running from the heaviness of the moment. "Thank you," I said and tucked a stray piece of hair behind her ear.

She wiped a tear from her eye. "For what?"

"For always being there for me. For always reassuring me I'm not alone. I'm glad you're here with me."

"Me too," she whispered.

I put my hand to her face, rubbing my thumb over her cheek. "We have each other, and that's what matters."

I pushed the lid all the way open. Inside were two bundles of black cloth, just like my memories recalled. I reached toward one and felt the familiar thrum of energy. It felt as if the blades were calling to me, excitedly singing my name.

I set it on my knees and carefully unfolded the blade from the cloth. I knew what it was before I touched it. It was an ancient nightshade blade forged in the moonlight of the temple of the gods.

It was the legendary blade once belonging to Astera Renata, Daughter of Darkness, heir to the Realm of Night.

My hands hovered, admiring the cobalt flames running along the sharp edge. The black wings wrapping around the hilt and onto the blade.

"What is that?" Archer breathed out in awe, staring at the blade.

"It's the nightshade blades. They have belonged to every eldest child of Orion since the first. And before that, they belonged to his wife, Astera Renata. The daughter of the Moon and Night. Wielder of Shadows and Flame."

"How do you know this?" Archer questioned, her voice still hushed, eyes fixated on the detailing of the sword before us.

"Cyrus." When his name left my lips, I realized I never told her about his death, though I imagined it was well known by now. But I had never told her of his last goodbye to her. "Archer, I...about Cyrus—" I stumbled over my words.

She looked to the floor, not meeting my eyes, and whispered, "I know. I didn't know how to bring it up to you either."

"I never mentioned it before, but he wanted me to wish you farewell. He said to give his little moon his love."

Confusion crossed her face. "Why would he tell you to tell me goodbye? Were you with him? Did he know he was going to die?"

I shifted uncomfortably but met her gaze. "It's a long story, but yes, I was with him the night they took him. I promise I will tell you all about it, but I need you to trust me that now is not the right time. Can you do that?" I hoped she would let it be for now. I would explain it to her, I knew I would, but it was too risky. I couldn't put her in danger with this knowledge. Not before I knew what to do.

She was silent for a long while, contemplating my request, but she finally said, "Okay. I trust you." She gestured to the blade in my lap. "Tell me more?"

I was thankful for the change of subject. I took a breath and calmed my mind, then continued, "Before he died, he gave me some ancient texts with some of the lost histories of the gods. Most of it was wiped away, but there was enough to put some things together. In the back of the book, he drew these swords, and when I saw them..." I sighed and gestured to the blade. "I remembered I had seen them before. Dad showed them to me long ago, promising me he would teach me to use them."

"Swords? As in more than one?" She met my eyes this time, and curiosity shone in them. I smiled and nodded, gently using the cloth to set the blade on the ground. I reached back into the chest and pulled out the blade's twin.

The humming only increased with both out in the open. I laid it next to its sister, and I swear the blue flames glowed faintly. I could feel it calling to me, telling me to hold them.

'Wielder of shadows and flame. Daughter of Darkness. We are together at last. We have been waiting.'

I shook my head. Was I imagining things, or had the blades whispered to me in my mind? Archer reached out a hand to touch them, but I stopped her.

"Wait," I said, holding her back.

My hands hovered as I hesitated, but I grabbed both gently. A rush of power ran through my hands and into my veins. It coursed through my body, filling me with an energy I had never known before. I felt powerful. Invigorated.

I gasped as I stared at the blades; this time, I knew I wasn't crazy because the flames did glow. Bright, cobalt blue.

I held firm, not wanting to let go of this new sensation, and rose to my feet. I took a few steps back, needing to stand to my full height. I twirled the blades, striking them against the ground, and electric blue sparks flared at the contact. I weighed them in my hands and knew these blades belonged to me.

They weren't strange or heavy, they were perfectly balanced. Like an extension of my arms as if they had been molded to fit me and only me.

I laughed at the ridiculousness of the notion and swung them around a few more times. I looked at Archer and grinned. Her face was still in shock and awe. "Those are...they—"

She couldn't finish, so I finished it for her. "Weapons of death."

I didn't want to let go, but I put them back in their cloth and wrapped them up. I looked back to the chest, curious if there was anything else in there, and a flash of silver, bright as moonlight, glinted in the corner.

I went to reach for whatever it was, but a hand on my arm stopped me. A look of wonder in Archer's silver eyes made me think that whatever was inside called to her.

It was narrow and long, nearly the length of her. She set it down on her lap and unfolded it.

The room brightened. It looked as if pure moonlight had been forged into a large silver bow. The quiver of arrows was made of the same material, tipped in nightshade, and glistened with gold and white decorations. Whorls of white shadows and stars speckled over throughout.

She ran her hand along the bow and stood, lifting it in front of her. She drew an arrow back, and the bow glowed. The moonlight in the room caressed her, creating a halo of light.

Our mother had been Moon Fae, this much we knew, but seeing Archer like this, she looked like she could be the Moon Goddess herself. Her silver eyes glowed. It was my turn to be in awe.

She grinned. "It's like it was made for me. It feels perfectly balanced. It was…singing to me."

"What did it say?" I asked.

She hesitated but eventually said, "It said, *'Our moon… my master. Hold me. Wield me. Bathe me in the light.'* Did yours say something like that?"

"It was a little different, but…yes," I replied.

We stared at each other for a moment, unsure of what had happened and what we had just found. We turned back to the chest, wondering if there was anything else that could be hidden.

She wrapped the bow back up, dimming its glow, and looked back in the chest.

There were a handful of things remaining like my mother's old jewelry box, father's clock he carved years ago, and a few random trinkets that had been on our mantle as kids, and a knit cap both Damian and Rellyn had worn. But underneath them were two cloaks of the same night-black material encasing our weapons. I handed one to Archer. They must have been our parents'. Still around the neck were two silver pins.

It was beautifully detailed, and the sight of it sent my memory back to a few months previous when we had gone to Alynta. Memories of Anya speaking to us in her shop, where she had described a couple in black cloaks—bearing the sigil of the Realm of Night—carrying a babe with raven hair and cobalt eyes. Then I remembered the archives with Cyrus where we had gone over the census information and found that my parents had been in Solterra for a time.

I stepped back, my breath escaping in a gasp, my lungs constricting.

I looked to Archer, and I knew she had made the same connection. I didn't know what it meant or what impact it would have on us, but finding these weapons, knowing our parents had left Asterion and traveled south to Firielle with me as an infant, meant there were more lies and truths I had yet to uncover.

The moonlight began to fade around us. We had been here too long.

We wrapped up our new weapons, grabbed what we could carry from the chest, and rode back to the castle as fast as we could.

I couldn't keep my mind silent. It swarmed with new and unanswered questions I wished I could ask Cyrus. I was still withholding many things from Archer, but I feared for her life. I feared for mine, too, but it meant more to me she was safe than the answers. I would do anything to protect my little sister. Anything.

The realizations of the night settled in as we rode.

I was the babe Anya described. Our parents had fled from Asterion, and I was from the Realm of Night. Our surname was Orion, and we were descended from Orion himself. From the goddess born of shadows and flame. And now, we had weapons that called to us. What did it all mean? And what in the gods' names were we supposed to do about it?

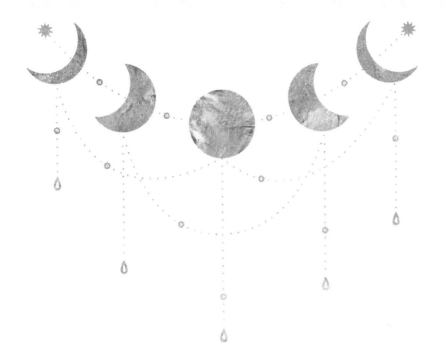

CHAPTER 33

We made it back in time, narrowly missing breakfast.

I knew it would be suspicious if I showed up with brand new weapons that were not standard issue. It wasn't out of the question for wealthier Fae to have custom-made blades or for those high ranking in the legion. But it wouldn't go unnoticed for me, especially when I had yet to master using only one sword.

I recalled how the blades had fit in my palms, and my left hand felt empty—unbalanced—missing a crucial part of itself. My training with Callax had begun to pay off some. It hadn't fixed everything, but he had been right about correcting form and strengthening my core. It annoyed me to acknowledge he was right, but he was, and for the first time, I saw significant improvement. I kept my distance from him during each session. While he put me on edge, he also set my senses on fire, and I needed to keep that at bay. It was difficult when we spent entire days together from dawn to dusk.

Thankfully, today was one where we rotated sparring partners. and I was partnered with Kaede.

I could tell he was going easy on me. We traded blows, and I knew he wasn't putting the full weight of his force behind them. While I appreciated that he didn't overtly desire to hurt me, I didn't want to be pitied.

"Don't hold back," I said, sweat dripping from my face onto the mat below.

"Are you sure you're ready?" He busied himself with the straps of his belt, not bothering to look at me.

"Maybe, maybe not, but I'll never get better if you don't."

He raised his sword, focusing on what I assumed to be my nose and not my eyes. It was getting increasingly frustrating, but I tried not to let it get to me. Yes, he had improved, but we could never move on until we confronted our issues.

"Why won't you look at me?" I finally asked, raising my sword and stepping forward. He brought his down on mine, and I felt the change. He wasn't holding back this time. I hadn't accurately anticipated the amount of force he now put behind the blow, and my knees nearly buckled before I adjusted and planted myself, engaging my core like Callax had taught.

"Because I can't." Two more blows. I was ready this time, but keeping my sword upright against him took more effort.

"It's been a long time, Kaede. I've apologized. Can't we move past this?"

This time I swung at him, and he parried with ease. Our swords clashed, the vibrations shaking my arm, and I pushed in, closing the gap.

"For the sake of our friends, for us, can't we move past it?" I pleaded.

"You've never apologized, Renata." His voice was stern.

"Yes, I have."

"Actually, you haven't. But that's not the point." The frustration was clear in his voice.

"Then what is? Do you truly hate me?" I shoved back against him, and his sword slid down the length of mine, coming dangerously close to my thigh. We still used dulled weapons, but they would leave nasty bruises.

"Gods, I don't hate you," he said through gritted teeth. He spun and tried to knock my legs out from underneath, but I jumped back in time. "The point is, is that I loved you and you knew. And despite that, you couldn't let it go.

Couldn't let me move on in peace. I was humiliated."

He brought his sword down, clashing with mine. The shock of his confession loosened my grip and it fell, clattering to the ground. I fell to the ground, his sword leveled at my throat. "You laughed at me in front of everyone. You laughed and then went about your day, your life, as if it meant nothing. Like I meant nothing."

Surely I hadn't been that callous. To laugh in my friend's face and walk away? I only remembered turning him down, but maybe I was wrong.

"I was young and stupid and in love, and the girl I stood beside my entire life suddenly disappeared in an instant. You stopped being my friend. You stopped talking to me, and eventually I couldn't bear to even look you in the eyes because it hurt. Even when I moved on, it hurt."

"I—I'm sorry, Kaede. Truly. I didn't realize…"

He swallowed hard, contemplating my words and whether he believed them. He looked to the floor, his sword lowering. "I know," he whispered, his voice cracking.

I slumped to my knees, my shoulders rolling forward in submission. I had spent the last years thinking so poorly of him, of my friend, not even realizing the extent of his pain. I was always so caught up in my own. "I hope you can forgive me," I whispered.

I waited for him to say something. Anything. But his shoulders sagged, and he dropped his sword at my feet. "I have," he said. "But I still need time. Forgiveness doesn't take away the pain. But for what it's worth…I'm sorry, too."

He turned and walked away. I wasn't sure relief was the right emotion to describe my feelings, but there was something there between us…hope, perhaps.

Whatever it was, I would take it. I would hold on to it and never let go.

The swords called to me as I strapped a new harness to my back. Most blades were carried around the hip, but with two, I needed to be able to access both easily without them banging around my legs. I grabbed them, feeling the rush of power that surged through my hands into my body. It felt good. It was similar to the energy I could feel when I was angry, but it was more controlled. Focused.

Callax was late. There were only fourteen hours left until the trials began. This was everything I had been training for, and I still felt woefully unprepared. I knew it wouldn't make a difference, but I wanted to fit in every minute of practice I could.

I gripped the blades and shook my head free of the thought. There was time to worry later.

I experimented for a while, running a few basic drills, getting used to the weight of two in my hands and how it changed my center of balance. Logically, it should be more difficult, yet it felt easier. Like something had finally clicked, and I knew what I was doing. If this was how the others felt, then no wonder they had so much confidence.

I rested between sets, catching my breath. The added weight required more energy for the same movements. I would have to get used to that. I let the tips of the blades sit on the ground, and blue sparks sprung from the contact. Curious, I lifted and dropped them again. Softly, this time, so as not to dull the blade on the stone. Again, blue sparks ignited. They sizzled out harmlessly on the mat. If a touch caused a spark, then what would dragging it do? I took my right blade and cautiously dragged the tip along the stone floor. Only a few inches and the sparks turned into a small blue flame. I panicked and lifted my sword, stomping on the fire, the smoke wafting to my nose.

Callax walked in just then. "What was that?" he asked, slightly alarmed.

I stood over the scorch mark on the ground, covering up the evidence of the small flame with my boots.

"Nothing." I placed the blades behind my back into their sheaths.

"Right." He lifted a brow and unpacked his equipment on the bench against the wall.

"Don't worry yourself. Like I said, it was nothing."

"Mmhmm. So, what's behind your back?" He eyed the two swords protruding at an angle from either side of my head.

"Oh, these? Family heirlooms. I just haven't thought to use them till now." I shrugged, trying to play it cool, but there was no doubt Callax saw right through me.

"You're not ready for two. We're still working on mastering one." He reached out a hand, waiting. "Let me see."

It wasn't a question.

I hesitated, not wanting to let anyone touch them, but he stared me down and reminded me of his rules…I must follow as he says when it came to training. He kept his hand aloft between us, waiting. I took a deep breath and reached behind me.

His eyes widened as I gently placed them in his hands. He tested the balance, tossing it from hand to hand, inspecting it closely. When his hand touched the wing curved against the hilt, he paused. For a moment, his eyes widened and looked from the wing to me as if waiting for an explanation for his unanswered questions. But I only stared back, unsure of what he was looking for.

With reverence, he whispered, "Where did you get this?"

"Like I said, a family heirloom. It was my father's. He promised it to me when I was a little girl." I didn't mention Archer's weapon.

"Be that as it may, you will continue to train with the standard swords." I could tell he didn't believe me, but he handed it back.

I was not expecting that. "What? Why?" I asked, demanding an answer.

"Because I said so." His mood changed in an instant.

I placed them behind me, resting between my shoulder blades, and crossed my arms. If he was going to be an ass, then I would be stubborn. "That's not a good enough reason."

"It is."

"No."

He growled, eyes darkening at my defiance. "Miss Orion, do not push me today."

"And if I do?" I kept my arms folded, settling into my decision.

"Then you'd best back up your words." He drew his sword from his hip and whirled on me.

I leaped backward, but not fast enough. The tip of his blade grazed my cheek, drawing a line of blood. I winced at the sharp pain and drew my blades.

"What the hell?" The energy had a mind of its own and was hungry for victory. I leaped forward, growling in anger. How dare he cut me?

"War is not fair." He parried my blows with ease, the ringing of clashing metal echoing in my ears.

"There's not a war going on right now," I quipped. He swung his sword down, and I crossed mine into an X, protecting myself from his slicing into my shoulder. He pressed harder, pushing them closer.

A dark storm rolled behind those multi-colored eyes of his. "You do not know what is or isn't going on. You live in peace in this castle, blissfully unaware." He spat those last words out, and I wanted to pull back.

I stepped to the side, rotating under my arms, pushing him away. We circled, waiting for the other to strike. The tension in the air was palpable.

"Then tell me. I am neither weak nor naïve," I snapped.

He laughed and brought his sword down with both hands, ready to end this sparring match. "You are both. No matter what you do, you cannot stop what is coming."

I wasn't done with him, nor with proving myself. I wasn't weak. I wasn't naive. But I was ready. I knew I was, and these swords filled me with an invigorated energy that told me so. It was only the other day he made me promise not to back down, to yield myself to no one, including him. Yet, here he was, calling me weak. Telling me to give up.

Had he changed his mind so quickly? Or was this another test?

We traded quick blows. He was fast, but I was confident. For the first time, I was fearless, and his arrogance drove me forward.

"Do not pretend to know what is best for me. I am not a child. Whether or not I can prevent an outcome does not mean I am any less worthy of knowing." I swept my legs underneath him, knocking him off balance, and stumbled back out of reach.

His mouth twitched into a smug smirk. "Maybe. Maybe not. But you have yet to prove yourself, have yet to prove that you are capable. So, I will do as I wish."

My mind raced with anger, the fire thrumming through my veins. I was not a child. I was tired of being underestimated. The king kept the entire group in the dark. We were supposed to be his weapons, his beloved Ira Deorum, and yet we knew next to nothing. Cyrus only shared his knowledge with me when he had no other choice. My parents had lied to me about where we had come from, from my heritage. Fynn refused to let me learn about his new life, keeping me from getting closer to him and from bettering our relationship. And now, Callax…

I took a running start and leaped into the air, bringing my blades above me. I drove my foot square into Callax's chest. He hadn't anticipated the move and fell, sword clattering next to him, defenseless. I placed my blades on both sides of his neck, letting them press on his skin. The smell of smoke wafted into the air, but I ignored it. I stared furiously down at him, and his brows raised in surprise. A dim blue glow emanated from around me, and I leaned forward.

"These sessions," I snarled, "this training—whatever this was…" I pushed the blades in harder, knowing I was cutting into his neck. "It's over. I want nothing more to do with you." I released the pressure and backed away. I stormed out of the room, grabbing my bag on the way out.

He called after me, "The trials are tomorrow. Is it wise to end your training when you need all the time you can get?"

"Burn in hell."

He was right, and I was terrified. I had pushed that fact from my mind for as long as possible, but a few extra hours would not make a difference. Not anymore.

CHAPTER 34

I slammed my bedroom door and leaned against it, sighing.

I dropped my bag, my heart skipping a beat at the shock. I hadn't seen him when I walked in, but Fynn sat on the edge of my bed, leaning forward, elbows on his knees.

"Gods, Fynn, you scared me." I clutched my chest, trying to calm my racing heart. We hadn't spoken in a while. I was thankful for the time apart, but I knew we couldn't avoid this conversation forever. I had hoped we would never have to talk about it.

He chuckled lightly, but there wasn't any humor to it.

"Can you come sit?" he asked softly. His eyes were tired, dark rings circled underneath, and he looked ragged. I nodded and picked up my bag, sliding it under the bed, hoping he wouldn't ask about the blades sticking out the edge.

I sat beside him, keeping some space between us. He noted the distance and looked hurt. Sad, even. I wasn't sure what to say, if I should say anything at all, so I remained silent. Waiting.

Yet even with only a glance at that familiar face, my anger seemed to dissipate. It was the one thing I never understood with him. Whenever I was in his presence, I became someone different. I wasn't strong or forward like I was around others, around Callax. No, around Fynn, I completely forgot about myself. As if my troubles no longer mattered and all I could think of was making sure he was happy.

He seemed to keep the weight of the world on his shoulders, and now as the Phoenix, he quite literally did. It wasn't fair for me to put more weight on him by being unjustly angry or irrational. I may have my own hopes and desires, but his would always come first and I could never make sense as to why.

But as I sat there, waiting for him to speak, I couldn't help but think of his actions. Of how he restricted me, keeping me confined to his side, asking me to be ignorant to his actions. My emotions rose and fell, never consistent, never stable. He had that effect on me and it was confusing.

Callax taught me to be strong, to yield to no one, but for Fynn…I yielded everything.

He had yet to speak, and I searched his face for an answer. For some hidden, silent apology.

My chest tightened, my throat closing around the words that wouldn't form. I feared what he might say or if there was another thing for him to be angry about.

His hand wrapped around mine. I inhaled sharply, but steadied myself, not wanting him to see me afraid. But I couldn't hide the way my heart wanted to rip out of my chest at the innocent touch. A touch I no longer wanted.

I was afraid of what he had become. I feared what he might do.

He had hurt me in the past, both physically and emotionally, and while I had moved past those things…I would never forget. It was impossible to erase the triumph on his face as he burned an entire town in the name of the king. He had reveled in that madness.

It was a cut that ran deep. One that still bled.

I wanted him to let go, to erase his touch, but another part—an illogical, needy, desperate part—craved him. More than ever I craved his warmth, his love, his comfort.

Gods, I missed him. I didn't think I had ever acknowledged that part and instead kept myself busy to distract my mind. It was confusing to want someone so deeply, yet despise their actions. My heart wanted him, but my body screamed to run.

Despite all of this, I was frozen. Unable to move.

"Say something," I said breathlessly.

"I don't know what to say."

My heart sank.

I wanted him to say something. *Anything*. To apologize, to scream, to cry. To yell at me for my actions or for not reaching out. To shout at the distance between us or to get on his knees and beg for my forgiveness. Anything but this.

Not *'I don't know.'*

"Do you not have anything to say?" I asked, trying to keep my building frustration from bursting out. I didn't know what I wanted, but I didn't...I didn't want him to leave me.

"I don't know, Renata." He shrugged, his shoulders slumping, his head sagging between them. He looked defeated. Broken.

Had I broken him? I couldn't face that reality if I had.

I was still angry and needed closure, but I hated seeing him like this more. And the part that felt sad for him always seemed to be stronger than the part that wanted to hold him accountable.

"What don't you know?" I felt like I was going crazy.

"What do you want me to say?" He was getting frustrated now, but he kept his voice low, still full of unexpressed emotion. He pulled me close, but I felt a thousand miles away.

"I don't know Fynn. Anything. Please." I tried to gently free my hand, but he clasped it between his, trapping it. My heart pounded faster, fighting against my chest.

I wanted out. I wanted him to let go... I didn't like this.

Leave. I needed to leave.

But I was stuck.

Stuck with him. Stuck in this room. Stuck in this cycle.

No, no, no…make it stop.

Please, make it stop.

"I'll fix it, I promise. I'll make it up to you," he whispered.

"How?" I asked, silently urging him to solve my panic with some unkown answer, to magically erase this moment and start over.

"I just will. I can't lose you."

My heart skipped a beat, but I knew it wasn't because his words comforted me. Deep down, I think I knew my heart was breaking. But I refused to acknowledge the small cracks that were forming. Because if I did, then the pain would become real and not something I imagined.

Unable to think of anything else, I said, "Okay. I believe you." But I didn't think I did. I just needed the pain to stop.

Please, make it stop.

"Can I hold you?" he asked, raising his head. I nodded and stood, slipping out of my training leathers and climbed into bed with him.

His arms wrapped around my waist, pulling me in close. He put his head on my shoulder, inhaling deep, rubbing his thumb silently over my bare skin.

The ache—the desperate ache that wound so tightly within my chest that my heart was in agony—only intensified as he held. Suddenly, I wasn't at home…I was suffocating.

I stared at the beautiful male I had spent my lifetime loving, and wondered what I had done to deserve this. To wait endlessly for a love that came only at his discretion. To offer everything I was for the hope of it all. Not a guarantee, not a promise, nor an open invitation, but merely a wish…cast out into the heavens, waiting to be answered.

But the gods did not listen. They never had.

So what hope did I have that he would?

I lay there, still and silent, while he kissed my neck softly, whispering, "I love you," over and over until the words lost all meaning.

I didn't move. I couldn't.

My mind raced, yet somehow felt entirely vacant. All that anger, that confusion, and frustration moved into my hands. I couldn't move without upsetting him, so I curled my fingers and dragged my nails over the pad of my thumb until I rubbed it raw.

Even then, I did not stop.

I held my breath until I couldn't breathe. Staring for what felt like hours into the empty darkness, searching for something to pull me from this. All I found was a reflection of my pain staring me down, daring me to fight back.

But pain was all I had known. So I let it feed. Devouring me whole.

I tried to convince myself that he was truly sorry for his actions. That he had to be, because he told me he was. I wanted it to be true. I needed it to be true.

So I told myself I believed him.

I believed him.

I believed him.

I believed him.

Right?

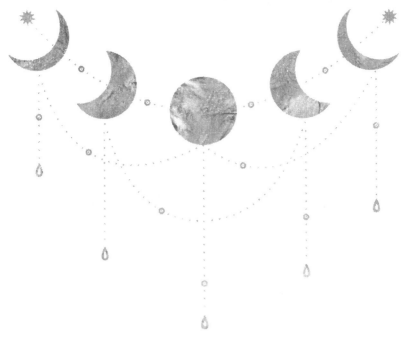

CHAPTER 35

I woke with a sense of dread.

I dressed, putting on the new black leathers they had given the twelve of us and walked out into the alcove between our rooms. I was the first out, but Emryn, Kaede, Senna, Skye, and Archer soon joined. Skye broke the silence. "Are we just going to stand here, or can we go eat? I'm starving."

Kaede chuckled softly at his sister, shaking his head in her direction. He grabbed Emryn's hand. "She's right, let's eat. We'll need it."

None of us said a word about the trials as we grabbed our breakfast from the kitchen.

Emryn said, "Let's eat outside and enjoy the sun before it gets too warm. And then, after the trials, we can come back out and enjoy the sunset together. I think it would be the perfect way to end the day."

Kaede squeezed her hand and smiled softly. "That sounds lovely, Em."

Maybe it was because of our shared moment the other day, or perhaps because of my issues with Fynn, but when I looked at the two of them, I didn't see them how I used to. I didn't see an arrogant male undeserving of my friend, I only saw a couple who loved and supported the other.

We sat in a circle on the cool grass and ate our breakfast. Skye told jokes, and Senna told us of her time training the legion and how she felt there would be a change coming soon. The training had become more intense, and she said she wouldn't be surprised if the king was preparing for an unknown war in the near future. It wouldn't shock me after the events in Alynta. A blow to his people like that would not settle the realm into peace.

Emryn broke the dismal talks of war and chimed in with her hopes and plans for the future and what we might do one day when we were the official Ira Deorum. She wanted to go back to Alynta and see what she could do to find the survivors and help rebuild. We would have the time between missions from the king to come and go as we pleased, and her ideas were quickly agreed upon by us all. We knew we had our duty to the king and didn't have a choice in the matter, but we still had our integrity. It was one thing I thanked the gods for. That as a group, we would still be whole, despite the trials set before us.

We spent the last of our free time recalling stories of the past; raucous nights in the taverns back in Firielle, embarrassing moments during training, hunting trips in the summer, practical jokes played between siblings.

Despite knowing that our lives would be forever changed after this meal, we didn't let it bother us. We knew we had each other, and we always would.

"I love you guys." Emryn beamed at all of us, meeting our gaze with her emerald-green eyes. "We're starting the day together, and we will end it together. As a team."

Her words resonated with me. I didn't know what made me say it, but I interjected, "As an inner circle—six friends, loyal to the end. We are the only ones we can trust and the ones we love. 'Til the Night rises." I had never uttered the phrase before with my friends. It was something only Archer and I had used, but it felt suitable for the six of us. They were my family as much as Archer was.

Emryn nodded, raising her glass of water in the air. "To our inner circle—until the Night rises."

We lined up outside the training room doors against the wall, the twelve of us in the order of our testing. I was at the very end, and I didn't know whether to be grateful or nervous.

My hands shook, and I wiped the clammy sweat that gathered in my palms onto my pants. We weren't allowed to use any outside weapons, which meant I would be back to using the standard-issued sword. I was still terrified that going back to the unbalanced weapons, even if I chose to use two, would make me fail.

King Tobias never specified any repercussions, but the implications were dire enough to know I would never leave these castle walls again. I wouldn't be allowed to exist outside of the capital at this skill level. I would be deemed a threat to the throne.

Footsteps sounded behind me, and I turned, expecting to see Therion. Instead, I only saw Fynn.

He wore a jacket similar to one Callax had worn the night I wandered into the Royal residential wing. But his was a beautiful crimson red, trimmed in gold detailing. A simple, gold circlet sat atop his head. He looked beautiful. Regal. He looked like the Phoenix.

The Light Phoenix, I corrected myself.

He grabbed my hands and craned his head down, kissing me on the cheek.

"Are you ready?" he asked.

"Honestly?" I sighed, shaking my head. "No."

He laughed softly and rubbed his thumb over my hand. "You'll do great, Renata. I know you will. And when you finish and show them just how strong you are. Soon, we will be equals. We can be together all the time then. Complete our missions from the king together." He smiled as if his words would comfort me.

They didn't.

I hid a wince. As if we weren't equal already. I knew his powers would outmatch any skill I learned. That was a given. But it felt more like an admission he didn't view me as worthy of him. As if I was undeserving of his respect until I proved myself.

Down the hall, Therion and Ilvar walked towards us. I turned back, not wanting to bother with the semantics of his words. I had bigger things to worry about. Instead, I said, "Thank you. I can't wait till it's over too. I can't wait to celebrate with you." I smiled, trying to reassure both of us I meant those words.

"You'll do great. You always do." He kissed my cheek once more. "One day, we will lead the Ira Deorum together. It's our fate, after all."

But that was the problem.

I didn't believe in fate.

CHAPTER 36

Three hours had passed since Callax started the events, followed by Soren, Mavenna, and Senna. All four passed their trials quickly. They were the ones who would impress the most, their skills enviable above all.

We waited outside the room as each of us was called in individually. Those who had yet to pass the test were not permitted to watch. I knew it was designed to push us, to strain our limits, but we weren't allowed to know the specifics until we faced them. Just as we would not know the limitations and capabilities of future enemies until we met them on the battlefield.

The hours ticked by agonizingly slow.

Panic filled my body, and I began to pick at my fingers. I needed to know how they did, how any of them did. I needed anything but to wait.

Finally, the large training room doors swung open with an ominous creak. Therion walked out and stood before me, grim and severe. He nodded and turned back, waiting for me to follow.

I swallowed hard. This was it—my moment to pass or fail. To live or die. I only hoped my extra efforts and additional training would pay off.

They cleared the room of all weapons and stations usually lining the walls. Where the regular sparring ring should be, stood another nearly three times its size. A single rack sat next to the ring, lined with all kinds of weapons we used over the last seven months.

Therion led me to the center, and standing on the viewing deck was King Tobias. Next to him, scuffed up and still in his gear, was Prince Callax. He looked serious and sullen. Deep grooves and scratches lined his new leathers. It brought me a small amount of comfort knowing Callax had struggled. But it disappeared quickly because if he had struggled, gods knew I would too.

On the king's other side was Fynn. I tried to get his attention, but he was staring ahead, unblinking.

"Welcome to your trial, Renata Orion." The king's gravelly voice echoed throughout the room. Therion walked to the back wall where the other eleven stood. I quickly noted Archer, beautiful as ever, a hair barely out of place. She smiled and nodded at me. Next to her were the rest of my friends, whom all looked just as well. Skye bore a slight scratch along her cheek, but it was barely noticeable from this distance. Kaede nodded in recognition, and Emryn caught my eye, giving me a quick thumbs up, mouthing, 'You got this.'

It comforted me a little, knowing all of them passed and were acting encouragingly. At least if I failed, I could do so knowing they would be safe.

"For your trial, we will test you on your ability to wield a sword. This has been your weakest technique in training."

That was it? Just swords? Would I not have a chance to show my skills in the other areas? My heart pounded with dread, racing at the thought. If I didn't have my other skills to back me up, or even my newly found nightshade blades, I didn't think I stood a chance.

No, I scolded myself. Despite how Callax and I ended things the night before, his words still rang through my head.

The strong do not falter.

"Choose your sword and enter the ring. If you step outside the bounds, or are killed, you are finished. Your goal will be to knock the opponent out of the ring or to kill them and avoid death yourself. If you lose, your end will not be swift. Do not disappoint me."

I swallowed hard. We were not using sparring weapons anymore. This was real, and the consequences of losing were real.

I wished more than anything I could have used the nightshade blades. They would have been a better choice than the ones before me.

I inspected the weapons. Some were chipped or warped from continual use, but all the edges remained sharp and deadly. I chose the same one I had used while training with Callax. It was the one I had the most success with, albeit limited.

I balanced it in my hand, feeling heavy and wrong. It didn't call to me or light with a faint blue glow. It was normal. Mundane. I would have to be one that was exceptional.

I walked to the center of the ring, turning to face the king above. I took a deep breath and counted to four as I waited for the signal to start. He raised his hand above his head, signaling, and the room's side door opened. Out walked two males.

Two.

Two giant Fae warriors that bore scars down their neck and arms. Two males who had seen fight after fight and lived to tell the tale. My breathing did little to calm me.

I looked around the room and locked eyes with Therion. He only glared and raised an eyebrow at my disbelief. He was going to be of no help.

I might stand a chance against one opponent, but two? It was impossible, and it seemed the king knew this too. I looked up, frightened, and the king sat with a smug smile. Fynn, next to him, sat unmoving and unfazed by the presence of my two adversaries. Callax, however, looked like he was going to be sick.

My grip tightened on the sword, and I readied myself. Fully prepared to live out my final moments in this world, here in a sweaty training room.

Shaking off the panic, I widened my stance, rooting myself into the ground and engaging my core like Callax instructed me night after night.

I was strong. I was capable. I would not falter.

I told myself this over and over as they stepped into the ring.

The king shouted, "Begin."

They launched towards me.

I ducked to the side and circled around the ring, assessing their movements as a pair and individually. I wouldn't win this battle on strength alone.

"Well?" the taller one asked, his stringy blonde hair hanging in his face. "Why don't you show us what you have?"

The other one, shorter but significantly stockier, grinned. His crooked teeth hooked on his bottom lip, and he wagged his eyebrows. Taunting.

I'm not sure why I antagonized them, but it felt better than succumbing to the panic. "Is that all you have? One attack and some taunts?" I tsked, "Seems like such a waste for such brutes."

The short one grunted in anger and flew towards me, aiming for my chest with his sword. I blocked and deflected quickly enough. The second following suit immediately, aiming for my ribs.

My feet moved without instruction, using instinct instead of thought. I stepped to the side and used my blade to push him in the opposite direction.

I circled for a moment more, my eyes darting between the two who looked too much like brothers to be anything but.

They stood on either side, closing in step by step. I was going to be trapped at any moment and needed to find a way out. Wicked grins spread across their faces, and they looked at each other, acknowledging some predetermined plan between the two.

My legs froze. They felt distant from my body as if they were no longer attached. I couldn't remember how to make them work.

I stood, frozen, as the brothers raised their swords and closed in. I moved without thinking. I threw my body forward, darting through the narrowing gap of their bodies. I hit the ground and rolled.

I landed in a crouch and flicked my braid behind with a swing of my head.

They whirled—faster with each step. One was coming from the side and the other straight on. I met the taller one's blow, and the loud clang reverberated in my ears, ringing in my head.

I twisted, trying to swing out from underneath, but I wasn't fast enough. The edge of his sword dragged along my upper arm, ripping through leather and cutting my skin.

I danced around the two, trying to separate them to meet their blows individually, prolonging my defeat.

I was on the defensive, and I needed to survive. I had to find some way to beat them.

The tall one came for me first. I twisted under him, bringing my sword towards his middle with as much force as I could muster.

I sliced through leather and caught his skin. Blood flecked onto the ground below. I kicked at his knees, making him buckle and lurch forward. His brother lunged forward, closing the gap between us, meeting my sword high in the air. He pressed down, and it was almost too much.

I gripped both hands to the hilt, pressing upwards with all my might, preventing him from slicing open my throat. I was being cornered. Inch by inch, my foot slipped behind me, bringing me closer to the edge. Closer to defeat.

A grunt called my attention, and I saw the tall blond I had knocked down rise to his feet. His hand was at his side, holding the cut I made.

My feet continued to slip. Don't move, I screamed to my feet. Don't fucking move. But they didn't listen.

Sweat poured down the side of my face, dripping into my eyes. My legs trembled, begging me to give up.

The blond advanced, anger and hatred written on his face.

I didn't have a choice. I released the pressure I was using and dashed to the side. The short one, not recognizing my move in time, shot forward, narrowly missing the edge.

I ran to the other side, as far away from them as possible. My arms were shaking.

They advanced together, blood dripping from one, a sneer on the face of the other. "You're going to die, and we're going to enjoy every drop we spill."

I snarled. Anger coursed through my chest, lighting my veins, and surging into power. It was like some mental block finally gave way, the thing preventing me from owning what I was capable of, disappearing along with it. I was done being weak. I was done allowing males to push me around, to succumb to their whims. Only Callax had pushed me, urged me to take that strength back.

I felt him in my mind, reminding me to fight back. So I reached out and stole that strength, made it my own. My body wanted to give up, but I refused.

The brothers lifted their swords, ready to strike me down. Anger and frustration flowed through my entire body, and a familiar rage ran through every pore, energizing me.

I thought of Archer and of my friends. Of the life I had yet to live. I would not leave them behind. I would not falter.

I launched to the side, avoiding one, but coming into direct contact with the tall, wounded one. I blocked his blow, the impact shaking my arms. I ignored the dread and brought my blade back around, slicing through his leather, down into his arm.

He screamed in pain and reeled, avoiding another cut.

"Watch out!" A voice, sharp and clear, sounded from the other end of the room.

I turned to see Emryn cupping her hands around her mouth, yelling at me to pay attention. From the side of my eye, I watched helplessly as Ilvar took Emryn by the arm and walked her away from the group. I paused, unsure what to do.

My hesitation cost me. While the tall one had stumbled to the side, his brother closed in. I raised my sword, but it was too late.

Pain roared through my side as he sliced into my chest. Metal scraped across my ribs, blade meeting bone.

I dropped to the floor with a scream, blood pouring from my body.

The short one rounded again, ready to pierce through my body this time, but I rolled to the side, forcing my body to move.

Blood lined my side, but I gritted my teeth and used my sword to help lift me from the ground. My mind screamed at me to stop, and slowly the pain ebbed, replaced with nothingness.

I was going numb.

I raised my sword and my skin cracked open, cold air licking at the edge. It was sick and unnatural, but it wasn't registering fully. I was losing too much blood. My vision blurred.

I shook my head, clearing my eyes, and grounded myself into the floor below as Callax had taught me. It was only his voice, his words that echoed in my ears. Telling me to fight. To live.

The male ran towards me, but I stayed still, waiting for the last moment. He closed in, and I turned once, knowing I needed to be quick if I wanted to survive. I stepped away and lowered my sword parallel to his neck, letting his momentum drive most of the action.

I pulled as hard as I could.

The sharp blade dragged across the soft skin of his neck, and he choked. His blood fell out of the wound like a waterfall as he collapsed to the ground, sword clattering at my feet.

One remained. My left hand gripped my ribs, putting pressure on the wound that would not close. It would be minutes before my skin began to mend, and even if it did, I would have to survive the blood loss first.

I staggered over to the injured one on the floor, knowing I needed to finish him off or drag him out of the ring. And seeing as I could barely keep my sword aloft, I had only one option.

I leaned over the male, blood soaking into his blonde hair. I felt sick. I had never had to kill another person. His pained face turned my stomach, and I swallowed down the bile. Given any other circumstance, I would have gladly spared him. But I did not want to die.

Mercy was not weakness, but the strong did not falter.

I blinked back the tears and steadied myself. In this one instance, I admitted to myself that he was right.

I couldn't spare any mercy. Not if I wanted to live.

I wanted to enjoy another day with my friends. To make things right with Kaede. To gossip at night with the girls and see the sunset we all promised each other. I wanted it all, and his death would be the price I paid.

I lifted my sword, ready to drive it through his neck and end his life. In the split second before my blow landed, his eyes widened, and I saw his fear.

I hesitated.

A fraction of a second too long.

The strong did not falter…but I had. I was too weak, too kind. And in that moment, I knew I had failed.

His arm jutted upward as mine moved down. A flash of silver and his dagger sliced through my open abdomen, embedding itself into my torn flesh.

My sword continued downward and drove through his neck, but it was too late.

Blood spilled from my side, and I dropped my weapon to place pressure on the deep gash overtaking my torso. I couldn't see the severity of it throughout the remaining scraps of my leathers, but I knew it was fatal.

Warmth seeped over my chilled hands, bringing back some heat that had been stolen as my body tried to conserve blood. But it was useless. I was losing more than my heart could replace. I had minutes left at most.

My world swayed as my vision blurred. I found Archer's face in my mind and held onto the image. She was the one thing holding me steady.

Across the room, her face frozen in shock, her hands clasped tightly to her bow as if she was hoping to jump in and save me. But there was no hope.

I was going to die.

Before I could mouth 'I love you' in a final farewell, a commotion came from above.

Blinking away the tears clouding my fading vision, I saw a petite form dragged to the king, held up by two guards

My world came to a crashing stop as a flash of silver arced across the form's neck.

Red spilled down faster than it had the right to.

Delicate hands clawed at their throat, trying to seal in the blood, but the wound was too great.

Too wide.

Too deep.

Too fatal to be held together by such thin fingers.

It happened so suddenly that none of the others noticed save for Callax and Fynn, both standing at the king's side.

The world tilted beneath my feet, and as I gave way, two guards grabbed me by the arms and held me there, facing the king. I slumped, unable to bear my weight any longer.

Panic raced through every vein in my body, infecting every inch of my mind. I never thought to pray before now. The gods were gone from this world and had no reason to listen to a dying girl's plea.

I had moments left, and knowing that this was my fault, that Kaede's suffering was my fault...praying was the least I could do.

And so I prayed.

I reached out my mind to any and all gods who would listen.

I prayed to the Moon and the Sun and to the gods of Chaos and Death. I prayed to Astera and Orion, to the God of Night, and to those who might remain in this cruel world—hoping there was one amongst them who would care to answer my desperate plea.

But there were none.

Silence enveloped me.

My mind slipped as my body succumbed to the wounds. Before I faded, I gathered my feeble strength to raise my head and met the king's dark, soulless eyes. I put every ounce of hatred into my gaze, and I swore in that moment, my skin burned with the embers of a fiery rage.

But whatever foreign power pooled inside me was snuffed out as I sank to the floor.

In the haze of the encompassing oblivion, a haunting wail broke through the fog, and I knew Kaede had seen.

Our friend.

His partner.

Emryn lay dead at the foot of the king.

CHAPTER 37

It was consuming me.

Roaring through the house, winding through my veins, it sought me out. Consumed me.

I couldn't move, I was trapped. I couldn't leave my bed to alert them. My family. My parents.

It wrapped its dark tendrils around my body and mind and devoured everything in its path. Its sharp claws digging through me, paralyzing me with the pain.

I lay frozen as I watched it wind through the hallway, collapsing the beams, trapping my mother and siblings.

Their screams.

Gods, their screams.

My father's hands wrapped around mine. Dragging me and Archer through the window to safety.

My father running back into the house. The red flames—no, blue—consuming my childhood home.

I screamed. The fire rose with my terror, encompassing the house, sealing them inside. Deciding their fate.

There was nothing left. No fear. No emotion. No pain. Only raging blue flames and screams of agonizing terror.

I too, was burning.

It was too warm.

My whole body burned, searing itself from the inside out. Flashes of Emryn's body haunted my every thought. Even my personal darkness was no longer safe from the world.

I forced my eyes open but saw nothing. Darkness surrounded me, and I tried to sit up. I needed to find my friends. To find Kaede and Archer. But strong hands pushed me back down, back into the bed soaked with my sweat. Why was I burning?

"Camilla, the water." Unfamiliar panic laced a hoarse voice. It echoed, their pain becoming mine, making everything intensify.

Smoke burned my nose, and flames raged through my body. My breathing became ragged and uneven.

"Camilla, now! Bring the tonic."

Male. The voice was male.

"Here, take it." Camilla's sweet lilting voice was filled with urgency and panic.

Why was everything so cold and so hot? Why were my hands burning? Pain flared into my back, a strange weight pulling me down, knotted between my shoulders.

"What?" I mumbled, trying to push myself back up. I needed to find my friends. But my world was blurry, dizzy, hot. So unbearably hot.

Something was being poured down my throat, and I started to choke, but strong hands tilted my head back, making me swallow the bitter liquid.

No. Stop. I needed to find my friends. Why didn't they understand? But the world only faded to black once more.

"Renata?" That familiar, soothing voice returned, and I felt my world align again. The fragments of my broken mind mending along the seams. Only that voice offered me a path back to reality.

I opened my eyes, but the world was still blurry. I could vaguely see a figure slumped forward in the chair next to my bed.

The figure held my hand in his and stroked my forehead, soothing me back to sleep.

I slept in fits, in and out for what seemed like forever. Thankfully, the memories and terrors stayed behind locked doors in my tired mind.

When I finally awoke, I was still in the infirmary. He was holding my hand, leaning back in the chair next to my bed, his eyes sunken in and dark circles carved beneath. A quickly fading scar below his temple marred his achingly beautiful face.

Sunlight illuminated the flecks of dust falling into his hair, the golden beams reflecting off the highlights of his cheekbones.

Everything seemed sharper—clearer. As if the fire that burned through me heightened my senses.

His eyes snapped open. "You're awake." I had never heard someone so relieved.

"What is going on?" I asked, my voice hoarse, unaware of how long I had been unconscious.

"Camilla, she's awake." His eyes lit with hope, and his shoulders relaxed slightly.

"Callax? What are you—where's Fynn?" I asked, worry and confusion filling my voice. A flicker of pain crossed his face at the name.

"They're gone. My father sent them on another mission. They won't be back for nearly a week at the earliest."

I rested my head on the pillow. "All of them?"

He nodded. "Yes."

"Did everyone pass?" I asked. Memories of the trials came back in pieces, two males, pain, searing pain, a scream, Emryn. I was going to be sick. Gods, Emryn. There was too much blood. But it couldn't be true, could it? Maybe it was just a trick of my mind, a false reality created in the loss of blood.

"Callax, what happened to Emryn?"

He swallowed hard, fighting the memory. "I'm sorry, she's gone...my father, he—I couldn't stop him."

No. It couldn't be. Not Emryn.

I swung my legs over the side of the bed. I needed to leave, but a wave of nausea and pain roared, and the heat flared through me again.

"You need to rest. You're still healing." He guided me back to the bed where I lay in defeat.

Tears fell, and I didn't stop them. I put a hand to my abdomen, where the pain seemed to radiate from. Bandages wrapped around me, and I remembered the dagger that had protruded from my side.

Callax noticed my hand. "I almost lost you," he whispered. There was only pain and fear in his voice. I had never heard him sound like that. "The blood wouldn't stop, but we got you here just in time. Camilla was able to stop it before your heart gave out. I...I don't know how you survived. But somehow, you held on." He looked relieved as he spoke the last words.

It had been his words that held me together for so long. I didn't tell him that, but it was true.

"How long have I been out?" I wasn't sure I wanted to know the answer.

"Two days, going on three. Camilla says you need to rest for at least a week. Physically, you've healed, but mentally and emotionally, you have a long journey ahead. She has never seen a Fae live through injuries quite so extensive, but it's a miracle. You've been blessed by the gods."

I scoffed. I was cursed, not blessed. A question formed on my lips, but I hesitated. If I had failed, surely the king would have ended me already, dealing out whatever consequence he deemed fit for my failure.

I wanted to suffer. I deserved it.

My failure was the reason for Emryn's death, for Kaede's pain. I heard the wail of agony when he saw her lifeless body, and it was something I could never erase from my mind.

My heart wrenched from the guilt.

My friend was dead because of me.

"What is to happen to me?" I asked, my voice low. I feared the answer I was sure to get. I had failed, and I knew there would be consequences. Maybe the king was waiting until I was healed so he could kill me himself in front of my friends. Make a statement.

"I was able to convince him that you didn't get a fair fight. One of your opponents cheated by bringing in an outside weapon, and that it is grounds for an automatic forfeit."

He rubbed his shoulder, tracing some invisible line beneath his collar. "He tried to convince Therion you should be disqualified and killed then and there, but...I pushed back."

"You?" I scoffed in disbelief. But he was here when no one else was. He had argued with the king...for me?

"I told him you clearly would have won if he hadn't had the dagger, and with some convincing, he finally agreed. You won on a technicality, but...you did it. You passed."

Relief flooded through me. I hadn't failed.

Which meant Emryn died for nothing.

"I stayed behind to ensure you were okay, but..." his voice trailed off.

Callax's hand grasped mine, trying to comfort me. I felt rough welts covering his knuckles, and I glanced down. Red marks stained his hand.

"Why aren't you with the rest of them?" I asked. He averted his gaze.

"I needed to make sure you were okay. I couldn't leave you like that. Not alone."

My heart skipped a beat. It should be Fynn who was here, not him. Isn't that what a good partner would do?

I let go of his hand, not wanting to be touched. I lay there in silence until sleep claimed me.

CHAPTER 38

The silence was unbearable.

Everything moved in slow motion. The days were unending, the nights even longer, all of it bleeding into one. My grumbling stomach and knots in my unbrushed hair were the only indications time had passed.

I had experienced death before, it was not a stranger, but this was different. I thought perhaps as I grew that the pain of losing someone would get easier to bear. That maybe the overwhelming grief that weighed down my soul was only because I was young when I lost my parents. It wasn't true.

Death gripped at my heart every waking moment, refusing to let go. It wasn't fair that Emryn was gone. But there was nothing we could have done to stop it. Except for me.

If I had done better…been better, none of this would have happened.

My door remained open, blankets strewn over the windows, shrouding the room in as much darkness as I could manage. Faint footsteps echoed across the stone and dark shoes appeared. I didn't move. Didn't react. I only lie there, soaking in the coolness of the floor, hoping I might melt into it.

A soft grunt registered as the figure sat beside my curled body. A tray of food was placed in front of me, and the smell of porridge and fruit filled my senses. I was tempted to lift my head, but the cracks in the floor remained more interesting.

"Eat," he said. His voice was soft and warm, a thread of light in unyielding darkness. A finger brushed my tangled hair from my eyes, tucking it behind my ear. "Please eat."

There was so much tenderness behind those words. So much empathy and sorrow. As if he too, felt my pain.

A tear fell as I blinked into the nothingness. I wasn't sobbing or making any noise, but they fell regardless.

He wiped them away.

I wanted to lean into the touch, but I couldn't bear to move. To admit that I was desperate for any semblance of warmth. Even if it was his.

He sighed softly, but remained by my side in the silence. Eventually, he picked up the untouched tray and left.

Three times a day, Callax returned.

Each time, fresh, hot food sat on a clean tray. Each time, he sat next to me, wiping away my tears and accompanying me in the silence of my pain. He urged me once with each new meal, trying to get me to eat, but I remained unmoving.

He placed a pillow beneath my head on the second day, and offered me a new blanket. I only caught glimpses of his hands as he did these things. His bruises had healed, and a strange sense of relief passed through me to see that no new wounds covered his body.

If only the mind healed as quickly as the body.

Three days passed like this—me, on the floor and Callax beside me.

On the fourth day, my mouth became unbearably dry and I could no longer swallow. Each attempt like sand in my throat. I stared at the cup of water on the tray and tried to reach for it. My fingers wrapped feebly around the cool metal. I tried to lift it, but it was so heavy, and my hand was stiff.

Strong fingers wrapped around mine. Callax lifted it, guiding it to my lips. Water spilled down my chin as I greedily drank. Gently, he lifted me up, helping me to sit.

My head sagged, and my eyes were heavy, but I drank more, this time swallowing it all.

"Do you need more?" he asked gently.

I nodded, shallow and slow. Without a word, he left me to get more. He returned seconds later, but it felt like an eternity without him. I had grown used to his companionship, his silence filling the lonely ache in my heart.

When I drank my fill, the cold water sloshing in my empty stomach, I grew tired again.

"Here," he offered, patting his thigh. I didn't have the strength to resist as I lay my head down. It was soft and comforting, far better than the floor. I could have stayed there forever.

A brush began to pull gently through my hair, like a parent might do for their child. "Can I tell you a story?" he asked.

It was a strange request, but I nodded.

"When I was a boy, my father liked to…punish me. I never knew why, only that he seemed to take joy in it. There was this post in the courtyard. He liked to call it the 'learning post' of all things." Callax scoffed at the memory. "Whenever I ended up in trouble, which was more often than I like to admit, he'd send me out to it. He'd make me wrap my arms around it and said if I let go, he'd chain me up and start all over again."

My heart ached at his words. Parents were supposed to love and guide their children. Not beat them into submission. "What would he do?" I asked.

"He'd whip me." I could feel, rather than hear, the echo of pain that lingered throughout the years.

I lifted my gaze, trying to find his, but he averted his eyes, focusing instead on my hair. I settled back down, letting him continue.

"Each punishment was assigned a different number of lashings, and if I let go or cried out, he started over. When I was younger, he went easier on me. But as I grew, so did my 'offenses.' And with each new one, his punishments became worse, often giving me new and inventive ones." He took a deep breath. "Once, I caught my younger brother, Madoc, stealing from the cooks downstairs. He didn't know any better, and the kitchen staff laughed it off. But my father was furious. He knew it was Madoc, but as he began to confess, I stepped in and claimed I had done it."

A pang of familiar protectiveness rose in my chest. I knew that feeling well. I would do anything, accept any punishment, to save Archer from pain. What was an older sister to do, if not to shield the younger one from the pain of the world.

"What happened?"

He shook his head and sighed. "I knew he would punish me for being so foolish. But Madoc was too young. I would heal, most of the scars he gave always healed, and I would be fine. But this time was different. After the lashings were over, he didn't permit me to leave. He told me I had been foolish to sacrifice myself. That a proper king would let an inferior suffer in his stead."

"Callax, I—" I tried to offer an apology, but he didn't let me.

"While I remained there, gripping the post—my back still bleeding—he brought my brother out and made me watch as he whipped him, too. I listened as he cried for him to stop. But he didn't." He turned his head, the brush in my hair pausing as he wiped a tear I couldn't see.

"I thought it was finally over, but he hadn't dismissed me. So I stayed. I stayed there, gripping the post for hours, my back exposed to the scorching sun. I wasn't permitted to move or call for a healer, so I remained here until night fell. When the moon was high in the sky, my father finally called for me to be released. I collapsed, unable to move, my back and wounds grinding into the dirt."

His heart sped up ever so slightly. I placed my hand on his, trying to comfort him, and said, "I'm so sorry, Callax. You didn't deserve that." And I meant it. No matter who someone was or how they treated others, no one deserved a father who cared so little.

Fathers were supposed to guide and protect, to nurture and teach. I recalled the love I felt from my father and wished I could offer that to him. How different would his life had been if had a father who loved him?

His mouth thinned, and he stared at his fingers, ignoring my words. As if he couldn't bear it. "I passed out from the pain, and when I woke, I was lying in the infirmary, my back exposed. The wounds should have closed in that time, but they remained open and raw. Camilla was there, young and still in training, but she tended to my wounds over the next days as my skin struggled to heal." His breathing deepened, his heart finally calming.

"Why didn't they heal?" I asked, pulling the tray of food closer. I had grown distracted by his story and finally succumbed to the effects of my hunger. Absently, I picked at the roll on the plate, tearing bits off and chewing them slowly as he spoke.

A small smile curved the edge of his lips as I ate. It softened his features and I looked away.

"My wounds had burned in the sun's heat, preventing the skin from sealing. And when I fell on the ground, the dirt infected the wound."

I stopped eating and looked at him now with horror and sorrow. "How old were you?" I asked, my voice barely a whisper. Was there an acceptable age for this kind of treatment?

"Twelve."

A tear slipped from my eye, and he wiped it away. I leaned into his palm, but he only pulled away and moved the bread back to my mouth.

"Do not cry for me, love. It's okay." His voice was soft, but I didn't believe him.

"No, it's not," I said. I was firm with my words because it was not okay. It was never okay for a parent to treat a child like that. "There is no world in which that is okay. Whatever you did or didn't do…you were a child." I held back the anger growing inside, the desire to rip the king apart for what he had done to him.

I kept my voice as comforting as I could, needing him to hear my next words. To believe them. "No child deserves to know the pain of a parent who cannot love."

His bottom lip quivered, his eyes searching mine. With hope or sorrow, I did not know.

I looked back down at my roll, taken aback by the emotions in his eyes. I sat up then, removing my head from his lap, the brush clattering to the ground.

"You should probably go," I whispered, my eyes downcast. He likely had more important things to do anyway than to tend to my needs. I didn't want to keep him. "Thank you for…for everything."

He stiffened, but rose to his feet. He paused for a moment at the door, turning back to face me once more, but thought better of whatever he was going to say and left without another word.

CHAPTER 39

On the sixth day after her death, I decided to leave my room, if only for a few moments.

Callax had not returned, nor did I expect him to. But with my wounds healed and my sister still gone, I had no reason, nor desire, to venture outside. I spent most of my days in the bath or back on the floor, reading and re-reading the books, but nothing new retained itself.

I pulled on a pair of loose linen pants and a soft white top and tied my hair to the side in a braid. It was oily after days of not washing, but I didn't have the energy to care. All my energy had been focused on merely surviving one day to the next and giving my body the time it needed to heal. However, my mind would take longer to mend. I wished for nothing more than to turn everything off. It would be so much easier.

There didn't seem to be a point in it all. Not when I was alive while she was dead.

I moved my old clothes from the floor to the bed and, in the process, knocked the unopened invitation to the ground. The Initiation Ball was in two days' time, and invitations were sent out immediately after the trials. It felt like a violation. It only served as an acknowledgment they were moving on without her. Like Emryn's death meant nothing.

Sighing, I picked it up. I turned it over in my hands, the deep red envelope and gold wax seal complimented each other beautifully, my name scrawled in perfect penmanship on the front.

I read the information and tossed it back onto the bed. A small card fluttered out, landing on top of the comforter. It had a shop and street name on the front, but on the back was scrawled, 'Please visit Oak. I have instructed her to take care of you.'

The thought of leaving my room or even moving seemed like a daunting task. Each movement required incredible effort, none of which I had. Every simple task, down to breathing, was harder than it should be. Every breath I took was a reminder that Emryn wouldn't do so ever again.

It wasn't fair. It felt selfish to enjoy anything. But if I didn't have a dress, then I would surely suffer more. And while I deserved it, I didn't want to give the king the satisfaction.

The shop was small, tucked between a bakery and a grocer. Just being near freshly baked bread made my stomach growl. I hadn't eaten a full meal in days, only bits of rolls Callax had offered in the days before. My normally full face was beginning to sink in, my cheeks less rosy and eyes dark with exhaustion. I desperately needed to eat and sleep, but I doubted either would come soon. The reminder of Anya and the baker from Alynta haunted me as I walked through the door. I tried to push back the nausea and disgust flowing through me at the thought. It was almost enough for me to turn around.

"Hello dear." A lovely middle-aged woman stepped out from the back room and greeted me with a wide smile, her eyes crinkling in the corners. She tucked a pencil behind her ear and walked towards me. "What can I help you with, my lady?" she asked.

I forgot this was how I would be addressed from now on. As a member of the Ira Deorum, we were all awarded the official title of Lord and Lady and would be given new living chambers soon, suited to our specific wants and needs. It wouldn't be fitting for the king to have such public use of commoners. Only titled Fae were worthy of serving the king in such an official capacity.

I shook my head, bringing myself back to the room. I plastered on a fake smile, my cheeks straining at the movement. "Hello," I said, "I was told to come here and that you could help me. Though I'm not quite sure who sent me." I fished the little card out from my pocket and held it up. "I found this. I know it's last minute, but I was hoping you could help me?"

Her bright features lit up at the sight of the card, as if she knew exactly who it was from. "Oh, yes, follow me." She turned and walked past the mannequins modeling her dresses and suits and took me back into her back room. Rounding the corner, I was met by a mound of fabric nearly as tall as I was and narrowly avoided toppling it over. I continued back until she stopped and pulled out a rack against the wall.

Lining it was a myriad of pieces, from dresses to suits to a mix of both, which I had never seen before. A rainbow of vibrant colors and textures wound its way through the fabrics. I sucked in a breath, admiring the beauty of it all. Each one its own individual work of art.

"They're beautiful," I whispered, reaching out a hand to run along the varied fabrics. I usually opted for simple styles when dressing myself, typically settling on all black or occasionally tan or white. It was easiest that way, no fuss or stress, and it saved me precious minutes of sleep every morning. But though that was my usual, I always desired the luxury of a life where I could stockpile fancy dresses and jewels for such an occasion as this.

"Do I get to choose one?" I asked, still fixated on the clothing.

"Oh, did he not tell you?"

I furrowed my brows. "Did who not tell me what?"

"I received explicit instructions and specifications from him to make you a custom gown for the ball. I sent it off this morning, and you should receive it later today. I'm sorry, my lady, I thought he would have told you."

What had been the point of sending me here if a dress was already chosen for me? And who was this 'he'?

"Who exactly ordered my gown?" I asked. I wanted to be upset, but I did not possess the mental willpower to muster the effort. I didn't like that yet another choice had already been made for me, especially by a male.

"I'm sorry, but I was told not to say anything. I fear I may have ruined the surprise already." She looked genuinely disappointed, and I didn't like that.

"No, please don't worry, it's quite all right." I smiled, trying to reassure her. It wasn't her fault I was upset.

She seemed to ease her shoulders a bit at my words. She turned to the rack. "This is what you're here for, actually." She gestured to the clothes in front of me. "He thought it would help for you to pick out clothes for your friends while they are gone, since they won't have time before the ball to have anything made."

Whoever this 'he' was, while terribly annoying, might be kind of thoughtful. I imagined it was Fynn. He had a habit of offering me gifts after a falling out or fight, and he mentioned he wanted to work on things. Now I was officially a part of the Ira Deorum, we would have all the time in the world to spend together. While still annoyed I didn't get a say in the matter, I was thankful to have a distraction from the grief. Even if it would be short-lived.

I spent the next few hours sorting through the rack of clothes, contemplating each of my friends' styles and personalities to match what would fit them most. The distraction worked. For the time I was in the shop, I didn't think of Emryn once.

At least not until I pulled out a soft pink tulle gown, long sleeves ending in lace, the neckline speckled with light green gems. I could have sworn the dress had been made with Emryn in mind. The colors would have matched her hair and eyes perfectly, and for a split second, I smiled, wanting to tell Oak that I had found the perfect one for my friend.

Then, a wave of grief knocked into me so violently that I stumbled back, nearly pulling the rack down with me. I held the dress, clutching it to my chest as if the fabric held some lost essence of her. Frantic sobs rolled through my body in aching waves.

Gone. She was gone.

Oak's tiny footsteps sounded throughout the room. She had been in the front helping another customer, but she must have heard the commotion. That or my loud sobs.

My breathing became jagged, and I struggled to inhale deep enough to fill my lungs. Instead, they became increasingly short and panicked.

She was gone. Emryn was gone.

She would never wear the dress, never get to dance with Kaede or see the last sunset we all promised each other. We'd never sit on my bed and gossip about boys or drink wine together ever again.

It wasn't fair.

She hadn't deserved to pay the price of my failure. I could still see her smile, hear her laughter, and feel the warmth of her chest as she wrapped her comforting arms around me.

What was I going to do? A vital part of my life had been ripped from me. Again.

Make it stop. The grief, the pain, the unbearable weight of it all.

I had known from the day I met Emryn our time together would be limited. She was not Select Fae, not even Half; instead, she was limited to the hundred or so years humans and Quarter Fae were given. I knew this, yet she still left us nearly eighty years sooner than I expected. She was too young, too vibrant, too vital just to be...gone.

Make it stop.

I couldn't breathe. My grip on the dress loosened as I curled in on myself and leaned towards the ground. Oak's soft, delicate hands pulled the dress from mine. She joined me on the ground, a perfect stranger, cradling me on the floor while I panicked over a dress.

"Shhhh, my dear, everything will be alright." It wouldn't be alright. Nothing would ever be alright again. But her soothing voice and the cold floor calmed me, and her hand smoothed my hair. I took a few shaky breaths and settled into her arms. I wanted to be embarrassed that a random stranger had to comfort me in her own store, but I couldn't manage the emotion. I was drained.

"You can leave now, my dear. I'll have my assistant pack up your choices and deliver them to your room. Go home and get some rest." She held my face in her hands and looked me over, tucking my hair behind my ear like some worried mother. "And eat something too while you're at it."

I tried to protest. I didn't deserve her kindness, but she shut me down with a look, and I didn't fight it. She folded the pink gown and tossed it in a pile by the door as she walked out.

A moment later, she returned with a smaller bag, and the smell…oh, that lovely smell. I knew she must have run over to the bakery next door because it smelled of bread and pastries. My stomach grumbled, and I thought that if the bag was for me, I might actually eat today. Her assistant packed up the items I had chosen for my five—four—friends and was about to call for a courier when I stopped her.

"No, please, let me take them. I need something to do anyway, and I'd appreciate the distraction." I insisted, and she nodded, leaving the bags on a bench nearby. I thanked her for her kindness and the clothing. She surprised me by giving me a hug. Her arms locked around me and squeezed. She was tiny, and her head barely met my shoulders, but I wrapped my arms back around her, relishing in the contact and warmth.

"Take care of yourself, my lady. And promise me you'll eat." She raised her brows sternly.

"I promise."

The entire way back, all I could think of were the pastries that lay inside the bag. I knew this promise was one I could keep.

CHAPTER 40

The bread must have contained some sort of magic because I felt better instantly. The weight of my loss was still there, but it was manageable for now. Maybe it was because I hadn't eaten in days, but I was convinced the food was magic.

I sorted through the bags and pulled out the items I'd chosen. I was impressed with myself at the choices. I hoped they liked them as much as I did. I fiddled with the wrapping and absently wondered what mine would look like.

I pulled out Senna's first. It was a skintight gold pantsuit that sparkled in the light; a deep red, floor-length overcoat paired with it, meant to be worn together. A beautiful gold clasp brought it together in the middle, and gold thread detailing throughout the neckline and shoulders. Senna was not one to wear a dress, and I hoped she would find this fitting and appropriate.

Skye's I picked to match her hair. A black strapless gown fell from the bag, and I placed it in her box with the silver harness to accompany it. The straps wound their way around the bodice, crossing over itself, and ran up the chest in three straps where they would wrap around her neck like a collar. Fierce and bold, just like her.

Kaede's was next. I readied the box for him and pulled out his suit. It was simple enough, a white linen top with a black coat, but I opted for special buttons to be added. Down the front lapel ran emerald gem buttons wrapped in soft rose gold. It was a simple nod to Emryn, and I hoped he would appreciate the gesture. I knew it wasn't much—and I owed him a long and deep apology that could never convey the sorrow we both felt—but it was something.

Archer's was last. I made sure to get hers perfect. I felt the soft silk fabric and stared. It was a deep blue that mimicked the hour before night fell. It had only one sleeve, and at the waist sat a beautiful silver pin shaped like the crescent moon. I folded it neatly and pulled out the last piece for her ensemble. The chains clinked against each other as I laid them against the dress. It was a metal sleeve of beautiful silver chains that would wrap its way up her arm.

Seven crescent moons adorned the metal. If the moon were high in the sky that night, she would look like its Fae personification. She would capture everyone's attention, I was sure of it.

My fingers trailed the edges of the boxes as I stacked them. I wished there was one more for Emryn. One filled with that beautiful pink dress. I remembered the moment in the store with Oak's kind words, and tears brimmed my eyes. I blinked them away. I would have time to cry later.

I closed the door behind me to Archer's room, the last of the gowns delivered. I rolled my shoulders, ready to crawl into bed and settle into the silence. I stopped when I saw the sunset peeking in from the open windows. Looking out, I knew what I had to do and wound my way down the stairs.

I crossed the courtyard to the wall bordering the cliff below. The cool stone pressed into my skin, the wind sweeping through my tangled hair. I hadn't bothered brushing it in days, and it was a mess.

The salty ocean breeze mixed with the floral blooms, and I inhaled the scent. It was a beautiful combination. My chin settled on my arms and I watched the sun descend over the horizon. It dipped beyond the edge of the sea, the sky shining a beautiful pink and gold hue.

Emryn would have loved this. This should have been a moment we shared. I sank into my arms and let the sorrow flow freely. I wanted more than anything to give up, to go back home and find some sense of normalcy back in Firielle. But I knew it was impossible. Too much had changed—I had changed. Going home without Emryn felt wrong.

A hand touched my shoulder. I jumped, whipping around to see Archer.

"I thought you weren't going to be back until tomorrow." I threw my arms around her, and she squeezed me tight.

Senna answered for her. "We finished early. Fynn made us ride through the night. He was in a rush." I tried to pull back from Archer's grip, wanting to give each of my friends a hug as well, but she didn't let go. I melted into the hug, giving way to the embrace.

"I missed you too," I muttered into her hair. She buried her head into my neck and squeezed harder, nearly winding me.

"Is everything okay?" I asked.

She pulled back and looked up at me with those silver eyes.

"No. I thought I lost you, and we had to leave before we knew if you had woken up yet and I have been so worried. I wanted to stay behind, but we knew the king wouldn't let me, and I have been praying to any god out there that you were okay." she paused to catch her breath.

I pulled her back in and gave one more reassuring squeeze.

I knew the feeling well, I knew how all-consuming the potential and realization of loss could be. A wave of comfort washed over me at the embrace and realized how terrified she must have been, not knowing if I had survived.

"I'm okay, I promise I'm okay," I reassured her. It wasn't a lie, but it wasn't the complete truth. I supposed being physically okay would do for now.

She finally released me, and I gave both Senna and Skye a hug, truly happy to see my friends. "Where's Kaede?" I asked, looking around to see if he was straggling behind, but he was nowhere to be found.

Skye shook her head, "He's not doing well. He's hiding it, but…" Her shoulders sagged, feet shuffling beneath her nervously. "We can tell it's going to take quite some time to get over it."

I bit my lip and nodded. We spent a while there, holding each other as we watched the sunset. Archer's head rested on my shoulder, Skye leaned in while Senna held her waist, and silently we honored our friend with the last precious minutes of the sunset.

Emryn would have loved this moment, the vibrant hues in the sky, all her friends together. She loved life more than anyone I had ever known and fully embraced each moment, finding light even in the darkest of times.

I sighed as I wrapped my arms tighter around Archer, holding on to the light she brought to my life. Sorrow and heartache pulled at my heart. This was going to be hard, that much I knew, but we had navigated grief and loss before, and we would do it again. Together.

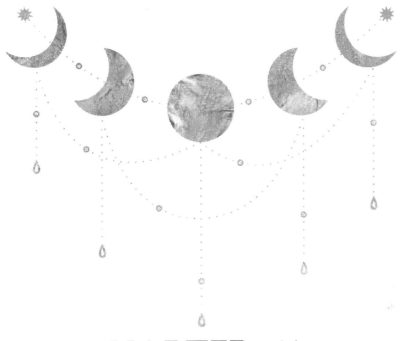

CHAPTER 41

Every part of my body still ached like it had been stretched, and torn, and beaten. A new weight settled in two large knots on either side of my spine, right between my shoulder blades. The pain woke me every night since the trials. I had become accustomed to a certain level of soreness since I began training two years ago, but this was new. I chalked it up to the lack of sleep and lying on the ground each night instead of my bed, but it was irksome.

I pulled a robe over my thin nightgown and headed to the infirmary to see if anyone was there. Maybe they had a tonic to help me sleep or soothe my pain.

I only made it a few steps out of my room into the hallway when I saw a dim light flickering. Archer's door sat slightly ajar, a still burning candle inside. Dawn was a few hours away, and she never stayed up this late.

She wasn't alone. Her door was closed enough I couldn't see who was with her, but I could tell it was a male. Maybe it was the scholar boy she had a crush on. Now I was really curious. I leaned against the wall and placed my head out of sight near the opening.

"I don't think I'll ever be able to look her in the eyes again, not when the image of Em's body is all I can see." Kaede's voice was broken. He sounded so full of grief it pierced through my heart. I leaned against the wall for support, knees buckling beneath me.

"I understand." Archer soothed Kaede with her tender voice. I knew the tone well, she had used it on me many times. "We all know how hard this must be, and you're allowed to take all the time you need. There's no wrong way for you to grieve." She sniffled, and I knew she must be crying.

Emryn had been close to all of us. Everyone felt her loss, but gods, I couldn't imagine losing her the way Kaede had. It had been so callous and cruel, and none of us had the time, or chance, to even say goodbye. There hadn't even been a funeral. The king disposed of her body, and we never heard anything else regarding it.

"No. I...I don't think I can," his voice was quiet but firm. He sounded as if he had already made up his mind.

My heart stopped.

"I—I just wish I could have said goodbye, or thanked her, or anything."

I strained to listen. I knew this was a private moment, that I should leave and let them have their privacy, but I couldn't tear myself away.

"What would you say? If I were Em, what would you tell me?" she asked. There was a brief pause like he wasn't sure if he should say anything.

"I'd say...thank you for the best years of my life. For showing me that love exists even in the depths of grief." My heart sank, and my breath left me. In my rejection, I had pushed him into Emryn, I had been the reason they ended up together, and now I was the reason they had been torn apart.

I wanted nothing more than to collapse to the floor, for the ground to open and swallow me whole.

"I'd thank her for being the reason I smiled again and pushing me to open my heart...but now, I feel like it's collapsing. Without her, I don't know that it'll ever feel again. I don't know if I can ever forgive Renata for taking her from me."

There was a long silence, and I moved away from the wall, ready to leave when I heard Archer. "I wish I could take it away, but know that I am here for you. We are all here for you." I could hear her sniffling between words. "Don't let the bitterness be the only thing you allow to enter your heart. Feel the pain—honor it—but don't allow it to make a home in your heart."

I held in my tears only long enough to grab the tonic. Still, I did not sleep.

I must have succumbed to sleep in the early morning hours. A large black box sat at the bottom of the bed. I rubbed my eyes and tried to remember if it had been there the night before, but I was almost certain it hadn't.

Before I could open it, a sharp knock sounded at my door. I left the box where it was and rubbed the remainder of sleep from my eyes. Fynn stood in my doorway. He leaned in and planted a kiss on my cheek.

"Good afternoon, sleepyhead." He beamed at me.

I managed a wary smile. "Where have you been?" I asked, "I missed you last night." It was the truth, well, partially. I hadn't thought of him much. I opened the door wider and stepped back, inviting him in.

"I can't stay long," he said, "I have a meeting with the king and his generals, but I forgot to give you this and wanted to make sure you had it for tonight. I want you to wear it for me. That way everyone knows your mine." In his hand, there was a small black box wrapped in a red ribbon. It matched the one on my bed.

I reached out and took it. His hand rested on mine, stopping me. "Wait until I leave. I want to be surprised when I see it on you tonight." He kissed my forehead and left.

My contentment faded with him. How could he look so damn happy? Emryn was dead, and I had no doubt he had just finished demolishing another town while I recovered, but I didn't have the heart to ask about the outcome of their latest mission. I don't think I could handle knowing.

Laying on crushed black velvet was a red ruby. It was inlaid on brilliant yellow gold and connected to a thin chain. I held it up in the mirror and placed it next to my neck. It was beautiful, but the red of the stone seemed to leech whatever color was in me, making me look drained.

Red was not my color, but I would wear it. For Fynn, I would make an effort. He seemed so happy, and while I wasn't, I didn't want to bring him down with me.

He promised he would try, and I supposed he was.

I tossed the box with the necklace back onto the bed, moving the bigger one to the center. This must be the dress Oak had mentioned, and if Fynn brought me the necklace, this must be from him as well. I had never seen him try to pick out something fashionable before, so I braced myself for something garish and red.

Inside lay the most striking gown I had ever seen. I pulled the bundle of fabric from the box, letting it fall to the floor in a cascade. It was a beautiful shade of black, fading to a blue so deep it mimicked the night sky. Speckles of silver floated throughout the fabric, and it flowed like liquid night when it moved.

I stared in awe, appreciating the amount of work and time that would have gone into creating such a piece of…art. This dress was art. I held it up to my body in the mirror. It dragged slightly, the deep blue pooling on the floor. The back dipped low, and the front carried two straps that didn't quite meet, and I wondered how they were supposed to stay up. I fiddled with the fabric pieces, looking for a clasp of some kind. Maybe they tied around the neck like a halter, but there was no clasp. Instead, it was another loop, like both ends hooked onto something.

I lifted the soft paper the dress had been folded in and realized I missed what lay underneath. I set the dress down gently on my bed, not wanting to wrinkle the fabric, and removed the rest of the wrapping. Beneath, lay an intricate web of solid silver. The way they looped together looked like…wings.

It looked as if it would fit itself perfectly on my shoulders, wrapping around like sleeves on a dress. I went back to the mirror and put it on. It was as if it had been made for me. The metallic wing design wrapped around my neck, the crest mimicking a collar of sorts on either side. Below, it wrapped around each side of my breast, ending at my waist, accentuating it.

I admired the detail of the metal, formed into outlines of feathers, and turned to look at the back. I gasped softly as I ran my hands along the edges.

It arced in the back, looking as if the metal was protruding from the sides of my spine. Precisely where real wings would be anchored if I had them. I rolled my shoulders, feeling the weight of the metal and the pressure of the back. I felt the strange weight once again between my shoulder blades. As if something heavy were missing from sight.

I stared at myself in the mirror, twisting and turning to see every facet of the silver overlay. I was so perplexed by their artistry I didn't notice Archer walk in. I was startled when I heard her gasp. "Whoa."

A wide grin grew on my face. "I know," I nearly squealed in delight. I had never seen something quite so beautiful before, and I couldn't believe Fynn managed to find something so exquisite, especially when the silver didn't match the gold of the necklace. But he was a male and chalked it up to lack of foresight.

Archer carried her dress in her hands. "Do you like it?" I asked, curious to know if I had done well in choosing for her.

"Like it? I love it." It was nice to see a smile on her face, on both of our faces. Part of me felt guilty for being happy, but I wanted Archer to be happy, so I focused on that instead.

"I wanted you to feel as beautiful as you are."

"Can you help me do my hair?" Her voice softened, her smile faltering. I knew why she had come to me. Normally she'd never trust me to help with her hair, but Emryn had been her go-to when it came to style. They had spent countless nights together when I was busy with Fynn, brushing and braiding their hair. It was their thing, and now, they would never have that again.

I took a deep breath and counted to four, trying not to appear as shaken as I felt. "Of course. Come on, let's get ready."

It was a nice change of pace to spend the day primping and preening instead of sweaty and gross after a long day of training. I was still getting used to a new schedule. We would no longer have endless days of training. I honestly wasn't quite sure what we were expected to do on a daily basis now since we weren't locked in a room from dawn till dusk six days a week. We would still train to maintain our skills, but not as frequently. I was sure missions would take up much of our time and become a regular occurrence.

My fingers stumbled through the complicated braid, but I managed to finesse it after three separate attempts. "There, I think I got it," I said. "Go look."

She rushed to the mirror, her face lighting up at the sight. My heart warmed instantly. She was beautiful. The sweep of the braid accentuated her face, and the few pieces I left out framed her silvery eyes. She looked like moonlight personified.

"Your turn."

I huffed a small laugh and ran the brush through my snarled hair. I finally bathed the night before, but it remained knotted.

"What do you want?" she asked. "I know you like it down, but I'm thinking a low-swept bun or braid since you have those beautiful silver wings to show off. I think they should be the focus." She was right, they deserved their own moment, and I didn't want my black hair covering any of their glory. She ran her hands through my hair. The sensation reminded me of when I was young.

My mother used to braid my hair nearly every day. My long, thick hair often got tangled in the branches of trees and caught on everything. It was one thing I missed most about my mother, and having Archer make the same motions made me nostalgic. She looked strikingly like our mother. I was sure they would be nearly identical if she were still alive today.

She finished, and I felt around my head, inspecting the work blindly. She braided it around my head like a crown, and pulled out strands to frame my round face.

It was perfect.

We finalized our ensembles by adding touches of colored lip salve and black kohl around our eyes. I found the whole idea slightly ridiculous, but she was so excited.

When I looked in the mirror, I was glad I let her. It made me feel feminine and powerful—alluring—and I enjoyed it more than I thought.

Kaede entered my room with a quick knock and leaned against the wall. I tried to offer him a smile, but he still would not meet my gaze. Even with the small amount of progress we had made, we would not be making any progress soon. I didn't blame him. But I would be there if he was ever ready.

"You two look beautiful," he said. He was handsome, wearing the suit I had picked out for him.

"Can we talk?" I asked.

He pushed off the wall, walking away. "I'll see you girls tonight." He closed the door behind him, leaving me with my hand outstretched.

"Give him time, Ren. He's not doing so well."

"I know. I just wanted to tell him how sorry I am." Tears choked me, but I leaned my head back, trying to let gravity stop them from falling. But it did little to stop the anger—the self-hatred—from flowing through me.

I wanted to scream. To break something and watch as it shattered. I was angry and confused and I didn't know what to do with all of it. I was mat at myself, at the world, at the king, and Fynn, and Callax... Heat rose beneath my skin, pooling in my hands, begging to be let out. My back ached too, and I needed to do something—anything—to release the building tension.

From the corner of my eye, I spotted the music box from back home, and I became blind with rage. My parents were gone. They were never coming back, just like Emryn. They had left me here to figure this world out on my own. They had lied to me about my heritage, about where I belonged. And all I knew at that moment was anger.

I stormed over to the dresser and grabbed the box. Without thinking, I hurled it across the room.

I watched it slam into the wall with a loud crack. It shattered into a thousand tiny pieces and I instantly regretted what I'd done.

I fell to the floor among the pieces and began to sob, smearing the black kohl we had carefully applied to my eyes.

Archer paused, staring at the broken box. Disbelief and shock passed over her face. She remained unmoving for a moment before she stiffened, burying whatever emotion she felt. She fished through the shards, picking up a pink figuring that had snapped off from the base.

"I'm so sorry," I whispered. I shouldn't have acted so rashly, but I couldn't stop it. It felt like some dark and twisted thing had infected my heart. This wasn't me. "Archer," I said, waiting for a response.

She shook her head, her voice raising. "I know you're angry. I am too. We all are. I am beyond disgusted we have to follow his bidding and one day we'll fix that…but you can't just—you can't break down. Not right now." The anger subsided from her voice in a sigh. "We have to learn to live with it. It's the only way to survive."

She was right. She was always right.

I reminded myself that I wasn't the only one grieving, that I wasn't the only one who carried this pain. It was easy to forget as grief was often isolating.

She helped me to my feet and said, "We can clean up later. For now, let's try and have some fun."

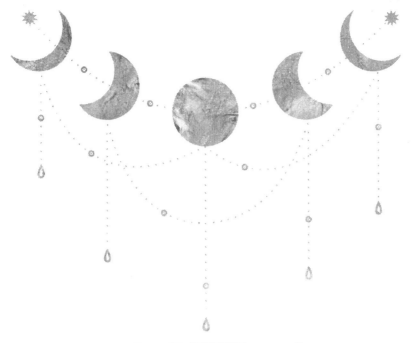

CHAPTER 42

Music floated down the long hallway. My hips swayed to the rhythm as we walked toward the throne room. The ball had already begun, and we were to make our grand entrance after King Tobias's speech.

His booming voice echoed out to the hall, droning on about the splendor and mercy of the Sun God, and how we should be eternally grateful to serve him. How Fynn had blessed our lands by becoming the Phoenix. That he would usher in an era of peace and harmony.

I tuned him out. Darkness swirled through my mind and urged me to run my sword through his gut, to watch the light leave his eyes. He deserved nothing less.

Fynn squeezed my hand, bringing me back. He would be the first to be recognized by the king but had requested we walk in together.

"You look beautiful tonight." He smiled. I should have felt my heart flutter at the comment, but it remained still.

"I have you to thank for that." I pulled back and gestured to my dress with my free hand, letting him admire the beauty of what he gifted me.

He looked me up and down, admiring my curvy figure in the dress, his eyes landing on the necklace at my throat. "Yes, the necklace is quite stunning on you. It matches you perfectly." It didn't, but I wouldn't say anything.

I touched the ruby. "Yes. But what about the dress?" I gestured once more, confused why he hadn't mentioned it and only the jewel on my neck.

His brows scrunched. "What about it?"

The doors opened, and the trumpets sounded, announcing our entrance. He stiffened, straightened his back, and wrapped his arm around mine, forcing me to do the same.

The crowd parted as we entered. My eyed immediately fell to Callax, seated next to his father. He couldn't be bothered to look at me and I wondered what I had done to erase the nights spent by my side. Perhaps I had imagined it.

Music continued softly in the background as we walked in a steady rythm to the foot of the throne. As cold as ever, King Tobias sat in his throne. To his right, the queen—whom I had never seen—and to the left, were his two sons. Only the younger looked like their mother.

Prince Callax Sundan sat slouched on his throne, legs spread, one hand gripping his thigh as the other propped his head up. His crown leaned ever so slightly to the side, his usual crispness and rigidity gone. He was the epitome of arrogance and as I approached, his eyes finally slid to mine. Something like hunger and rage filled them as he noted my arm wrapped up in Fynn's.

The king's voice boomed throughout the room as he stood, demanding attention. "Tonight, you will bear witness to the appointing of the most elite. These Fae before you have proven themselves worthy, not only of the titles of Lord and Lady, but as the Ira Deorum."

I was disgusted. I had once been hopeful—proud, even—to bear this title, to serve our king. But now…now I couldn't stand to look at him. To hear his voice. To see him still living, knowing he had killed my friend.

"Tonight, we honor them." His grin was wicked, full of sick joy, promising death and destruction to those who dare defy him.

Fynn let go of me and straightened his lapel as the king called him forward, first to be crowned.

A servant approached, carrying a red velvet cushion. On it sat a gold circlet, and on another lay one of the most beautiful swords I had ever seen. Strange power emanated from it and my stomach churned, a wave of nausea rolling through me. I felt dizzy, as if being near it was too much.

Fynn knelt on the step and bowed his head. King Tobias picked up the circlet and placed it atop his golden hair, crowning him as the Phoenix before the world.

He picked up the sword next. It shone brighter in his presence, as if it recognized him—his power.

The thought of my own blades, their fiery blue glow, flashed through my mind. They were opposite, yet so similar.

Holding out the sword reverently, the king presented it to Fynn. "What you see before you is the blade forged by the Sun God. The sunstone sword." He announced it triumphantly, and though his back was to me, I knew Fynn was grinning ear to ear.

I fought the continuing dizziness and watched as he sheathed it around his waist. The king offered him a place by his side and called me forward.

"Renata Orion, please step forward and take your rightful place in the Ira Deorum."

I grimaced. I knew he didn't mean it, but he couldn't let them know. He had given me my place on a technicality. One that Callax had fought for. I did not return his smile.

I swept my long skirts behind me, kneeling. The high slit in my dress threatened to expose the entire expanse of my leg.

His scent was sickly sweet, like fruit ripened to the point of rotting. Cool metal slid onto my head. He leaned lower, letting his hand press down hard, digging into my skin. Barely audible, he whispered, "If you can't manage to follow the rules, you will find that your sister will meet the same fate as your friend." He gestured for me to fall in line next to Fynn.

I shook with rage, clenching my fists to keep it in check. I wanted to explode—to unleash everything I kept buried inside—to rip out his throat and let his blood spill onto the carpet. It roared in my ears, begging to be set free, screaming for release.

But I obeyed, watching blankly as the rest of them were crowned.

Callax was the last to be crowned. He took of his ornate, princely one, and traded it for the simple circlet his father offered. I noted the detail on it as it fit snugly against his black hair. Two snakes intertwining gilded the front. It was similar to the realm's sigil, but with only flame between the snakes, not the sun.

The king motioned for us to stand before him. "Bow before the Ira Deorum, for they are the hand of the king, the blade of the Phoenix. The wrath of the gods."Obediently, they bowed before those who would forever be tasked to punish those who yearned for a better life.

"Let the dancing begin," the king shouted, and the crowd rose once more.

Fynn took my hand and led me to the dance floor.

I only knew the waltz well enough not to stumble over my feet as Fynn clumsily twirled me around the room. We hadn't said much to the other, too swept up in the dance to focus on anything else.

Fynn was a terrible dancer, barely moving in time. It was nearly comical that someone as imposing as him couldn't lead his partner. At the end, he landed on my foot and I held back a wince.

The next song picked up and I longed to dance, to forget my troubles and just disappear into the crowd. But Fynn said he didn't want to dance anymore, so we didn't.

Instead, he led me over to a group of gruff looking nobles with graying hair, and began conversing. He held my arm tightly in his, trapped to his side, parading me around like some pretty jewel he was afraid to lose.

I couldn't stand it any longer, so I excused myself. He nodded, barely acknowledging me as I did so. I made my way through the crowd and over to the side tables. I spotted Senna and Skye slowly rocking back and forth in the other's arms to the slow-paced music. It was a beautiful sight and my heart filled knowing they still had the other to rely on.

I turned, gasping as I slammed into a solid mass.

My eyes wandered over him. Broad shoulders draped in a fine black suit, lapels embroidered with silver threads concealing the body of a god beneath. Prince Callax Sundan stood before me.

Callax was well and truly a sight to behold, a prince of the realm, heir to the throne. He was beyond handsome. He was devastating. Regal. His dark hair brushed against the gold crown atop his head. His stunning, star-flecked eyes were as deep and endless as they had ever been.

I had to consciously stop myself from quaking in his presence. At the power that emanated from him.

His eyes lingered on my shoulders, where the silver wings wrapped around my shoulders, dipping to the curve of my breasts. He looked ravenous. Full of a hunger and desire I shied away from. No one had ever looked at me the way he did.

Slightly elongated canines flashed as he shook his head. "Gods above, that dress…" His voice was thick and hushed. "Miss Orion, you look absolutely divine."

I ignored his comment. The way it made my body heat. "No 'Realm of Day red' for the prince tonight?"

"No. It angers my father that I refuse to wear the horrid color. Especially on a night like tonight. Which is exactly why I did so."

"You wish to anger your father on purpose?" My brows rose. It didn't seem like the princely thing to do, but knowing more about him now, I understood why.

"Yes."

The music stopped, pausing briefly between songs. All eyes in the room fell on me as Callax bowed low, extending his hand as he looked up at me through dark lashes. "Dance with me."

Not a question, but a command.

I slid my hand into his. "If I must. I trust you know how?"

He drew our bodies close, placing his left hand on my waist. My breath hitched, electricity jolting through me as his fingers laced through mine, the hand on my back now laying flat across the bare expanse of skin.

I was tugged closer. Not by him, but by some invisible force, a threat winding its way around us, tying our bodies together.

The notes of the song rang high and clear, a violin singing above the orchestra, lifting my soul with its crescendo.

Callax's hands were commanding and clear. He knew what he was doing. He knew how to lead, how to drive me through the room. The music was our guide as it flowed through me and into him, connecting us. His eyes did not leave mine once as we danced in complete harmony.

He did not need to look away to know where he was going. Wherever we moved, the crowd cleared a path, and I simply followed his lead. We became a symphony of movement, my skirts billowing behind me, the silver of my wings glinting in the candlelight.

The music rose in a crescendo, horns blasting low and the strings high, building to a climax—a pinnacle of beauty and art. Callax threw my arm above my head, flinging me out in front of him in a frenzy of controlled spins. He was my center, and I danced under his touch. Free to become whatever I wished, like a bird in flight, and him the wind beneath my wings.

Round and round I went, my skirts flying behind me, the room blurring. The music rose and lifted, climaxing with an explosion of harmonies. My heart expanded inside my chest, the darkness retreating as it filled with light, basking in the attention we commanded.

I knew they were all watching, and I reveled in it.

The last note blared triumphantly. Callax pulled me back in, our eyes locking, wildness dancing through them as he dipped me low.

I arched my back into his reassuring embrace, my gown pooling like water on the floor. My chest heaved with exertion and I threw my arm over my head, fingers grazing the floor. I knew at that moment with complete certainty that even the king could not keep his eyes from me. From us. And I did not shy away.

We danced and dance, and I lost track of time. During the third, or fourth, or fifth dance, Callax finally spoke. "Leave him."

"What?" I gasped, unsure he said what I thought he had. This wasn't happening.

"Leave him. He doesn't deserve a second more of your time. Of your heart."

"What do you know of my heart?" I meant for the words to be harsh, but instead they were soft with disbelief.

He gripped me tight, his voice fervent. "I know it is good, that it is better than I ever imagined. That it is wasted on someone like Fynn."

"That is not your decision to make." I pulled back, still dancing, but placing distance between us.

"I see the way he treats you. The way he ignores you when he wishes until it suits his needs or you are of service to him. Even tonight he has yet to steal you away from me, knowing far too well what it means to dance at my side."

I shook my head, refusing to make sense of his words. "He's... he's busy. He has an important job."

"*Bullshit.* He doesn't care about you. He never has."

"He *does* care, Callax. I know he does. But it's none of your concern." It felt as I might be trying to convince myself more than him.

"It is my concern when I have to stand by and do nothing as I watch him drain the life from you day by day. Do you know what that's like? How agonizing it has been? How much control it takes to stand by and do *nothing*?"

"Control," I scoffed. "Do not talk to me of control when you throw yourself on top of me every chance you get."

He growled with frustration. "And why do you think that is? Don't act like you don't enjoy it. I saw how you reacted. I felt it, just as I can feel it now." He pulled me back to him, his lips brushing against the shell of my ear. "When I am near, your heart races. I can hear the small noises you make when I pull you close, the way your breath quickens and your eyes flutter like a hummingbird."

I swallowed, unable to deny it. It was true. Even now, my body reacted to him. Called to him, waiting for the moment he answered.

"It is your choice, as it has always been. But know that you deserve so much more." He turned to the side.

I couldn't read his face, and normally the thought of someone so territorial might make me irate, but dancing with Callax, being this close... I yearned to fix whatever this was between us. No one had ever made me feel this seen. This known.

"Maybe...maybe we can start with friends?" I asked, hopeful.

He snarled, and looked past my eyes into my soul, holding me tight within their depths. Yet with complete calm, and the utmost sincerity, he said, "I do not want to be your friend."

I pulled back, distancing our bodies as the dance continued. The words hurt more than I could have ever imagined.

"I want to be the ground you walk on. I want to worship at your feet and between your knees. I want to make you hum in anticipation from a single glance across a crowded room." My knees shook, and I gripped his arm for support as the room disappeared around us. "I want to be the one you trust and the one you turn to. I crave your body, I long for your mind, and I weep at your touch. If you let me, I am yours, Renata Orion. Body, mind, and soul."

There was a pounding in my chest, and my heart threatened to burst. He had never said my full name before. The way it rolled off his tongue nearly brought me to my knees.

"If you'll have me, I would paint the heavens with your wrath and bring the kingdom to its knees before you. But he..." He glanced to Fynn, hatred gleaming in those beautiful blue eyes. "He would rather watch you burn along with it for the sake of glory. The choice is yours. So choose wisely."

I dropped his hand, and it lingered in the air between us. Empty. Waiting.

I was shaking as I stuttered. "Callax, I—" The memory of being pressed against the wall, his thumb on my lip, every stolen glance and moment shared between us... But also the cruel words and constant pressure. It was too much.

I took a step back and knocked into Fynn. I was thankful for the interruption.

I left Callax standing where he was, hand still outstretched, supporting the empty space I left behind.

Fynn wrapped his arms around my waist, noticing that I was visibly shaken. "Is everything alright?"

I nodded unconvincingly, unable to form words as we swayed together in time to the song. I rested my head on his chest and forced my ragged breath to calm. But there was something off about the way my head felt against his chest. It used to fit perfectly, like it had been made for me, but now it only felt cold and unwelcome.

The unanswered question between us burned through my mind. I pulled back and looked into his amber eyes. "Thank you for the dress," I said, trying to ease my mind.

He scrunched his brows in confusion. "The dress?" He stared down at it. "It looks lovely, but I only got the necklace." He nodded to my neck where the ruby burned a hole straight into my breaking heart.

"Right. My mistake." The already formed cracks in my heart began to spread. And I watched, utterly helpless, as the walls of a home we had built together crumbled around me.

We finished the dance in silence. When it was over, he pulled me back toward the males from before. "Enough dancing. I want to speak with a few other nobles from the north. The king and I are working to form new alliances for labor trades and—" I drowned him out, my mind leaving my body, traveling far away.

He hadn't gotten the dress for me. It shouldn't have bothered me, but it was the one bright spot in a very long week. It was carefully thought out, made to fit me exactly, to complement my skin and hair. So much thought and effort had gone into it, and if it wasn't him...then who?

My next thought was Callax, the feel of his hands on my bare skin and the words he had confessed. My heart lurched at the thought.

No. It couldn't have been him.

He would rather watch you burn along with it for the sake of glory.

I didn't want to believe it. Refused to.

I snapped back into my body and pulled my hand from his. "Fynn. I need to ask you something." He paused, hesitating at the demand in my voice, but he nodded. "I know it sounds impractical, but be honest. If it came down to it, me your duty as the Phoenix—to the realm and the king—which would you choose?"

His laugh was a punch to the gut. "Where is this nonsense coming from? What has gotten into you?"

"Answer the question." The room spun despite remaining still.

He threw his hands up in exasperation. "Renata, you know the answer. You know my duty is to the realm as the Phoenix. You know what that entails. You can't possibly think I would give that up."

There it was. The answer I knew he would give, but dreaded nonetheless. The weight of the world crashed around me, and I wanted to collapse.

He reached for my hand as if nothing changed. "Come on, let's get back to the party."

But I couldn't. I pulled away, disgusted at the thought of letting him touch me again. "Fynn, stop." Tears formed in my eyes as I finally realized what I wanted. Who I wanted. And it wasn't the golden-eyed Phoenix before me.

I had lost myself, and I wanted her back.

I had given myself to him so entirely I had forgotten who I was. I disregarded everyone in my life in search of his approval. I love him…but love wasn't supposed to feel like this.

It wasn't supposed to be this painful and demanding.

I tried to make myself fit—bent my pieces until they were beyond repair, and still…they did not fit. Still, it was not enough.

How much more would I have to break before he saw how I had torn myself to shreds to be worthy of his love?

No matter what I did, no matter how I begged and pleaded, I could not make him love me.

I finally broke. "I can't…I can't do this anymore. I'm done, Fynn. *We're done.*"

I shook my head and backed away. I needed to get out of there. I was suffocating.

He reached for me, but I held up my hands, placing a barrier between us. I knew deep down this had been coming for some time, but I had been too afraid to face it.

Somewhere along the way I buried myself in broken dreams and drowned in the pain of unrequited love. He had promised me a life together, and I tried to chase it. But his words dripped sweet like honeysuckle lies.

The heart was a fickle thing, and mine had broken.

I stood in front of the one person I thought I loved more than anything and realized that while he was my sun, I was his shadow. I was not enough for him. I never would be.

He held up a finger, pointing it at me. "You can't leave me. We are fated for each other, and you know this." A new kind of anger painted his face—a silent, hurtful rage.

But I only shook my head as I turned and ran, my gown trailing behind me.

CHAPTER 43

(Please be aware that this chapter contains mention of attempted sexual assault. If this triggers you or believe it may trigger you, please skip this chapter.)

I caught Archer's gaze as I stormed out of the throne room, away from the dancing and merriment. She was dancing with Kaede.

"Where are you going?" she asked, placing her hands on my arm. I paused, wiping the tear that fell from the corner of my eye, trying to hide my emotions, wanting her to spend her night here enjoying what she could with our friends. But being the ever-attentive sister she was, she noticed. "What's wrong? Is everything okay?"

I painted on a fake smile, trying to hide my disappointment. "I'm fine." I rubbed her hand and took it from my arm. "I'm just tired. I'm going to go to bed and call it a night."

"Oh, thank the gods, I am so done with this already." She looked relieved and leaned in, whispering with a grin. "Kaede may be handsome, but he is not a good dancer…I can tell you that." I sniffled through a laugh, caught off guard by her humor. "Wait here. Let me tell him we're leaving, and I'll come with."

"Are you sure?"

"Please, you're saving me." Her look told me as much, and she disappeared back into the crowd to find Kaede. Across the room, Soren and Caldor stared me down with a strange look on their faces, like they were predators and I the prey. I was instantly uncomfortable.

"Okay, I'm ready, let's go," she said, and I couldn't have been more excited to slip out of the beautiful dress into my robe and curl up in bed with Archer.

From behind, I heard someone call out my name, it sounded like Callax, but I wasn't in the mood to speak anymore. I ignored it and continued with Archer instead.

Relief swept over me as we exited the throne room. I took a deep breath, feeling lighter already. Once we were around the corner, I stopped and pulled Archer in close, needing a moment of familiarity and reprieve. She leaned into the moment and wrapped her arms around me, pulling me in tight. I could feel my heart find Archer's steady rhythm and mimic it, connecting us.

I loved her so much. So much that it hurt sometimes, though I hadn't always expressed it to her. I needed to. I wanted her to know I would be here for her. That I wouldn't leave her, and I would be there no matter what came for us. I was her older sister. That's what we did. She was too precious for the cruelty of the world.

"I love you so much," I whispered into her hair and breathed in her fresh lilac and jasmine scent. I wished I could wrap her up and protect her.

"I know," her voice cracked with emotion. "I love you too. Just promise you'll never leave me."

"I promise. I will always be there for you."

I wiped a tear from her cheek and held out my finger. "Pinky swear."

She grinned and held up hers, intertwining it in mine. "'Til the Night rises?" she asked.

I nodded and kissed our hands.

"'Til the Night rises."

We walked lazily down the hallway, winding our way back to my room. A brush of air wound its way up my bare spine, and my hair stood on edge. I hesitated. Something was wrong. I couldn't quite explain it, but I pulled Archer close, and she stopped.

"What is it?"

I shook my head, convinced I was being paranoid, "Nothing, I just thought—" The words died in my throat as a rough hand pulled me away, and I watched in slow horror as they ripped Archer from my arms. Her screams echoed in my ears, the sound forever burned into my memory.

Without thought, I lunged for her, grasping through the shadows of the darkened hall to find her. To bring her back to me. But she was out of reach.

Two sets of firm hands grabbed my wrists, slamming me against the wall. My head cracked against the rough stone with a sickening sound. My vision blurred, and I tried to shake my head to clear it, but it didn't work. The musky scent of a male wafted through my nose and filled my senses. It took a minute to recognize the sick scent. Caldor.

There was another, but I couldn't place his scent or see his face.

The torches lining the halls were almost nonexistent in the late hour of the night, and shadows danced around the other male's face. I couldn't place him, no matter how hard I squinted. I screamed, thrashing against their arms. My head pounded.

There was a loud crunch, and Soren swore from across the hall, "Shit. You nasty little bitch, you broke my nose." I heard Archer spit in his face, and I welled with pride. Good, she was fighting back.

"Leave her alone," I screamed. The sound ripped through my chest with a deepening growl. Low laughter and the sound of bone smashing against stone filled my ears. I winced, unable to tell in the dizzying darkness what was happening.

I screamed again, my throat raw with the noise, and pulled against the hands restraining me. I kicked out to the side, trying to hit anything. But Caldor and the unknown one twisted my wrists behind me, forcing me to my knees. My teeth bit down on my tongue, and blood welled in my mouth. I tried to move, but the angle of my arms made it nearly impossible.

I had to get us out of here. I couldn't let them hurt her.

Soren prowled from the shadows, dragging Archer by the hair. She fell limp, and blood trickled from the wound on the side of her head. A primal instinct flared to protect her at all cost. Rage ignited through me, lighting my senses and setting me on fire. I wanted to tear his throat open, to feel his bones break under my hands. I stared at him with all the malice I could muster, but with my pounding head and aching arms, there was only so much I could rally.

A deep rumble of laughter rippled through his chest, and he threw Archer to the floor. She lay still. Unmoving. I bared my teeth.

"Why so angry?" Soren leaned down, running his hand along my face and neck. I snapped at him and bit down, latching onto the tip of his finger. I tasted blood as my head snapped to the side.

"You bitch, you'll learn your place. You and your pretty little sister."

Red flashed in my vision, and I spat in his face. He wiped it away, trailing blood from his bitten finger onto his cheek. The acrid smell of alcohol wafted from his breath, and I bit back the urge to vomit.

"You know," he whispered, utterly void of the anger from a moment before. "You used to be off limits when you belonged to the Phoenix."

"I belong to nobody."

He smirked. "After that little show you put on—flirting with the prince, then publicly breaking it off with Fynn—looks like those rules don't apply anymore." I watched in disgust as his eyes wandered around my neck to my heaving chest and then farther down to the high slit in my dress. His eyes flared with lust and greed, and underneath my anger, I was scared.

I had never experienced a male other than Fynn. And even then, he was my first and only. I dared not think of the horrendous and cruel things Soren had in mind as his eyes roamed greedily over my restrained body.

He stood and nodded to Caldor and the other. They obeyed his silent command and twisted, pulling me to my feet. Pain roared through my shoulder, down to my wrist, and a small cry of pain escaped my lips. I was terrified. My heart raced and fear crept in, stiffening every muscle in anticipation.

Run, move, fight, do something. I screamed at myself, but it didn't matter. I was paralyzed from the terror.

Fight, damn it. But again, nothing.

My arms splayed to the side, forced back against the wall. I watched in horror as his hands roamed down my neck to my low-cut top, his fingers tracing the seam of the dress. My heart pounded in my chest, threatening to tear it open. Terror seeped into every part of me, weighing me down. I couldn't fight off all of them. I was utterly helpless.

If I stayed still enough, it would be over soon.

I could scream, but I feared what might happen to Archer if I did. If I broke free, there was no way I could take her with me, her limp body making a quick getaway impossible. So instead, I remained still, vacating my mind from my body, attempting to feel as little as possible.

His hand continued down past my navel, trailing along my hips until he found the slit in my dress. I cursed myself for not strapping a dagger on earlier, hiding it under my gown.

For a brief moment, his hand left my body. I sighed with short lived relief before he pulled me in close, pressing himself forcefully against me. I tried to tear away from his massive body, but there was no point. The other two held me back, my shoulders straining in their sockets, threatening to pop.

I turned away, closing my eyes. It would easier if I couldn't see. But his fingers gripped my face and squeezed, pressing my teeth into my cheek. He forced me to meet his dark stare. There was nothing but cruelty in his eyes. He wanted to hurt me. To make me suffer. And I was going to let him. As long as Archer remained untouched, I would allow him to do as he pleased.

"When I'm done with you, your sister is next. No one will hear you scream as I make you watch. Your plea for mercy will make it all the more enjoyable." Blood ran down hi face from his broken nose, staining his teeth.

Rage boiled inside my blood. I could handle whatever he threw my way, but knowing he had no intention of leaving her alone drove me over an edge I didn't know I had.

"I will kill you," I spat. My breathing became ragged, all control slipping from my body. Flames flowed through my veins and I didn't bother to suppress them. I would use anything I could to my advantage, to keep their filthy hands from my innocent sister.

I wanted to break every finger, remove their hands so they could never touch another female again, and then burn them all to ash.

Behind them, Archer stirred. Her eyes shone with terror as she sat up, finally awake.

"GO," I shouted, flinging my head toward the stairs behind her. She shook her head, but again I yelled. "GO. NOW!" This time, she listened.

Screams pierced the air from the two males, as the scent of burning flesh filled my senses. Soren backed up in surprise, too shocked at what had happened to realize Archer was getting away.

I focused my energy into my legs, pulling back and kicking high and hard until my foot slammed into his chest. His head slammed into the wall with force and he crumpled to the ground. He wasn't out cold, but he clutched his head, blood pouring down the side.

Behind him, I could barely make out the blurry figures of Caldor and the other male, making their way down the hall, clutching their burnt hands. But watching with satisfaction as they ran cost me precious time.

Soren's fist slammed into my cheek, his rings cutting into the edge of my eye. Pain shot through my head once again, and I spat blood.

I swung, aiming my fist up and under his chin, ignoring the bark of pain in my shoulders. I put all the power I had left into it, channeling whatever power remained in my veins. It flowed through me at will, pouring into my hands. I swore my veins glowed as my fist made contact.

Cold, blue flames roared to life over my skin. It burned his face as he screamed.

In shock, I pulled back, and the flames died with it. But it had done enough damage.

He looked to me in horror, clutching his smoking face. "You'll pay for this," he hissed.

But I was already running. My foot hit the stairs and I only made it up one flight before I tripped. I could barely see, my eye nearly swollen shut and I knew I wouldn't make it back to my room. It was too far. But I couldn't stay here, bloodied and broken.

I looked up and recognized the crimson banners and ornate doors I had stumbled upon only once before. I leaned against the wall for support, my body broken and exhausted. Using those flames had sapped my remaining strength and I collapsed to the floor. I crawled the rest of the way, stumbling until I found the door.

I prayed I would be safe here.

CHAPTER 44

Everything was a blur.

The safety of the shadows gave me permission to let my tears fall. I couldn't think straight, and I knocked into a large tub sitting in the corner of his bathing room.

A bath.

Clean.

Clean water.

Wash it off.

My thoughts pieced together in string of words. There was no cohesion in the shattering of my mind. I wasn't strong enough.

The only thing keeping me together was knowing it hadn't been Archer who he touched. The invisible weight of his rough hands lingered against my bruised skin. Dried blood still caked to my palms and I didn't know whose it was.

The water was cold and stale, but it was clean. I wanted—no, needed—to wash off the stain of their touch.

I peeled off my torn gown, the fabric falling into ribbons on the floor. I braced my arms against the raised edge, but they shook. It took everything I had to keep from collapsing back to the floor.

I was vaguely aware of a door being thrown open, but I didn't care. Let them find me. I hadn't the strength to even keep myself upright.

I began to collapse when strong arms hooked under mine, and lifted. Gently—cautiously—they helped me step into the cold water. The shock of the temperature sent me into violent shivers, but the cold was barely noticeable.

I stared vacantly at my knees, barely registering anything happening around me. There was a blur of movement and a fire crackled to life. A pail scooped out the cold water, replacing it with the heated ones.

I was a prisoner in my body. The droning buzz of my empty mind echoed throughout me. My violent shivers slowed as I relaxed into the now warm water.

I slipped below the surface.

The peaceful oblivion was a weight of comfort. The searing in my lungs echoed the pain in my mind, melding into one until I couldn't tell where one ended and the other began.

I was drowning, and I didn't care.

I let the water rush over my head, abdicating to the dark weight of its silence.

Firm hands pulled me from the water. I gasped as air filled my burning lungs and I broke from my trance.

I started to cry.

Violent, soul-racking sobs.

My head hit my knees as I curled into a ball so tight that even with the hot water and lavender salts, my muscles protested. I continued to sob and wail as the gentle hands dipped a cloth into the water and softly scrubbed my bloody and bruised body. The faint smell of tobacco and vanilla broke through the scented salts of the tub.

Water ran over my back, down the sides of my arms, and eventually my hands as he washed me clean. I should have pulled away. The thought of being touched was enough to make me sick, but something deep inside, some instinct I was unaware of, told me I was safe with this stranger. That I need not worry.

The hands dipped mine into the water and scrubbed the blood from under my nails. When they were clean, free from any remainder of the assault, they were placed back on my legs.

Warmth rolled over my head. Whoever was here gently lathered soap into it, massaging my hair and rinsing it out again and again.

After a few minutes, I was clean. Or, I assumed I was, as I had yet to lift my head from my knees.

Footsteps registered somewhere in my mind as heavy feet shuffled in. "My prince, we—"

"Get out," he growled, a low rumble ripping through his chest. I had never heard a noise so protective—aggressive. "Find the sister and make sure she is sent to a healer. Make sure they're all okay."

The door clicked shut.

Softly, his hands wrapped under my arms and pulled me up. One hand guided my leg over the edge, the other draping my arm across broad shoulders. A robe wrapped around my body as he guided my arms through the sleeves, then secured my wet hair into a towel.

Blankets and pillows lined his bed and he let go for only a moment to arrange them into a nest of warmth and comfort, like they might somehow shield me from the world. He let me fall into it, my head laying against the soft pillows.

A soft body curled up against my back. My sobs were less violent now, only silent continuous tears instead. He tucked a stray piece of hair behind my ear and up into the towel. A deep, protective growl resonated in his chest. "Who did this to you?" he asked. "I will rip out the throat of whoever dared touch you."

He waited for my answer, but I couldn't form the words, his name acid on my tongue.

Instead, I curled up as small as I could, wanting to disappear. The world was closing in, and I wanted to feel as little of it as possible.

I let my mind float away, unable to handle the racing thoughts any longer.

Cold glass was held to my lips, a vial tipping back. I drank the liquid, not caring what it was, greedy for anything other than this misery. He stroked my face, quieting me with a soft whisper of my name repeated over and over again.

It didn't take long until, blissfully, consciousness left me, and I drifted off into the welcoming embrace of oblivion.

Flashes of cruel faces. Of hands wandering my body—pain and horror—played through my mind as I thrashed around, trying to escape them.

I woke with a start, and screamed.

I screamed and screamed, wailing into the night. Hands wrapped around my arm, and I flung out, making contact with whatever was close to me. Touching me.

The blue light emanating from my arms allowed me to see strong cheekbones shadowed by dark curls.

"It's me," he whispered. "You're safe." He held his hands up and away. "I'm here," he said, showing his intentions were not to harm, not to violate. He backed off the bed and stood some ways away, allowing me space to breathe.

Memories of that night came rushing back, reminding me it was not him I should be afraid of. I nodded and settled back against the headboard, permitting him to crawl back next to me. I should have been afraid, but some hidden part of me trusted him.

Now awake, unable to hide from the horrors of the world in my sleep, it all returned in a crashing wave. My breath quickened into sharp, pained gasps as my chest collapsed inward, suffocating me.

No, no, no. I can't do this. I can't.

Pain wrapped its greedy claws around my neck and squeezed. I couldn't think, couldn't breathe. Air caught in my throat, and I sat there, clutching at my heart, clawing at it, wanting to rip its wretched hold from my body.

It was a tidal wave of grief, and pain, and sorrow. Of hopelessness. Everything was too much. I was feeling too much.

Fynn, Emryn, Archer, my family, Anya, and countless unnamed others. Gone, or dead, or betrayed, or lied to.

No, no, no.

I can't. I can't. I can't.

The words raced through my mind as I struggled to breathe. Heaving sobs came up empty as I gasped for air. I was suffocating from the pain. It grabbed me in a chokehold, and threatened to snuff out whatever strength—whatever life force—I had left.

I didn't know how much more I could take before I shattered beyond repair.

My breath racked my body as I heaved. Emotions ripped through me and built to a pressure I could no longer stand. The impossible task of breathing took all my focus.

I curled into a ball so tight there was no way I'd ever be able to relax again.

My hands didn't know what to do, felt foreign on my own body, so I ran them through my hair, clenching tight and pulling. It brought me back to my body, allowing for a new avenue for the pain to follow. But it did little to fix it. So I dug my nails into my head as I rocked back and forth, my breath returning in another pained sob.

Make it stop, make it stop, make it stop.

I can't, I can't, I can't.

It was an endless loop. Those words repeated over and over until there was nothing left.

I must have muttered them aloud because Callax pulled me closer and onto his lap, settling me between his legs. "Oh gods, I'm so sorry." His soft plea was unbearable. "I should have been there, I should have followed you."

His empathy was too much.

My nails dug into my scalp, tearing my skin. Warmth pooled at my fingertips and I knew I was bleeding.

"I'm here," he said. "I'm here, I'm here, I'm here."

His words began to replace mine, his tender hand wiping my tears. He held me for a long while. Not asking me to stop, not telling me I would be okay, but simply holding me. He seemed to know what I needed without asking, and all I wanted was to curl up and fade into the blackness of the night.

Hands caressed my head as he gently removed my fingers from the bloody mess. "I'm here. I will not leave you. Never again." The words pierced a hole in my already torn heart. "I will *always* be here for you."

I wanted his words to comfort me. I wanted to be consoled by them, knowing that he made sure Archer was safe, that he was taking care of me and I made it despite the odds. But none of it mattered.

Nothing mattered anymore.

I wanted to fade away. To let the darkness consume me. I was from the Realm of Night—a daughter of the darkness—so let me return to it. Let me embrace it.

Fire flared once more under my skin and I wailed at the agony, of its fight to be free. Callax pulled me close, my head resting against his chest, and held me tight, trying to calm me.

Over my shrieks of agony, I could feel his shaking cries.

He was crying with me. For me.

"What can I do? What do you need?" He sounded frantic, like my pain was his. Like every emotion racing through me passed down that thread and into his heart.

All I could manage was a strangled cry. "Make it stop."

He was shaking. "Let it go." His voice was barely more than a whisper, but it was a command. He held tight. "Let it go, Renata. Turn it all off."

His words gave me silent permission for the relief I sought. It comforted me in ways other words could not.

The overwhelming outpour of emotions faded in the wake of his darkness.

It rose then, shadows fighting against the light my flames. It was a strange, new sensation, but the shadows beckoned to me, reaching.

I let it build, adding layer after layer, using it as a cloak to shroud the pain in my heart. I will them into a wall, a fortress of obsidian so thick nothing could break through. Without question, they obeyed.

I embraced the darkness like an old friend. It flooded over me, and my sobs stilled.

Callax, still rubbing his hand over my hair, ebbed into the background as every emotion faded away. One by one. Replaced with nothingness.

This was better. This was easier. I couldn't handle the pain anymore...so I wouldn't. I wouldn't feel anything at all.

A light flickered, a dying ember of a once warm flame, finally snuffed out. And it was in the darkness that I could finally see.

I need not fear the dark, for I was the dark.

Callax relaxed beneath me, my breaths finally even. "Fate may have dealt you its hand, but you alone are free to choose your path."

For once, I listened.

I followed their rules and they called me complacent. I broke them, and they murdered my friend. But one thing they'll never call me again...is weak.

Whatever cord tethered me to my emotions was severed by the vicious shadows that solidified around my heart. There was an emptiness there instead. I could see the pain inside, but I felt...nothing. No more heartache, or loss, or grief, or sorry. Only anger and rage.

So much rage.

CHAPTER 45

I felt lighter than air.

I raised my hands above my head and leaned into the stretch, arching my back and yawning loudly. The morning light streamed through the windows, bringing a smile to my face as it warmed my skin. I turned to my side and was slightly surprised to see Callax, still fully clothed, lying next to me. I brushed my finger against his nose, and his eyes snapped open.

"Good morning, dear prince," I chirped. Both brows raised. "Care to explain what you're doing in my bed?"

He looked slightly concerned as confusion warped his handsome face. "Do you not remember what happened last night?" He propped himself up on one elbow, looking down on me. Flashes of the night before flickered through my mind, but there was no hurt, or shame, or fear. Instead, all I felt was anger. But I pushed it down, making a note to deal with it later.

"Right, that…yes, I suppose I do."

He continued to study my face, and leaned back, skeptical. "Are you okay?" he asked. "You seem…different."

"Never better." I looked around and realized I was wrong. He wasn't in my room, I was in his. And in his bed, no less. I shrugged. "Well, I best be going, then. Wouldn't want to miss breakfast."

I untied the robe he had put on me and let it fall to the ground, baring the entirety of my backside to him. I picked up one of his tunics that lay strewn across his chair. I turned, holding it up. "I'm sure you don't mind, do you?" I didn't wait for his response before sliding it over my head, barely grazing mid-thigh.

When I turned back, picking up my torn dress from the floor, I smiled and winked. He stared, confused and open-mouthed, at my brazenness. I liked seeing him like this, at a loss for words.

I only waved over my shoulder as I closed the door behind me.

I knocked on Archer's door and peeked inside, not waiting for a response. She sat upright and launched toward me. She had a bandage lining the side of her hairline, and I grunted in surprise at the strength of her hug. I was still bruised and sore, but I let her embrace me.

"Good morning to you too," I chuckled. I pulled her away and held her shoulders, inspecting her to make sure she was all in one piece. "Are you okay?" I asked. She nodded, waving her hand in dismissal.

"Don't fuss about me. Are you okay? You made me leave, and I went to get help and found Kaede. I explained what happened, and he went after them, and I searched for a while for you, but finally a guard found me and told me you were with the prince and that you were safe. And what are you wearing?"

I smiled at her rambling concern. She often did that when she was nervous. "I'm fine, I promise. In fact, I feel great." She looked taken aback, but it was true. I did feel great. Better than I had in a long time.

"How?" she asked, rubbing her wrists absently.

I shrugged. "I just turned it all off."

"Off?" What does that mean?"

"I just can't be bothered with all the woes of the heart and all that nonsense. It's easier to deal with things when I'm not constantly worried about repercussions. Like breaking things off with Fynn or all the stuff from last night."

"But enough with that. I feel great, and I'm going to kill those fuckers that hurt you, and that's all that matters. Ready for breakfast?" She gave me a strange look, but didn't push it. I patted her on the shoulder reassuringly. "We've got a bit meeting today, and if I'm not going to be tempted to open a window and toss myself out, or murder the twins in broad daylight, I'm going to need some food."

"You can't just kill them. They're the king's lackeys. He'll kill you too."

"Let me deal with that. For now, let's focus on breakfast."

She shook her head, still unsure how to handle this improved version of my myself. But she finally agreed and I headed back to my room to change.

A new uniform lay neatly folded on my bed. Now that we were officially the Ira Deorum and no longer in training, we had been given upgrades. Not just to our rooms, but to our clothes and status as well.

I buckled the straps around my waist, securing my weapons and noticed the new insignia around my left arm. Branding me. I brushed the lint from my top and held back the snarl that came from the sight of the large sun across my arm. I would remove it soon enough. If I had my way, I would never have to see that symbol again.

Grabbing my usual black boots from beside my dresser, something crunched beneath my foot, jabbing into the soft skin. I winced and pulled away, looking to see what was there.

Shards of intricately designed wood lay scattered over the floor. I remembered then that I had thrown the music box across the room in anger. I shook my head in disbelief at my actions, ashamed I let myself become so encompassed by unchecked emotions.

I began cleaning up the pieces, not wanting to leave the mess for later. Part of me felt like I should be sad about this, that I lost one of the few ties to my parent's and had cost that same loss for Archer. She would care about it, so I would see what I could do about getting a replica made for her. But nothing else rose in my heart. It was…peaceful, almost.

The base had stayed mostly intact, but as I set it aside, I noticed a large crack splitting the bottom panel in two, revealing the gears of the music box beneath. I stared into the fragments of the remaining mirror laid in the center and looked at my reflection. There was something new within my cobalt eyes. Flames flickered beneath the surface, reminding me of how Fynn's had looked whenever he used his powers. But I blinked, and they were gone.

A strange sliver of white, just inside the broken pieces, caught my attention. I brought it closer, inspecting it. There was something tucked inside.

I braced my hands on either side of the solid piece of wood and brought it down on my knee with a snap. I placed the two parts on the dresser and picked up the small envelope that had fallen to the ground.

There was familiar handwriting on the front. One I never thought I'd see again. It only said, 'Renata' across the front. It was my father's handwriting. The way the R curved below the E in a flawless hook made me realize I should have caught on long ago that he had to have been raised with a good education, and not lived his life as a lumber worker as he claimed.

I opened the letter.

My darling girl,

If you are reading this, then your mother and I were never never able to tell you of our honored heritage. We always feared something might happen to us, and we should have told you long ago, but know that we only wanted you to have a normal life. One free of responsibility and the weight of our past.

We loved our home in Asterion, but we knew that if we stayed, you would be burdened with a life you didn't ask for. We brought you into this world against all warnings not to. You deserve to have a choice, to have a life before everything changes.

We knew one day you would come into your own and learn to harness your powers, but we hoped that being far away from the Realm of Night might dampen them. Might give us more time. But that wasn't the case.

You expressed signs of your powers at such a young age, despite never going through the rituals we assumed necessary to access them. From the beginning you have defied all the rules and made them your own. You have always been headstrong and that will serve you well in the years to come.

My darling girl, you come from a long line of powerful Fae. Asterion is home to many who have honed their affinities from the old gods. Your mother and I among them. She was a strong healer, and I fell in love with her when we were young. I was high ranking in the legions, a soldier just like my namesake, but we were not allowed to be together. It had been forbidden long ago for the Orion line and any descendant of the original rulers or Moon Fae to bond. Their potential offspring was prophesied by the Matron to be volatile, full of darkness and power that had been held back for thousands of years since the Dark Phoenix herself.

But your mother and I hid our love, and knew if we were to be discovered we would be forced apart. We kept it secret for years, stealing every moment we could. I took a job in another court and she moved around for me, to be with me at all times. We had already confessed to her family, they had known for a while, and when finally they convinced us to approach the Obsidian Council so we might be together publicly, we discovered she was pregnant.

We were terrified, but beyond ecstatic. We knew we couldn't keep it a secret any longer, but because of you, they could never force us apart. You saved us.

When the council realized your mother was pregnant, they were furious. But since we were mated and with child, they permitted us to remain together under the condition we gave you over to them after the birth. We were allowed to stay with you, to raise you, but you would be educated and controlled by the council.

We tried to find a way out, but there was none. So we agreed.

The Lunar Priory looked after your mother, ensured everything went smoothly, but the council wanted answers as to what you would be. How strong you might become and how much they had to fear.

They could tell you were a reincarnation even before you were born, but the future was uncertain, unpredictable. Your birth would usher in a new era of power and peace, or it would shroud the world in great darkness, bringing about the end of the Night as we knew it.

From the moment you were born, they wanted to subject you to training.

They wanted to oversee every step, every food you ate. They were going to hone you into a weapon to use against the Realm of day.

We knew King Tobias was bound to discover you one day and send his legions after us. He was crafty enough that it was likely he might even find a way through the wards and slaughter us all. You included. But we didn't want that future for you.

We already loved you so much. We didn't want you to be molded into a weapon without choice. You would have to decide one day when you came into your powers, but you were only a child. It was too much.

So, your mother and I fled. We knew your powers would flourish in Asterion, and it was our hope that they would be dampened if we left, until you were ready to face the truth. We also hoped that living within enemy territory would hide us from the king, as he would not be smart enough to look for a child of the night within his own lands.

But we realized as you matured, that your powers had manifested without the usual rituals. Anytime you became angry, or upset, or frightened, fires would start. They were small at first, easily disguised, but they continued to grow with you. Sometimes, you would light your blankets on fire while in your dreams. We became concerned and reached out to old friends. We rode to Alynta and dispatched letters to Asterion, hoping someone could offer help, but we never heard back.

I know this may be scary and overwhelming, but this is who you are. You are the Reincarnation. The only reincarnation of Astera Renata—the Dark Phoenix. The only one to exist, besides you.

She is your namesake, and names hold power. You are the rebirth, the renewal. Your full name, Renata Orion, means the rebirth of a warrior. And one day, if you choose, the Realm of Night will be yours to rule and protect. You alone have the power to claim this birthright.

Do not fear what you are. Embrace it. Nurture it. Use it to keep your family safe. Regardless of this responsibility, you are and always will be our daughter—my little Phoenix.

Your mother and I love you and your siblings so much. It is our wish for you to take your fate into your own hands.

'Til the Night rises once more.

—*Cassius and Claudia, your loving parents*

The letter nearly fell from my hands as my mind reeled.

All the accidental fires, including the one that killed my parents, were caused by me. All because I couldn't keep my panic under control. Questions swirled in my mind, and I wished more than ever that my parents or Cyrus were still alive.

I folded the letter and looked at the symbol sealed in the wax—the sigil of the Realm of Night. I could see it clearly now, the symbol of the Dark Phoenix. Of me.

No. I shook my head. It wasn't true. It couldn't be. If I was the Dark Phoenix, I would have been able to save Emryn, and I could have beaten Soren and Caldor in the hall before his hands stained my body.

I hid the letter under my pillow, not wanting anyone to see it. I would tell Archer later. She deserved to know since this affected her as well, but it would have to wait until after the meeting.

I finished lacing up my boots and returned to fetch my sister. She was putting the last of her daggers into her belt and noticed the two additional ones strapped to each thigh and one against each ankle. She looked at them, then at me, and we exchanged a knowing glance. We knew why we wore our weapons outwardly. Never again would we be caught defenseless. "Come on, let's go," I said. "I want to eat the good food before its all taken."

CHAPTER 46

The war room was silent save for the sound of scraping chairs as everyone adjusted themselves, waiting for the king. Each side of the table was set with six chairs, with one at the head of the table.

Kaede, who sat next to Archer, had a fading black eye and his knuckles were swollen and angry. He gave me a once over to make sure I was alive, but returned back to his sullenness. I have him a nod, silently thanking him for whatever he had done last night to ensure Archer's safety. We may not be on speaking terms after Emryn, but I was thankful. I owed him for that.

The back door flung open and Soren and Caldor walking in, Kell right behind them. In the back of my mind, I wondered if Kell had been the other male in the hall. The three were typically together, and Kell their lapdog.

I narrowed my eyes and raised my brow at their audacity to walk in with heads held high. I might not have reacted emotionally like I used to, but they would pay—one way or another.

They sat across the table from me, the only open seats left. I had arranged it that way on purpose, arriving early to make sure the other seats were taken. The bruises around Soren's nose were still healing, an angry red burn running along his jaw. Caldor had bandages around his wrist, and a few new scratches and bruises covered all three, thanks to Kaede.

They hesitantly met my stare, assessing. I raised my brow and let a wicked, rueful smile cross my face before leaning forward and winking.

When Caldor flinched, instinctively moving his wrists, I laughed. The room stilled. "I wish I could say it's a pity your face was ruined, Soren, but...I'm not in the habit of lying."

Skye choked on her water, covering her mouth. Pyne and Mavenna narrowed their eyes, but remained silent.

Oh, I was going to enjoy this. Even if I wasn't planning on using whatever gifts I had, I would make sure they knew what I was capable of. When they died, I wanted to make sure they felt ever second of it.

I leaned back in my chair, rocking it onto the rear legs, placing my boots on the table. Callax walked in just then, seating himself next to me. He scooted closer and leaned in. "Are you good?"

I leaned back farther, angling toward him. "Never better." I put both hands behind my head, settling in the chair.

"Okay," he said unconvincingly. "You just seem...different today." He nodded to the bruises still marring my cheeks and hands, but I ignored it.

"Is that a bad thing?"

He smiled. "No. I like the confidence, it suits you."

The doors opened once more, and in walked he King, Fynn right behind him like the obedient boy he was. We all rose as the king took his seat.

I turned to Callax and teased, "Does daddy have a new favorite?"

Callax scowled, rolling his eyes. He kicked my leg under the table.

I stifled a laugh, the king finding my interruption less than amusing. He stared me down and I simply leaned forward, resting my arms on the table, and stared back. My face was bored and expressionless, but I held his gaze unwaveringly. Daring him to test me.

Now that I had this secret, I had no reason to fear the king. I had no problem pushing the limits of my position as an official member of the Ira Deorum no matter how short lived it would be.

He made the mistake of letting me in. Now, I was going to tear him apart from the inside out.

There was a flicker of uncertainty in his eyes, and his upper lip twitched as he looked away, clearing his throat. I tried to get Fynn's attention next, but he kept his eyes straight ahead, legs planted wide, arms behind his back. Ever the dutiful soldier. It was a pity because he could wipe out the entire room at any given moment, but he had chosen to follow blind orders instead.

The king cleared his throat, and began. "The rumors of rebellion are no longer only rumors. We hoped to squash those who wished to flee when we burned down Alynta. But those who wish to stand against me, against your Phoenix, are growing. We have confirmation that there have been some who escaped our group and made it through to Cresslier Pass. We do not know their fate, as none who entered have returned, but this cannot be allowed. We cannot allow them to hope."

None had survived that he knew of. I thought back to my parent's letter, how they had left and survived. So making it through the pass was possible, but the how was still a mystery.

"I have gathered intel confirming that the Realm of Night is readying for a fight. And, to make it worse." His voice lowered, and it sounded almost as if he was afraid. "They have a Reincarnation on their side."

A hush fell across the table. We all leaned in and exchanged glances. A Reincarnation was unheard of. According to everything I had been taught, the old gods were dead. They hadn't come back in any form since the Great War all those years ago. A Reincarnation not only meant they were immortal, but contained great power. Was it truly possible?

"How do you know this?" I blurted out. I was becoming more brazen, no longer caring for the consequences. But even this—to speak out of turn in the king's presence—was pushing it.

His eyes flared with anger. "What I think Miss Orion meant to ask politely, was how I gathered this information. First, let me make it very clear that this is none of her concern, but trust that I have my sources. Some that might come from inside sources. Second, hold your tongue until I have finished, or I will have Fynn remove it for you."

"He never complained about my tongue before." I smiled at Fynn and he reddened, keeping completely still.

Soren snickered and I snapped at him. "What are you laughing at? I don't need Fynn to remove your tongue, I'll happily do it myself."

Callax coughed to cover the smile that brightened his face. The king shouted at me to be quiet once more and I backed off, sitting back in my seat. It was probably wise to not push my limits too far the first day on the job.

"As I was saying, we cannot allow the Realm of Night to exist with such power. The fact that they have existed this long outside of our control is reason enough. We cannot allow them to continue their existence in such open defiance of the laws of the land. The Realm of Night must be conquered, and the new god must die."

I glanced to Archer, checking in with how she was holding up, but she sat still as a statue, focused only on the king's words.

"I have suspected for some time that this day would come. I have planned to conquer the city my ancestors failed to acquire, for some time. But this moves my agenda along much faster. Instead of waiting out until the end of the month, You will all set out in two days for the war camp at the base of Cresslier Pass. The generals are there waiting for you, with a few thousand men already. Senna and Mavenna will stay behind to ready the remaining troops. We want to attack as soon as possible, giving them less time to prepare.

"When we get there, they may be ready for us, or we may have to brave the pass and breach the city. Either way, the existence of the Realm of Night must come to an end."

I was not expecting to leave so soon. I figured there would be weeks of war councils and endless planning strategies, but was this something he and Fynn had been planning behind our backs for some time?

I didn't like this. I already had mixed feelings about the Realm of Night and its people, the council that had displaced my family…but they hadn't provoked our realm. Had done nothing to deserve a full on attack.

Those who had fled, apart of this so called rebellion against the king had done nothing but hope for a better life. Was I truly willing to be a part of this?

The king dismissed us with instructions for the following day and left us to make our final preparations. We rose from the table, acknowledging the king with a salute and chimed in as the realm's elite soldiers. "Long may the Day last."

CHAPTER 47

I was supposed to be packing—preparing for a war I had no interest in fighting.

It would take us nearly a week to ride that far north, and that was only if we swapped out horses in each city we passed. I didn't want to think of how sore I would be, or the possibility of facing the unknown horrors of Cresslier Pass if we were forced to cross through. There were stories told about the beasts that lie in wait in those parts of the mountain, the kind that were meant to scare you, and actually did.

Power rose through me as I unsheathed my blades. I hadn't handled them since the night before the trials when I had sparred with Callax. I kept them hidden away until now, as it would have been foolish to try and flaunt them without my position secured.

Testing the balance out of habit, I swung them around. They were still as perfect as ever, just as they had been the first time. The faint blue glow was more pronounced now. Brighter than before, the etched flames now dancing with the embers of real ones.

My vision filled with red, coating the world around me, reminding me that I had been helpless as I watched my friend murdered right before me. I waited for the agony to consume me, to fall to the ground in mind numbing pain, but nothing came. Only the red remained, a lingering fury I felt for everyone who had ever wronged me.

I imagined the two males I fought as they advanced. I replayed the fight and followed the motions. Block, parry, blow, swing, sidestep, finish. Over and over I fought the fight in my mind, correcting any poor form, swinging both swords over my head instead of just the one. I was not weak. I would not let anyone die because of me again.

It was a dance—delicate and deadly. Power roared in my veins, urging me forward, lighting a fire beneath the anger that lived inside.

They would pay, as would the king. I would make sure of it.

Again and again, I followed through with the movements until each strike was deadly and precise, no faults to be found. Without my mind second guessing my actions, constantly worrying if I was good enough, it was like I was someone else entirely. A beast waiting to rip them apart.

The dark metal sang as it sliced through the air. They had been made for me. For the Dark Phoenix. For a god.

Fire pulsed through my veins, igniting every inch of me until I was a blur of movement. Every step, every swing of my blade was for Emryn, for my family, for every person I had loved who was dead. With precision I had never before wielded I tore through the room and with a roar of anger, I brought both swords down, ready to finish off the mental image of my enemies.

My blades slammed into the ground, tearing through the hard surface of the platform. I watched in a mix of horror and awe as they were consumed in fire. Raging, cobalt fire. They flickered in my eyes, and my first instinct was to back away, to extinguish them, but it pulled me in. Their movement hypnotizing.

I was shaking as I pulled them free from the floor below. I had feared fire my whole life, the consequences that always inevitably followed. I started the fire that killed my parents. I burned down a forest, all because I was frightened.

But I was no longer scared.

I didn't want this power. I didn't ask for it. But it was here, and it was mine. I could either cower like a fool, or embrace it.

I lifted my hand before me and let the fire spread over my palm.

A loud crash sounded across the room, and I gripped my swords tighter, readying to fight. I pulled all that energy back into my core, storing it away, and the flames extinguished.

I turned to see a stunned Callax, staring in awe at the sight before him—at me—smoldering with the remains of my fire.

Before I could say anything, convince him not to be scared or run away, he drew his sword from his side and stalked over to the sparring platform. He took a defensive stance, sword raised. "Again," he commanded.

I knew what he meant, and I appreciated the silence, the lack of acknowledgment or fear. I wasn't ready to discuss it, and he knew that.

We danced together, trading blow for blow until I lost track of time. Sweat dripped from my face as I battled the crown prince. He was an expert swordsman, trained from the time he was a child, but he had taught me well. With the advantage of two blades to one, along with he harmony singing between me and the nightshade, we were an even match.

Time disappeared, and it was only Callax and me. Fighting together, as one.

He seemed to predict my every move as I matched him with equal force—a dance of metal and strength.

"Harder," he growled, twisting out of the lock I had him in. "Bring me to my knees. I am not afraid of you."

I felt no panic, no moment of fear, nothing blocking my way. His foot slipped in a puddle of our sweat and I saw my opening. I took a running start and launched into the air, bringing both my swords into an X as I came down.

The force of my blow brought him to his knees and I poured all my effort into it. He strained under the pressure and I grinned. I was going to win and he knew it. Still, he did not shy away.

I let the pent-up anger flow through me as I pressed down, his eyes equally wild. The blue glow of my blades illuminated his face. When the razor edge neared his throat, he conceded my win. But I wasn't finished.

He moved, thinking I was going to back away, but the moment he shifted his guard, lowering his sword, I pressed mine back to his throat, relishing in the victory.

Callax held perfectly still, no hint of fear or terror as he held my gaze, staring deep into my soul. It sent a shiver down my spine as he saw me—truly saw me—for the thing I had become.

Turn it off.

It was Callax who encouraged me to do this. He released me from the prison of my own making, freeing me from the turmoil in my mind. I was a weapon.

I pulled my blades up, moving his head with them. He rose obediently.

I didn't know what overcame me, but in one fluid motion, I sheathed my blades and gripped the fabric of his lapels, and pulled his tall frame down—crashing his mouth into mine.

I was consumed by him. We were a clashing of lips, and tongues, and teeth. The fire burned again. This time, it was a pleasant, warming sensation that lit inside my core. There was no breath except his as he moved me to the side of the room.

He shoved me up against the wall. I tossed my head back as he ran a line of kisses down the side of my neck to my collar. He nipped playfully, his sharp canines grazing my skin, and it heightened every sense in my body.

I moaned, the sound resonating deep in my chest. I pulled him back up, wanting his mouth on mine. My hands found his hair, and I ran my fingers through his thick, black hair. I tugged, holding him at my mercy. Gods I had wanted to feel this—him.

A moan of pleasure escaped his lips as he grinned through the kiss, the tug of his hair. I laughed, pleased at the evidence of his enjoyment.

My hands ran down his chest as I pushed, turning our bodies in harmony. With his back now to the wall, I shoved him down to the bench below.

I took in the sight of him below me and my eyes flared with greed—roaming over his muscular body—legs splayed, leaning back against the wall. I stood over him, curling my lips. My body hummed in anticipation at the mere sight of him.

"Miss Orion," he growled, his words full of need.

I put my finger to his lips, silencing him as I straddled his hips. I rocked back and forth, grinding against his hard length as I settled on him. He tried to say something, but I pushed harder, digging my hips in, needing more friction.

I shook my head, my eyes never once leaving his. "If you want what comes next, I expect you to stay silent, is that understood?"

His eyes were deep with lust and desire, but he nodded, the words dying in his throat.

I bit my lower lip, hiding my grin as he leaned forward, trailing fervent kisses along the sensitive skin of my neck. My head tossed back in ecstasy as I circled against him, moving in rhythm with the growing pulse of my desire.

I fumbled with the complicated clasps of his top, but gave up and moved my hands down to his belt instead. Much easier.

His rough hands rand down my back, and even through the thick leather, the force of his nails raked against my spine. I shivered, the hair raising on my arms. A sound of pure pleasure escaped my lips as I freed him from his belt, opening the top of his pants.

He lifted his hips in compliance as I slid them down past his hips, releasing him.

I slid off his lap and knelt before him, smiling with wicked intent. He had no idea what was coming. I gripped his knees and pressed wider, bringing him forward. I let my hands slide up his thighs…closer.

Callax twisted beneath me at my teasing touch. I lifted my gaze from his impressive length, to his eyes, and waited until they opened expectantly.

"Beg." I commanded.

He raised a brow. Not in defiance, but rather in surprise at my forwardness. I was not afraid. I was not weak or scared, and I belonged to no one. I yielded my power to no one. Including him.

He twitched beneath the whispering touch as I ran my finger along the length of him, my eyes never leaving his. I wrapped a hand around him and pressed my thumb into the soft underside, eliciting a gasp.

"I said, *beg*."

He huffed in defeat, realizing what I was doing, that this was my repayment for everything he had done these past months. It was his turn to be left shaking.

"Please, Miss Orion." He closed his eyes and whispered greedily, his voice trembling. "I am begging you."

Victory.

I leaned in, gliding my tongue along his length—tasting him—then rose to my knees, closing the space between us. He wrapped his hands around my neck, pulling me in tight for a kiss.

Merely an inch from his mouth, I stopped, my free hand between us, the other still firmly wrapped around his cock. His breath was hot and heavy, and full of anticipation. I could feel the desire between us. The need. I could taste it.

I licked him from the side of his jaw to his ear, and whispered, "I win."

Without another word, without another touch, I stood and sauntered out of the room, not once looking back. Leaving him shaking with desire behind me.

CHAPTER 48

It was impossible to keep the smile off my face.

Never before had I experienced anything like that before. That intense. That intoxicating. It had taken all my strength to not strip myself bare and fuck him right there.

"What are you smiling for?" A familiar, hateful voice took me by surprise as I rounded the corner. I gasped a little, but schooled my features back to neutral, not letting it show that he phased me.

I crossed my arms. "That is no longer any concern of yours."

"Don't speak to me like that."

I clutched my hand to my heart, feigning shock and worry. "Where are my manners? I do apologize dear Phoenix, but I believe that when I ended things between us, that severed any required concern on your part. You're free."

He barely contained the rage, taking a step forward. I didn't back away. "No, you don't get to speak to me like that, because I had no say in the matter. I never ended things, and neither did you. You were just upset. You didn't mean it. Not really."

"Why? Because I can't know my own mind? Because I'm some weak and defenseless female?"

He shook his head in exasperation. "Not anymore, no."

"Not anymore?" I nearly shouted. "So you did, then. You thought that the entirety of our relationship?" I shook my head, some part of me still not believing it even when it was put so clearly in front of me.

"Yes." He exploded with frustration. "You have failed at everything you've ever done. Gods, you're so thick sometimes. I got you here. Your pathetic life finally has meaning, finally has purpose, because of me. Me." He pounded his finger against his chest for emphasis."

"You got me in. I earned my keep. And that…had nothing to do with you. You are a pathetic excuse of a male. Keeping me at your side for what? for show? Because it wasn't becoming of someone so highly revered to lose the girl at his side? No, because if you lost that, then who are you to win a war, right? Win us peace?"

I laughed, low and lifeless. "No. Fuck you, and fuck your peace." I took a step forward, letting him see me for who I was, what I had become. "You didn't want me, and now you've lost me. Make peace with that."

I turned and started to walk away, brimming with rage I only kept in check because this was not the place to tear him apart.

"This isn't you," he shouted after me. He gripped my arm and spun me around. His face was red. Shaking. "This isn't you, Renata.

"Isn't me?" I roared. "No, the old me was at the end of a very long rope, and I cut that bitch free. So this? *Me*? I am a monster of your own making."

I ripped my arm from his grip, freeing myself at last. Fire sparked in his eyes, but it was just that. A spark, and nothing more. He wouldn't kill me here. Not when it would be evident what happened.

When we faced each other next, it would be for the last time. Because all of it—all the betrayal and lies, the frustration and wasted years—I would wash it away with him. Let it all disappear for good when he was lying dead on a battlefield.

I walked away, his defeat sweet on my tongue. "Do not waste your tears when I tear you apart.

CHAPTER 49

I slipped into the scalding water, praying it would soothe my aching body and release the remaining tension.

The fire crackled—the only light in the dark room—and the burning driftwood mixed with the lavender and lemon salts, filling my senses. I leaned back against the cool metal, resting my neck on the roll of towels folded over the edge. It was a trick my mother taught me when I was young. She did it nearly every time she bathed, and I often found her hours later, still soaking in the lukewarm water, engrossed in a romance book.

I sighed, content with being alone in the peaceful silence, and added some foaming soap into the water. This was likely one of the last nights I would have like this for some time. So I relaxed into the feeling, blissfully unaware of the world around me.

In that solitude, I failed to notice my door slowly opening, or the male now leaning against the frame, until he cleared his throat loudly. I sat up, my chest barely below the surface of the dwindling bubbles.

Callax's damned crooked smile sat lazily on his beautiful face. Without my mind occupied with Fynn every waking moment, it was so easy to let myself appreciate everything he had to offer. But he hadn't come for me it seemed, as my equipment back dangled from his hand.

Shit, I must have left it in the training room, carelessly forgetting it in my triumphant exit. He distracted me so thoroughly, it was easy to lose track of my own mind around him.

He kept his eyes on me as he popped a grape into his mouth. My untouched dinner tray sat on the dresser near the door. "By all means, please continue." He lifted another piece of fruit to his mouth and winked. "I do love dinner and a show."

I gathered the sparse bubbles, trying to cover my breasts with some sense of false modesty. I would allow him to see whatever I wished, but only when it was to my benefit, and his appearance just now hadn't been under my control.

"Leave," I demanded, but the word caught in my throat. The memory of his bare lower half submitting to me, made it hard to resist that invisible pull. The need to have him near me. Inside me. It stopped all the authority I tried to summon.

Callax set my bag on the ground and stole a strawberry from the plate as he stalked to the edge of the tub.

He had changed clothes. His loose cotton tee was unlaced, drifting open as he squatted down, revealing a smattering of black hair covering his well-defined chest. I resisted the urge to run my fingers through it. To pull him in the tub with me. I pulled my lower lip between my teeth, imagining what it would be like to have that chest on mine—

"Distracted, Miss Orion?" His drawling voice snapped me back to reality.

Two could play this game. I had no reason, no desire, to hide from him any longer. I smiled slyly and leaned back, leaving my breasts exposed. I spread my legs, letting one dangle over the edge. How much longer could I tease him before one of us finally burst? "Leave, before I—"

The strawberry pushed into my mouth before I could finish my false threat. I bit off a portion, chewing the sweet fruit. Juice dripped down my chin, and his calloused thumb dragged through it.

"Before you what? Hmm?"

I swallowed in silence, not once breaking eye contact.

"If I recall correctly, part of your training conditions were that you were to take care of your body." He brought his thumb to my lips, pushing the juice against my tongue. He held my mouth open. "That means you eat every meal in its entirety, or I will punish you accordingly. Is that understood?"

I swallowed, his thumb still hooked against my lower jaw. I nodded.

He washed his sticky hands off in the water, dragging the tips of his fingers through the rippling surface then down my thigh. Higher, and higher, until—

I gasped, my breath shaking as he slid a finger inside me. His thumb brushed against my clit, and my body tensed, my exposed breasts lifting from the water, begging to be touched.

Too soon, his hand slipped from me and I whimpered at the loss of him. The need that remained. Burning me from the inside out.

He bracketed my throat, bringing me up toward him. Soft lips brushed against the shell of my ear, nipping at the edge as he purred, "Good girl."

A wave of lust roared through me, the water instantly reheating. My cheeks flushed, undoubtedly as red as the strawberry he forced between my lips.

His lips twitched upward. The skin of my neck tensed as he tightened his grip. I fought every urge in my body that screamed to submit to him, to give in to the mysterious pull—to let him has his way with me then and there, ravaging me—but I wasn't quite ready.

I couldn't let a male have this much control over me so soon.

"You need to leave." My words were breathless, his effect on me all-consuming.

He bit his lower lip and leaned over the edge. "Don't let me catch you breaking my rules again." He stood then, giving me one last once-over in appreciation and walked to the door. Before he left, he turned and looked over his shoulder, shadows dancing around him. "Or do. Could be more fun that way."

He winked, closing the door behind him.

I sank below the surface and remained there until my body calmed down.

CHAPTER 50

I wrapped my blades back in their cloth. I would need to hide them from the king, but I wanted them close by. I had warned Archer to do the same, knowing she would want to use her bow. In the heat of battle, it would be easy enough to hide the weapons, but we could not carry them so openly unless we wanted to draw attention. I wasn't sure the king or the others would know what nightshade was, but flaming swords would be hard to hide, especially since I didn't know how to control them.

"Are you ready?" Callax's voice startled me, but I remained still as I held the covered blade.

I nodded. "As I'll ever be."

Dawn broke over the hill as we rode into Alynta. We rode for what felt like days straight, ragged and worn. King Tobias sent us ahead of the legion, trying to get us to the base of Mount Cresslier before weeks' end. Senna, Kell, and Mavenna all stayed behind to lead the legion, chosen by the king as generals. Their duty to the Ira Deorum remained, but things were bound to change in times of war.

The town of Alynta was completely decimated in the wake of Fynn's fire.

We hadn't stayed to watch the town burn to the ground, only to ensure its destruction. It all seemed like a lifetime ago.

I thought of Anya and her tiny dress shop, the baker and his son who had been so kind to us. My breath caught in my throat as I thought of all the innocent souls lost to his power. Fiery rage danced beneath my skin, but I shoved it down, capping it. I wouldn't allow myself to resort to the same actions. My fire would be of no use here.

No one knew except for Callax, but I was unsure of how much he saw last night in the training room. Even then, I had yet to confirm what I knew myself to be. I still denied it.

"We'll camp here for a few hours. Don't bother setting up the tents. The sun will be up soon. Just roll out some blankets and try to get as much rest as you can," Fynn instructed. "We'll ride through the day before we stop."

A communal groan rolled through the group, but no one said anything. Fynn was our official leader now—the mouthpiece of the king. We were to follow his every word.

We watched silently as he dismounted his horse and brought his magnificent wings into existence. I stared in awe—despite my growing hatred for him–and watched the early morning sun glint off his golden tattoos and highlight the deep red of his wings.

He gave me a once over, nothing but disappointment and disgust in his glare. "I will be back in a few hours." With a thunderous downbeat, he followed the rising sun into the horizon beyond.

My back ached like it always did when I rode and wished once more I had his wings to fly instead of ride. As if in response to the wish, two heavy knots ached between my shoulders, and I felt the weight bearing down on me. I rolled my shoulders, stretching them out, and dismounted my golden mare.

Archer was two horses away, Skye seated between us. I had pocketed the letter the night before, intending to give it to her. The grass crunched under my feet as I made my way to her.

"Here." I held out the letter to her. "I want you to have this."

She took it, looking at the seal, then at me in confusion, hiding it quickly. "What is this?" she asked, voice low.

"It was from mother and father. It has a lot of… information. Get some sleep, and read it when you have time. We can discuss it when this mess is all over, okay?" She nodded and tucked it into her saddlebags.

It was near impossible to fall asleep with the sun rising in the sky. But Archer and I doubled up our blankets, blocking out as much of the morning dew as we could, and curled up next to each other.

She laid her head in the crook of my shoulder. I ran my hand through her hair, comforting her. "It's been a strange year," she said.

I laughed. That was an understatement. "Yeah, it has." I kept my eyes closed, trying to convince my body to relax.

"Do you think mom and dad would be proud of us?"

My eyes fluttered open in surprise. "What?"

"Do you think they'd be proud of this? Of us?" She gestured to the air around, and I knew what she meant.

I sighed. "I don't know, honestly. I like to think they would. I don't know that they'd agree with the king's actions and that we follow his orders, but we also don't have much of a choice." She nodded silently. "And, I think they would understand."

I thought about the letter, of how they fled Asterion to give me the choice of who I wanted to be. What I wanted to be. They left to give me a choice, and here I was heading off to war against people I didn't know. A realm I was supposed to lead. But they weren't my people; they never had been. I owed them no allegiance, no honor, no loyalty.

Those had to be earned.

But they also didn't deserve the war we were bringing to their home. It was a confusing line of thought.

I shook my head. "I think they would want us to make our choices, and whatever they were, they'd be proud of us for choosing for ourselves."

Fynn returned sooner than I would have liked.

The rest of us packed our bedding in the quiet of the early morning. We shook off as much of the dew as possible, but it soaked through. I tied the corners of the blankets to the straps of our saddlebags and hoped that the rushing air would dry it. My muscles protested as I threw my leg over my horse. I patted her shoulder and silently apologized for having to carry us so far and so quickly. I was sure they were feeling the exhaustion as we were, but they were better soldiers and never complained.

Fynn folded away those burning wings of his and mounted his horse. "We'll stop at dusk to rest, but we need to make it to Pyrrhos as soon as possible. There, we will resupply and rest while we strategize our plan of attack and wait for the legion to arrive." He spurred his horse with a swift kick, and we raced off over the hill.

I watched as we passed by the outskirts of Alynta. A few shopkeepers milled around in the rubble…rebuilding from what they could. At least some had survived. I wondered if Anya and the baker made it, though it wasn't likely.

I thought of all the husbands and sons in the distant mountains, mining for sunstone. I thought of how they would come home when their service was up, only to find their entire lives burned to the ground. It made me sick, and I added it to the mental list of reasons the king, and Fynn, deserved to die.

As we rode, I had no option but to let my mind wander. There was no room for conversation, the wind deafening as it ripped past our ears. We wore our hoods to protect us from the growing cold while we continued north. The south was sunny, warm, and inviting. But as we moved further north, past Alynta, the air grew less welcoming, as if it warned us to leave. It wasn't freezing, but the wind brought a bitter chill, and my cheeks flushed red.

The passing mountains reminded me of the sunstone that lay hidden there and the sunstone sword the king gifted Fynn. A weapon of death. One passed down from host to host and used to kill the only Dark Phoenix.

If I was Reincarnation—no, I scolded myself. I was no such thing and would not allow myself to think like that.

Hours passed before Fynn let us stop to relieve ourselves and eat some food. I leaned against my horse, snacking on the dried meat and stale bread we had packed.

Skye broke the silence, "Do you think we'll make it?" she asked, her voice shaking the tiniest bit.

"Don't think like that," I stated and bit into my bread. "We can't let that be our mindset going in. Of course, we'll make it."

She nodded, but her head hung low. "We've just never faced anything like this. All we've done, all this training…it's been untested. We know we're good—"

"Great," I corrected.

The corner of her mouth twitched a little. "Right, we know we're great, but…I worry about Senna leading the charge with the legion." I wrapped my arm around her, trying to offer some comfort. I knew she was scared for her mate. Rightfully so. It was war, after all, and none of us had ever lived through, let alone fought in one.

"I think," I mused, still eating my bread. "That King Tobias could send Senna—and Senna alone—into the fray, and she'd be the last one standing."

Skye huffed out a short laugh. "Yeah, you're probably right. My mate is a badass."

"That is an understatement. I honestly think she's holding back most of the time. The only thing that could give her more advantage would be if she could fly." She gave me a rueful smile, and I knew I was right. "The day we see Senna unleashed upon the skies is the day Albionne will tremble in fear and bow to their great commander." I smiled at the thought. "What I would give to witness that."

We finished our bland meal and continued north. There were no towns on the main road between Alynta and Pyrrhos. We passed a few travelers and merchants hauling their wares to and from the cities, but it was the end of the harvest season, and they were few and far between.

The terrain grew sharp and rocky, and the soft rolling hills of the southern grasslands slowly faded into the rocky mountains of the north. I had never been this far north before. Alynta was the farthest I had ventured. Well, I suppose it wasn't entirely true. I had been born in the north, a daughter of the Realm of Night, and according to my parents, the north was mine. But I didn't remember my life there—nor did I particularly care—so I didn't count it.

The days blended together, and more than once, my eyes drifted close, nearly falling off my horse. When the sun faded behind the nearing mountains, I sent a small prayer of thanks to the gods. We eventually stopped, finding a clearing not too far off the road. The leafy trees I was accustomed to were exchanged for beautiful pines and evergreens. They were stunning, and their fallen needles made for extra padding on the hard floor.

Archer, Skye, and I set up a shared tent. Kaede, Callax, and Soren shared another, and Pyne, Caldor, and Fynn shared the last. I was surprised Kaede opted to tent with the other males, but without Emryn here, he didn't need to share a space with three females. We were his friends, yet I imagined being near me was still hard, so I didn't blame him.

We hadn't spoken since the night of the Initiation ball. I was happy to give him time and space, but I hoped we could mend it sooner rather than later for the sake of Skye and Archer. Of all people, I knew what grief could do to a person. How it tore through one's mind and made reason lose all sense.

The wind picked up, rattling the tents with their cry. "Can we put our beds together?" Skye asked. She was the smallest of us all and often got cold.

"Of course," Archer chimed in, happy for the comfort our proximity would bring. We moved our bedding to the center, and I was glad I aired out the blankets from the morning. They were stiff, but dry.

Skye lay between the two of us, soaking up the warmth. We all huddled next to each other, trying to relax, when Archer said, "I miss Emryn." It was moments like this when I was thankful I couldn't feel anything. A dull ache flared in my chest but brushed it off. Now was not the time to mourn. Not when we had a war to fight. A war I didn't want to take part in.

"She held us together," Skye whispered.

"She was," Archer agreed, pulling the blankets closer to her chin. I couldn't see her face clearly in the darkness, but I could tell there were tears in her eyes. I always knew what she was feeling. It was something I had always been able to do, even from a young age.

"I feel like we're losing Kaede." Skye's words surprised me.

"What do you mean?" I sat up on my elbow.

"I just—he's my brother, and I can feel it. Our connection feels…broken somehow. Fragmented. Like losing her broke something vital in him and released this dark chaos." I knew what she meant by the connection; Archer and I had it too. It must be a sibling thing. "Its been hard on all of us, I know that, but...I didn't realize he relied on her as much as he did. He always hid it so well, but I think she was what made Kaede, Kaede."

"I've felt it too," whispered Archer. "I've talked to him a few times, and he seems different—not fully here. Kaede and I have always been close, but even now, he seems lost."

The blankets shifted as Skye sat up. She sniffled, "What am I supposed to do?" Her voice was breaking.

"I don't know that we can fix him." I tried my best to comfort her, and I reached a hand out to rub her shoulder. "Grief is its own beast. It doesn't tell you what comes next or how to prepare. It leaves you guessing, reaching out aimlessly in the dark for hope." I surprised myself with the tenderness of my words, but they were true. It was what I would have wanted to hear. "Hope is there if you know where to look, but if you're alone, it makes it near impossible. I think all we can do is reach out a hand, let him know we're here for him through it all."

Maybe I was a hypocrite for saying these things when I had given up on hope despite the outreach of others. But it had been too much, and though I couldn't claim to know how Kaede's compared to mine, I vowed to myself I would never stop reaching out. Even if I couldn't follow my advice, I owed it to him, I owed it to Skye, and I owed it to Emryn.

"I suppose so." There was a small smile of agreement in her voice, and I wrapped my arms around her, holding her the same way Callax had done for me.

Archer joined in, and we sat there for a long while. The two of them cried silently, and I sat wishing, and hoping—praying—their grief would dissipate quickly. Unlike my own.

It had been nearly a week since we left Sunsbridge. The city of Pyrrhos now lay in sight and was larger than I expected. It wasn't exactly a coastal town, as the ocean was an hour's ride away, but it was close enough that tradespeople lined the main streets. Many tried to sell us their wares, but the rest kept their distance, unsure of our presence in their home.

As we made our way through the streets, I saw evidence of libraries, schools, large education centers, and public spaces. Pyrrhos seemed to thrive on learning and education. I could see Quarter Fae mixed in harmoniously with the Select and Half, a rare sight amongst the other towns in southern Albionne. Most Quarter Fae I grew up around were shunned to the outskirts, forced to sell their merchandise in run-down markets. It was inspiring to see Fae of all kinds milling about with each other.

We wound our way up a hill to an overlook, and Fynn stopped us there. Just beyond it were ten or so large, white tents with people walking in and out. I couldn't make out what the occupants were doing, but before I could ask, Fynn interrupted. "Set up camp. We will meet with the generals stationed here and rally their troops in the morning. The legion is expected to be here within a week. We will need to make the most of it."

CHAPTER 51

The next few days were spent waiting around as Fynn flew reconnaissance and monitored the pass, waiting for signs of their legion. We had been introduced to all of the important people and I did my best to avoid the rest as we waited for the rest of our legion to arrive.

Archer and I went hunting one of the nights, trying to find more food for the rest of us as the males under General Branan's command ate like pigs, and acted like them too. Avoiding them was an ideal way to spend our time.

General Branan, a gruff-looking male, sat at the head of the war table. Maps lined the tables, along with lists of coordinates, and statues indicating parts of the army and the enemies as well.

Skye, Archer, and I exchanged glances and scrunched our noses. The smell of sweaty, old men filled this entire place. Even with the entrance pinned open, a soft wind blowing through, it overwhelmed the entire tent. If the males made note of it, they didn't let it show.

"We believe Asterion's legion will attack by the end of the week."

Kaede leaned forward, facing the general. "That soon?" he asked.

Soren, who sat across from Kaede, his massive broad sword strapped to his side, taunted, "Are you nervous?" He goaded him with a look, testing his temperament, but Kaede only stared back, unamused.

Kaede's scruff had grown out over the last few weeks, not bothering to keep up with his usual perfect grooming. He was shaggy and unkempt, shadows lining his eyes. He wasn't sleeping, and he looked worse than I had seen him in some time.

He ran a hand through his stubble. "If I recall correctly, you were being thrown to the ground under my fists not that long ago, Soren." He spat the name with disgust, but the general raised his scarred hands, intervening.

"Boys, let's leave the fighting for the battlefield." They settled back in their seats and he pulled out a map.

I furrowed my brows as I looked at the expanse of the Realm of Night. Only a handful of small cities were marked across the map. No major roadways, no large cities, save for Asterion, were marked down.

I waited until he finished his long-winded explanation over something I didn't care about, then asked, "Why are there no more settlements and cities marked on that map?"

The general looked confused. "There are no more than what we have shown here. We believe this information to be accurate."

I could tell he was uncomfortable with me putting pressure, so I applied more. "I understand that by comparison, the Realm of Day is much larger. That much is undeniable, but are we really to assume that in the entire expanse of the Realm of Night, there are no more than a handful of small cities, all focused around the capital?"

"These are the maps we were given by the king, it is not my place to question—"

"But why has he spent decades gathering and training so many loyal soldiers when, what…their numbers reach only forty thousand?" I pointed to the maps. "Are we really foolish enough to believe that in the last thousand years, their populations have not grown? That all of this land, from the sea to the mountains, are barren? You'd be foolish—"

"Renata, enough." Fynn growled, stepping into the tent. His large wings folded tight behind him, shimmering into the aether as he took his place beside the general.

I bit my tongue only for the sake of everyone else in the room. Callax placed a hand on my thigh, steadying me, but I brushed it off.

Fynn leaned over the table, pointing to a location at the mountain's base. "From what I can gather, we believe they will come through here. Now, we can take the foot soldiers—we easily have the numbers to overpower them on land—but it's their aerial forces I'm most concerned with."

We all exchanged worried glances. The king had been amassing his legion for a long time, but in all that time, we had nothing that could…fly. Well, besides Fynn.

I was about to question the general again, but Callax cut me off, taking the brunt of it this time. "Am I to understand correctly that the Realm of Night has both land and air forces, while we only have the one?" He leveled Fynn and the general with a harsh look.

The general swallowed. "Yes, my prince. We were uncertain they still existed until just this last week or two. We received confirmation from our intel that the Night Stryders have returned." His voice faded as if he was ashamed he hadn't told us.

This time, I interrupted. "What are the Night Stryders?"

General Branan cleared his throat, and seemed to look to Fynn for permission. He nodded, and then continued. "They are an ancient, elite force of aerial warriors dating back to the Great War. Perhaps even earlier. In ancient times, they were split into two groups, each one led by…by one of the old gods. The Axan mares were led by the Goddess of War. They are soulless, carnivorous creatures, torn from the darkest of nightmares. They may resemble their equine counterparts, but they are anything but. Long horns spear back from their head, deadly and dangerous. Their wings are that of a bat, thick as their hides and twice as wide as they are tall. Their teeth and hooves are razor sharp, tearing apart whatever they touch. When in battle, they wore golden skull masks, their manes dripping with the blood of their prey and their eyes… are as red as fire."

A chill ran down my spine.

"They are demons incarnate and are said to fight like them too. They are rumored to be the demons that lie in wait for those crossing through the pass."

Had all those who fled to the realm met this fate? How had my parent's gotten past them? I made a mental note to never go near one if the time ever came. I think I would rather take Soren on with my hands tied behind my back than face a creature like that.

"The other half of the Stryders fly into battle on Starlax stallions. These are rumored to be magnificent creatures, though just as deadly. They were said to have been bred for the God of Night himself, to ride the heavens with his queen."

Fynn cleared his throat, and the general turned red, realizing how openly he was talking of the old gods. If war wasn't upon us, I imagined Fynn might have killed him then and there.

"They were pulled from the storms and forged from the sky. Starlax are thunderous war horses, and embody the storms they were pulled from. They are massive and brutal and the Stryders who rode them in battle were led by the Goddess of Storms. Their feathered wings stronger than that of the Axan. Yet despite flying, it is said they prefer to ride the storms they create, using thunder to cover their war cries, and the strongest of them can even manipulate lighting to jump distances in a matter of seconds, giving them an edge in battle."

Equal parts awe and terror coursed through me. It was a pity we had nothing of comparison. I would have loved to have grown up around such mighty creatures.

"Thank you, general. If that is all…" Fynn moved to leave, but the general held up a hand, halting him.

"My lord, there is one more thing." The general pulled out an arrow beside his chair—a silver arrow made of white wood bound in silver thread. I looked to Archer, and we exchanged an uneasy glance. They must have found the boar, her arrow still lodged in its chest. Thankfully, she had left her bow and quiver back in our tent, but we had been foolish to even take them hunting this close to the border. Still, she adjusted her body uneasily in her seat.

"What am I looking at?" Fynn asked, obviously confused.

"This was found around the same time a few of my scouts went missing at the base of the pass. It's the arrow of a Quivershade." Fynn threw his hands up, still unaware of the meaning. "I know little more than the name of the females who once wielded such weapons, but these arrows... all I truly know is that they were once used by those in the guard who protected the Moon Goddess herself during the Great War."

Fynn whipped his head, calm rage seeping into his features. "Do not continue to speak of the old gods, you fool, or it will be the last thing you do." The general backed up instinctively and bowed his head in shame. "Whatever threat they throw my way, I will level them to the ground." He opened his palm, and a spark of red fire ignited. He stared down at it as if it held all the answers. His fist closed, and the fire disappeared just as quickly. I wasn't sure which realm had more to fear.

The air was crisp, biting at my nose as we all left the tent. My stomach grumbled and I sighed at the thought of having to scrounge for food amongst so many males.

Callax's hand brushed against mine and I turned, letting him lead me far away from the prying eyes of the camp. If Fynn saw us together, it wouldn't end well for either of us.

"Yes?" I asked, raising my brows at the hand he kept around mine. He touched me every chance he got, as if he couldn't get enough.

"I was going to go down to Pyrrhos for the night. Take a walk through town before it gets dark and perhaps get to know it a little before...before everything changes tomorrow."

It was cute watching him try to find the right words. Strong advances, sexual encounters, brazen words...those he never had issue with. But this, something so small and intimate...I laughed a little. "Are you telling me your plans or are you asking me to come with you."

His cheeks flushed. "Would you join me, Renata?"

I looked back to Archer, who now sat underneath a tree, reading. I tried to come up with an excuse to sit with her and stay, but her eyes lifted, and she shook her head. As if she knew what I was thinking. The little traitor.

"I suppose it wouldn't be an awful way to spend my night."

He smiled, broad and wide, extending an arm.

CHAPTER 52

Callax made me laugh like I never had before.

When it was the two of us alone, there was something entirely different about him. Something I had never noticed before. There was a lightness that shone in his eyes, the stars that reflected there dancing like he had placed them there just for me. And when he smiled, one dimple appeared at his left cheek.

I spent most of my life despising him, and it wasn't for no reason, but lately he had shown himself to be a true friend. More than a friend, really. But I appreciated it all the same. With Callax I was…me. More so than I had been in quite a long time.

We passed through street after street together, stopping to sample local food and fresh meat. We even tried some sort of crispy potatoes that made me squeal in delight. I had never them prepared in quite that way before, and I was determined to speak with the cooks about it. I would even spend hours in the kitchens with them if it meant we could replicate the delicious, greasy, concoction. Even Callax was speechless at the way they tasted, his eyes rolling back in his head.

The people in Pyrrhos matched the energy of the mountain air around them. They were kind and caring, and reminded me so much of the people from Alynta. I still felt a twinge of sorrow when I thought of them, but it was mainly anger toward the injustice they faced. I feared that the same fate awaited Pyrrhos if we weren't careful.

They were so close to the potential battlefield, and still, no one seemed to be even slightly concerned. It was odd. "Callax?" I asked. He was busy still inhaling potatoes and looked at me, mouth full, oil dripping from his finger. I stifled a chuckle, covering my mouth.

"Hmm?" he muttered between bites, not quite looking up from his food.

I let him finish, then asked, "Do you think the people here are scared? I mean, where will they go when war breaks out? Are they not aware of why we're here?"

The carefree look on his face faded and I almost regretted asking. He swallowed before answering. "They're aware." He looked down at his feet, kicking some rocks as if the question made him uncomfortable. "They know, and yet…they refused to leave. My father sent the order for the town to be evacuated a week ago. Yet, when the scouts reported back, they all said the same thing. They said they knew that 'she would come to save them.'"

"She?"

He gave me a knowing look that made me turn away, not wanting to face the fact that he seemed to think I knew what it meant. But he let it go. "We have no clue what any of it meant. One man said the heir had finally risen, and he had faith she would be the one to bridge the gap, to lead them all into a millennium of peace." He took a deep breath, steadying himself. "Of course, my father ordered for him to be executed."

Callax looked around, not quite meeting my gaze. Whether from shame at his father's actions or something else, I didn't know. "But it seems to be the consensus between them all, and they refuse to evacuate. I suppose stationing our war camp here is a punishment of sorts. I think my father assumes they will be destroyed in the casualties of war."

He looked as disgusted as I felt. It was one thing to not allow traitors to live, but having hope—having the desire for peace and equality—wasn't deserving of death. "You don't agree with his politics?"

We had yet to talk about any of this. I knew he disliked his father, loathed him even, for what he had done to him growing up. I was still bitter about that fact. But we had never talked about how we aligned politically. What that might mean if we stood on opposing sides.

We slowed our walk, stopping in the center square. A beautiful fountain sat in the center, surrounded by strings of lights and candles that all reflected in the water. It reminded me of Firielle and the town square where my life had changed forever. It had only been less than a year, and somehow it was a lifetime ago.

I looked to Callax, waiting for his answer. He tilted his head back, admiring the beauty of the night sky, far above the strings of lights. "I've never told anyone this, but I far prefer the night sky to the sun. There's something so peaceful about the chill that sweeps over the world at night. It's calming. Inviting." He looked back to me, his eyes twinkling in the light. "But to answer your question….no. I do not agree with father. I never have, but I've never had the luxury of opposing him. Every act of defiance was met with punishments so severe that it made me cruel in turn." He wrung his hands and then sat on the edge of the fountain, rubbing at his knees as if they bothered him.

"I'd be a far worse king than even he, if I did. To have seen the atrocities we have, and then to take the throne and continue as if none of it mattered…" He scoffed and shook his head. "I have to hope there is more to this world than what he has shown me. That I can be a better king."

"Do you even want to be king?" It was a foolish question. Treacherous, even, if heard by the wrong ears.

I could outrun my fate, I had been given the chance. But to be born into it, to have it thrust upon him at such a young age…I wondered if he had ever thought otherwise. If he would oppose if I were to steal him and run far, far away from here.

"That…is a complicated question."

"How so?"

"I've never had the opportunity to think I'd be anything else. That there might be a life for me somewhere besides the palace walls." He rested his elbows against his knees, leaning forward, his hands clasped. "Renata, my entire life has been a string of awful events that have led me down one singular path. To endure it without breaking, I became who he made me to be. Existing only as some wretched mirror of my father's actions. I never believed I could be anything or anyone else." He wrung his hands, the words pained and sad. "I spent my entire life calloused and angry. And I believed it was all life had to offer. Until you."

I stumbled over my words, my breath catching. "Me? What...what did I have to with that?"

He laughed, almost disbelieving and turned his dark eyes to mine. "Everything." His hand cupped my cheek.

I instinctively leaned into it, pressing against the warmth, the only thing that pierced into the cold shadows around my heart. And it frightened me. I moved away, inhaling sharply, refusing to let my mind wander back to the night he confessed everything. The same night when I had to become someone else in order to save my mind and heart.

"Is everything alright?" Genuine concern filled his face, and a crack formed in my frozen heart. But it halted, sealing back over when a young boy, no older than ten, tugged on my sleeve. He looked so familiar, but I couldn't place him.

"It's you, it's really you." There was no question to his words, only certainty as he pulled me behind him and toward a woman selling jewelry in a corner stall. He pointed excitedly at me as he shouted, "Auntie, Auntie, look who I found. It's the lady dad told me about. She's come to save us, just like he said."

A loaf of bread sat uncut on the edge of the stall, and suddenly the boy's face clicked into place. A baker's shop in Alynta, the kind man who loaded a bag with the tastiest pastries, and a young boy helping his father. I sank to my knees, meeting his face, and gripped his arms in my hands.

I was breathless. "Where's your father? Could you take me to him? I'd like to speak with him."

His face fell, and he shuffled his feet nervously, refusing to meet my eyes.

"He's dead." His aunt answered for him. She brought a hammer down on some bent copper with such force I feared the table might split beneath it. "The king ordered him killed, all for daring to voice his hope for this gods forsaken land. First, he burned his home, then took him from his boy." Her lip curled in disgust at the two of us, obviously not knowing, or caring, who we were.

I turned my attention back to the boy as Callax apologized to the woman. "What did you mean when you said I would save you?" I searched his face for an answer, unsure of what his father had known and told him. What he had died for.

A smile lit his face, proud to repeat the information. "He said you were sent from the heavens to save us. That you would bring us all to Asterion and rescue us from the wicked king. He said there were stories about you, that we've been waiting for you for a long time."

I stayed silent for a while, unsure how to answer. How to tell him that I had no intention of ever claiming that part of my lineage, that I wasn't the savior they were looking for.

"You're going to save us, right? That's…that's why you're here?"

"I…" I did my best to smile, to bring him some sort of comfort when I wasn't sure I had any to offer. "I'm going to try." I patted his arm and smiled with as much warmth as I could manage. His father died for this hope. Passed it on to his son who now burdened me with it. How could I offer him any reassurances when even I did not believe in myself?

Silently, I added his father to my growing list of people who had died because of me. For the hope I gave by simply existing. It was growing increasingly difficult to stand by and do nothing.

Even if my parents had warned me that the Realm of Night would use me as a weapon, there was never a chance to prove them right or wrong. Maybe they had been right to want that. To protect the hope of their people. Even if I was destined to only ever be a weapon, fighting against King Tobias, against the Realm of Day…it seemed like a damned worthy cause.

I wanted to get out of there. I needed space to think. To breathe.

I turned and walked away, leaving Callax and the baker's son behind me.

The night air fill my senses, cooling my skin. If I had kept my emotions intact, I would have been overwhelmed it all.

All the grief, and loss, and pain would have broken me—left me shattered on the floor. But now, it all fell flat, sliding off my frozen heart with ease. It was better this way. I could think clearly. Act without outside influence. Whatever decisions I made were wholly for my benefit and no one else.

It was easy to see the night sky here. If the south was meant for the sun, then the north was made for the night. Endless expanses of open sky trailed on far past the horizon, disappearing into mist over the sea. The moon hung above, nearly full in its glory, shining like a beacon of hope.

I was reminded of the stories my father once told, the lore Cyrus had shared with me in his books, and what my parents had written. If all of it was true, then the moon had been stuck, just as I had been. Trying to break a perpetual cycle that seemed to trap so many.

It felt as if I had been doomed to repeat her fate. To disappear beneath the hands of another. To give more than I ever received and to only ever love in vain.

It was sad to think about. To view my memories of the girl I used to be, the one I longed to be…all for him. Pain had been the only thing I knew, and instead of letting it go, I kept it tied to my hip, ready to pull out whenever I needed. Happiness was fleeting, promises were never kept, but pain…pain was always there. Reliable.

It accompanied me in the shadows, and no matter how long the daylight lasted, night always fell, and I was there…ready to fall apart in the safety of the darkness. Because when I was happy, I had given him my heart. He held the delicate little thing and crushed it without thought, crumbling it into dust.

And I had stayed with him. After all of that, I had stayed with him. Let him demolish me so completely I forgot who I was.

I thought loving him was the answer. That if I loved him more with each passing day—choosing him even when I could not choose myself—that he might reward that effort like some loyal soldier.

But no matter how I tried, I could never have forced him to love me in the way I wanted. The way I needed.

The realization crushed my soul.

When I thought of it, it had all been some desperate attempt to prove to myself that I was worthy of his love. But I shouldn't have wasted the energy because I was more than enough. I always had been. Even when I couldn't see it.

Could I really blame myself when the moon only shone as the sun allowed?

But I was not the moon. I was my own damn light.

I had freed myself from him, and I would no longer spend my life hidden in his shadows.

I mourned the Moon Goddess, for the pain and despair she must have endured for centuries at the hands of another. We were alike, her and I. And if it were true, if by some strange twist of fate I truly was the—no…I wouldn't say it. Wouldn't breathe it into existence. But if I were like my namesake, rather than the Moon, then we couldn't be further apart.

I had no mate, no devotion to a realm. I was torn between the fate I was born with, and choosing my own path. And no matter where I looked or who I turned to, I was lost. Truly lost.

No amount of walling off my heart, could spare me from that feeling. The helplessness of it all.

I curled my knees to my chest, hugging them tightly, staring over the hill to the city beyond. The stars hung low, shining bright, decorating the path in the sky carved out for the moon.

It didn't take me long to find Orion. The line of three stars always brought a smile to my face from the familiarity, and suddenly I was back home in Firielle. My father sat beside me, his arm around my shoulder, hand lifted to the sky. "See there, my darling girl, do you see Orion?"

I nodded, eager to please my father. I memorized the outline of the warrior's belt, the large bow he held aloft in the heavens.

"Orion was a true warrior, loyal to the Realm of Night. He fought so bravely for his mate and their love. He loved her so much, that when she died, he took her weapons and fought for her honor. He even died for her too."

I remembered being confused, not understanding the finality of death at such a young age. "Why did he have to die?" I had asked.

"Sometimes, when you love someone, you would give everything you have, everything you are, so they can live on. Even if it's only in their memory. And for mates—"

"Like you and mama?" I interrupted, proud to have made that connection.

He chuckled, squeezing me tight. "Yes, my darling, like me and your mama. Sometimes, people are too precious to let go. Too loved to live a life without them."

The memory faded, and I continued staring at the stars. A single tear slipped from my eye, but the pain was still no more than a dull ache. Begging to be let out. Demanding to be felt.

Callax lowered himself in the grass next to me. "Where were you?" he asked, his voice gentle as the breeze. He had known I was lost in my own mind.

"I was eight, sitting in our yard beneath the oak tree. My father had just shown me Orion." I smiled and pointed to the constellation above. "He loved the stories of gods and stars. But the one of the starblessed warrior was always his favorite."

"Tell me about him?"

My frozen heart beat once, softly. So I told him of my father. I told him of the jokes he would tell, and the way he treated my mother with such kindness. How he loved his work and the people of Firielle. How he wanted nothing more than for his girls to grow up and be strong and capable like him.

"He was a wonderful father and even better mate. He always knew how to make me smile. When I was angry or upset, he would take me outside to cool me down and show me the constellations. He always said that whenever I was angry, I could always talk to the stars." My lip trembled a bit, but I bit down. "*'The stars listen,'* he would say. *'If you can find one and wish, they will always answer.'*"

I loved that memory, those words.

"Do you still wish?" he asked.

"I stopped wishing a long time ago." The hope for a brighter future, for a world where I was happy again, died with my family. Perishing in that fire along with them.

"It should have been me," I choked. I wasn't sure where the confession came from, but it was like the shadows around my heart let Callax through, recognizing him as their own. But the words spilled out of me, and they did not stop. "I think I caused the fire. I think somehow in my night terrors, I started the fire that stole my family. My parents knew….they knew and they didn't fear me. They knew I was dangerous and kept me around anyway."

With each word, it was like a weight lifted. Like by holding back this unspoken truth, I had drowned in the guilt of it. But without the heaviness of grief—my emotions locked away—I was able to find the truth hidden beneath them.

"They lied to protect me about who, *what*, I am. And they suffered for it." I looked over the city beyond us, the lights growing brighter in the darkness of a storm slowly rolling in. "But these people here, they shouldn't suffer the same fate when I might have the power to stop it. I just—I don't know what to do, Callax. Tell me what to do."

He took both my hands in his, pulling me close. "Whatever happens tomorrow, Renata…" My name slipped off his tongue like a melody in the wind, an ancient song that filled my cold heart. "Whatever comes our way, we will face it together. I will be by your side until the Night rises."

The words shook me. Had he known that was something I said to my sister, to my friends, to prove our loyalty? There was no way he had known, and yet he uttered the four words that somehow opened me up to the idea of him.

I turned away, pulling my hand free, no longer able to look at him. The devotion in his starry gaze.

We sat in silence for a while, watching the clouds roll closer. Thunder echoed through the valley, and rain fell against my skin. I savored the smell. It reminded me of some long-forgotten memory I couldn't place, but rather felt in my soul.

"Can you ever forgive me?" The question was soft. Almost unspoken.

"What for?" I had a feeling I knew what he was referring to, but I wasn't sure I wanted to be the one to bring it up. Not if he didn't remember it. If he didn't realize it had been me.

He took a shuddering breath. "For all those years ago. When I—if I had known then that—"

I held up my hand, stopping him before he could finish the thought. "Don't." I didn't want to think of that day. Not now. Not when so much had already happened between us.

"I truly am sorry." He turned his head to the sea, staring into the distance as the wind tousled his hair. I wanted to run my hands through it.

"I know," I whispered, my voice distant. I found myself staring, fixated on his profile.

He had let his hair grow a little, no longer swept perfectly to the side or tucked beneath the weight of a crown. In the evening light, he looked…soft. A faint shadows of stubble lined his jaw and he tensed, a muscle feathering there as he sniffed, wiping the rain from his face. When he looked back, his eyes glistened.

I absently chewed the inside of my lip. I wasn't nervous, but something deep tugged within my chest, begging to be let out. I reached inwardly, testing the barrier of shadows that lay encasing my heart. I was relieved to find it still secure. What lay inside scared me more than the possibilities of tomorrow.

I could leave nothing to chance. Not even him.

I broke his gaze and fiddled with one of my daggers, twirling it in my hand, tossing it up and letting it fall in the grass. I distracted myself like that for some time, and he sat with me in companionable silence until the rain petered out. The clouds thinned, and the stars shone brilliantly once more.

I pressed the tip of the blade against my finger, testing the boundary of my skin, hissing sharply when it broke the surface. A drop of crimson welled against the tip.

Callax took my hand in his and removed the dagger from my grip. I tugged lightly, wanting to wipe the blood away, but he didn't let go. Instead, he turned my hand over and pressed the blood against his palm, tracing it across his skin.

His skin against mine sent a rush of electricity through my chest and down my spine. I gasped softly. A foreign sense of recognition resounded in my mind and I stared in bewilderment at him. Though there was nothing on my arm, I could have sworn a tiny thread of light wound its way around his hand and over mine. But I blinked, and it disappeared.

The tiniest smile at the edge of his lips was the only sign he felt it too.

When his eyes met mine, the stars within shone brighter, and the night seem to wrap around him like some perfect shadow. And as it did, the softness disappeared from his face. The only way I could think to describe him, was regal. A king.

His hand left mine, leaving me cold and empty. Like he was the only thing keeping me warm. He pulled a chain out from beneath his shirt. Resting at the end was a plain, silver ring. It was beautiful, but simple. He lifted it from his neck and held it delicately in his palms.

"It's beautiful," I said.

"It was my mother's. It's the only thing I have left of her."

I furrowed my brow in confusion. "Is your mother not—" The question halted in my throat as he shook his head silently, twirling the ring between his fingers.

"Oh." How did I not know? "If the queen is not your mother…then who?"

"My mother was murdered the moment I left her body." Tears welled in his eyes, and I reached out my hand. I knew the pain of losing a parent. His brows furrowed together, his lips thinning.

"I'm sorry," I offered. But he didn't react.

"It was my father." His demeanor hardened. "He slit her throat before they could place me in her arms. Before the cord was ever cut." He stared into the distance, and I could feel the loss echo off him, the memory still real to him.

"I resent my father for many things. But when my stepmother told me…" His voice trailed off as he choked on the words. A tear slid free, and I wanted to wipe it away for him, to rest my hand on his cheek and let him know he was not alone. But I stopped. "I grew up thinking she was my mother. She was as kind and as loving as she could be to a child that wasn't hers. But I was the product of an indiscretion, and some part of her always resented me for that." He twirled the ring in his hand. It was evident he cherished it.

"My father could not allow for such a mistake to be made public." Hatred dripped from his words and my ire for the king only grew. "My stepmother never left the castle or wandered into Sunsbridge. My father kept her under a tight leash, so ti was easy enough to hide that she wasn't the one pregnant. My father ordered anyone who knew to be killed. He replaced the staff save for a handful of loyal servants. There was never a chance of the secret being made public. Not even my half-brother knows."

Everything cruel and calculated I once saw in him faded with the wind. Callax had made mistakes over the years, but I was beginning to think that he only followed the actions exemplified to him.

He was raised as a reflection of the king's mistakes, but he was not the king. He owed the world no penance for the transgressions of his father. Yet still, he paid the price.

Before I could speak, he removed the ring from its chain. He held it closer now, and I watched as he pulled it apart.

Hidden inside the solid outer ring, was another, smaller one. It fit perfectly inside, molded to its shape. The smaller of the two was made of twining strands, winding around each other. A beautiful, knotted pattern ran throughout. Inlaid in the center, were tiny, flattened stones of sapphire. The gems were small, and they shone brilliantly in the moonlight.

He slipped the solid ring over his index finger and extended his hand, waiting for mine.

I pulled back. "What are you doing?"

"Do you trust me?"

I tilted my head to the side, studying his face as he waited for my response. Trust wasn't something I freely gave, and I wanted to resist, but I couldn't get myself to say no.

"I want to," I said, and it was the truth. I did want to. I just wasn't sure how.

He looped the ring back through the chain and offered it to me. "We'll get there." I let him place it in my hesitant hand. "Consider it a promise. To you, to me, that come what may on the battlefield, or in the days to follow…that I am yours." The ring warmed in my hand and I fought the urge to both slip it over my finger, and to hand it back to him.

It was too much, too intimate, too thoughtful to be given to someone as broken as me.

Callax wrapped his hands around mine, closing my fingers over the ring. His touch centered me, and my racing thoughts slowed. "If you'll have me, I promise to be by your side until the Night rises. And if you ask me to defy my father and fight by your side—whichever side you choose—I will. And if you ask, I would paint the heavens with your wrath."

He brought my hand to his mouth and kissed the closed edge of my fingers. There was a tenderness to his touch I had never known. A devotion that came from the deepest parts of his soul. I knew he meant it. And the thought worried me. I feared what we might become if I let my emotions free.

A whispering echo pushed me to accept the gift, and I finally nodded.

His shoulders sagged with relief, and I let him take the chain, placing it over my head. The ring fell between my breasts and I ran my thumb along the raised edges.

We lay together under the stars that night, not caring that the wet grass soaked through our clothes. And despite my better judgment, I let him hold me until the sun rose over the mountains, signaling the start of a new day.

The dawn of war.

CHAPTER 53

The king's legion arrived late in the night, their thundering footsteps waking the world around them. It was impossible to go back to sleep. Not only were my nerves shot and the thought of battle too consuming, but I had made my decision.

Kaede remained silent, his body half turned to the sea as I told my friends my story. Of my history and where I was from, how my family came to live in the south, and what all of this meant for us. And when they questioned Callax's presence, our closeness, I told them of how it was him who had trained me. How it was him who stayed by my side through every moment. They were still wary of him, and rightfully so, but if I trusted him then it was enough for now.

Every choice we made going forward put us all at risk, but now that they knew, there was no going back. Either they were on my side, or they weren't. The choice was theirs.

Callax held the small of my back in his hand, steadying me as I called it to a vote. When every hand raised, it took both our strengths combined to keep me from falling to my knees. I still didn't understand their unending loyalty or what I had done to deserve it.

Noticing my silent question, Skye stepped forward. "Emryn called us an inner circle once. But we're more than that. We're family." She turned to Kaede, pulling him closer to us all with a simple touch. "All of us."

Archer offered a reassuring smile. "I think I speak for everyone when I say we trust you, Ren. And if this is what you need from us, then…then we will give it. Not just for today, or this battle, but for the betterment of our world. For a brighter future."

I looked to Kaede, hoping he would offer some sort of confirmation that he believed in this more than a halfhearted nod. He didn't raise his head, but he said, "It's what Emryn would have wanted. For her, I will do this."

My heart skipped a beat, but I swallowed it down. It was enough for now.

It was Senna who answered. Her voice a command and a call to action. "Then let's figure a way out of this, together. One where we all come out on the other side."

We traveled before dawn to the base of the pass. A cold wind blew over the rocky ground, whistling between the stones. The tall peaks of the mountain range rose into the clouds, their cliffs dark and imposing, just as terrifying as all the stories described.

It was to our advantage that their forces would cross through the pass. There was only one way in or out that we knew of, and from it, we could see them coming the moment they broke through. And if they retreated, we would be sure to follow, using them to lead us inside.

I stood beside Callax, Archer, and Skye. Kaede lingered to my right. We formed a line as the legion approached behind us. Like a drumbeat, their feet pounded into the ground, a steady rhythm of impending doom. And then they halted and formed their ranks.

When they stopped, the silence was deafening.

A shuffle of weapons broke the silence, and I turned my head to see Senna and Kell breaking from the front lines to join us. We were stood above them all, the Ira Deorum waiting atop a small hill to choose our own advantages. Senna took her place next to Skye, their hands brushing against the other in silent acknowledgment.

Hours, or at least what felt like it, passed as we waited. Only the wind, and occasional scrape of metal filled the silence.

Eventually, King Tobias rose through the crowd of warriors. Even the golden horse striding beneath him seemed to carry himself with pride. Fynn remained there at the front, waiting for the king. And when he arrived, banners held high, Fynn flared his glorious red and gold wings, expanding them out into the world so all could see. He was their beacon, their symbol of hope.

But to me, he was everything I hated in this world. And I would tear him down.

A familiar ache settled between my shoulders, weighing me down. I shrugged it off, telling myself I'd deal with that problem later as I watched Fynn draw his sword. A small wave of nausea rolled through me, even at this distance.

That thing was a god-killer. Meant to tear me down as it had my predecessor all those centuries ago.

I twirled the ring around its chain on my neck, fidgeting in anticipation. This was the worst part. The waiting. We were ready, but there was no enemy to fight yet. We stood in complete stillness, silence echoing throughout the world. Hours more seemed to pass and still, nothing came.

I clenched my fists open and closed. I wanted to move, to fight, to do something other than stand here and wait. Callax's fingers brushed gently against mine, letting me know he was there. That the promises he made the night before still held true. It stilled my heart.

Then the shrieks began.

Haunting, blood-curdling screams echoed through the passages of the mountains. Never before had I heard something so horrifying. Their cries pierced through my mind with a shockwave of pain, a high-pitched whine spearing through my head. Soldiers behind us cried out in agony, clutching their ears as blood ran down the sides of their head.

"Gods save us," breathed Callax, pointing to the sky beyond. I followed his finger, and there, cresting above the point of the mountain was a wall of black—an imposing mass of pure terror.

Axan mares. Bat winged horses—demons of the night.

Their cries only increased in a grating cacophony as they approached. The front line wavered, the grips on their bows slackening in terror.

"Archers at the ready." King Tobias held his fist in the air, commanding the front lines. He held still, waiting until they were in range. And as they approached, the more I could see.

Two lines, one atop the other, descended upon us, spearing down from the heavens. Lightning cracked through the sky, and the smell of rain filled the air. General Branan was right. We were at their mercy.

Another clap of thunder sounded and they were on top of us in an instant. Too soon for the king to even predict. "Fire at will," he shouted, but it was lost under the boom of the storm sweeping in as the league of Night Stryders dove into the legion.

They dropped from the sky, great warriors falling from their backs, hitting the ground in a dead sprint as they made their first attack.

Fynn took to the sky, launching in a wave of fire. I flinched.

The other half of the Ira Deorum did not wait for us as they ran down the hill, eager to shed blood.

A swirling battle of lightning and flames illuminated the sky above. I turned to my sister and friends and held out my sword. I reminded them of our plan, and that no matter what happened, we would stick together. Emryn's death would not be in vain.

Archer placed hers atop mine, then Callax, and Skye, the rest of them following suit. "We cannot let them win. For the sake of the world, for the freedom of this land, for our friends, we will fight together. 'Til the Night rises once more."

There was nothing but sheer determination as I rallied us. They had chosen me and my cause. I would not let them down.

They all nodded, echoing my sentiment, and sealing their fate.

As one, we turned against our king.

CHAPTER 54

I held on tightly to my determination, using it to carry me through the slew of bodies.

It took longer than I expected for the foot soldiers to realize the six of us were fighting against our own. Once they did, they launched toward us in droves. I thanked the gods that Soren and the others were distracted with the Night Stryders, dipping in and out of reach. We just had to make it through this first wave and then we'd be free to run and make our move.

A few archers hit their marks, dropping the large beasts from the sky. I watched in a mix of horror and delight as the Axan lived up to their legend and tore apart soldier after soldier, an army of their own—even without their riders atop them.

Blood stained their razor-sharp teeth as they ripped into any spare flesh around them. It took nearly three men to take one of the mares down. Their ferocity nearly unmatched.

The Realm of Night was not as ill-prepared as it seemed. But even with the sheer amount of riders attacking from above, they alone could not take on the numbers the king boasted.

I unsheathed my blades, pulling them free from behind my back as carved a path of destruction, trying to make my way to a clearing. The perfectly balanced blades hummed with power and seemed to delight in the blood spilled before them. I didn't want to admit it, but it was almost…enjoyable. I had been searching for a way to release this rage for some time. Each strike was a breath of relief.

A trumpet sounded in the hollows of the mountain. A brilliant war cry echoing across the battlefield. The Night Legion had come.

This was it. This was what we were waiting for. I glanced to the band of red, emblazoned with a large sun on my arm. The only thing marking our allegiance. With a savage grin, I ripped it free. To my left, Callax did the same. The symbol of the Dark Phoenix sat bold and bright atop my armor.

In that moment, the five of my friends all turned, waiting for my command, for the moment we would let everything about our old lives slip away.

"Now," I shouted. Together they pushed back any surrounding opponents. The base of the mountain too far now, and except for the dozen or so soldiers around us who had been fighting us off, the king and the rest of them would only see us as overly eager warriors, determined to spill the first blood of the enemy.

The cries of 'traitors' were lost in the noise, swallowed by the screams of the Axan. Lightning struck the ground to our right, a Starlax falling to the ground in a blaze of fire and electricity. I stumbled, but Callax gripped my arm, hauling me forward with him.

A roar of anger ripped through the sky, a blast of heat sending bodies flying across the ground.

He knew.

"Run," I screamed, propelling myself forward as fast as I could go, making sure we were all still together. I knew what would come next, and I didn't want any of us to still be in the open when Fynn rained his Phoenix fire down on us. Not even I would survive it.

Brilliant red and gold light illuminated the clouds, splitting the rolling storm. In the aftermath, loud thuds echoed across the ground, armor and severed limbs flying as he slaughtered them without mercy.

A wild blaze stung our heels as he threw a wall of fire down on us. We narrowly dodged it, the sweat evaporating from my brow. I leaped over a charred corpse as we neared the front lines of the opposing army. We were so close.

Ahead, Skye and Archer screamed for them to stop, to lower their weapons as arrows began to dash against the rocks, some too close for comfort. Atop a tall, dark horse, the Night's General called out, "Lower your weapons."

I did the same to my friends, sheathing my blades behind my back, glancing only once to the army behind us, knowing we had little time before they were within reach. I held up my hands in surrender.

I approached the general and was met with a spear to my throat, ready to run me through. Behind me, Callax stiffened, but the general held up his hand. "Hold," he said, and in unison, his soldiers relaxed. "Archers, fire at will."

I flinched, but the direction of his other hand pointed across the field. No words were needed as his eyes met the sigil across my arm. The same one on all of our arms. A flicker of recognition ran through him as he took in my hair and eyes, the blades across my back. His eyes widened and I knew he understood.

With a curt nod, he gestured for us to line up with the rest. "Welcome to the fight."

Together, we marched against the king. Against the only home I had ever known.

Burning flesh overwhelmed my senses, drowning out everything else entirely with a wave of heat. Suffocating men and women scraped their half burned bodies across the ground, scrambling for any kind of shelter. But there was none to be found.

Senna took charge, seeming impervious to the sights around us. "Kaede, you and Archer take the left flank, Skye and I will advance. Ren and Callax, you two take the right. We need to eliminate the rest of the Ira Deorum before they can form against us. They're our biggest threat." Not wasting any time, we all agreed and split up, pulled apart by the tides of war.

There were endless rows of warriors, a veritable sea that stretched on for what felt like miles. But I didn't give myself time to overthink any of it. It was either fight, or die.

Blood spattered my face, dripping down my armor, staining me as we made our way through the melee. Behind us, Fynn retreated from the sky and began decimating those around him in waves of fire. He darted in and out, using his sunstone sword to bring down anyone who dared approach. He had slowed some after the first few hours, no longer able to focus on one opponent, but it wasn't enough to make a difference.

I prayed to whatever gods would listen that we would make it, either through their graces or sheer luck. Whatever worked in our favor. Yet for each one I slew, two more took their place. I fought in a desperate frenzy. I would not let the king win.

A circle of large males surrounded me, some strange coordinated attack to take me down. Sometime in the last few minutes, Callax had wandered from my side, lost somewhere in the haze. They advanced on me and while I would fight no matter what happened, I wanted him by my side. I needed to know he was okay.

"Callax," I shouted. I braced myself, planting my feet. There was no response and I shouted again, letting his name carry out into the mass of endless bodies.

For the first time in a week, my heart raced. There was a growing chance we wouldn't make it out of here alive. I needed to find Archer, to make sure she was safe, too.

I took a steadying breath and met the first male's blade with my right, ripping through his stomach with the other. The one to my left raised his sword, moving too quickly to parry and I dodged the blow just in time to see a dagger embed itself directly in his eye. I turned and two more lay on the ground, Callax towering above their bodies as he turned. Face bloody, he said, "You called?"

We stood back-to-back, fighting together as droves of soldiers descended on us.

"Gods, could your timing have been any more off?" I shouted above the clash of metal. My arms moved wildly as I fended off two soldiers at once. I cleaved a man's head in two and forced myself to not empty my stomach as pieces of his skull ripped apart.

"I do apologize for the—on your right." I whipped to the side and let go of the blade I was trying to dislodge from someone's chest. I picked up a spear from the ground and threw it. It impaled him to the ground.

"I'll consider it," I said.

"Consider what?" He grunted as he slit a man's throat. I shouldn't have found that as attractive as I did, but gods...this male would be the death of me.

I pulled a dagger from my thigh, one of the last and aimed it just passed his shoulder, stopping an attack from behind. "Your apology."

We went on like that for what felt like days, surrounded by nothing but bone and blood and the screams of the dying. But I did not tire. Not with him by my side.

It wasn't until blood coated my eyes, and I paused to clear the red from my vision, that time seemed to start again. From across the field, I saw Kaede kneel on the ground, Archer only a couple yards away. I was ready to shout at him, to figure out what exactly he was doing on the ground, when Archer took a running start and launched herself off his shield. I watched in stunned awe as she lifted her bow to the skies. Her hair gleamed in the light, and I could swear that in the moment she was airborne, her bow became the moon—a sharp crescent hung in the sky—waiting to be harnessed.

She launched two arrows skyward, and a soldier fell from the back of a Starlax where he was attempting to attack the rider. It seemed she was doing just fine without me.

A loud, bellowing laugh ripped through the world, carried on the wind as Callax returned to my side. The male atop the horse turned and descended. The Starlax landed with a thud, any soldiers in the vicinity blasted back in a strange gust of wind that didn't seem to affect the four of us. A silver haired male equipped in ornate silver armor assessed us. I took a wary step back, positioning myself in front of Callax, taking his hand.

I met the stranger's silver eyes and nearly collapsed. They were Archer's eyes. My mother's eyes.

"What great timing," he boomed, his voice deep and commanding. "We've been waiting two decades for you to come and visit." A straggling solder charged forward from the side. I gripped my blade, but merely lifting his hand, the silver-haired male reached out a tattooed hand and closed his fist.

The soldier collapsed to the ground, clawing at his throat.

He was suffocating him.

I looked back in horror, my jaw nearly on the floor.

"My gods," Callax whispered, his eyes wide in recognition. No Fae alive could conjure magic like that. And I knew exactly who—what—he was.

"God, actually. Singular." He winked at Callax and dismounted.

The silver-haired Fae turned to me. "Pleased to finally make your acquaintance, cousin." He flicked the arms outward, keeping the oncoming soldiers at bay in a swirl of wind. "I can't hold them off forever, but long enough to give you a rest and properly introduce myself."

He extended a hand, and hesitantly, I took it. I expected a handshake. Instead, I was yanked forward and wrapped in a tight embrace. "You're all grown up, Rennie. But I could spot you from a mile away. You look just like your father."

I broke free from his suffocating hug and asked, "Who in the hell are you?"

He laughed again, a loud crashing sound that carried above the wind. "The name's Vallen Sora. God of Air." He turned a questioning gaze to Callax, looking thoroughly unimpressed. "And you are?"

"Prince Callax." He extended a hand.

Vallen ignored the gesture and made a face as he looked him up and down. He turned his attention back to me. "Glad to see you chose the right side. Now, let's get back to kicking some ass."

With a flick of his hand, the wind disappeared. He leaped back on top of the massive horse, charging forward into the slew of bodies around us, drawing a black, blood-stained sword.

Even with Vallen appearing, the dent we made wasn't going to be enough. There were just too many to fight off at once. And the longer we waited, the longer we fought and the more I tired...our chances dwindled. We couldn't beat them with numbers, but if I could take Fynn out of the equation, then perhaps it would be enough to make them withdraw.

I told Callax what I needed and he hesitated, not wanting to throw me into likely the last fight I might ever take part in, but he nodded.

We searched as we fought, trying to figure out how to get to him, when a wave of fire roared to our right. It was like he had wanted us to come to him, clearing a path. The sun descended behind him, illuminating his silhouette in deep shades of gold.

"Renata, watch out," Callax shouted a moment too late.

Kell's blade sliced through my leather and down into the bone of my shoulder. I cried out as pain seared through me. I nearly let go of one of my blades, but the fire flared beneath my skin, urging me to hold on. It slithered under my skin and up to the open wound. I winced as blood sizzled, the fire cauterizing my wound. It still roared with pain, but the bleeding had stopped.

Kell doubled back, taking advantage of my wonderment at what just happened, but I blocked just in time, wincing at the effort.

We had only been sparring partners a handful of times this last year, so his fighting techniques were strange and unpredictable. He carried a sword in one hand, a hunting knife in the other.

I watched his left hand. A sword would pierce clean through, but that serrated blade would rip, and tear, and open me up. He grinned and lunged, and if it hadn't been for all this persistent training, those nights spent with Callax until we were both run ragged, he would have ended me right then.

A cry of pain stole my attention, and for a split second, despite my better judgment, I glanced away, searching for him. To make sure he was okay. But that precious second cost me.

Kell swung his arm around, halting my movement and ripping through the leather across my stomach. I gasped, clutching at the wound as his other hand connected with my jaw.

As if in slow motion, his fist moved into my field of vision, and I caught a flash of warped, red skin, hidden beneath his sleeve. Wrapped around his left wrist was a scar. A handprint of burned flesh that had never healed right.

I let white hot fury burn against my palm as I sealed the wound on my stomach closed, letting the pain melt away into nothing as hatred took over every sense.

How dare he touch me.

He had been there. He was the other male the night Soren and Caldor attacked me. Flashes of terror and pain that once consumed me, swallowed my mind as I was thrown back into the memory. Not in fear, but as a reminder of what he had done, the cliff he and his friends had shoved me over. But I was not that same girl anymore.

Fire raged beneath my skin, and I grinned. He was mine. I would enjoy every second it took as I ripped him apart.

With a roar indistinguishable from some beast of hell, I attacked. The first blow sliced through his chest, my other piercing through his thigh. He was at my feet in seconds, sword and knife on the ground. I wasn't me, wasn't Renata in that moment, but something else. Something far darker and menacing than I had known myself to be capable of.

There was nothing in my mind except for blinding rage as I ripped through his body, tearing him open—exposing him to the world as he had done to me.

My name rang through the bloodlust, breaking through the darkness like a beam of light. A hand grasped my arm, stopping the next blow.

"Renata, enough." I turned to see Callax, my hand still raised. But he did not shy away. "He's dead. Do not waste anymore energy on him."

He tried to pull me away, but his death was not enough. I needed to know he could never use his hands again. But death wasn't enough. I wanted justice.

I wanted revenge.

I nodded to Callax, and he released my arm, thinking I had given up. But he only watched, eyes wide, as I brought my blade down, severing Kell's hand. I picked up the hand and tossed it into the air as an Axan mare flew overhead, eyes blazing with hunger. It caught the appendage, devouring it in one go.

"There," I said, wiping my bloody hands clean. "Now I'm done."

He cocked his head to the side, like he was admiring the sight of me covered in the blood of my enemies. We could revisit that thought later.

His leg bled, a cut on his upper thigh making me worry. I reached out to touch it, but he said, "I'm fine. It was a shallow cut. Caldor is the one who should worry."

I sighed with relief, silently cursing myself for letting myself get so distracted with his well being. There was no reason I should worry this much.

Like Callax said, Caldor lay on the ground behind us, clutching a nearly severed arm. His legs kicked frantically against the dirt as I approached, trying to escape my wrath. He had seen what I had done to his friend. Callax had made him watch.

"Please," he whimpered, holding out his good hand.

He would live to see another day, but only because I deemed it so. He would meet the same fate as Kell soon enough, but only when his wounds were inflicted solely by my hands. I wanted the honor of seeing him suffer.

I kicked his uninjured arm free, digging my heel in, pinning him down.

"Please, I won't—" he cried.

"Won't what?" I asked, squatting down. "Won't trap me against the wall while your brother drags his filthy hands across my body? Won't watch and laugh while my innocent sister is thrown around, waiting for you to have a turn?"

"It won't happen again, I promise." He was frantic. Pleading.

I pulled a dagger from my waist and drove it through Caldor's palm, pinning him to the ground below. "You're right," I said with satisfaction. "It won't."

I smiled as his screams filled the air.

CHAPTER 55

Burning corpses filled my vision. They were everywhere. Everyone, everything—burning.

Agony and death surrounded me, all because of him. Children would never see their father's again, families ripped apart and destroyed all because of him.

Callax asked me only once what I needed before he went about giving it to me. I wanted Fynn. And I wanted him dead.

Somewhere in the distance Soren and Kaede battled it out, Archer nearby. But he would protect her. And she would be fine.

My mind filled with a singular purpose, one last reason for all this death.

Callax carved a path for me, just as the God of Night had done once for the moon. This time it was through an ocean of bodies and not the stars, but the purpose was the same. To let me fulfill my destiny.

My nightshade glowed in my hands as I walked behind him. Men screamed as they died at the hand of their prince. He didn't need my help, didn't need my worry as he tore through body after body, lying them at my feet as I stalked toward the hill Fynn fought atop.

When we reached the base of the hill, Callax gripped my arm, pulling my focus. The rest of the way was mostly clear, the fighting concentrated mostly to our back. "End this," he said. And his voice was filled with such belief and determination, that my body filled with renewed strength, as if he had offered me hope in this dreary world.

I made one last sweep of his body, ensuring he was safe. And then I turned back, just once to see my friends. If this was the last time, if I died alongside Fynn, then it would be worth it. Perhaps Emryn's death would have meant something after all.

I checked off their names as I found them, a weight releasing as they all were accounted for. The only one left was... Where was Skye?

Callax's face went white, and he called my name, shouted for me to look.

A flash of black and silver caught my eye as my friend darted up the other side of the hill, her short hair torn loose from her braids.

No.

"*Skye, no!*" I shouted, the sound ripping through my throat. But it was too late.

She was fast, too fast for me to run and stop her. But I ran anyway. Tore up the hill as fast as my legs could carry me. I tore the gauntlets from my arms, the extra weapons at my hip, hoping it might somehow spur me forward, give me some sort of momentum to reach her in time.

Fynn's glowing red eyes met mine as he tore his sword free from the fallen soldier at his feet. A charge of heat electrified the air, my fire pounding against my mind to be set free, as if trying to protect me from the imminent danger. But I wasn't the one at risk.

Wicked and cruel, Fynn smiled, knowing exactly what this would do to me. To my already broken heart.

I didn't have time to react, to scream another warning or call for Senna to save her mate, before he raised his sword.

I could do nothing but watch as the one I had spent a lifetime loving—the one I would have once given my life for—drove his sword through her chest.

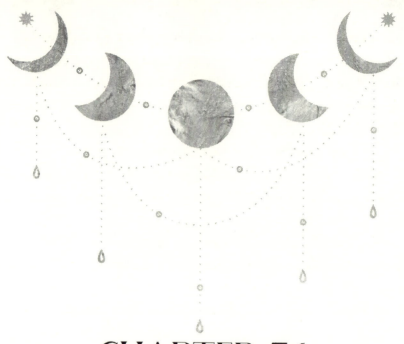

CHAPTER 56

The world stopped.

My breath left my body in a violent scream. Paralyzed, I watched in horror as Skye's body slid from his blade.

I followed the direction of her gaze as she fell, somehow locking in on Senna from across the battlefield. In a blaze of black and gold, soldiers fell at Senna's feet in a perfect rhythm. She was the epitome of war and power, and she glowed with it.

Skye's hand reached out, frozen in a longing grasp toward her mate.

I tore my eyes from her, and looked back to Fynn. His eyes remained locked on mine, lips tightening into a wry smile.

I knew he was loyal to the king, self-righteous to a fault, that would never change…but this?

Kaede. Oh gods, Kaede… His little sister lay only a hundred yards from him, bleeding out on the soiled ground. His back remained to us, and he didn't know. Didn't know his sister was moments away from her last breath.

Unbridled rage ripped through me, igniting every ember in my body as I struggled to maintain control. I advanced, blades at the ready.

Fynn waited, fire igniting in his palm, his blade in the other. Waiting.

Fury's twisted arms curled in my chest, sinking its talons into my still beating heart. My breath dissipated in the growing shadows of the night. The last dredges of kindness flickering in the wake of my rising darkness as I snuffed them out.

Skye reached her hand toward me as I passed, pleading for help. But I heard nothing, felt nothing, as I stepped over her limp body. She had agreed to this. She knew the risks when we rebelled and stopping to save her…it wouldn't end this. It wouldn't fix anything.

Everything within me succumbed to the darkness, and all I knew was godly rage. If he was the embodiment of the Sun, then I would be the Night's wrath—Darkness incarnate.

I took a final, deep breath as I closed the space between us. Power rushed through my blades, glowing a brilliant blue in contrast to his, renewing my determination.

His sword crashed into mine with an unexpected force. We had never once fought the other. Not in this capacity.

A wave of nausea rolled over me at the proximity of the sunstone, of what it meant if it tore through me. I could tell my nightshade had a similar effect to him. Good.

The heat of his flames and clashing weapons was strong enough to singe the hair that came loose from my tightly woven braid. Smoke burned my nose as he lifted his blade again, and again, each strike stronger than the last.

He pushed me back as I narrowly spun from a death blow. My foot caught on a stray rock, and I stumbled as I rolled to the side, his sword slamming down where I had been only seconds before.

He stepped on my foot, holding me in place, the momentum carrying me in the wrong direction. There was a crack, and my ankle buckled beneath me. Pain seared through my right foot as I fell to the ground. My right foot at an odd angle.

My left blade flew from my grasp, leaving me with only one.

Fynn took advantage of my misstep and without giving me a second to recover, swung down, aiming for my heart.

I caught the edge with my remaining blade, holding on with all my strength.

He was stronger than me, he always had been, and I knew I'd never be able to beat his brute strength alone. Not like this. His wings flared behind him and he used it to push himself closer, bearing down on me, shoving his sword within inches of my throat.

I knew I couldn't kill him with just one of my blades. And if he died without me using both, he'd come back soon enough, it's what a Phoenix did. But it could give us enough time to regroup.

I gripped both hands on the hilt, keeping him at bay, but he only pressed harder, the flames of his sword licked against mine. I watched in horror as the heat began to warp it. There was only one way to stop him, but I wasn't ready to give in to the sweet release of death. Not yet.

The pain from my mending ankle jolted through me, giving me hope.

"They should have ended you when they had the chance," he spat. "Did you know it was the king's idea to bring two opponents into your trial?" He flashed his teeth, and the air around him chilled. "But I was the one who gave them the dagger."

My foot snapped back into place, still sore, but secure. He didn't notice as he continued.

"Why?" I demanded, disbelief running through me. We had still been together at the time. He had taken me to the ball after, paraded me around like some prized gem, pretending to love me.

"We suspected you were up to something, but we couldn't prove it. It would have been too much of a spectacle if a member of the Ira Deorum suddenly wound up dead, so had to devise a proper way to dispose of you. A way where no one would come asking questions. And when you failed to die, I suggested to the king he break you instead…I told him to kill Emryn."

The memory of her falling at his feet, blood pouring from her throat, Kaede's scream… All I saw was red.

He laughed mercilessly as he pushed me over the edge. "You were never going to be my equal. You were weak and pathetic, and once I realized you weren't worth my time, I knew that killing you would only be that much more satisfying."

I planted my feet beneath me, leveraging my hips as I pushed up, sending him off balance. I jumped to my feet, his eyes wide with surprise and disbelief. He glanced down to my foot that had been broken only a minute before. Even Fae did not heal that quickly. But he had been wrong when he said we weren't equals. I wasn't Fae. I never truly had been.

For so long, I begged the universe to let me be, to give me control over my life, and now...here I was, with the chance to finally take that control.

I let myself be reminded once more of the girl I used to be. Scared and helpless. To remember what it was like to be weak. I had been so afraid of the power I held—afraid I might burn up with it—that I cowered in the safety of his shadow. I let him control me. But no more.

No more would I let another dictate my life.

If my powers were to be my ruin, then let them. They were mine by blood and birthright, and if I was to burn out with them, then let me fucking burn.

Fire roared through my veins, demanding to be released. And this time...I didn't stop them.

My blade ignited along with me. The blue of my flames danced in the air, illuminating the world, battling his for dominance.

If I couldn't stop him, there would be no one left to prevent the destruction of an entire realm. I may have failed my family, but I would not fail my friends.

I swung the warped blade around in a circle, testing the balance. I mocked a bow.

"You wanted an equal? Well here I am."

He screamed in anger, and in his frustration he dropped his sword. Using both hands, he unleashed a torrent of fire that surrounded us, cutting us off from the rest of the battlefield.

I didn't budge as he pressed the walls in closer. Instead, I stared at my palms, willing my power to form, to take shape. It was new, its limits unknown, but I stopped fighting and instead, listened. Letting it take the lead.

Wild and uncontrolled fire ignited in my palms spreading up my arms. The fabric of my sleeves burned away with it, my armor left scattered across the hill.

"How?" he whispered in disbelief.

I didn't bother with a response. I flicked my hand outward as I had seen Vallen do with his air. It knocked into his chest, and Fynn scrambled backward, tumbling to the ground as he tried to put it out. Over and over I unleashed streams of fire in his direction, laughing.

His wall around us fell, and he focused on deflecting. He wasn't used to being inferior. Being underneath someone.

I leaned in, towering over him. "Tell me," I hissed. "How does it feel?"

He spat at my feet, refusing to answer, indignation raging behind those golden eyes. He reached for his sword, but grasped at empty air when he realized he dropped it was no longer there. It lay somewhere behind us near my second blade, but I didn't dare risk turning my back to retrieve it.

I looked down on him, nothing but anger and disgust in my gaze. With my warped blade—now more reminiscent of a scythe—I lifted his chin.

I tilted my head, asking again. "How does it feel to know death beckons you at my hand? How does it feel to know that you cower at my feet?"

The world around me moved in a spiraling fracture of madness as I lifted my sword, slamming it down through his abdomen, pinning his body to the ground. He screamed in agony, writhing beneath the blade. I ignored his cry as I stalked to where my remaining blade lay.

A volley of arrows launched through the sky, aimed directly at me. By now the world had seen us. Knew what was happening. A line of soldiers rushed up the hill, ready to defend their Phoenix. But I would not let them.

I centered myself with a breath, letting the fire within rise and fall with it. I extended both hands outward, and a wall of cobalt fire roared to life around me, sealing us off from the rest of the world. Fynn's death was between him and me.

I returned with my blade. Each step brought me closer to my inevitable and self-made ruin. But I didn't care. I had once promised myself I wouldn't be like Fynn. That, for the sake of my soul, I couldn't be.

But circumstances change.

And promises can be broken.

Standing over his body, I rent the blade free, and he choked in a gasp of air. The nightshade weakened him, leaving him temporarily powerless. He attempted to rise to his knees, and I let him, knowing it wouldn't change the outcome of his fate.

In my arrogance, I didn't see the blade hidden in his hands. Pure sunstone drove through my side and up into my lungs. Dangerously close to my heart.

An ungodly wail of agony ripped through me. I had never known such pain.

In the searing torment, my concentration faltered as I fell, my flames sputtering out, leaving us exposed to the battle below.

"Surrender," he demanded, but his voice wavered, still weak. "Before I remove you from this world."

My vision blurred. I wrapped my shaking hand around the gold hilt of the dagger. I yanked it free, gasping as relief flooded through me. This wound would take longer to heal, the sunstone sapping my strength, rendering my flames nothing more than a spark.

Blood poured from my wound as I rose to my feet and slammed my heel into his wounded abdomen. He doubled over with a groan.

When he gathered the strength to face me once more, I lifted my blades, placing them on opposite sides of his neck. My reflection shone in his defiant eyes, and I looked vengeful.

Arrows whistled through the air, and I held back a hiss of pain as two pierced through my shoulder, another in my back. A crooked smile spread across my lips. "I am a god. I am not so easily removed."

With a triumphant roar, I tore through his neck. Even with one blade bent, there was no resistance.

The Phoenix's head rolled to the ground, mouth frozen in a silenced scream.

More arrows tore through my back, and one scraped the edge of my heart. Blood filled my lungs as darkness clouded my vision. There was a cry of pain somewhere in the distance. A name—mine—shouted like a prayer, a desperate hope for me to hold on.

I knew I would die, but I would also rise again. Reborn in the ashes of victory.

I fell to my knees as I gave in, surrendering to the darkness.

Cobalt flames exploded over every surface of my body, and the world disappeared into oblivion.

CHAPTER 57
Callax

Callax slammed his sword into Soren's, locked in a battle of strength. He would kill this male for what he had done to her. He would rip him to shreds and let her watch. No one touched her and lived. She was his.

Pain ripped through his side as he held on for as long as he could, the wound Soren dealt him was deep, but not fatal.

Flashes of red flared through the sky, and Callax dared not look to Renata, afraid of what he might see. This was her fight. Her kill. If she died—no, he would not let himself think like that. She would make it. She had to. He had ensured she was as skilled as possible because the thought of losing her again—of being left alone in this world—it threatened to unravel him.

He had suspicions of her powers, the strength that lay dormant underneath, waiting for her to claim.

There was a shift in her presence after the trials. Something new surfaced that night—some dark and ancient power that called to him—but she refused to accept it. The loss she had gone through with Emryn only held her back. Tormented her.

Her pain had become his as he watched her fall apart in the madness of grief. He didn't know how she handled such immense pain. He could barely stand it himself. It was why he encouraged her to let it all go, to stop feeling entirely. It may not have been the wisest decision, but he would have done anything to end her suffering.

Even his father had been suspicious of her for some time. Fynn continuously fed him information about her whereabouts and her constant inquiries about his power. The history of the gods. If there was one thing his father hated, it was a threat. And that was what she had become.

Wherever she went, or whatever she did, her friends followed. And if he lost half of his beloved warriors…the king couldn't risk it.

The red-tinted sky shifted, and in a flash, was replaced with a brilliant blue. A wall of flame swirled atop the hill, shrouding them from view. Even Soren paused their fight to gawk. But whatever flames she summoned didn't last long.

A scream pierced the sky, rocking the world beneath him.

A cry so full of rage and pain it sang through his body, waking up something ancient and cold.

Her fury echoed across the battlefield and out into the world. That thread that connected them both, tightened. Something was wrong.

The wall of fire shook and fell as he watched Renata pull a blade from her side, the Phoenix at her feet. Arrows whistled through the air. He screamed a warning, but it was lost to the world.

Fear ate at his heart. He watched, utterly helpless, as arrows pierced her body. But even so, she did not falter. Something ached within him at the thought.

The fragile girl he once knew was no more. Instead, before the entirety of Albionne, stood the most divine creature he had ever seen. Rising in strength and glory, she lifted her blades.

The battlefield came to a screeching halt as Fynn's head toppled to the ground, landing at her feet.

She had done it. Relief swept through him.

But he spoke too soon.

Arrows continued to tear through her body, and he knew they hit her heart. He knew because he felt them too. Felt her slipping away from him.

The ground shook beneath him, a great world power awakening, as cobalt flames blasted from her body in a radius so vast he was glad he hadn't been any nearer. Any soldier within that vicinity turned to ash before his eyes.

He'd seen that shade of blue before, the same one he had surrendered to. The one that held so much loss and grief it had broken his heart. The same cobalt blue as her piercing eyes.

A chill rippled through the air as her flames disappeared, and Callax gasped in the air that had been stolen. His lungs filled painfully with each breath, his eyes scanning desperately for her. Where was she? The damned smoke was too thick to see through.

He launched into a sprint. Panic gripped his heart with each bounding step, knowing there was no way she could have survived something that powerful.

He had never learned of a god with flames like hers. Rumors had spread, whispers between his father and advisors of an ancient, Dark Phoenix, but it was impossible.

Callax skidded to a stop as the smoke cleared.

It wasn't her. Not anymore.

Smoke billowed off Renata's charred corpse, and he sank to his knees. Whatever caused this hadn't the mercy to spare her.

Callax hit the ground, the impact knocking into her charred corpse.

Cracks spread through her body, and without a whisper, she fell…into a pile of ash before his eyes.

Renata Orion was dead.

CHAPTER 58
Callax

Callax began to cry. He began to—to scream.

He screamed to the gods above as if his soul had been ripped from his body. Shaking, and screaming, and tearing at the ground beneath him. He had never known pain like this. The mortality of even his long life flashed before his eyes.

Grief expelled from his body in a shockwave of shadows as dark as the night—pure, unfiltered agony.

His mind went blank, and all he knew was that she was dead. Renata was dead.

Callax had never known such agony. He clawed at his chest, wanting to tear the useless heart from his body—a gaping hole where she used to be. It might as well have died alongside her.

He dug deep into his mind, searching for the invisible string that tied them together, but he found nothing. Only darkness remained.

Callax lurched forward. He was going to be sick.

He dug through the ashes before him, scraping his nails into the ground. In his desperation, he raked through them as if somehow, he could pull her from this—bring her back to him.

Please. Please come back.

Something solid and round his his fingers. He pulled the object from the rubble and dusted it off. In his palm, a perfect match to the one on his finger, was the ring he gifted her only the night before. It was all that remained.

Sobs racked his body, and then Archer was there.

Tears flowed from her bright silver eyes as she lifted him from the ground, wrapping him in a tight embrace. She held more than twice her weight as Callax leaned into her, still shaking. She was the only thing left of her.

"We have to go," she said, barely more than a whisper. "We have to go, Callax. It's Skye, she—we have to go." Her feigned bravery did little to hide the sorrow shaking her voice.

Pocketing the ring, he followed Archer to where Senna and Kaede crowded around Skye's limp body, her chest heaving with effort.

But something stopped him. He could have sworn the ashes moved. A tug pulled on his heart. Soft and gentle, but there. He shook his head, convinced it was a trick from the insanity of grief, and continued down the hill.

But it wasn't a trick. He turned around, his knees weakening at the sight, and gripped Archer's arm for stability.

The ashes coating the charred ground swirled around each other, lifting into the air.

No. It...it couldn't be.

Whatever rationalizing he had done, vanished. The swirling stopped, and a flare of bright blue light burst from the ashes, launching into the sky.

Pain seared into his back and down his arm like he had been branded with a white hot iron. Archer made a similar noise as he clutched his arm to his chest, a chill washing over him.

The ground shook. The rising flames exploded, clearing the smoke and pushing back a storm rolling through the evening sky. The final rays of the sun disappeared behind the mountains as night finally settled in.

Large, black wings tipped in cobalt exploded from the flames.

Phoenix wings.

Archer shielded her eyes from the light, but he couldn't take his eyes from it. From her.

"Gods above," he breathed as her body rose in the air, encompassed entirely in blue flames.

He dropped to his knees, the legion behind him following suit, bowing in respect to the newly made god before them.

To the Daughter of Darkness, wielder of shadows and flame. The Dark Phoenix. Heir…to the Realm of Night.

The Night had finally risen.

Long may she reign.

TO BE CONTINUED…

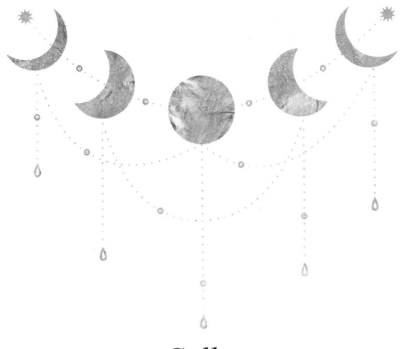

Callax

Callax awoke to Renata still in his arms.

She was so peaceful when she slept that he had been tempted to stay awake, watching her.

The early morning sun glinted off the ring he had given her. It meant the world to him to have her accept his gift. He had never known his mother, only stories passed down in secret from the few that remembered. Even then, it had taken years to coax the stories from them, the few servants that remained alive after her murder.

All he knew was the color of her eyes. Not even her name remained for him to hold on to.

Callax spent a long portion of his youth hoping that his stepmother, the queen, would offer some sort of relief from his pain, that maybe she could take her place. But despite her kindness, she had never stepped into that role.

He didn't blame her. She had another son to take care of—one that was her own. He liked to think of himself as a protective older brother, he had taken many punishments for him over the years, but he was nothing in comparison to Renata and Archer.

The way she protected Archer was with the fierceness of a mother. She had let herself be torn to shreds because of that loyalty—would likely lay down her life if it came to it.

It was that fierceness, in part, that drew him to her. She was always one step ahead or partially guarding her sister, even when they walked down the halls. And despite her shortcomings at the start of her training, she never once backed down from a fight. Or from him.

He brushed his finger against the ring. It had fallen free from her top as she slept. Her heart beat steadily beneath it and he let himself linger for a moment, feeling that rhythmic pulse echo into his veins, soothing his own aching heart.

Something like pain, or rather...an ache he could not place, threatened to burst from his chest when she accepted the gift. Like some ancient ritual bonding the two. As long as she wished, he would be by her side. As a friend, a lover, or perhaps something...more. Something vital.

But he could not let himself think of it. Not when the outcome of this battle was still unknown. Denying himself such simple pleasures was not a foreign concept for Callax.

The march of the legion, a far echo that beat into the ground, came to a halt as they arrived in the late hours of the night. He cursed them for waking her. She needed her sleep, needed to be at her full strength.

Renata stirred, a confused hum passing through her lips. Callax fought back a smile, his chest constricting at the mundaneness of it all. She rubbed her eyes, pushing up from his arms.

He chuckled slightly at the state of her hair. The long black strands stuck to her face, imprinting against her soft cheek, while others stood nearly on end.

She flashed him a look that said, don't you dare say anything, and he kept his thoughts to himself. But he still stored the memory, keeping it tucked safely away.

"Good morning. Sleep well?" Callax asked, smirking.

She stretched, raising her arms above her head, and groaned. The smallest sliver of skin peeked through between her waistband and top and Callax had to steady his breath, and control the urge to lay her back down and sink himself deep within her. Everything about her drove him mad with desire.

She looked confused at the dark sky around them and noted the torches of the legion in the distance. The shuffling sounds as they moved around.

"Well enough. You?" she asked.

He smiled at the pleasantry, wondering if this might be a ritual between them going forward, or if allowing him to hold her was a one time thing. He couldn't stand the thought of never holding her again.

"I suppose. Though, there was this obnoxious sound that kept waking me. Almost like someone was...snoring."

She scoffed and threw her shoe at his head.

Callax only laughed and swatted it away before it smacked him in the forehead. He stood, brushing his dark pants off from the damp grass. He extended his hand, and she took it, walking beside him as they sought out her friends.

Somehow, this unruly female had walked into his life, and swept him off his feet in more ways than one.

When he looked at her, he did not see a broken-hearted girl, but rather a warrior. A survivor.

And one day, if the gods shined down on them...his queen.

Acknowledgements

Writing a book is not something I thought I could ever do. It wasn't a life-long dream, nor a career I wanted to pursue. But one night inspiration struck, and I knew I had a story to tell. It was my story, and I had never had the courage to share it so publicly before. But with the power of TikTok, a little bit of therapy, and an insane amount of ADHD, I wrote my first draft in five weeks. It was a crazy endeavor, but I loved every minute of it.

Renata Orion is deeply rooted in who I am as a person, and it is terrifying to share her. She encompasses everything that I am, down to how I think. (Though please know that I have never actually killed anyone). But telling her story has allowed me to heal in so many ways. Over the last few years, I left an abusive marriage, separated myself from my lifelong religion, moved across the country, traveled to Scotland solo, and survived a worldwide pandemic. Many highs and lows went into forming this story, and while it was all extremely hard, I don't regret a single thing.

I have to start by thanking my amazing little sister, Bethany Talley. Not only was she the perfect inspiration for Archer Orion, but she is also the entire reason this book exists. Thank you for the countless nights where I sent many voice notes describing my crazy ideas, for answering my facetime calls to explain a new scene idea, and for encouraging me to write this story. I would not be who I am without you, this story would not exist without you, and you continue to inspire me on a daily basis. I love you so much.

Next, I have to thank my incredible support team who never doubted my abilities: Kelli Kabetzke (my beautiful and strong best friend who holds my entire heart and knows every secret), Benjamin MacDonald (my wonderful cousin who loves me more than I deserve), Morgan Nebeker (the friend I never expected but definitely needed, you always amaze me), and Kris aka Scottish Boy (whose last name I still don't know after years of long-distance friendship and text messages. Thank you for swiping right on tinder and for being a constant source of encouragement. I owe you some donuts.) And to my roommates (Allie and Lauren), and my many, many wonderful TikTok family members who encouraged me every step of the way. You guys are the best.

And a special thank you goes to my therapist...none of this would have happened if you hadn't helped ensure I was mentally stable. You are the one who encouraged me to write and find peace from my grief. My life has forever been changed for the better because of you. And without you, I would have never known I had the power to do this. You are the absolute best.

And finally, to everyone else who offered endless amounts of encouragement and showed up for me when I needed it: Mom, Dad, Jacob, Ruth, Stetson, Denver, Bethany, Brooke, and Sawyer. And thank you to my aunts, uncles, and cousins that supported me along the way.

And lastly, thank you to Sarah J. Maas, who created characters so real and a world so intoxicating that I fell back in love with reading.

'Til the Night rises.

Made in the USA
Columbia, SC
25 July 2024

38741872R10233